RIVER

ANNE GREGOR

 Created with Vellum

PREFACE

Phytophthora infestans is a water mold— a fungus-like microorganism— and the cause of Ireland's potato blight. The Irish Potato Famine began in 1845 and hung on through 1852, killing a million men, women, and children— losing at least another million to emigration.

Many emigrants seeking cheap passage to America found themselves on overcrowded 'coffin' ships that had no regard for passenger safety. Little food and water during the six-week to three-month voyage. Squalid, close quarters below deck caused thousands to die during the journey, with more perishing from typhus once in port.

Countless Irish immigrants during the famine years landed in America poor, malnourished, lacking a trade, and speaking little English. They set up small ghetto communities on the eastern seaboard where the ships' passengers disembarked at the Boston and New York ports.

Their lack of skills and literacy forced the Irish into accepting the worst jobs. Working long hours and receiving little pay. America's expansion push called for cheap labor, and

Irish immigrants fit the bill. They built roads, canals, bridges, and laid track for railroads.

It was after the Civil War that the Irish began pushing westward alongside the railroad companies, helping the transcontinental crossing lay track across America. Many of these same Irish settled along the track, bringing their culture and religion with them. Atoka, Oklahoma, is one such place.

In 1852, Joseph Byrne, barely out of nappies, survived the eight-week voyage from his family's beloved Ireland to America's coast. Starting out in his young teens, Joseph survived working the transcontinental railroad line for eight years. By 1872, the Missouri—Kansas—Texas Railway, or Katy, reached Atoka, and Joseph found his home. In 1873, the twenty-three-year-old Irish railroader met the love of his life, Neakita, a Choctaw native. His wild Rose.

THE IRISH WOLVES TRILOGY FOLLOWS THE LEGACY AND DESCENDANTS OF JOSEPH BYRNE.

RIVER

Why do tragedies have to be so damn tragic? In Proverbs, King Solomon's sage advice of laughter being the best medicine has merit. However, laughter is also the best cover-up.

A person can hide embarrassment or loneliness with laughter. "Hugh! I'm so happy you haven't eaten yet. I got back earlier than expected and I can join you and Tilly for lunch."

Misdirection. Who laughs when sad?

Comic relief. It's a public service, right?

Laugh instead of frown. Laugh instead of cry. Laugh instead of scream.

River. Raven. Rowan. Sisters forever. In good times and bad.

... but remember to always...

Laugh through the bad.

1

THE DOMINION HOUSE, GUTHRIE, OKLAHOMA – DECEMBER 23 (TWO MONTHS AFTER THAT NIGHT)

Tonight was Patrick Prohibition's first official day of operation, River's new pop-up venture, and she wasn't just an employee. She was the president. There would be no more obsessing over Patrick O'Faolain on her part. Cheers to mental fortitude and stealthy evasions... and whiskey.

Though River was excited about her new enterprise, tonight was also the Oklahoma Historical Society gala to honor and raise money for a select few Oklahoma university professors. Raven's husband, Bran— and wasn't that crazy that her sister was married— sat on OHS's board and had come up with this year's charity ball idea after hearing their parents' story. It was one of many reasons why River had forgiven him for hurting her sister and loved him like the brother he now was.

They'd been back in Oklahoma for a few days and had a packed schedule. A wedding, done, a charity gala, currently in full swing, Christmas, and New Year's Eve at Irish Wolves Pub & Eatery to finish off the trip. Admittedly, River was most excited about Wolves. She was dying to see how Triskelion's design for the bar turned out. Bran had kind of ruined that project for them last summer when he'd broken up with Raven, her older sister, but she had faith in the O'Connors following Triskelion's vision.

Josephine O'Connor was River and her sisters Raven and Rowan's best friend. The O'Connors ran a hospitality business, opening and managing restaurants and clubs all over the world. It was a shame Jo had a previous engagement because she was the life of every party and could have distracted her from 'He who must not be named'— Spoiler, River wasn't talking about Lord Voldemort.

Jo and Honey Bunny (Jo's nickname for the behemoth always attached to her side)— i.e., Thomas MacGregor, owner of a security firm and Jo's personal guard and favorite man to argue/flirt with— were attending an O'Connor holiday event. Not even River's grandma, Nan, or Matilda, Bran and Patrick's grandmother, could make it. A real pity since they were both really good at making awkward situations bearable.

Dinner and speeches were over, and River was currently standing with her sisters in the ballroom, drinks in hand. The music was proving to be quite eclectic. River highly approved.

"I think I've clocked ninety-nine men checking you two out. If you aren't whisked away by the end of the night by some glorious warrior, I'll eat spam for a month," Raven declared, making a gag face.

"Spam is a food of the gods, *soooooo*, not really a hardship, but I agree, the three of us killed the 'dress to impress' assignment," Rowan deadpanned.

While they were still in Dublin and knee-deep in Raven's wedding plans, they found *the* dress they wanted to wear tonight. It was unsurprisingly the same dress except in different colors. They planned on doing something similar for New Year's Eve at Wolves. The three had long black hair to their waists and hazel eyes, thanks to their mother's Native American heritage, and alabaster skin, thanks to their father's Irish heritage. River, Raven, and Rowan weren't vain, but that didn't mean they didn't enjoy the theater of making a scene. Dressing like one another on occasion made an impression.

Raven's precious seven-month baby bump didn't stop the fun either. River's off-the-market sister may not need any male attention besides her husband, but she and Rowan sure as hell still wanted it.

Tonight was an ode to shades of blue. Raven was in Italian blue, River was in Cendre blue, and Rowan was wearing Calamine blue. The dresses were modest in the front and a party in the back. Tight crew neck, short sleeves, body molding, floor length, and then naked from behind. Bare back to the crack. Kind of *Sense and Sensibility* on the front, and Elle King's *My Neck, My Back* walking away. They all did a similar natural makeup palette with subtle differences. Raven's gloss was slightly darker to accentuate her full lips— River would die for her older sister's pout. River smudged a darker, smokey brown around her eyes to accentuate her naturally sultry cat eyes. Rowan didn't need to accentuate anything. She just needed to smile. Her dimples had men tripping over their Prada loafers effortlessly.

Guthrie, Oklahoma— You are fucking welcome.

Bran had been called away moments ago for more meet, greet, and schmoozing, taking his father and brother with him. The sisters had to swallow their laughter because he made no bones about how sexy he thought his wife was, pregnant belly included. He didn't want any man talking to her without an O'Faolain arm draped over Raven's shoulders. Jealousy and Proud Papa mashup. It was way, way too cute. Raven was sighing and blushing in equal measure.

River casually perused the cavernous room. It truly was a splendid venue. All done up in reds, golds, and pine wreaths. Simple and elegant. River pondered what her life would have looked like if the O'Faolains had never stepped foot into the first Triskelion Territory Designs they'd started in Eufaula, Oklahoma— before Bran had hurt her sister and sent the Byrnes running to Ireland. Maybe they would have been the ones to have gotten hired to decorate for the gala tonight. Sighing, she shrugged off the what-ifs. It was neither here nor there now. River would never wish they'd never met the oil billionaires. Raven was too happy to contemplate an alternate reality.

Rowan must have noticed her study of their surroundings. "It's a beautiful space. Bran chose well."

"My husband has good taste. Obviously," Raven announced, grinning, speaking of

herself, not the room.

All three of them had a good laugh over that. Lord, it still seemed impossible after the last several months that Raven was happier than she'd ever been, married, and about to be a mother.

Raven deserved her fairytale. They all did. A couple of months ago, River thought she might get *her* happily ever after. Patrick's intensity that evening in Dublin when he'd walked her home from a pub, and they stood outside Triskelion had certainly *felt* pivotal. The force of his dark eyes pinning her to the door had created some passionate fantasies on her part, but... nothing had come of it. After that night, Pat avoided being alone with her. They rarely texted. They still laughed and smiled at one another— fake gaiety... River's specialty in times of stress. She got a few pats on the shoulder and even a couple of dreaded side hugs.

Friendly.

Friends.

Crushing.

From the moment she'd walked down Triskelion's stairs in their Oklahoma office— when her eyes had found and locked on

Patrick O'Faolain —River had wanted nothing more than to be lost in that man's intense amber gaze. Forever.

But *That Night...* Christ, *That Night* when Patrick had trapped her body between the cold wooden door of Triskelion and his warm chest haunted River. Her feelings for Patrick had always been a buzz, tingling her nerves. After... they became a sting; uncomfortable, hot, and feverish.

Where others saw a fun-loving jokester, River had always found Patrick's presence steady. He was certainly a man with ghosts. The O'Faolain brothers had both been marked in some way by their horrible mother. Patrick was a man who always appeared to be searching for... something. On the flip side, Patrick made her feel special. He listened when she spoke. He knew when she was being less than honest with her ready smiles and laughter. Patrick always could see... *her*. Why couldn't he see *them?*

That Night, as River mentally referred to it, Patrick had shown her new web page developing tools as they chatted, sitting next to one another at the bar. She'd asked him about an issue she was having with Triskelion's contact page. Every now and again, Pat's knee would touch her knee. His barstool would swivel that little bit too far. While she was showing him the contact problem on her phone, he rested his hand, his very large, long-fingered, warm hand on her thigh.

Never too high. Certainly, not high enough.

Each smile or slight touch lit River's insides like wildfire. Being in love with a friend was excruciating.

They took selfies.

It felt like a date.

It wasn't.

And then... *"Have you dated anyone since you left Okla-homa?"* It had taken River a moment to understand what Patrick was asking.

Pat's normal animation had been missing. His body language was stiff. She could only look at him. Confusion had surely painted her face. It was so off-topic that River had been temporarily speechless. Why would he ask? Realization finally bloomed horribly bright. It was only a question. A query any *friend* would ask. River imagined his discomfort was probably due to her being a female friend instead of a male.

River recalled wondering if she would ever get used to inhabiting space with her obsession. It had felt impossible then, and it felt impossible still.

River cringed as she replayed that evening. It had been wonderful, horrible, and awkward, but trumping all that, there had *definitely* been sexual chemistry. Maybe? River had replayed every moment from *That Night* a million times over. No stone left unturned, so to speak. Patrick's whole demeanor *had* changed after he'd questioned her dating. River just didn't believe that her unrequited love for the man had skewed her perception *that* much. Patrick had asked River if she'd gone on any dates. She'd answered honestly.

"No, we've been way too busy." But added, so she didn't seem so pathetic, "I'm thinking of accepting a date from a great guy who lives here in Dublin. He's asked several times, but like I said, we've been swamped."

A change of subject would benefit her sweating armpits, so River tried Raven's trick of a rapid conversation segue. "I'm sure Bran will be staying by Raven's side until Baby O's arrival, but what are you and your dad thinking of doing?" There, an easy family question.

"Who's the guy?" Patrick asked, staring intently at his whiskey on the bar.

Dog with a bone much? She was so not having a bro talk with Pat about potential dates. Offense then. "Jesus, Pat, like you care. Move on. I'm not discussing my love life tonight."

Patrick jerked his head up and gave her a weird look before turning his attention back to the bar top. He shot back his Jameson Cask Mate, visibly trying to shake off 'a mood.' Men— did they have monthlies like women? And when in the hell did she start sounding like Nan?

The rest of the evening went well, with overly descriptive speculations about Bran and Raven's bedroom gymnastics (thanks to Jo), Triskelion, and Jo's plans for the rest of her stay. The evening ended up being lovely despite pining for the guy sitting at her side.

It would get easier to enjoy Pat's presence once River mastered her feelings. Or rather, mastered hiding them from herself.

After a few more drinks, everyone was ready for bed. Jo and Honey— why start calling the man Thomas when Honey Bunny was so precious— headed to their hotel.

River said her goodbyes, told Pat she'd see him tomorrow, and started walking to the flat. She needed to remember to keep a smile on her face when she told Rowan how great the evening had been.

It took River a moment to realize that Pat was a step behind her on the sidewalk. Slowing, she glanced back and asked Patrick what he was doing.

"Walking you home."

Okay... "Good grief, Pat. Don't go out of your way for me. I know where I live. It's only two blocks over. Head on to your hotel. I'll see you tomorrow." River smiled and gave a goofy half-wave.

Stubborn O'Faolain. "I'll see you home. No one should walk alone unless they have to." He then doubled down by moving to her side and putting his arm around her waist. Tingles shot up her spine.

Thoughtful. So friendly and thoughtful. That's Patrick. In

no time, they reached her door. With keys at the ready, she unlocked the heavy door, ready to shove it open. River glanced back to tell Patrick goodnight— again. The words stuck in her throat.

Pat's intense dark eyes were staring at her from directly over her shoulder. So close. Moonlight made his white hair shine and greyed his features and clothes. He looked like a black-and-white photo.

Stark and stunning.

His left hand hovered behind her neck before landing. His callused thumb, like a hot brand, brushed her nape. River's breath caught. Her throat dried. Words? None.

P at, the easy-going, confident, youngest O'Faolain, appeared unsettled, wary, and hesitant. She slowly turned to face him. Pat's grip on her neck adjusted to the front. His fingers now cradled her jaw and neck in a light grip. She let her back rest against Triskelion's door, no longer interested in twisting its handle to escape.

Patrick stared at her face and her mouth for what seemed like hours. His thumb slowly brushed her lower lip. In River's nervousness, she licked her dry lips. Her tongue briefly brushed against his skin.

He groaned.

She panted.

Patrick braced his other hand against the heavy door at her back as his body curled closer to hers. Each breath between them was a puff of white in the cold Dublin air.

Had River misunderstood his feelings? If there was a chance, any chance, she would take it and damn the consequences.

River arched her body off the door, bringing their mouths even closer. She placed her hand against his chest, running her palm up the black wool lapel of his coat until her fingers rested against Patrick's throat.

"River. Jesus, River," Patrick rasped, her name sounding like a benediction on his lips.

"Please, Patrick." Please what? Anything, Lord, but a side hug. Anything.

At River's words, Pat's eyes closed. As if not closing the distance between their mouths was unbearable.

Why did he struggle against their attraction? At least River knew the attraction was mutual. This behavior did NOT exist in Platonicville. Not even adjacent.

Oh God, he moved. Each of their inhalations and exhalations were shared. The smallest increment— the eye of a needle—a grain of sand— separated their lips from coming together. Do it. Do it. River wanted to scream, 'Do IT for fuck's sake!'

The hand not holding her jaw fisted and slammed the door, rattling the front window, and right before he shoved away from her body, taking every bit of warmth with him, Patrick O'Fuck-ingFaolain whispered against her lips.

"Don't go on any dates, River."

River had yet to register his words before Patrick had stormed down the sidewalk. Several minutes passed before River could peel her body from the cold wood at her back wondering what the hell had just happened?

River had to find a better way to guard her heart because her temporary feelings box was shattered— it had exploded the moment his skin touched her own. Don't go on any dates, River. Did that mean... did he want to say... did he want her to date him? Don't go on any dates unless they were with him?

As River made her way up the stairs to the flat, her lips tingled and felt full like they'd actually been kissed. If wishes were made flesh...

Christ Almighty! River was NOT supposed to be thinking about any of *that*. She'd decided that tonight would be the night she would stop dwelling on the youngest O'Faolain and enjoy the evening and her family... enjoying her life. His obvious embarrassment and regret over the encounter forced her to reassess how she would proceed. If her eyes snagged overly long on his white head and broad shoulders upon occasion... habits weren't broken overnight.

If she didn't get a handle on... this... thing, it might break open the new and improved, well-constructed 'feelings box' she'd only finished soldering before walking into the gala— and as welding was only a fictional hobby— she didn't want to test the seams.

Expectations and hope rarely matched reality.

River was about to discuss Auntie names to distract her thoughts when Raven said, "Oh look, the guys are already headed back our way." River inwardly groaned but took a deep breath and pasted on a smile.

"The music's started, Rave. I bet Bran wants to dance with his baby mama," Rowan said, gently poking Baby O. "It's kind of weird not having Thomas MacGregor and his Merry Scary Men guarding us, isn't it?"

"A lot less crowded. That's for damn sure." Since the Byrnes and the O'Faolains were all together, Thomas agreed to let them take only one guard to drive them to the gala and stay with the vehicle. Sam Delton, their families' persistent stalker, and all-around sick fuck, had yet to be found. He may have been quiet, but Delton's poisonous fog hung over all of them still.

"If Bran wants to dance, I hope the floor isn't crowded. We need space," Raven's eyes sparkled as her hands slid around her belly.

"Lay off the chicken and dumplings, sis," River teased. All three sisters laughed at that. Raven had barely gained weight. It was all baby.

The three O'Faolains walked up as the sisters were laughing at Raven. Bran didn't stop until he bent at the waist to hug her sister and kiss her tenderly. It was lovely to see. Hugh stood slightly outside the group, and Pat looked angry about something. Wow, Raven was definitely the only winner in this group tonight.

River elbowed Rowan lightly in the side and whisper-asked if she wanted to go the bar with her once Bran asked Raven to dance. Her answer was two thumbs up.

A minute later, Bran asked Raven to dance— shocker. Rowan smiled an *I told you so* to Raven, who only smiled and shrugged. As they were about to walk away, Raven turned and asked, "Would you all dance with us this first time? I don't want to feel like a Baby On Board display. You two will distract everyone with your bodies," Raven nervously laughed, which meant she really did want them, but *come on*! Torture.

Lord, have mercy. Rowan looked like a deer in headlights, so River went with her earlier plan. "Row and I were about to go to the bar. Go on, you're the most beautiful woman in the room. Plus, you wouldn't even know we were there. You'll be staring at Bran, and you know it." Grabbing at Row's hand, they were about to escape when Patrick decided to insert himself into the conversation.

"I'd like to dance, River." With a strained smile, he grabbed her hand and started pulling her toward his brother. As she was being unceremoniously tugged in Patrick's wake, she heard Rowan telling Hugh, "Okay." He must have asked her to dance.

Fine, she'd do one dance. Patrick looked ready to endure it, so she would too. Then, plan B. B stood for bar.

Where was their easy camaraderie? Why was he being weird? To her? As if *she* had done something wrong— like almost kissing *him* two months ago. No, that was *all* on him. If he felt some kinda way about it, she didn't care. That was a Patrick problem. Getting annoyed now, she pulled her hand from his. He looked sharply at her, a brow arching in question.

"I don't know why you're being such a shit to me, Pat, but I haven't done anything to deserve your coldness." He seemed shocked, opening and closing his mouth soundlessly.

"I... damn... I have been a dick." He looked chagrined and a little lost.

Join the club, O'Faolain.

They stood staring at each other for another minute. She was not going to break the silence. He could explain, or she'd walk away and be a party-of-one at the bar.

"Jesus, Riv. I'm sorry. I have been a moody bastard. Please dance with me. Let me prove to you that I can be something besides an asshole."

River knew she would follow him. She would follow him anywhere.

She was weak, damn it!

He didn't say one word about Dublin, which shouldn't surprise her. He'd remained mute since that night.

He regretted the emotional display.

He regretted showing her anything other than friendship.

She hadn't imagined that moment but... had she?

River swallowed. Knowing the only way forward, for the whole family, was to pretend a nonchalance that was absolute shite, as Nan would say.

She forced a smile. Happy. Happy. Happy.

"Apology accepted. Let's go dance with our family," she half laughed. Looking around his tall frame, she could see Raven and Rowan standing near the dance floor, watching them with concerned expressions. River cringed at the barrage of questions sure to come her way later.

Patrick slung a *very* casual arm around her shoulders and moved them toward the others. Damn, she'd really thought tonight was her night to get her O'Faolain shit done and dusted.

Now she had to endure having the muscular arms of her obsession touching her body for, please God, under four minutes.

Picturing a double shot of Jameson Black Barrel, she walked confidently onto the floor. She would make this dance her bitch. She would overcome her feelings. And then— the band did a Camylio cover for *Strangers*. *FML*. The irony of it all. They *did* make better strangers. If she'd never met Patrick O'Faolain, River wouldn't compare every man to him.

Patrick may not want her romantically, but River truly believed he was the only man with the capability to see... her. He listened. Her words mattered— to him —or they used to. Every thought, every dream, always came back to Patrick.

No one would ever, *could* ever, compare to the youngest O'Faolain.

2

River was in his arms. Patrick could have groaned at how good it felt. She wasn't meant for him, but she felt so right. He had to remember that he wasn't a one-woman man. He wasn't a man who thought past pleasure. He chose women who wanted the same things from him. Nothing more than a night.

Why, then, was the one woman he could never ruin, never hurt, never let down, in his arms? Why was his left hand splayed against her lower back— her very naked lower back? He had noticed several men looking at her. Speculating if she was there with someone. Patrick had never been much of a rager, but his emotions were on edge.

Two months ago, he'd made a mistake. He'd asked River if she was dating. She hadn't been, which was a relief. Selfish? Absolutely. But then, she confided that she planned to accept some offers. Fuck. That. He'd seen red.

He wanted to find out every name and ruin them. River was his. But she wasn't. She was his best friend, but she was a best friend that he regularly jacked off to at night... anytime, really. He pictured River in his bed. River naked in his shower. River smiling. River against a wall, bent over a couch, in the dining room, the kitchen, the elevators... She was everywhere.

Mentally unstable, thy name is Patrick Brandon O'Faolain.

As they moved across the dance floor, River seemed to be avoiding looking at him. She was smiling at everyone else. He had really hurt her feelings, and she was pretending it didn't matter. That it didn't bother her. That her feelings weren't important. That *she* didn't matter— to him.

This is exactly why he didn't screw around with 'good' girls — with friends. It was a complication he'd successfully avoided for years. Not difficult, as he hadn't met River Byrne then. He'd met her now, though, and that had been causing all sorts of problems for months. He needed her smile, her laughter, her raunchy jokes, and her brilliant brain— but he needed the relationship to stay platonic. She wanted him. He most definitely wanted her. It could never happen.

Relationships were folly. Patrick learned that lesson young. If he did do this... this *one thing* that had the potential to hurt his family— hurt River's family— he would never forgive himself.

But damn, she felt so good in his arms. Her skin was soft. She smelled... edible. He wanted to kiss her. He'd imagined it a hundred— a thousand— times. How it would feel to devour her mouth.

He didn't like her ignoring him while she was in his arms.

As they made a slow half-turn, Patrick used the hand at River's back to bring their bodies just that bit closer. Her breasts now grazed his chest— thank Jesus for heels— and her eyes jumped to his, right where they should have been, where he wanted them to stay.

"You look beautiful tonight, River." He really needed to NOT speak. "Your dress is... stunning." What should he ask next? *What color are your panties, River?* Oh God, maybe she wasn't wearing any. Swallow. Cough. Dry mouth.

River's tongue briefly flicked her lower lip. Pat barely held in a groan. "Raven and Rowan are wearing the same dress. The only difference is the shades of blue we chose." Inward cringe. He hadn't even looked at her sisters' dresses.

"Oh... right. I see that now." He saw that he only had eyes for River. Perfect.

Pat made the mistake of glancing below her collarbone. Mistake. He could just make out the slight pucker of her nipples. The same nipples that were occasionally pressed against his chest. Clenching his jaw, he prayed his moan didn't escape. Praying his sex didn't express his 'inner feelings.'

Patrick squeezed his eyes shut. Christ, have mercy. Lord, have mercy. That's it, Patrick, think Mass thoughts. Hell. Damnation. Sinning. No, damn it. Not sinning.

"Pat?"

Hearing River's voice brought him back. Kind of. Once his eyes were open they fixated on her lips. Her mouth.

He was fucked.

"Patrick! Good Lord, are you falling asleep?" Pat winced. He did keep closing his eyes. To pray, damn it, not sleep.

"Sorry, Riv. I have a headache coming on." Great. Maybe he should admit to menstrual cramps. Bran was waving them over. Hopefully, his 'embarrass himself streak' was over. He gave River a smile, and what do you know, bad decisions were still going strong. Pat placed his hand on the small of River's back— way too possessive— to lead her from the dance floor to where his family waited with a photographer.

"OHC hired a few photographers to document the fundraiser. I would love it if the six of us could take one together. We're all dressed up, and Baby O Boy's looking good too. Would you guys mind?" Raven asked, smiling hopefully. As if any of them would tell someone as sweet as his new sister-in-law, no.

The photographer, who had one helluva crazy long mustache, fiddled with his giant camera for another minute.

"Okay folks, let's have the ladies in front since they're just a tiny bit shorter than you gents," the goof guffawed at his own joke. Patrick barely controlled an eye roll. "You three giants stand behind your lady."

Stand behind their lady. Panicked now, Pat looked at his father. He looked a second away from implosion.

Mustache wasn't done with the fun instructions.

"Ah, so you're the lucky father then," looking at Bran already standing behind Raven. "Okay, young lady, lean slightly back into your husband. The relaxed pose combined with your evening dress will make for a spectacular picture."

In the meantime, Pat, his dad, River, and Rowan hadn't moved a muscle. Like they were AI robots with dead battery packs. And, oh look, people were starting to watch the circus. Better and better.

River unstuck herself somehow, she's amazing like that, and suggested she and Rowan stand to one side and Pat and his dad on the other. Irritating, but brilliant.

"No, no, no. The height differences will throw everything off."

Mustache then hung his three-hundred-pound camera around his hairy neck, took Rowan by her arms, and placed her next to Raven's right. The cameraman then turned to River, moving her to Raven's left. "Okay, fellas. Same pose as Bran and Raven."

Patrick was startled when the photographer knew their names. He supposed it was common knowledge. Bran was on the Oklahoma Historical Society board. Pat watched Rowan and his dad stare at each other. Dad looked at Pat before assuming his position behind the youngest Byrne sister, looking as though he'd rather be at the wrong end of a firing squad.

"Let's get this done, Pat. I have a bar calling my name," River teased. As usual, she was trying to deflect the tension. Dang. She must have sensed his hesitation. He didn't want to stand behind her like a... husband. He also didn't want to feel her body against his— afraid of what he might do when he did.

Mustache began walking backward, giving the 'lovebirds' instructions as he went. "Okay, ladies. Lean only slightly back against your men. Bran, perhaps place a hand on your wife's tummy. You other guys, place a hand on your lady's hip."

Going with it now, if for no other reason than to stop the torture, Patrick's hand grasped River's hip, perhaps more firmly than strictly called for. She reclined just that little bit against his body. Intense heat roared through him. He was insta-hard. So erect it was like his dick had served in the military.

Pat shifted, attempting to ghost-the-wiener somehow, only managing to have it poking the exposed lower back of the woman currently gasping in surprise in front of him. Like he had thought earlier, and a hundred times since— this night kept getting better and better. He really needed to ask Gran if there was a patron saint of embarrassment.

Mustache clapped his hands in... satisfaction? Show over, the other attendees moved on, and he would too just as soon as Papa Boner left the building.

PATRICK HAD A HARD-ON. Pressed into her back. What in the hell was going on? Raven and Bran were now facing one another. Bran looked at her sister like her smile housed the sun, and River believed, to him, it did. Sadly, Raven and Bran's love story didn't eliminate River's current porn star moment. Patrick the Penis was making shit *super* awkward.

One of them had to do something— anything. "Umm... so... Pat?"

Patrick's hand, still attached to her hip, flexed once, then twice before dropping to her side. He must have leaned down because his deliciously warm breath touched her ear, shooting shivers through her body.

"If you wouldn't mind walking in front of me and heading to the back hallway where the restrooms are, I'd be indebted."

Rowan chose that moment to see if River wanted to head to the bar. Think. Think. Think. "Save me a seat, Row. Pat and I are going to run to the restroom real quick." Rowan smiled and waved as she headed in the direction leading to the rows of whiskey— to salvation.

River, all cool, no erectile aggression to see here, confidently strode from the room. Patrick kept perfect time with her shorter stride. As soon as they reached the darker hallway leading to the restrooms, Pat opened the door to their left and grabbed River's hand, pulling her in behind him. As soon as she passed the threshold, he closed the door, locked it, and had her pressed against the solid wood within seconds. The only illumination was shown around the door frame.

Breathless. Excited. Nervous. Confused. All of the above. But also curious, desperate, and out of patience. "What the hell is going on with you, Patrick?"

His hands flat against the door on either side of her body, he leaned in, putting his mouth very, very near her own. "I don't know. I don't fucking know, Riv," he admitted with a desperate edge.

Where Patrick O'Faolain was concerned, the phrase *in for a penny, in for a pound* struck true more often than not. "Well, your dick seems to know something. Why don't you ask it?"

"Why are you making this so difficult?"

Incensed, River snapped. "Me? *I* am the one making things hard? Pun intended."

"Damn it, River! I'm not the man you need. I will only hurt

you. I know it. If I hurt you, it would kill me. Please. Please be stronger than me and walk away."

River gasped in surprise. Every one of her hopes and dreams where Pat was concerned were laid out before her. This moment. This was the one single moment she'd been dreaming about for months. "I'm not walking away, Pat. You may not be the man I need, but you're sure as hell the man I want. The man I choose."

His penis might have pushed them into this room, but she hoped it was her words that would keep them there. "River. River. River," Patrick said against her forehead, her cheek, her lips— finally, finally, finally, he kissed her. His tongue, his teeth, and his very breath scorched her body. River would be surprised to find the room anything but ashes.

Patrick kissed— desperate and frantic —perfect. As his hands grasped her hips, pressing her body against the door, her hands explored— every bit of territory comprising Patrick's body that she'd ever desired to touch. His neck, shoulders, chest, abs, and that very hard, very masculine anatomy straining his pants.

As Patrick's tongue warred with her own, as their breath and bodies shook and spasmed, River ran her palm firmly against his suit-clad erection. Patrick groaned and pressed tighter against her hand. "You undo me, baby. I could come from your hand alone. Keep stroking me. Just. Like. That."

As her hand worked his body, his hands found her breasts. Through the silk, Patrick rubbed, tweaked, and full-on pinched her nipples until River was all but quivering. "Patrick..." River needed— everything. One of Pat's hands bunched her dress, wadding the material until it was high enough to reach her thighs. Yes. Yes. Yes!

And then knocking. Knocking on the door her back was currently plastered against. She heard someone ask how the door got locked. River's eyes had adjusted to the dim light enough to make out serving carts, platters, and glassware. Oh God.

Patrick breathed a 'No Way' against her lips, his fingers just shy of brushing against her damp center, her fingers still wrapped around his clothed dick. This was... this was the worst moment to be interrupted. The. Worst.

"Pat," River panted. A question?

"Riv. Just... give me a moment, and I'll get us out of here."

Patrick removed his hand from beneath her skirt. So, River reluctantly removed her hand from his zipper. He didn't help matters by pinching her nipple one more time before fully separating their bodies.

Gently, he moved her slightly west of the door and, at a sloth's pace, flipped the lock, opening the door to the bewildered waitstaff waiting beyond.

"So sorry, guys. We thought this was the coat closet."

River died over the ridiculous lie but followed Patrick out, smiling and so sorrying as she went. Zero eye contact. River did *not* want to see the knowing smirks. As they neared the restrooms, River said, "And... the Awkward Olympics Award goes to... Patrick O'Faolain." Elbowing her in the ribs, Pat suggested they use the restrooms to... sort their clothes out and then meet at the bar.

River couldn't help grinning at Pat. She was giddy. Ecstatic. Patrick wanted her like she wanted him. Finally, holy shit. Just thinking about where her hand had been two minutes ago had her blushing but reveling in her daring as well.

River leaned toward Patrick before he went into the men's restroom, thinking he might kiss her. He backed away suddenly and gave a quick glance at their surroundings. As if... as if he were making sure no one would see them together. Embarrassed now, she gave Pat a small smile before backing away. "See you in a few, then."

"Of course," Pat said, already turning away.

It was the last time River laid eyes on him that night. She met Rowan and a hovering Hugh for a drink, made the room rounds again, and then, *finally*, it was time to go home. It was just under a two-and-a-half-hour drive to Muskogee. They had a driver so everyone could kick their shoes off and relax.

During the car ride, Bran said it sucked Pat started feeling bad and had to leave early. He'd paid an Uber driver some ungodly amount to take him all the way to Muskogee.

A real shame, that.

River closed her eyes, leaning her head against the soft leather headrest. She'd started the evening determined to let the idea of a relationship with Patrick go, only to find herself in an absolute state of euphoria, to the utter dejection of its finale. She sat up when someone took her hand. Rowan. She was looking at her in question. River could only shake her head no, mouthing *I'm fine*. Rowan wasn't convinced but dropped it.

She was fine.

She wasn't dying inside.

She didn't want to cry.

3

___

His mustache itched. Ignoring the irritating facial hair, bushy eyebrows included, Samuel Delton continued to mingle amongst the glitz and glitter of the Oklahoma Historical Society's gala elite. Cheese motherfuckers. Getting hired by the OHS as a professional photographer for the event was a breeze.

He smiled at just how well-acquainted he was with cameras. The only difference was the people he was taking pictures of tonight knew he was doing it. Admittedly, not as much fun.

For this occasion, he was a paunchy middle-aged man with no interest in scaping his hairy body. He'd had to go above the usual costuming since the O'Faolains had surely been made aware of his identity after the Tulsa detectives discovered he'd been behind some tampered pictures that were sent to James O'Connor and Bran O'Faolain... of their girlfriends. They also discovered some of his cameras and followed them to his home—Sam sure missed the lady's gym locker room feed.

So, the wrong people would know his identity and what he looked like. Sam had been very careful coming back to Oklahoma for that very reason. He knew the detectives were still hot to find him. They wouldn't.

It galled Sam each time he was forced to remember what Hugh O'Faolain had done to Sam's father, Thomas Delton, and the reason he found himself in costume tonight. His dad had been a loyal accountant to that fucking family for years, and they dared accuse him of stealing! His father didn't take anything from those bastards that he wasn't owed. He only professed his guilt so the great Hugh Almighty didn't prosecute and ruin the Delton name. His father wouldn't allow that kind of shame to fall on his son or his wife— of course, that thankless bitch left her husband and son soon after, anyway.

Unfortunately, Thomas Delton had basically been black-balled in Oklahoma. He could never hope to work for any prestigious companies again. The stress forced his father to resort to prescription pills to cope with the brutal betrayal. He died shamed and depressed. The coroner tried to rule it a suicide, but Sam knew better. It was an accident. His father would never leave his son alone. Thomas Delton's death could only be laid at the feet of one man. Hugh O'Faolain. Ruining the alpha oil wolf, his whole family and their best friends, the O'Connors, were simply cherries atop his revenge float.

So, shocker, Sam was way ahead of the detectives' efforts. He'd left his RV at a park in Arkansas, a beautiful state, and drove his tiny, nondescript car to Guthrie. He had a new life, a new purpose, a new identity, and time. Time being the most precious thing. It was time to expand his @SammySoGood— King of Twisted Love Stories business, and, even more importantly, time to plan new ways to destroy the O'Faolains.

So, what had he learned tonight? First, Bran was shelved for the moment. Sam could tell he was a total Stage 5 wife clinger. There wouldn't be much opportunity for a while. Second, old man Hugh watched the youngest Byrne with an intensity rarely seen without some sort of sexual interest attached. Sam wasn't concerned. Yet. He had plans for Rowan Byrne.

Third, and the best bit, was that Playboy Patrick was smitten with the middle sister. Keep it in the family much? Patrick was fighting the attraction, but his tented pants didn't go unnoticed through Sam's camera lens. Sam also didn't miss the two slipping away together.

When River emerged from the back and ordered a double shot of whiskey, Sam was giddy. Something went amiss behind closed doors. Patrick never showed his face in the ballroom again. He wanted River but was fighting it. Once a playboy, always a playboy. Sam would have to watch the youngest O'Faolain boy.

Whatever pictures he took would have to be sold to gossip blogs instead of sent directly. Public was better than private for Sam's plan to work anyway. He would spend a few more days in Tulsa before heading back to Arkansas. He had to think of the perfect travel disguise for his trip to Ireland after all.

4

<hr>

It was Christmas morning. Two days after Patrick had bailed on River at the gala. Two days after he'd hurt her feelings. Again. He needed to talk to his brother or father, but each time he started to, the thought of admitting what he'd been doing— leading on the sister of Bran's wife— he hated himself enough, but to see a look of disappointment on the faces of the two men he loved most in the world would crush him.

How had things become... this?

He absently flipped bacon before putting hashbrowns in a huge cast iron pan. When Patrick turned to grab the bowl of waffle batter, he let out a started yelp. Hugh the Harbinger of Doom was leaning against the center island, big arms crossed over his chest. Staring.

"Jesus, Dad. Are you trying to make sure I burn myself on a pan?" Patrick went back to the bacon, turned the waffle iron on, wiped the already clean counter down, and pulled the bacon to put it in the warming drawer. And still, the bastard didn't say anything.

Pat really, really didn't want to make eye contact. His dad could still make him squirm like a naughty five-year-old.

Without turning around, Patrick asked, "Is the table set for breakfast?"

Forty-five seconds later. "Mom and Bébhinn are seeing to it."

"I'll keep working on the food. Let me know when everyone is ready." In other words, dismissed.

"Patrick."

Fuck. Patrick felt his shoulders stiffen but soldiered on. *Ignore him, Pat.*

One minute and fifty seconds later. "Patrick. Turn around. Now."

There was no ignoring his dad, apparently. Turning the gravy to low, he turned.

"Yes?"

"I see you are wanting to test me this morning. Consider me unimpressed."

"Fine. What would you like to say to me?" Even Patrick knew he was pushing his dad's patience, but for fuck's sake, he was in the middle of a self-made crisis.

"River." Pat flinched. "Tell me."

Oh God. Patrick should have known. His dad missed nothing when it came to his boys. Sonofabitch, he should have talked to him before now.

"I fucked up with her, Dad."

"How far has it gone, Son?"

Patrick pressed his fingers against his eyes, trying to relieve the building pressure. Knowing his dad would always love him helped him get the story out. He told him everything. The nonstop texting, always calling her, loving her laugh, loving her smile, loving... everything about her.

Pat admitted he went too far in Dublin, asking her not to date. He admitted to trying to stay away from her. Admitted it wasn't working. Admitted to hurting her feelings with his on and off again bullshit. Admitted to kissing her at the gala. Admitted to leaving her alone and confused after the kiss. Admitted to avoiding her since then. Admitted hating that he wanted her to be only his but knowing he wasn't ready for that type of commitment.

Admitted to feeling utterly and totally lost.

His dad was silent for a moment. One of his best and most irritating qualities was that Hugh O'Faolain thought about every word before he spoke it, and he never spoke until he was good and ready. Patrick waited.

"It's Christmas. Not ideal. We are spending New Year's at Wolves and heading to Dublin two days after that. Again, not ideal timing."

"Not ideal for what?"

"Once we're back in Dublin, you are going to sit down with River and explain you have commitment issues. You need counseling, Patrick. I think your mother skewed your thinking." Dad raised his hand to stop him from interrupting. "Hell, I don't think. I know she did because she screwed up your brother and — me. So, you'll explain. She'll wait for you to get your shit together, or she won't. You don't like hurting her, so stop fucking doing it.

"Use your words. She will hear you. Maybe you should try to talk to her before going to Dublin. I don't know. That's up to you, but do not let this continue as it has. You're hurting River, but you're also hurting yourself." At this pronouncement, his dad put his bear paws on each of Pat's shoulders and leaned in close. "And I won't tolerate you hurting yourself. Are we clear?"

Wow. Intense. "Clear." Swallowing past the lump in his throat, Pat added, "Thank you, Dad." He only nodded and left the kitchen without another word. Well, he didn't know about the counseling thing, but he did owe it to River to be honest.

Before they left Oklahoma or after was the question.

It was Christmas morning, and River was trying her best to put on a brave face— and make it stick. She and Patrick had managed to avoid each other since yesterday. Small mercies. River snuck out of her second-floor bedroom and made it downstairs without her sisters hearing or seeing her. She knew a reckoning with them was coming. Just please, God, not today. On Christmas. She heard Matilda and Nan scaping the dining room table and headed in that direction.

"Oh wow, this looks amazing, you guys! Holy shit, these pinecones are flipping huge." River picked up the eight-inch cone in wonder.

"Language, young lady," Nan scolded. Matilda just smiled and gave River a wink.

"Patrick's in the kitchen cooking breakfast if you want to go see what's left to do," Matilda suggested.

River fumbled the pinecone, earning a sharp look from her grandma. That woman was way too intuitive. "Oh, I'm sure he's got breakfast under control. I thought I'd help you guys finish the table."

"Mmm, sure, sweetheart." Matilda was also too sharp.

Hugh walked into the dining room, glower in place. He surprised the shit out of River by walking straight to his mom and placing a gentle kiss on her cheek. "Merry Christmas, Mother." River saw Matilda blink furiously before wishing him a Merry Christmas too. River saw Nan turn quickly before anyone saw how Hugh's sweetness affected her. Damn, how she must miss her own men desperately at times like this.

Hugh, proving he was as amazing as his mother thought him to be, circled the table and placed a kiss on Nan's cheek. "And Merry Christmas to you as well, Bébhinn."

Nan couldn't hide her slight sniffle as she patted Hugh's

cheek and softly said, "So sweet." Hugh... sweet... will wonders never cease. River caught his eye and mouthed thank you. Hugh nodded in acknowledgment and left the room. Hugh was Shrek. There were so many, many layers to that onion.

River could hear her sisters and Bran descending the stairs. Game face engaged.

EVERYONE ENJOYED the breakfast Patrick prepared. He hadn't. Everyone was happy and laughing. Even River. Except Patrick knew her well enough to know her teasing and smiles were covering up her unease. The unease that Patrick had caused.

Patrick decided that today was a day for family. He would talk to River after Gran and Bébhinn left. Two days. Two days, and maybe he could figure out a way to have peace between them again. He needed River. He just didn't want to need her so much.

They all sat in the big living room around the giant Christmas tree. Mimosas and laughter. Bran sat behind Raven. His hands cupped their son. They whispered and kissed. Pat wanted that. But... but surely it couldn't last. He hoped for Bran's sake that it was forever. It just seemed impossible.

He would rather have River as a friend forever than a lover for a moment.

Bébhinn and Rowan were passing out Grandma gifts. They'd drawn names before leaving Ireland to see who they were buying gifts for except the grandmas. They got gifts from everyone and gave everyone gifts.

Patrick glanced at River, excited about what they'd done for the matriarchs of their families. She smiled back, but her eyes clouded almost immediately before she looked away. Damn it. Patrick squeezed his eyes shut tight for a moment. He didn't want River upset with him. He never wanted to disappoint her, and yet, it's all he'd done lately.

Hugh announced, "Mom and Bébhinn, you only have one gift each this year. We all went together."

Patrick didn't care what he got. Any present was just plain awesome. Both women smiled at each other and untied the red ribbons adorning each box. When they lifted the lids, there was a single letter inside explaining that they each owned an apartment in Dublin to use when they visited their family. Each woman had carte blanche in decorating and outfitting their apartments courtesy of Triskelion Territory Designs.

Of course, tears, hugs, and thank yous took thirty minutes. It was one of the best Christmases Patrick ever remembered having.

He wished River was sitting in front of *him*, like she was his and he was hers. Like Raven was with Bran.

It took everything River had in her not to ugly cry. She was so happy that her grandma was so happy. Both older women were in tears. Excited to be included in their children's and grandchildren's lives.

Nan knitted scarves for her granddaughters and Hugh and the boys. They were lovely, warm, and perfect. The boys each put theirs on and gave Nan big hugs. She and her sisters loved that. Matilda gave Raven a trunk of Bran's baby toys and trinkets. Raven was still crying.

She gave River a delicate white gold necklace with a single sapphire soldered to the left of the chain over the heart. Her husband had given her the necklace for an anniversary. Because, she said, blue was River's favorite color, she wanted her to have it. Matilda tried to act like it wasn't a big deal that she was giving

River something that her beloved husband had given his wife. Now River was the one tearing up. Matilda gifted Rowan an antique Native American woven wicker flower basket. Rowan... was dabbing her eyes.

'Tis the Season of Tears. What amazing and thoughtful grandmothers they had.

It was time for the younger people's gift exchange. Thank God she got Bran, and despite the tension between Patrick and her, River was totally stoked about her gift for her brother-in-law.

Hugh handed Raven her gift first. As Raven peeled back the tissue, her face turned pink, then red, then *redder*. What had Hugh gotten her to cause that reaction? It was in a hallmark Tiffany blue box. Hello... Tiffany.

Raven stuttered while Bran looked perplexed at her reaction. "Th... tha... thank you, Hugh. It's all so beautiful."

"Well, sis, share with the class already. What is it?" River asked.

Rowan moved over and looked in the box, squealed, clapped her hand over her mouth, and resumed her seat.

What in the hell was in that box? She looked at Patrick, who shrugged, seeming as perplexed as she was. Nothing for it but to examine the gift herself. Raven was too busy folding the wrapping paper to fill her in. River hopped over in front of her sister and started tossing the tissue to the floor. It was a full Tiffany set of baby dinnerware, combs, frames, cups— all engraved with Baby O.

Oh. My. God. River had started the Baby O, short for Baby Orgasm/O'Faolain, during Raven's first trimester. No wonder her sister's face was beet red.

River looked at Hugh. "Well played, old man." His expression of boredom never changed, but the asshole of assholes winked. Impressive. He knew what it meant then.

Raven got Hugh a soft, gray (ugly) graphic t-shirt with Best Gpa on the pocket. He shot a grin at Raven. Success.

Bran got River three cases of Jameson Black Barrel. "You rock, bro," River crowed, holding her loot. Bran smirked and said, "I'm very aware."

Finally, she got to give Bran his prezzie. River tossed him the gift, which he easily caught. He tore off the paper like a three-year-old, which River loved, and read the card inside. She'd gotten a session with one of their favorite potters in Dublin. Once Baby O was born, she would cast a mold of Bran's open hand with his son's hand in his palm. "I've seen some of her newborn work. It's breathtaking, Bran. Seriously, I think she'll create something you'll treasure always."

"River. Jesus. This is an incredibly thoughtful gift." He got up and hugged her tight. "Seriously, Riv. Thanks." Bran sat down by Raven again. He looked at her sister with so much love. Perfect.

"You're welcome. Much love to you both," River added. Raven was looking at River with love and joy. Her sisters' happiness was everything.

Patrick gave Rowan an exclusive pass to tour the Glenmorangie distillery in Scotland and the Slane distillery in Ireland with her own personal tour guide and tastings included for as many people as she wanted to take with her.

"Patrick," Row exclaimed, "You didn't have to do something this amazing. Thank you. Seriously, thank you."

River could see Rowan's gratitude made him uncomfortable, but he was also pleased that she loved the gift. Rowan surprised Patrick with tickets to see Deadmau5 in Vegas.

"Jesus, Row. This is the best gift ever! Thank you." Patrick stood up and grabbed Rowan up in a bear hug, making her laugh along with everyone else. It *was* a great gift.

Gift draw presents out of the way, it was time for the last

few gifts from people who wished to give a gift to someone who they hadn't drawn.

Hugh gave his mother a month-long trip to Italy with an extra ticket for her best friend, Diana Gaines. "Oh, you sweet boy," Matilda O'Faolain cooed at her only son. Hugh's cheeks pinkened. Precious.

"You mentioned wanting to see the Vatican library, so I got you and Diana a palazzo in Italy. No big deal." Hugh was trying to deflect. He only made it worse. Watching Hugh squirm was better than going to the movies.

"No big deal? Hugh— I've dreamed of a palazzo in Italy. Thank you, sweetheart," Matilda gushed.

Bran jumped on Hugh's embarrassment. "You are the sweetest of sweethearts, Dad."

Patrick added, "Dad, you truly are the sweetest boy in the whole wide world."

Hugh was a half second from launching out of his chair and tackling his sons, but Raven, unfortunately, stopped the beat-down by handing a present to Bran.

"I have something for you, babe."

River already knew what it was.

Raven had made Bran a loaf of sourdough bread using the starter he'd gifted her in Ireland. You would have thought Raven had given Bran the key to the answers of the universe. After Bran kissed her, a hair longer past comfortable to watch, he announced he wasn't sharing. River saw Patrick glance at the box. He was so going to steal some.

Rowan handed Hugh a small package, causing the older man to turn the color of a ripe tomato. It took multiple promptings to get him to unwrap it. Rowan had commissioned an artist to hand-tool a leather cover for a rare copy of *Pride and Prejudice.*

"For your library," Rowan prompted, when Hugh said nothing. "Bran and Pat mentioned you have a library on the third floor. I thought…" Rowan stopped. Please Hugh, River thought, be kind.

He opened the cover, it really was stunning, and read the inscription her sister had written.

To Hugh
RCB

"It's beautiful, Rowan. Thank you," Hugh said, carefully closing the book. His fingers gently ran over the cover. "You are welcome to see the library." Holy shit. A third-floor invite.

Crisis adverted. Row smiled. "I would love that."

There were two gifts left, and River prayed— heavily and on metaphoric knees —that the gifts would be ignored.

Nan said, "There are only two gifts left."

Thanks, Grandma.

"Oh, it was only a small thing for Patrick. No biggie. Let's get drinks and talk about your apartment renovations." Why hadn't she swiped her gift from the tree? Whyyyyyy, River moaned in her head. She'd placed the present under the tree when they'd first arrived at Hugh's— when she'd still held out hope that Patrick would drop his good buddy bullshit.

Rowan and Raven were picking up River's wish to move on and chimed in with, 'Yeah, Nan, I'm so excited,' and 'I already have some ideas, Nan.'

River saw Bran look at Hugh and then Patrick. Clearly picking up on the weird vibes. Her face was so hot it had to be red. Before she could extricate herself from the living room, a large hand holding a present appeared in front of her face.

Game face, River. Now.

Glancing up at Pat, she took the gift from his hand. "Oh, geez, Patrick. You didn't have to get me anything. Thank you."

Keeping her holly jolly smile, even when she noticed he was holding her gift to him, she continued, "Oh good, you found your present. It's just a simple thing... like a funny gift." Cringe.

Well, she singlehandedly managed to escalate the awkward. Now everyone was silent and staring. Lord, give me strength— or strike her dead. Either would work.

Patrick sat back in his chair. Watching River. "Let's open them at the same time."

Yes! Get it over with faster. "Sure." Smile. Chuckle. Nothing uncomfortable happening here.

River pulled back the tissue to see a framed picture of Pat and her taking a selfie at a pub in Dublin. Oh my God. River quickly looked at Pat. He was holding a very similar picture in his hand.

Raven broke the silence. "Did you guys frame the same picture for each other? That is crazy, Riv. How cool."

Forcing herself to respond, as Patrick was back to staring at the picture, she said, "How funny. We each took selfies with each other that night." Well," River began while standing, to begin picking Christmas paper off the floor and putting it in a trash sack, "thank you, everyone, for everything. It was an amazing Christmas."

Rowan was already up gathering trash, too, as everyone said thank you again. Hugh said he'd brought the screens down around the patio and turned on the heaters earlier so they could enjoy the morning outdoors. They agreed it would be fun to chill with Bloody Marys— nonalcoholic for Rave— and cards.

"Hey, Rave, I'm going to run upstairs and grab a sweater. Our yoga pants will be warm enough with the heaters. Do you want me to run to your room and get you a sweater?"

"Would you? Thanks. I'll help Bran make the drinks— that I can't have," she laughed.

"Put a ton of olives, celery, and pickles in some tomato

juice," River suggested. "It'll be almost the same," she teased. As River started to run upstairs, Rowan yelled to get her a sweater too. "I'm on it."

Rowan and River were in one room, so she grabbed a soft navy cashmere sweater for herself, planning on trying on her new necklace and a lovely cream cable knit sweater for Rowan. Running across the hall to Bran and Raven's room, she found her sister a lovely green cardigan, easy to wrap around her growing belly.

Excited for the day, River hustled through the bedroom door and smacked straight into Patrick's body. If he hadn't caught her arms, currently full of sweaters, she would have fallen on her ass.

"Oomph," Patrick grunted.

"Jesus, Pat. Sorry about that." Smiling, she started to move around him. He stepped in her path.

"Can we talk?"

River wanted to reply with 'not a snowball's chance in hell,' but opted for, "Sure, I'll see you on the patio." Smile. Flee. Again.

"No, River. I mean, can I talk to you alone." He must have seen her flinch because he added, "Please. I want to explain."

River didn't want to have the 'It's not you, it's me' talk. "Not necessary. I get it. We're still friends. No worries." As she started walking away, Patrick grabbed her free hand, gently pulling her back around to face him. Now, she was getting pissed. Did he really think she was so ignorant she didn't understand a brush-off?

"Jesus, River. Please, just give me a minute."

River almost relented. He looked distraught. She *did* believe he never meant to hurt her feelings. She *did* believe he valued their friendship. She knew he had to have issues from his mother hurting him as a child. Still, it didn't give him a pass to play with her feelings. And that's exactly what he'd been doing.

"How about I tell you what I already know so we can move on and never, ever address this again. You almost kissed me two months ago in Dublin. You asked me not to date anyone. The 'else' was assumed. Meaning, I assumed, incorrectly, that you wanted to date me. Then you ghosted me.

"The wedding was brilliant and fun, and we laughed like we used to. Then you ghosted me. The gala— Patrick, you don't understand— that night, I had decided, for my own happiness, to move on from wanting you. Then you mic dropped your hard-on against my back."

River had let the sweaters fall to the floor at this point and was glaring at him, arms crossed over her chest. Patrick tried to interrupt, but she wasn't having it. "And before you think I still believe you were excited because it was me, I don't. I get it. I'm a woman, and any will do."

Patrick flinched.

"The service room... I'm no coward. I fully admit you never made me any promises. Hell, I was willing to let you fuck me against that door, and YOU HAVEN'T EVEN TAKEN ME ON A DATE!" she whisper-yelled, unwilling for the family to bear witness to... this.

"That's on me too. What isn't on me is after... that... moment, I thought you were as into me as I was to you. I tried to kiss you in the hall. You were mortified, looking around like someone might have seen you with me." River took a deep breath, willing the tears threatening not to fall.

"And then you left. Then you ghosted me again." Chuckling, River shook her head as she bent to pick the sweaters off the floor. "So, you can see, Pat, I don't need anything *explained* to me."

River went to the stairs, stopping without turning around.

She took several deep breaths. She hated what she'd just done. Hated that she and Patrick were in such a rotten place.

Still facing the stairs, River quietly, and much calmer, asked, "Pat?" She heard him move behind her. Not attempting to touch her, thank God.

"Yes?"

God, he sounded upset. That made two of them. "I'm sorry. I—"

"God, River, don't—."

"Stop. Let me finish. I am sorry. I spoke to you as if we had something other than friendship. You did give me mixed signals, but we were never a thing. Not before, not now, not ever. I just want to be friends again. It can work if we both try, to like, you know, fake it until we make it. Not just for us, but for our families. For me, Pat, please, let's enjoy today. Play games and laugh. Our grandmas are leaving in a couple days. We've New Year's at Wolves, and then I go back to Dublin."

"We. We go back to Dublin."

"Yeah, that's what I meant," she sighed. Though, to be honest, she wished he wasn't going back there. "Will you try to be friends like we used to be? I do miss that." River held her breath. Patrick's big body at her back cast shadows down the stairs in front of her.

"I can do that. I miss us too."

River nodded. One step forward and Patrick's hand landed on her shoulder, stopping her forward momentum. "Patrick," River warned. It took a moment, but he finally released her. She continued down.

This time, Patrick let her go.

5

———

Days of apartment designing for the grandmas— until they'd left Oklahoma— friendly banter, game nights, music, dancing, baby names, and eating meals family style— all satisfactory. He and River had been practicing the 'fake it until you make it' mantra for days— all satisfactory too.

Except for every night and every minute. The need to grab River and hug her tight, kiss her, touch her, talk to her about anything and everything— not fake talking for the family— but really talking, was eating him alive. Moments where she told him her secrets, and he told her his.

Jesus, God, he was lost. He wanted her— but— forever? No. Maybe if they dated. Casually? No, River wasn't casual. He knew that, which is why he'd tried to avoid... this. Fuck. Everyone decided to turn in early since tomorrow night was New Year's Eve, and they were celebrating at Wolves, driving the fifty minutes back to Muskogee that night, then packing everything for the trip back to Ireland.

Patrick showered. Paced. Tried to jack off— to River's image, of course— definitely didn't quash his infatuation with the woman.

What to do?

What should he do?

What was he willing to do?

What would she let him do? Shit, not where his mind needed to be.

Dad asked him if he'd spoken to River. Patrick said they'd spoken. Technically true. She had, at any rate. Each and every word was carved into his skin. Excuses were no longer an option. He had hurt her. And, oh look, he was still contemplating seeking out her bedroom. When she'd let him have it outside Bran's room on Christmas— there were no words to describe the agony. He'd been a breath away from begging her to be his in truth.

You never made me any promises... I was willing to let you fuck me against that door... you haven't even taken me on a date... you were mortified to be seen with me... then you left... you ghosted me... I'm a woman, and any will do... we were never a thing— not before, not now, not ever...

He was done. No matter how hard it was to stay away, he would never willingly hurt River again, which meant sticking to the plan. *Fake it until you make it.*

Midnight. The kitchen, then. Maybe he could put together a casserole that could be put on early for brunch. Perfect.

Patrick made his way downstairs, not bothering to put anything on over his boxer briefs. It was him and the kitchen— and the kitchen didn't care what he was wearing.

As Patrick neared the kitchen's open sliding barn door, he heard voices.

River.

He should leave.

He wasn't leaving.

"I hope I didn't wake you. I just missed you and wanted to hear your voice."

Patrick saw red. His body heated and expanded. River missing someone that wasn't him. No. No way. Rage burned all rational thoughts. He stormed into the kitchen, seeing River's small frame sitting on one of the center islands, an oversized t-shirt pulled over her bent knees, and a tiny arm wrapped around them. Her other hand held a phone to her ear.

Talking to someone she missed.

Pat stormed over, placing his body directly in front of her tiny feet. Body language all *What the Fuck Do You Think You're Doing?* Completely unfair. He even added a *How Dare You?* look. Faking it until they made had been a dumb idea anyway.

River startled. Of course, she was startled. Eyebrows raised, all WTF. Patrick raised his own brows back at her. River took the phone from her ear and pressed the speaker.

"Hey, Nan, Pat just walked into the kitchen, say hello."

Pat could have died. *Should* have died at his presumption.

"How is my sweet boy doing, then, Pat?"

River stared at him. Daring him to make a scene.

"Starving, Nan. I miss your butter rolls already. I miss you too," he added. Mentally trying to find a way to get out of this unscathed. River's nostrils flared— she was pissed.

"I'll see you in a few weeks, Patrick. I have an apartment to design and a great-grandbaby to kiss. Be good to my girls."

Patrick had a lump in his throat. "I will Bébhinn. See you soon."

"I love you, Patrick. I love you, River Aster. You call me whenever you need me. No matter the time or day. Promise?"

"Promise. I love you, Nan. See you in a few weeks."

Patrick knew he'd fucked up. Like really, really, really fucked up. River ended the call and set her phone on the counter. She didn't say a word, successfully rocking his father's favorite silent intimidation technique.

"I'm sorry I interrupted. I was going to put a casserole together for brunch tomorrow." Credible.

"And what exactly were the theatrics about?"

Patrick considered weaving some ridiculous tale until River added, "Please don't lie. I'm too tired, Pat."

Patrick noticed the skin under her eyes looked bruised like she hadn't been sleeping well. Patrick's ever-present guilt crashed through his body. Torture.

So, he told the truth. "I couldn't sleep because I only think of you even though I don't deserve you. I refuse to put our friendship in danger again, but when I heard your voice, I couldn't turn back around. I did intend to make a casserole for tomorrow until I heard you talking on the phone." Here, he paused, gauging just how much truth she needed— wanted. She looked like it was all truth or nothing. Truth then.

"I didn't know you were speaking to Bébhinn. You told someone that you missed them and that you just needed to hear their voice. I was pissed, and jealous, and everything in between. And before you hand me my ass, I know I have no rights to those feelings, but... well, you're the one who asked for honesty."

River *HAD* *ASKED* *FOR* *HONESTY.* A mistake? No, she wouldn't lie to herself. It thrilled her to hear Patrick's explanation. He'd been jealous. As revelations go, it was giant. But... it changed nothing.

It changed everything.

"I appreciate your honesty, Pat." River started to slide off the counter. Better to remove herself from... her destruction. But Patrick stepped closer, and River, for the first time, realized he was in his underwear and— he was happy, really happy, to see her.

"Patrick?"

Pat inhaled deeply, letting it out nice and slow, as if yoga breathing would cure his... upward-facing dog situation.

"River," Pat practically growled as he placed each hand on either side of her body, gripping the white granite like a drowning man would a life preserver.

Everything about this moment was a neon precursor sign to disaster. She didn't care. Not anymore. Not tonight. Perhaps not ever again. She was even willing to chance him ghosting her again.

Her body and her mind were made for Patrick Brandon O'Faolain.

Five days had felt like a long time. When she considered what forever might look like... Never sharing breath with Patrick or her dreams. Never have her body caressed by Patrick or share a peaceful silence. She wanted what her sister and Bran had. A bond without end or question.

Patrick was every fantasy River might conjure.

The freedom to explore his body was intoxicating. She started by running her fingers through Patrick's thick, white hair, a straight sheet that fell over half his beautiful face. Then she ran her nails over the short stubble where he'd shaved one side. The moonlight painted Patrick with a Viking brush. Ragnar Lothbrok come to pillage and conquer.

She drug her fingers over his lips and neck. Traced his broad shoulders. He was naked except for those sexy, silk boxer briefs. It felt like tracing marble, but where a statue was cold and hard, Pat was heat. Smooth and hot.

Patrick gripped both her thighs, spreading her legs wide so he could step between them, dragging her close until their centers aligned, wrapping her legs around his hips. They both moaned at the contact.

"Holy fuck, River. If you only knew how often I thought of touching you like this," he whispered against her lips.

"What did you think of doing? Where did you think of touching me?" River wanted to know everything— wanted to *feel* everything.

Patrick pulled back just enough to stare into her eyes. "Do you want me to tell you or show you?" He lifted his brows in question. A challenge?

"Show me."

Pat groaned. River leaned close, whispering against his lips, "Then I'll show you what I've been wanting to do to you."

"Oh, fuck. Yes, show me."

River felt close to orgasming from his words alone. Then Pat kissed her. If a person were to imagine the opposite of soft and subtle, slow and gentle, sighs and romance— *that* would describe their kiss.

Patrick lifted her off the counter, one hand cradling her ass, the other hand braced the back of her neck. It was hard and blatant, fast and rough, moans and thrusts. His long, strong fingers were digging into her ass cheeks, skating close to her slit.

"Bed," Patrick spoke into her mouth.

"Your... room. Rowan... mine," River stuttered out between Patrick's tongue stroking in and out of her mouth. Reaching between their bodies, she boldly fisted his sex. She felt the dampness of precum against her palm. God, she wanted to feel that part of him... taste. Her fingers slid beneath the boxer's waistband.

"Oh, God, Patrick," River moaned. Patrick thrust his hips slowly, using her hand like he would his own. Swiping her thumb over the head, she carefully pulled her hand from his briefs and made sure she had his attention before she sucked the drop of cum off her digit.

"I'm going to fuck you so hard, River," he warned. Patrick grasped her waist, pulled her up his body, and wrapped her legs around him. River circled her arms around his neck and held on as Pat strode out of the kitchen, ran up the stairs, entered his room, and slammed the door shut with his foot before dropping her on his bed.

RIVER WAS IN HIS BED. Jesus, God, he'd dreamed her here so many times it didn't seem real. His lungs were pumping, swelling his body with uncomfortable pressure. Her hair was splayed across the white sheets— her body so small, so delicate, so beautiful, so his.

Pressing his legs against the side of the bed, he leaned over River. If there was a more perfect woman, Patrick would not believe it. She was looking at him with her cat eyes, slightly tipped up at the corners, and lips slightly parted, slick from tangling with his mouth. He groaned, fighting for control. Patrick pulled her giant shirt over her head. Her tits were... he might explode.

Patrick leaned down and sucked one nipple and then the other into his mouth— fuck, like candy. "Baby, want to suck and lick every inch of your body." Her only response was to bow her back, pressing her chest more firmly to his mouth.

"Don't stop, Pat," River begged.

"I've got to leave these for now, sweetheart," He gave a parting lick to each puckered nipple. "There are so many places I want my mouth, but your deepest heat tops the list." Pat heard River's soft yes as he pulled her panties down her hips. He took a moment to take in the exquisite body of River Byrne before hooking her legs over his shoulders.

She was bare and slick and so close to his face his body shook with desire. Patrick never dreamed this would happen between them— forgot all the reasons why he ever thought it was a bad idea, only frantic to try everything he'd ever fantasized about doing to her.

River was squirming and panting, clearly desperate for him too. "Is this what you want, baby?" he asked once her eyes met his. Patrick let his hot breath fan over her center.

"God, Pat, yes," River moaned.

Patrick swiped his tongue across the length of her seam, flicking her clit before sucking the bud into his mouth. "You taste delicious." As Patrick drove his tongue into River's core, her moans and cries were music. He loved music.

Patrick was relentless, driving into her again and again. When he added his finger, he almost came from how wet she was. He felt River stiffen, her thighs squeezing, her pelvis jerking.

"That's it, River. Come for me, baby." Muffling her scream against her own palm as she quaked and spasmed, Patrick gentled his strokes, letting River ride her climax as long as she could.

"You want to know how you taste on my tongue?" River had gone limp. Her legs dropped to the bed, her body still shuddering with aftershocks. Looking at River, like this, replete, in his bed, her taste on his tongue— he felt absolute satisfaction and absolute unease. He needed more. He needed everything. He needed River to a frightening degree.

Her eyes opened at his question. Surprising him— she always surprised him. River answered, "I would." And then smiled, shifting into a better position to allow Patrick to cover her body with his. They looked at one another, wonder, and... things best left unthought.

He kissed her then, soft and gentle until River licked a circle around his lips. "Mmm, I do taste delicious. You're welcome, Pat," she laughed, poking his side.

"You naughty little shit," Patrick chuckled before grasping her waist and rolling. Now River was lying on his chest. He grabbed her ass, pulling her tight against his erection and groaned at how good *that* felt. River sat up, her full breasts swaying at the movement— mesmerizing. Their hot and aching centers aligned.

He wanted to tear off his underwear, but River needed to be the one to decide how far they went. River started to crawl backward toward his feet, her wet center grazing his legs. "Jesus, babe," Patrick's groan was cut off when she grabbed his briefs and started sliding them down his legs. His erection sprang free — that movement alone almost had him coming.

"River? We don't have to do anything else." *That* had to be the hardest thing he'd ever uttered.

"And waste all of Raven's detailed instructions? Surely you jest, Pat," she laughed while throwing his underwear to the floor.

"Instructions," Patrick asked, slightly stunned at Raven being discussed— *right now.*

"She gave me all sorts of things I could try on you. Well," she amended, "things to try on a man, not just on you. Raven said," River began, eyeing his groin, "Bran loves what she does to him."

His brother's wife telling River how to suck his dick momentarily threw him, and not even his specifically— over his dead, fucking body would she practice on anyone but him— but then her lips neared the swollen head of his arousal, and uncomfortable sibling thoughts burned away.

Patrick's body was extremely tense, anticipation swelling and locking his joints and muscles. Heart pounding, heavy breathing, and clenched fists, and she hadn't even started. "You can do anything you want, Riv."

~

RIVER'S MOUTH was an inch from Patrick's dick. What rabbit hole had she fallen into? And her orgasm... she'd had no idea they could be so intense. Hopefully, she was about to give Pat the same experience.

"Oh, I plan on it, Pat," River flicked her eyes to him, sitting back up. She slid a hairband from her wrist to put her hair in a bun. "Patience, O'Faolain." Leaning over again, testing the waters, so to speak, River purposely bypassed the main event. Raven said the anticipation would kill him. Lick and suck everywhere except where he wanted it most.

River let her warm breath puff over the swollen head before dipping further, placing hot, wet licks and kisses over his thighs, sucking the creased area beside his balls. *That* made Pat groan and twitch. She moved away just far enough to run her hands up and down his thighs, massaging his muscles until her thumbs were grazing his sac.

Patrick was focused on her. As her massage moved to the base of his dick, he thrust his hips.

"River, God, you're killing me," he groaned.

River decided to put Patrick out of his misery. Not breaking eye contact, she smiled as she licked the precum from his slit. River wasn't totally naïve about foreplay. She'd had a few dates in college where things had gotten pretty intense, but— this was Patrick. She wanted to do this right. She wanted him to want her like she did him.

Raven told her there was no wrong way— the phrase 'A for effort' was never truer than when giving a man head.

Finally, she allowed her mouth to cover him, her throat to cradle him. Her tongue stroked his length, her mouth sucking and gliding in time with her fist. River loved having Pat in her mouth— loved that he lost control. Patrick had begun to pump his hips, gripping her hair and begging her to take him deeper.

"Fuck, Riv, I'm going to come!"

Patrick tried to pull from her mouth. River wasn't having it. She wanted the full experience— and that meant swallowing everything Pat gave her. She placed one of her hands over his stomach, holding him still while working him with her other hand and mouth.

"River, Oh God, baby... yes... there... now!"

Pat's sex swelled right before he came. It was everything like she'd read it would be and nothing like it at all— she'd done *that* to Patrick— and if his shouts of pleasure were any indicator, she'd done a damn fine job of it.

As he softened, River let him slide out of her mouth. His *fuuucccckkkk,* made her smile.

"River... you... your mouth... killed me, baby."

Smiling, River crawled up his body, lying at Pat's side, her face in the crook of his neck. His pulse was pounding. "I hope you've been taking your vitamins, Pat because we aren't done."

His body shook with silent laughter. "I don't need vitamins to get hard again— not with you."

"I'll believe it when I... feel it," River teased.

CHUCKLING AT RIVER'S PLAYFULNESS, Patrick pulled the hair band from her hair, running his fingers through the silky strands and massaging her scalp.

In the dim light of his bedroom, he was happy, content, blissful even. River was molded to his side. He wanted her there always, but— they were young. He had never been in a relationship. He wasn't sure he wanted to be in one. He wasn't sure he could.

River was kissing his neck, and her hand was lightly gliding over his chest and stomach. Pat felt his body responding to her touch.

"You never got that breakfast casserole put together. Do you think if we tell our families why, they'd be understanding?" River asked.

"I'm sure they would. I could tell Bran how I ate you out instead. Give him some pointers for Raven," Patrick casually said. He knew that would set River off, and he wasn't wrong. She sucked her breath in so fast she choked.

"Don't you dare, Patrick," River hissed, pushing off his chest and glaring down at him.

"What's the big deal, Riv? After all, Raven told you how to give me head." He tried not to laugh, he really did, but River's face, all red and outraged, forced it out.

At his laughter, River slapped his chest. "You're an asshole, O'Faolain," she grumbled.

"Why you love me," Patrick teased. When she responded with 'probably,' Patrick froze. Did she love him? Like— Bran and Raven love? Forget that. He wasn't going there.

Oblivious to his internal freak out, River's hands were busy tracing Patrick's body. She stretched herself across his chest and licked across his lips.

"You want to know how you taste on my tongue?" River asked, parroting his words. And fuck if he wasn't hard and wanting.

"I would," he repeated River this time.

They kissed and kissed and touched and kissed and touched. At some point, Patrick switched their positions. River was on her back, their bodies aligned. His sex rubbing between her thighs— so hot and warm and welcoming. Gently, he traced the small tattoos on the side of her breast. A triskelion and Native American river symbol. He'd never seen it before. Her swim tops, as small as they were, still covered it.

"Your tattoo is beautiful."

"Thank you. We all have them."

"Do you want me inside you, Riv?" Patrick was aching and pulsing. He had one thought, one goal only— to be inside River Byrne.

Scratching her nails across his ass and pressing her hips against his, she answered, "Past, present, and in the future, Pat. Fuck me already."

Patrick took her mouth in a desperate kiss, positioning his sex against her own, sliding in with every intention of seating himself fully.

He felt resistance.

A barrier.

She stiffened.

He stopped.

He started to back out, coming off her body like he was avoiding gunfire.

"Don't you dare stop, Patrick. Don't you dare," River growled. "I'm a virgin, not a leper."

With that announcement, she bent her legs, taking him deeper.

Patrick moaned at how good River felt.

So hot.

So wet.

So tight.

"Christ, River," he gritted out. "Are you sure?"

"I'm sure, Pat," she answered seriously, looking up at him like... she wanted *only* him.

Bracing his weight on his knees, Patrick looked at where they were partially joined. "Jesus, I love seeing myself inside you." He traced his hands up River's sides, squeezing her breasts and pinching her nipples. When she started to writhe beneath him, he pushed past the thin barrier, seating himself fully.

River gasped as he moaned. "So tight. Christ, River." Leaning over, he kissed her softly. "Tell me I didn't hurt you, Riv."

"Not from lack of trying, Pat," River chuckled, making her channel squeeze even tighter. "Your weapon should have come with a warning," she teased, leaning into him before kissing him gently back. "I feel good. Promise," she whispered against his lips.

Patrick felt tingles from his scalp to his toes at the intimacy of— all of it. Before he started spouting poetry, he teased, "Only good, huh?" He slid back, practically leaving her body before thrusting back in. "And now?"

"Practice makes perfect," she gasped as Patrick's body started moving faster and faster.

River's hips met his in a beautiful dance. He chanted her name, and she chanted his. His balls were slapping her ass, her fingernails were gouging his.

He wasn't going to last long and reached between their bodies to rub her swollen nub. She went crazy, gyrating her hips, begging for release.

"Come for me, baby, and then I'm going to fill you full." Patrick felt the moment she surrendered. She became hotter, wetter, and tighter. As her body started to clinch and spasm, Patrick went off like a bomb, exploding.

He collapsed on one side of River's body, not wanting to crush her but also not ready to separate. River was caressing his chest, arms, shoulders, and face. When she started gently scraping her nails against his scalp, he moaned.

"Jesus, that feels so good." River had always seen him. Always felt him. Always made him feel like he was the most important person in the room— the most important person to her. And that scared the shit of him.

They were quiet for several minutes before River broke the silence. "I'm glad it was you."

Patrick didn't pretend to misunderstand. "Me too." He was humbled and— horrified. What would happen now? What did she expect to happen? One of River's breasts was next to his face, thankfully distracting him from deeper thoughts. Before he could think better of it, he turned her toward him, still connected, and drew her left leg over his legs.

PATRICK'S READJUSTMENT put her boobs snug against his face.

"A feast to be savored," Patrick murmured as his hot tongue started licking and sucking, hands kneading and pinching.

River couldn't stop the moans leaving her mouth. She felt Pat growing hard again and whimpered at how sensitive her body was.

"I could play with your tits all night, but I want to slide my dick deep in your heat more."

Pat talking filthy while pushing inside her caused a lightning-fast but intense reaction. River could only pant his name and beg for, "More, Pat, more."

River gasped as Patrick barrel-rolled her. She was now straddling his hips, his big hands grasping her hips, slamming her down as he thrust up.

"God, baby, you're so beautiful riding me," Pat admitted. She and Pat were both gasping now, hot and slick with passion. "You ready to come again, Riv?"

Patrick increased the speed. She felt like a rag doll in a tornado. River couldn't leave the storm— didn't want to leave it. She could feel her body start to quiver as Pat relentlessly hit that perfect spot inside her. "Now, Pat."

"Yes. I feel you locking me up. God, babe, going to come."

Patrick was frantic. She felt desperate— and then there were no thoughts. Just the two of them sharing the most intimate, private, life-altering moment two people could share.

As they floated down from the high, River was... wasn't River anymore. She was a part of something else... someone else.

"Patrick," River whispered, kissing the lovely spot where Patrick's shoulder flowed into his neck. "I love you."

She knew she'd fucked up the moment she spoke those three words. Pat's body stiffened, and though she was still lying on top of him, he'd clearly pulled back. Attempting to rescue the moment and stop her feelings from being hurt... worse, she added, "I meant, I love you because you're like a brother to me." Pat's eyes finally found hers in a WTF look of horror. "No, no," River tried to salvage further, trying, "Not brother," har har har, "like family." Not any better. "No, geez, I mean... I...," she stammered. Service Announcement: All sexy sex thoughts have evacuated the building.

Patrick gently moved River to his side, his penis sliding out of her, causing both their breaths to catch. "I'll go get us warm washcloths to clean up."

River barely heard him over the mantra repeating in her head: *you fucked up, you fucked up, you fucked up...*

～

PATRICK FLICKED the bathroom light on, catching his wide-eyed stare in the mirror. He was shaking like a scared little kid. River said she loved him. He loved her too. They were family, after all. Oh, God. That didn't sound any better when *he* said it.

Okay, Patrick. Move on. They were just words. His eyes started cataloging his body, noting each scratch and suck mark. Fuuuuccckkk— if they didn't make him want to take her again until they both were screaming and senseless —no words of love.

Sighing, Pat wet a cloth under warm water and washed his dick off while wetting a second cloth for River.

Blood. Barely there, but traces of... of River's blood were there.

She'd been a virgin.

She wasn't a virgin anymore.

This was turning into a 911, send the paramedics, deep shit kind of situation. His brother would be so pissed at him if he didn't make this right. His dad would just kill him.

He'd hidden in the bathroom way longer than he should have and firmly decided he had to leave the tiled sanctuary. Walking back into the bedroom, Patrick gave himself a pep talk. Tomorrow was New Year's Eve, a party at Wolves, and back to Dublin the day after the New Year. They would be so busy there really wouldn't be enough time to have a serious conversation. It was better to leave it until they were back in Ireland.

Patrick had never been a procrastinator, but in this, he was willing to see how it worked out for him. As Patrick walked to the bed, even after his mini freak out, he was still exhilarated at the thought of River waiting for him in his bed. He was met with mussed white sheets.

No River.

She'd left.

He'd fucked up.

Embarrassed her.

Damn it. He should go to her, but what would he say—what could he say? *Sorry, I freaked out. I took your virginity but I'm not ready for a serious relationship.* No. Talking tonight would only make things worse.

6

She and Patrick had sex.

It was amazing.

He ghosted her after she told him she loved him.

River was currently trying on dresses with her sisters and Jo. It was their big New Year's

Eve party at Wolves tonight.

Smile. Laugh. Tease. Take a sip of Jameson. Ignore the soreness between her legs. Lie about the small bruise on her breast, currently on display in the extremely low-cut dress she was supposed to wear— that she'd *been excited* to wear until she'd seen the suck mark. Oh, and ignore the looks her sisters kept sending her.

To take the heat off herself, she asked Jo, "What do you think Honey's going to think of you in that dress?" The four women had gotten slinky, barely there, sequence dresses for Wolves before leaving Dublin. They wanted to look like four disco balls. River's was turquoise, Raven's was bright green, Rowan's was silver, and Jo was currently trying on her gold.

Jo's cheeks pinkened. Score one for River. "Pfft, as if that man looks at anything but escape routes, shadows, and threats," Jo airily announced.

Even Raven wasn't buying Jo's story. "Mmhmm. So, you're saying when he has other guards in the room to watch over us, and I catch him staring at you like he wants you naked and in his bed... I was mistaken?"

"You are so full of shit, Raven! He does not. I irritate him. Honey barely tolerates me."

Rowan weighed in. "Yeah, Jo, about that. Thomas stared at you for so long the other night, and this is no lie, he adjusted his... Peter Rabbit."

The sisters were in tears, they were laughing so hard. Jo looked horrified before sheepishly admitting, "I do, sometimes, *rarely*, try to push his buttons. Still, I am just a job. You guys know he'll leave when they finally catch that weirdo."

That sobered things. "I can't believe he's still out there. I admit, I like having Thomas' crew living with us. Those pictures he took of me and sent to Bran still give me chills," Raven admitted.

"The FBI contacted his security firm a few weeks ago. They've worked with Honey's company before and wanted to make sure each group had all the pertinent information."

"Was there anything new, then?" River asked.

"I asked the giant asshole. He grunted and walked away. There are moments when I've thought of how satisfying it would be to kick him in the ass with a *very* pointy shoe."

"So, Riv," Rowan began.

And here it was. The interrogation. She didn't blame her sisters. They'd given her time to tell them what was going on with her and Patrick since returning to Oklahoma. She hadn't, and she should have. Now she had even more things to tell them.

"It's time you tell me, Rave, and Jo, what the hell is going on with you and Pat."

Slipping out of her dress, River put on a robe. "You three might as well get comfortable for this. We don't leave for a while, and this will take a minute to explain."

Once everyone was settled on the bed, River admitted she'd had feelings for Patrick for a while. They all nodded in agreement, quite aware, obviously. She told them she knew Patrick wasn't interested in having a serious relationship, but she'd still held out hope. How he would touch her back or leg or hand on occasion— and they weren't super brotherly.

She told them about the night he walked her home from the pub. How he'd almost kissed her. How he'd asked her not to date anyone.

"That was the night that I thought... that I let myself hope... we might finally get together. I thought he wanted to date me," River admitted. Closing her eyes briefly and sighing. Looking at the three women in front of her, she could tell they wanted to ask questions but were honoring her 'no questions' until she finished rule.

"He avoided me for the past two months since that night. Then, at your wedding, Rave, we seemed to find our way back to each other. I was relieved but still unsure of what he wanted from me. If he wanted anything." Then she told them about the night of the gala. His behavior. Her anger. The dance. The room. How far they'd gone that night.

Her sisters and Jo wore identical *What the Fuck* looks, small smiles starting to form on their lips. Until she told them about the hallway. River told them that he didn't want to be seen with her— that he left that night, by himself, without a word.

"Christmas was awkward between us. We hadn't spoken since the kiss. After presents, you guys remember me running up to our rooms to grab sweaters?" They both nodded. "He cornered me coming out of your room, Raven. I said I had nothing to say. He insisted. So, I'm not proud of how I spoke to Patrick, but I made it clear he needed to leave me alone. That we could work on eventually being friends again for the families' sake."

All three ladies broke their silence. Jo said, "I would have kicked him in the balls."

Raven just looked crushed, "I had no idea what you've been going through, Riv," she sniffled.

"I'm telling Hugh," Rowan said furiously.

"Wait, what? Hugh?" Jo looked confused.

"It's his sons that have hurt my sisters. Screw that. I know Bran has his shit together now, and" Rowan looked sheepishly at Raven, "loves our sister to distraction, but Patrick just keeps proving he's a dick."

"And you want to tell his dad... why?" Jo asked, brows raised in question.

Rowan seemed to realize she might have revealed too much. She shrugged her shoulders, mumbling to River to finish her story.

River looked at Rowan a moment longer before finishing. She told them that, after five days of them faking it, she was miserable. How she'd gone to the kitchen last night at midnight and called their grandma. "I told Nan that I missed her and just needed to hear her voice. I didn't realize Pat had come into the kitchen by then. He heard what I said on the phone and thought, like an idiot, that I was talking to a man."

"Jesus, help us. Men can be such morons," Jo said, shaking her head.

"Exactly. When he realized it was Nan, they talked. We hung up. Patrick apologized. We made out." River knew the silent oooos stretching each lady's mouth was the calm before the storm. "After that, we went to his bedroom. We had crazy sex. I told him I loved him. He didn't say anything. He went to the bathroom and didn't come out. I finally left and came back to our room, Row."

Silence. Crickets. Explosion. They all jumped on her at once, well, Raven and Baby O kind of rolled on her, peppering her with questions and Oh My Gods, and I can't believe it, and then finally...

"What do you mean he never came out? Did he come to find you?" Raven asked, sitting up and giving River her, *I better like your answer* look.

"No. And he's avoided me all day. He went to his house, I believe. To work," River air quoted. "At least that's what I heard Bran tell Hugh this morning."

"I'm shocked. Really shocked," Jo quietly spoke.

Raven added, "He can't mean to leave things like this."

Rowan leaned over and placed her forehead to River's own, and asked, "How are you, sis? Truly."

River squeezed her eyes closed, attempting to force her tears away. She looked at her best friends and answered honestly. "I'm confused and... hurt. I think maybe he's just overwhelmed. Maybe he'll come around tonight and talk about it— talk to me. But we all need to remember that I was a willing participant. He never said it would mean anything to him and... and I didn't care. I suppose," River stopped to swallow down more tears, "I should be grateful I lost my virginity to someone *I* loved even if it isn't reciprocated."

Realizing that she had single-handedly crushed every drop of joy from their New Year's Eve night, River attempted to shake off her drama.

"Okay, guys. I realize my situation is a bummer, but I refuse to let it ruin a night we've all looked forward to for weeks. Let's put our sparkly minis on and have fun!"

As best friends and sisters do, they fist-pumped, whooped,

and put on some dancing music. Raven and Rowan each took one of River's hands and squeezed. They would put what happened aside for now, but not forever.

~

THE FOUR WOMEN descended the stairs like goddesses. Four scantily dressed goddesses. Next to him, he heard Bran whisper, "Christ." His father growled, "No." Even staid Thomas grew red and clenched his fists.

Rowan "whispered" to the other women, "Looks like Peter Rabbit brought some buddies to the party." She smirked as the other women threw their heads back and laughed.

Patrick couldn't breathe, let alone speak. River, in a metallic blue dress cut to her navel, looked so fuckable, so... fucking *his*, he wanted to claim her in front of everyone. Bran had no qualms. He met his wife halfway, circling Raven's waist, "Christ, woman, let's stay home tonight."

Laughing, she kissed his brother's jaw and told him, "Not a chance, O'Faolain."

Thomas met Jo at the landing and must have said something she took exception to. Her eyes flashed and through gritted teeth, she told her guard, "I'm not changing." Jesus, those two... Stranger still, Rowan went to his father. Touching his hand, she whispered something to him. He nodded to the youngest Byrne before shooting a fiery glance Patrick's way. Oh fuck. River's sisters knew then.

River was in total fake it 'til you make it mode. She smiled and laughed and complimented all the men on their sharp attire. She never met his eyes.

He needed her eyes. He wanted her to look at him. If she really loved him, why was she ignoring him?

Because he'd hurt her like the idiot he apparently was. Because he didn't deserve to breathe the same air as her.

Bran, the only one brave enough to question the women's attire, asked, "Hey, babe, do you think you guys maybe— didn't realize how," and here, his brother waved his big hand in front of his chest, "revealing your dresses are?" At Raven's sharp look, Bran's eyes went wide. Patrick would have enjoyed the moment if he weren't in the middle of his own crisis.

"Am I too pregnant to be sexy on New Year's Eve?" Oh shit, even Dad sent a warning look in Bran's direction.

"No. No, my love. Not at all. You all look amazing." Nice save.

"I will be reporting your inappropriate attire to your father at my earliest convenience, Miss O'Connor."

Jo looked like a pin-free grenade. River, Raven, and Rowan moved to Jo's side. All three women trained their eyes on MacGregor. River asked MacGregor, "Do you think Jo doesn't look good, Honey?" Raven asked, "Do you hate the color? It's gold, like your hair after all." Rowan clenched his demise with, "Should I solicit several men's opinions once we get to Wolves? Take a poll? Maybe you're the only man who thinks Jo should change."

The guard's stare never wavered from Jo's. Obviously admitting defeat, Thomas said, "Miss O'Connor is... beautiful. In the dress," he tacked on quickly. His words loosened the stiff necks from all the women. "However, I will double my guard to ensure she has no unwanted attention tonight."

Jo didn't take her eyes off MacGregor when she asked, "So, by double my guards, what you really mean is, it'll still be just you, but doubly annoying?"

"Correct."

Jo sighed in defeat.

Damn. MacGregor was good. Patrick needed lessons—desperately.

His dad suggested they head out.

River never looked at Patrick.

~

AFTER FOUR HOURS of watching River drink, laugh, and dance with her many admirers— her perfect tits perfectly visible with her perfectly hard nipples puckering her dress— Patrick had reached his tolerance level. Dad and Rowan disappeared forever ago to tour Grandpa's memorial. MacGregor was hovering over Jo, who looked like she was about to explode from either anger or an orgasm. Take your pick. Bran had never let go of Raven. Ever. They were currently dancing to *Oklahoma Smokeshow*.

James and Jane showed. Patrick hadn't seen either of them for months. There was still stiffness between the two, but James made it very clear to anyone looking that they were together. Jane seemed withdrawn at first, but after Jo and the Byrne sisters hugged all over her, and Raven, he noticed, spoke separately to Jane, enveloping her in a warm hug, she seemed to relax.

The love of James' life seemed to unfurl from her protective cocoon. James looked at Patrick and smiled. The first genuine smile he'd seen on the man's face for a year. James drifted to the women, standing slightly back and to the side of Jane. Bran grabbed Raven's hand again, sitting down, his wife in his lap, and MacGregor was crowding Jo against the bar where no one could accidentally touch her— but himself, obviously.

A brunette in what must have been ten-inch heels appeared in front of Patrick, blocking his view of River and interrupting his visual stalking. Annoying. Deigning to look down at the woman's overdone face, Pat heard a red alert blare in his ears. Shit. He recognized her. A self-absorbed socialite near OKC that he'd fucked in a club over a year ago.

And as his luck was holding strong, Megan Thee Stallion's *Flamin' Hottie* started bumping over Wolves' system, and River began dancing her way to her sisters, encouraging Jo and Jane to join. Raven pushed off Bran, busting some pretty impressive pregnant moves. Rowan had finally shown up from her 'tour,' parting ways with his dad, and Jo— she looked at Thomas, lifted a brow in defiance, and danced her way to the other women.

River's eyes found him just as *Miranda's* sticky tentacles attached to his chest.

Fuck. Fuck. Fuck.

River closed her eyes briefly before taking a deep breath and turning from him.

The hurt on River's face destroyed him. It was as though he'd slapped her, but *he* felt the pain. Patrick watched in horror as she faked a smile and grabbed a man from the bar who'd been eye-fucking her for over an hour and took him to the dance floor.

Shit went downhill after that. River was dancing and gorgeous, as only she could be. Patrick's anger and jealousy skyrocketed. Octo-Miranda was whispering in his ear to follow her outside, and— fuck him if he didn't make the worst... the absolute worst decision of his life.

7

A FEW HOURS EARLIER.

It was New Year's Eve, and Sam had his telephoto lens all polished. He planned on capturing the party at Wolves tonight. A few patrons here and there— average Joes. He also hoped to capture an O'Faolain in a compromising or unflattering position. If he mixed innocent pictures with salacious ones, the Tulsa World lifestyle editor wouldn't be able to resist publishing them.

It took little intellectual deduction to realize Patrick O'Faolain was about to screw his personal life up. Hopefully, it would send the youngest son into a tailspin and embarrass his family. Small potatoes, obviously. Screwing with Patrick O'Faolain was a last tiny 'screw you' before he fucked their women over— literally.

Honestly, Sam couldn't wait for all of them to go back to Ireland. It would be much easier to get closer to the younger Byrne sisters and Josephine O'Connor. He wouldn't have to work so hard to dodge the Tulsa detectives. O'Connor's personal guard might be challenging to step around, but one way or another, Sam knew these women would eventually star in his films. It would ruin them and destroy their families.

He could live his own happily ever after then.

Alas, tonight Sam found himself going to Wolves Irish Pub &
Eatery at the unfashionable hour of five o'clock on New Year's
Eve. He, or she rather, as Sam was a gloriously rotund woman,
squeezed into a sparkly black sweater dress— black to allow for
dick concealment— atrocious silver ballet slippers— he wasn't
getting a disgusting bunion for a bit of good fun— and a brassy
blonde wig, curled and hair sprayed to within of its life, was all
he needed to secure a single table in the shadows.

He'd give his hostess her due. She smiled and kindly asked if
he had a preference for seating.

Hoisting his ugly, black, pleather bag further up his shoulder
— heavy because of multiple cameras— he used his best 'older
woman, I've smoked for forty years' raspy voice and answered,
"Thank you so much, young lady. If you have a small table for
two somewhere out of the way, that would be perfect. An old high
school girlfriend is supposed to be meeting me as soon as she gets
to town. At this time of year, I'm afraid her flight may be
delayed."

"Oh, of course. There is one little table near the back that is
close to the back garden, and even when it's this cold, the heaters
and shades make the space so nice," the hostess gushed.

"Sounds perfect, bless your heart. And don't you worry about
checking on me much. I'll order a few things while I wait for
Mags and read a new juicy book I just started." So easy. People
see what they expect to see. Looking too closely is considered
rude, especially with the younger ones. She either thinks I'm a
badly dressed, odd-looking woman or a man dressed as a woman.

As it was so early in the evening, the hostess doubled as a
waitress, so Tina helpfully took his order. Sam made sure to order
two mixed cocktails, a large water, and two appetizers. No need
to come back anytime soon, sweet girl. Just forget this little table
in the shadows was occupied.

Sam decided to take a walk around while his order was working to get the lay of the land. He left his sparkly coat on the back of his chair and his novel tented on the table, cover up to display the scantily dressed couple. If the waitress came back before him, she'd know he was coming back.

The garden was a warm winter wonderland paradise. He could imagine quite a few couples having a private moment outside. The women's restroom had a plush seating area with full-length and tabletop makeup mirrors for clothing tweaks and lipstick touchups. The perfect setup to hear gossip— and witness an occasional nip slip during tit adjustments. Sam could admit that Wolves was well done. Everything was new but comfortable, rich but understated. He hoped it burned to the ground.

8

———

The second Patrick's foot passed through the garden's doors, he knew he was fucking up. Not just a tiny fuck up, but a life-destroying fuck up.

He didn't think anyone in his group noticed Miranda and him slipping out. He was about to tell the woman he'd made a mistake— changed his mind— loved someone... loved someone more than he should.

Patrick didn't recognize himself... this scared, unreliable person he'd become.

Miranda ignored his disinterest or was so uninterested in anything but herself that she didn't notice his lack of enthusiasm. They were in a part of the garden that sported several wooden benches and standing heaters. Patrick found himself sitting on one of the benches with Octo Hands straddling his hips. Patrick's thoughts were muddled. He knew he was uncomfortable and only wanted to get back inside.

He stupidly allowed her one kiss before gently bracing her arms and moving her off his lap. "This was a mistake. I'm in a relationship." One he'd already fucked up and just cheated on. Definitely not winning the Best Boyfriend Award anytime soon.

Patrick was sickened by his behavior. Sick that Miranda was the type of woman he usually chose. Just... sick.

"What the hell, Patrick?" She asked, looking bewildered that he wasn't already balls deep in her willing body.

"I don't know." Patrick attempted to explain, "I just don't want to do this kind of shit anymore."

Miranda stood, straightening her dress as she stood. "Whatever, Patrick. If you change your mind, come find me. I'm going to head back in and find my friends." She looked at him curiously for a moment before walking away.

Patrick stayed sitting on the bench, letting his chin drop to his chest. Christ. He'd had everything. River loved him, and he loved her too, damn it! Why hadn't he just said it back when she gave the words to him? Why didn't he talk to her after... after what they'd shared? How she must have felt when he didn't seek her out that night or the next day.

That version of Patrick needed to die. He never wanted to be so self-centered or so afraid of loving someone again.

He would have to tell her.

If he told her everything, begged her to let him prove he could change— was changed— maybe she would forgive him.

The question was whether he should talk to her tonight or wait until they were back in Dublin? They were flying out on the second of January. Not long, but still, Patrick disliked leaving things unsaid. Pushing off the bench, he decided to feel out River's mood first. She'd seen Miranda touch him, but hopefully, she was too busy dancing to notice Patrick had gone outside with the woman.

Slipping back into the pub's warmth, he was relieved to see the women still dancing. No one glanced his way. He used the restroom before joining the guys, who were all entranced. He was happy to see that Jane was dancing with the other women. No men were around them. Thomas must have made sure that wasn't an option. Thank God for the guard's diligence.

Bran briefly glanced his brother's way and nodded. "It's almost twelve. What do you guys think? Should we join our women on the floor? I don't know about you clods, but I'm kissing Raven at midnight— bring the New Year in right," Bran said, grinning.

James and his dad stiffened at Bran's suggestion— Patrick felt his body freeze. Pat knew his expression must resemble the other men. A combination of yearning and fear. Their eyes were all trained on the dance floor.

Noticing their hesitation, Bran looked to James, saying, "You realize this might be your chance to at least hold the woman you love." James stood immediately. "And Pat, you need to fix shit with River, brother." Great. Raven must have told him.

Before Bran turned to follow James, he glanced at their father's stony expression. "Dad, for fuck's sake. Don't leave Rowan by herself." Clever, clever, Bran. Make it about not leaving Rowan embarrassed by being the only woman without a partner and not about Dad being so into the youngest Byrne he barely functioned in her presence— as if it wasn't the biggest unspoken non-secret in the families.

"Fine."

As the four men passed Thomas, Bran told him he could guard Jo better from the dance floor.

River watched the men walk toward them. Everyone slowed their dancing, noticing the synchronized testosterone marching their way. River felt her sisters scrunch next to her sides.

Raven asked, "I can claim exhaustion and sit this dance out. You can join me, Riv." Rowan followed with, "They're obviously making Hugh dance with me. He'd rather cut his beard with a dull razor. I'll sit out too. No problem. Really." Rowan bumped River's side casually while swaying to the song.

River didn't want to cause an awkward scene like she had at Christmas. And— she really didn't want to disappoint Bran and Raven. They didn't have too many more party nights out before Baby O made an appearance.

She'd seen that woman touch Patrick and fully admitted she was so jealous and so hurt she could have cried. Thankfully, River didn't think her sisters or Jo witnessed the woman, so she threw herself into dancing and did her best not to look for him. When she finally glanced over to where the men were sitting, Patrick was next to his brother, sans the brunette. Oh, sweet relief.

"Let's dance. It'll be fine. What more could happen," River joked, laughing off the tension. "And Row, I don't think you're the Hugh Whisperer you think you are. He always looks like he's in pain. Deep down, I bet he's so excited his Benjamin Bunny is ready to give you a whirl!" Raven let out a whoop of laughter, and Rowan elbowed her side. "Bitch," she whispered.

And then it was go time. Bran grabbed Raven first, bending down to whisper in her ear, causing her sister to blush. As soon as he moved her further out on the floor, the music switched to the traditional *Auld Lang Syne* by The Irish Rovers. A slow song meant conversation, sighing to herself, River knew it needed to happen sooner rather than later, but— if the words 'it was a mistake' came out of his mouth— there may be a murder at midnight.

Thomas had already pulled Jo into his arms. James was holding a hand out to Jane. James looked so damned hopeful, River let out a relieved breath when Jane put her hand into his. Then there was only Rowan, Hugh, Pat, and her. She heard Rowan tell them they could sit the dance out, to which Hugh put one of his giant hands at her sister's waist and began to slow dance toward the others.

Down to two.

"Dance with me, River. Please."

River finally met Patrick's eyes. He looked about as hopeful as James had only a moment ago. "Okay, Pat." Patrick had her wrapped in his arms and next to their friends and families in two heartbeats. Both of his broad hands palmed her back, pulling her tight against his body.

River placed her hands against his chest. His heart was pounding. Could it be that he was as affected by her as she was by him? Pat leaned his head close to hers so she could hear him over the crowd.

"River... I have some things I want to tell you and explain." River stiffened in his arms and attempted to put space between them. "No, babe, don't stop dancing. I do need to tell you some things, but right now, I only want to tell you that you're it for me. I should have told you this before now, but I do love you. Very much."

River was shocked. Tears sprang to her eyes as they continued to watch each other. She had hoped... really hoped... "I love you, Patrick," she mouthed quietly, knowing he could read her lips. The song ended, and the DJ was announcing the New Year with a fireworks light show. Pat leaned down— River stood on her toes— and then they were kissing and kissing and kissing.

The crowd was cheering the holiday. River was cheering her future. The DJ cranked up some crazy dance song, and the floor became a crush. Patrick led River back to their table, the other couples following. River looked at everyone and was happy to see James' arm wrapped around Jane, who was looking at James with a small smile. Jo started to move away from Thomas to go talk to some friends who had just waved from the other bar.

Thomas grasped his charge's arm and whispered something in her ear. Surprisingly, Josephine stayed put. Hmmm. Questions for later.

Everyone agreed they were ready to head home. James and Jane were staying in town. As were Jo and Thomas. Jo wanted to spend some time with her family and Jane, but she would be coming to Dublin in a few weeks and staying until Raven had the baby. Thomas was sending several of his men with them. River was thankful for the protection, but good grief, she wished Delton was behind bars already.

Bobby, the O'Faolain pilot called Hugh earlier that evening to let him know a storm front was headed toward Tulsa that would likely ground flights by January 2. He was prepared to take them tomorrow if they wished. Hugh had already told Bobby he could fly the private plane to Massachusetts to visit his family and stay for an extended paid vacation before bringing the jet back to Ireland, so none of the pilot's plans would be messed up if they left for Dublin a few days early.

After returning to the Muskogee, Raven and Bran went to their house, and Patrick asked River if she would spend the night with him at his house. Pat hadn't stopped touching her since they left Wolves. Her sisters grinned at her anytime their eyes caught.

Something had sparked this change in Patrick's demeanor. River was curious what the catalyst had been but didn't want to overanalyze.

She hoped it was permanent.

River wasn't nervous about having sex with Patrick. She *was* nervous about *after* having sex with Patrick. Last time, he'd hidden in the bathroom until she'd finally slunk back to her room, confused and embarrassed.

This time would be different. It *had* to be. He'd told River he loved her. He said she was it for him. She believed him.

But if he ghosted her... again.

River's internal debate escaped in a squeal as Patrick picked her up the moment they entered his house and started running toward his bedroom. "Patrick O'Faolain! Put me down so I can see your house," she laughed, slapping the arm banded about her legs.

"You can see it tomorrow, babe. I'll give you a tour of my bedroom now, though," he grinned back at her.

"I'll allow the manhandling then," River deadpanned. As Pat entered his bedroom and flicked on the dim surround lights. River gasped at the space. He set her down and immediately started taking his boots off, but all she could do was spin in a slow circle to take it all in. "Pat, it's beautiful." All cream and soft blues. Sumptuous. She and Pat had eerily similar tastes.

One whole wall of the bedroom was made of glass panels that completely opened to a wraparound veranda overlooking the Arkansas River. She couldn't wait to see the rest of the house.

"Holy shit, River! You're still dressed," Patrick complained.

River laughed when she saw Patrick was already in his boxers, and she'd yet to take her shoes off. "There's just so much to see, Pat," she remarked, looking at the vaulted white ceiling. River wanted to spend days combing the property and this house.

"It's almost two in the morning. Barely enough hours left to do everything I want to you."

That made River's body shiver in anticipation. "And sleep?"

"On the plane tomorrow. Now come here. Let me help you get

out of that dress." River slipped her heels off, sighing as her bare toes curled into the thick nap of the area rug. Patrick's hands rested on her shoulders, fingers curling lightly about her neck— a seductive collar. "This dress had me hard from the moment I saw you walking down the stairs. I know Bran was serious when he asked your sister to stay home because it's exactly what I wanted to do."

"Was it worth the wait?"

"I would wait a lot longer than an evening for you, River. So yes, very worth it."

As the hidden side zipper released, Patrick pushed the dress from her shoulders, letting it fall to the floor. "Christ, have mercy. You... your... this is all you were wearing under that dress? All night!"

She smiled wickedly at Patrick's awed expression when he realized she was naked except for a tiny blue silk thong. "Not much room for extras in that dress," she teased. River's thumbs hooked the edges of her panties. Patrick appeared mesmerized. "I'll strip if you strip, Pat."

Patrick grinned as he hooked his own thumbs at the top of his briefs. They both slid the last of their clothes from their bodies, standing before each other naked and wanting. Patrick closed the space between them. He gently placed his hands at her waist, lifting her body until she was able to wrap her legs around his waist, and their mouths were a breath apart.

"Patrick."

"River."

Patrick's mouth sealed over her own, tongues playing, moaning, panting, and begging for more. Without releasing her mouth, he laid her gently on his bed, following her horizontal position until he covered her much smaller frame.

River ran her hands over every bit of his exposed skin as Patrick traced the shape of her breasts with fingers and tongue. "I don't want to wait, Pat."

Patrick took her mouth in a soft, sweet kiss as he rubbed his sex against her own. River arched her hips, her legs falling apart. They both groaned as he pushed inside. There was no pain or pinch, nothing but a tight fullness. Completely seated, he stopped and rested his forehead against hers.

"I don't deserve you, River," he admitted, "but I will never let you go." At that, he began to move. Slow glides in and out. They both moaned at the friction.

Their mouths never stopped touching, breathing. *I love you. I need you. You are mine.* Tender touches... necks, cheeks, lips. Patrick lifted his body, raising his chest from hers. River used the separation to gently scratch her nails up his arms, across his chest, and down his stomach. His abs contracted as she moved her hands to where they joined.

Pressing into Patrick's hard length with her thumbs. Each of his in-and-out strokes had him closing his eyes and panting her name. His thrusts came harder now— faster. "Don't stop, River. Touch yourself, baby." Patrick leaned further back to watch as she did as he asked. Fingers already damp, River slid them over herself faster and faster until her hips were shaking, and she was meeting each thrust with frantic abandon.

"Fuck, River, I'm about to fill you up, baby."

Patrick's raspy growl finished her. "Pat," River gasped as she felt her body begin to contract around his sex. She screamed at the intense throbbing, repeatedly squeezing Patrick's length. He stiffened above her, driving home as deep as he could go before stilling— his body filling her with everything he had.

Collapsing, hot and heavy over her body— blanketing her. "God, Pat," River breathed, too wrung out to move a muscle.

He answered by licking her distended nipple and sucking the swollen flesh into his mouth, causing both their sexes to continue to throb and pulse. "I love you, Miss Byrne. Forever."

River knew they both planned on hours of hot, glorious sex,

but what they had just shared... it felt momentous. A commitment. A promise. They fell asleep tangled against one another.

"I love you, Mr. O'Faolain," she whispered against his chest.

River wasn't sure how much time had passed when she felt Patrick's arms link tight around her middle. "River?" he breathed quietly into the dark.

"Yes?" River asked, kissing his chest before melting once again against his chest.

"Will you promise to love me always?"

River tensed as she decided how to answer. Why had he asked? In the end, there was only one response that she knew to be absolutely true.

"I will."

~

PAT TRIED to pull a pillow over his head to block out the noise. Someone was pestering him to get up— River. Throwing the pillow to the floor, his eyes adjusted to the light until he could finally see her sweet face.

"About time! You are a bear to get up in the morning." She didn't appear to mind since she was grinning. "I love learning new things about you, babe," she teased.

Patrick finally noticed River was dressed, and her hair was damp. "Hey, why didn't you invite me to shower?" That thought made his dick twitch.

"Umm, well, let me see," she stopped to grab a pillow and hit him with it, "I did! You stuck your head under the blankets." She smirked, adding, "Such a shame too. Raven told me some of the things she's done to Bran in the shower. I wonder if you would have liked them," she sighed and shrugged her shoulders. "Like I said, such a shame."

She was about to slide off the bed, but Patrick was faster and snagged her by the waist, flipping her to her back, his knees pressed tight against her outer thighs. Her surprised squeal turned into a moan once he leaned close, dragging his lips up the side of her neck, sucking and licking until reaching her lips.

"First, can you never, *ever* discuss your sister and sex with my brother when I'm in bed naked and hard for you? A small courtesy. Second, I think you need another shower," he whispered against her lips.

River chuckled before she deepened the kiss, her hands clasped his head close as they devoured one another. Her nails scratched across the shaved side.

Breaking the kiss, she breathlessly explained that Raven texted and said they needed to be at the main house in twenty minutes— less now. "Rain check?" She grinned.

Patrick's answer was to climb off her and yank her yoga pants clear off— panties followed. "I'm packed, and I only need five minutes to shower and dress, five minutes to load the truck, and three minutes to get to Dad's. Which means, babe," grinning, he finished while stripping the rest of her clothes, "we're having a quickie."

"You? A quickie?" She asked doubtfully.

Patrick lifted her bottom off the bed and slid his length in fully.

"Pat, God!"

"That's right, River," Patrick said before driving into her body once again, "you're going to feel me inside you during the entire flight." As she arched her hips into his, he heard her murmur, "I'll always feel you."

Pressing one palm against her most sensitive flesh, Patrick leaned forward, trapping his hand between their bodies while his other palm rested by her head on the pillow, their bodies tight, friction creating fire with each thrust.

"Now, babe. I need you to come with me now," Patrick

demanded. Their bodies stilled, tightening, until spasms dragged moans from them both.

"I love you, Patrick," River panted, trying to catch her breath.

"I love you more." With a light kiss, Pat sat up and announced he had to shower or suffer the wrath of Hugh. "But you, River, aren't showering again." Bending toward her mouth once more, he whispered against her lips, "You're going to feel me soaking your panties for hours."

9

____

As it turned out, most of the pictures of Patrick O'Faolain in the garden at Wolves were too racy for the newspaper's social edition, so he didn't add those. Sam did send several to the paper's editor that showed Patrick looking down at the woman before they stepped outside. He also made sure to send pictures from the whole evening so the paper would believe he'd been hired by Wolves to promote the opening.

The really good ones— of the rando brunette straddling the youngest O'Faolain's lap, kissing and dry humping their little hearts out— went to an Oklahoma blogger with an impressive following, SocialOK. The blog's writer thrived on scandal and gossip. Right about now, she was probably orgasming over the winning lottery ticket he'd sent her.

Of course, Sam had to send the file under a fake name and photography business. Smiling at how clever he was, he only asked that she give his business credit since it was new and needed exposure. As soon as he knew the photos were live, Sam would erase the email and shut down his little webpage, Event Photography, so that nothing could be traced back to him.

Sam admitted to the thrill he had felt at the bar. He'd walked *around in his ugly dress and gaudy slippers, big wig, thin eyebrows, and garish red lips, rubbing occasional elbows with every person he planned on ruining.*

So much for O'Connor's security— the behemoth spent more time drooling over his charge than potential threats.

He wished they knew how close he had got to them.

How much closer he planned on getting.

Sam had had plenty of time before the bar's patrons started rolling in. After he'd scouted the rooms at Wolves, he'd spent considerable time working out the logistics of getting to Ireland undetected. His plan was brilliant. The lovely little hostess had given him the idea. He would go as a man dressed as a woman. He would make it obvious. People may look— but they would not study him. How rude would that be?

Smiling in the dark, Sam peacefully drifted off to sleep. So many fun things to look forward to tomorrow.

Happy New Year...

10

P atrick felt his ears burning. One of the guards was driving the six of them to the airport in Dad's new Jeep Wagoneer. The sisters all sat in the backseat. Whispering. An occasional gasp, 'no way,' and 'damn' peppered the whispers. Thank God his dad was in the front seat talking to Charlie, or he'd never live down his blush.

"Hey, Dad, could you turn the Weather Channel on?" Anything to cover River discussing their sex life. Without answering, he did as Pat asked. Thank God. Snow predictions were a vast improvement to the disgusting thought of the girls comparing him to his brother. Christ, sisters were... something.

Unfortunately, his brother was all too aware of what the sisters were discussing. "You'll get used to it," he laughed.

"Doubtful," Patrick grumbled. "Tell me, did you know that I've had to hear about your sexual preferences while I'm in the middle of *my* sexual preferences? Do you know how weird that is?" Patrick snarled quietly to Bran.

Bran had just taken a drink of his water and, to Patrick's satisfaction, choked and sprayed the back of their dad's seat.

Dad swung around to yell at his brother. "Goddammit,

Bran. I just had this detailed." Then he threw a box of tissues at Bran's head and told him to clean it up.

Patrick couldn't *not* laugh. Sometimes, paybacks were better than expected. Raven patted Bran's shoulder. "Are you all right?"

"Fine," Bran began to clean up his mess. "Just swallowed wrong."

Bran side-eyed Patrick. Pat only shrugged his shoulders. "You'll get used to it," he mocked. That earned him two middle fingers. Patrick was happier than he had ever thought was possible. Everything was as it should be— except confessing to River about kissing another woman.

"Damn it," Patrick cursed quietly. He should have told River last night, no matter what. He couldn't do it now or on the plane, but once they landed, he would. He was ashamed that he'd been so childish— because he was afraid of getting hurt, he tried to destroy the connection first. It was juvenile bullshit behavior and not worthy of his family.

He'd felt strongly about River from the very first meeting at Triskelion in Eufaula. He hadn't been as courageous as his brother. Bran knew Raven was his, and he'd been relentless until she truly was. Bran had fucked up too, and Raven forgave him.

River *had* to forgive Pat, too.

The O'Faolain flight attendant, Brenda, made sure both families were settled and comfortable before takeoff— bottled water, blankets, and snacks. To River, the blanket screamed naptime— needed after Patrick kept her up late and... this morning. The man was getting his wish. She still felt him between her legs.

Patrick's hand was currently resting across her thigh. Possessive. River stretched across the armrest and kissed his cheek gently. "I love you," she whispered against his mouth. Patrick's dark brown eyes looked at her with an intensity that gave her shivers.

"I love you too, Riv."

And... wow. She sat back and fluffed out her blanket, getting ready for a few hours of sleep. Before she forgot, she asked Raven, "Have you made a final list of what you need for Baby O's room? Row and I can help get the rest of the stuff picked up."

Rowan added, "I was thinking of planning a small baby shower and birthday combo since you're due so close to your birthday. How exciting would it be if Baby O came a few days early? Late February fifteenth, start running up and down some stairs, she advised, "then we could have two birthdays on the sixteenth," Rowan laughed in excitement.

"Raven isn't going to chance breaking her neck running up and down stairs. When our boy finally gets here, it will be the perfect time," Bran grinned at Raven, hugging her tighter to his side. "But I do like the idea of celebrating Raven's birthday at the same time as the shower. That means it won't be just a girls-only event, and I can come."

"Honestly, Hugh, tell me," Rowan looked at the older gentleman with exasperation, "are you as romantic as your boys?" She started to laugh before her laughter turned into more of a choked cough. Realizing too late that it sounded like she might be asking for her benefit.

Damn it. Row definitely was into the O'Faolain patriarch, and he always did his level best to ignore her. Men could be so... insufferable.

Thank God Pat saw her younger sister's discomfort and made some joke about Bran and him getting all their best qualities from their Gran. Just then, Brenda let them know they would be ready to taxi in about twenty-five minutes. The runway was packed with holiday travelers trying to return home before the winter storms grounded all the flights.

River noticed Bran staring at his phone before laughing and showing it to Raven. Raven, however, looked stricken and tried to grab Bran's phone. What was going on? Bran didn't notice her sister's distress, and River was about to intervene when Bran said, "Jesus, Pat. The outdoor garden at Wolves wasn't meant to be a personal playground for you and Riv." Bran laughed until he saw his brother's face. River was looking at Patrick as well.

He looked sick.

Had he done something with another woman right before he'd told River he loved her— for the first time? The same night she'd told him that she would love him forever.

"River," Patrick practically moaned her name as if he was in physical pain, his face white. His eyes were pleading. River's brief hope that this may have been another stunt by Delton to hurt their relationship ended.

River cut him off. "Let me see the picture, Bran. Please." She held her hand out, watching her brother-in-law fight the need to keep it from her. Raven looked at her then. She was crying. Not good, then.

"Give her the phone, Bran," Raven urged.

Rowan was already kneeling at River's feet, her hands grasping her knees.

"Please don't look, River. I can explain... I... I planned on telling you," Patrick begged. As she took the phone from his brother, Patrick moaned.

River slowly turned the phone over. She and Rowan both gasped. Patrick, and it was clearly Pat, his white-blond hair a stark contrast in the dark photo, sat on one of the garden benches, a petite brunette in his lap— one hand on the woman's back, the other on her ass— clearly kissing.

River's hands were shaking bad enough to blur the image, the phone dropping to the floor from her numb fingers.

Agony. Anger.

Devastating.

River felt cold. So cold. She knew everyone was talking, but it was like white noise had invaded the jet's cabin.

Irrevocable. That's what this picture was.

She glanced at Patrick. He had his head lowered— face in hands. Shame? Regret? River would never know because this was the last moment she would ever speak to the man. Grasping Rowan's hand while looking at her older sister's tear-streaked face, she told them in a decently even voice, "I would ask that you let me off the plane, Hugh. I will come later." She would not— could not— be on a plane with… him.

Raven stood quickly, dislodging Bran's arm at the same time Rowan stood. Both sisters looked ready for battle.

River only wanted oblivion.

Raven spoke first. "Leave all three of us here."

"Like fucking hell I'll leave you!" Bran yelled.

Hugh only growled, "Rowan. Please." Row only shook her head. No.

River cleared her shaky throat and told them, "I will get an Uber to Jo's. I'll come once the weather passes. I promise."

"No."

"No."

Patrick broke the stalemate. "No, River. I caused this. I fucked up. I'll stay behind." He stood then, tears falling down his deceitful face, and asked his dad to tell Bobby that he needed to disembark. He stopped by River's chair, her sisters still crowding around her, and begged, "Please, River. Please allow me to explain. If not here, then Dublin."

Patrick's imploring look did nothing to melt the ice encasing her body. River looked up at the love of her life. "Do not ever approach me again. Do not call. Do not text. If you have an ounce of compassion, Patrick, you will do this for me." River gulped down her anguish so she could finish. Damn it, she was crying now. "Raven forgave your brother. Those pictures weren't even real, though. Yours are real. I will never forgive you." With that, her body folded in on itself. She curled into a tight ball of grief; her sisters' arms wrapped tight around her.

How would she recover from this? She heard Hugh speaking to Bobby over the intercom and heard Patrick's footsteps as he slowly walked away.

And she'd thought being ghosted by Patrick was the worst thing he could do.

It turns out her imagination wasn't as incredible as she'd believed.

Her sisters had put the chair divider up and maneuvered River between them. Hugh and Bran looked visibly upset. It was like *déjà vu*. Except Bran had been the one to destroy a Byrne that time.

"River." Raven wanted River to look at her. When she felt fingers gently touch her cheek, the sisters' sign of intense emotion, a way of saying *I'm here* or *Are you okay*. River lifted her eyes. Placing a hand on her own chest, Raven spoke through choking tears. "I know, Riv," slapping her chest again, "I *know*."

Bran was out of his seat and grabbed Raven, pulling her into his body. "I can't bear to hear you speak of that time. Please," he whispered against the crown of her head. Lifting his eyes to River, he said, "I don't understand how my brother and I could hurt you both. It wrecks me that Raven still hurts." He swallowed, pinching the bridge of his nose, attempting to corral his emotions. "I do know this. We are a family. We *will* heal together."

River could only nod. Christ, what a mess.

"I'm fine now, Bran," Raven said, touching her palm to his jaw, "but I need to finish what I was saying to River."

Bran finally let her go, and Raven sat back beside her. "Sorry. It is hard to see you so upset. It made me realize how tough it had to have been for you and Row to see me like you are now. I want you to recognize that I understand. That you aren't alone."

Rowan grabbed each sister's hand. "You will never be alone." Rowan and Raven shared a look before facing River. "And I hate to do this to you, but we're going to turn your logic back at you." Rowan let go of her hand before placing her finger gently on River's cheek. "You are going to sleep this flight away. Rave and I will channel our inner River and begin an outline of what the next few months are going to look like for you."

"That's right, Riv. All three of us have a lot to do, and if we have clear parameters and guidelines, we'll all feel better."

"Day by day."

"Day by day."

River took a deep breath. "All right then. Day by day."

Rowan patted her leg before standing. She turned to Hugh, who was sitting ramrod straight on the edge of his seat. "Hugh, could you call Brenda back here and see if she has any type of sleep aid onboard?" He immediately pushed the call button.

"I don't need a sleeping pill."

"You do."

"And I'll turn this loveseat into a comfy bed for you," Raven added.

They'd just taken off. River desperately wanted to be home and forget Oklahoma ever happened.

Brenda came rushing back. "Sorry, Mr. O'Faolain, for the delay. I was just serving Bobby a coffee."

"Not a problem, Brenda. Do you happen to have any sleep aids available?"

Brenda's eyes briefly landed on River's puffy eyes and tear-stained face before quickly looking back to Hugh. River would be embarrassed if she wasn't so numb.

"I have a personal prescription for Ambien, sir. I don't sleep well in hotels."

Rowan asked, "Would you mind sparing one for my sister?"

"Of course. I will get it now, along with water. It works faster on an empty stomach." Before she left, Hugh also asked her to get every spare pillow and extra blankets for her and her sisters. Brenda spoke directly to River. "I'll get the bedding, but first, I'll grab your pill so you can start to relax while I get everything situated." Her smile was kind. River mouthed a thank you as she didn't trust her voice.

Brenda was back in a flash, pill and water in hand. "You know, there is a small bedroom behind the partition," she said, pointing over Hugh's head.

Her sisters both said, "Here will be fine," at the same time. They wanted her surrounded by everyone. River nodded in agreement. Rowan sat back by River while they waited.

"Raven, while Brenda gets the bedding situated, come sit down and put your feet up for a moment. You keep rubbing Baby O, and it's freaking me out."

Raven smiled softly as she moved to do as he asked. "Your son is doing somersaults."

Once her couch was made up and the lights dimmed, the Ambien started to do its thing. Her sisters kissed her goodnight. "When you wake, we'll have shit figured out. Just sleep now, and know we are close."

11

―――――――

It took five days for the weather to clear enough for flights to safely resume. Five fucking days. Patrick was going out of his mind. He'd stayed in Tulsa during the snowstorm, doing nothing but sitting in the dark brooding over all the ways he'd wronged River— and there were many.

She'd blocked him from her phone and social media. Her sisters blocked him too. Patrick assumed his dad and brother would like to block him as well, but then they wouldn't be able to yell at him. He deserved it. He deserved worse.

His dad was so angry that the first time he called Patrick, he only said one word. *Why?* He asked if Bran was there. He was. He asked to be put on speaker. And then he told them every way he'd had hurt River. He attempted to explain his irrational fear about commitment, but he floundered for words.

He told them about Miranda. That she was someone he'd hooked up with before. He admitted to being confused by his feelings for River and had made the worst possible choice. When Miranda asked him to step outside in the garden, he agreed. He regretted the decision immediately but allowed her to climb on his lap.

He'd kissed her.

He was so ashamed.

He believed River would never speak to him again. Forgive him.

They were silent as he tried to get hold of his emotions— to stop crying.

Finally, Bran broke the silence. "You aren't the only O'Faolain around here to fuck up. I lost Raven for a while and almost lost the chance to be a part of my son's life. I understand screwing up, Pat. It's what you do from here on out that matters now. I'll stand by you because we're family, and I love you, but I won't step between the sisters."

"You have an uphill battle, Son, but I will never hold your mistakes against you. We all make them. I agree with Bran, though. I won't go against what the sisters want. River needs time to heal, and they've thrown up barricades all the way around her, even from us. It will take time."

Knowing his family was disappointed but still loved him meant everything to Patrick. If they abandoned him— he didn't even want to imagine it.

So, here he sat on the O'Connor's private jet, wanting to vent his rage at how long it would be before he reached Dublin — before he was in the same city as River. However, desperate anger wasn't any more productive than despair. River was a planner. She was the best at it. He needed to become a better planner. He needed to spend every hour of every day working toward winning her back.

Josephine O'Connor was distracting him from his thoughts. She sat facing him. And she looked like she was half a second from flying across the aisle to bash his head in. He'd tried to talk to her three times already, and she'd refused to speak.

"Thank you again for letting me share the flight." He

sounded as stiff as his father. His emotions were so raw. Barely leashed.

"You're here because you asked my brother. This is a shared family jet. If it were only mine, you wouldn't be here." Her voice shook, she was so pissed.

"Nothing you say could possibly make me feel worse than I already do," Pat sighed, running his hands through his hair. "Fuck, Jo. Don't you think I know how badly I've fucked everything up? Don't you realize I'm dying inside knowing how I've hurt River? I knew the minute I touched that other woman that I'd fucked up." Pat leaned back, staring up at the interior lights, trying to calm his breathing.

Sitting forward, he made sure to make eye contact with James' sister before he said, "I was scared and running. I knew that night, after the garden, that I never wanted another woman except for River. She is it. I realize it will take a miracle for me to ever get her back."

Jo was sniffling. She was a good friend to the sisters, and he was thankful for it. She picked up Thomas' hand and started to rub his fingers between her two much smaller hands. Patrick didn't think she even realized how she was soothing herself. The bodyguard looked shocked as well.

Jo was wrestling with what to say to him, he could tell. He deserved any amount of vitriol spewed his way. He would take it, swallow it, and continue to plan.

Sighing, Jo said, "Listen, Pat, I know people make bad, really bad decisions." As she continued to speak, she was moving her hands, one of which was tugging and pulling Thomas' along with it.

"I realize you are dealing with your own fallout. I've just been dealing with not being there to comfort one of my best friends when she needed me. I feel... Oh," she finally realized she was holding her guard's hand like a safety blanket, "sorry, Thomas." She quickly dropped his hand back in his lap, twisting her hands together.

Thomas took her hand back and just kept it still on the armrest that divided their bodies. Jo went still before she looked back at Pat. "I'll feel better when I see her. That's all," she shrugged, running out of steam.

"I'm glad she has you and her sisters. I promise you, though, I will never stop trying to get her back."

"I don't think you deserve her," she admitted without heat, leaning her chair back as a huge yawn cracked her jaw.

"I *know* I don't deserve her."

Patrick watched Jo's eyes slowly close, her head listing to the side. Thomas watched her for a few minutes until her breathing evened into sleep before scooping her out of her seat and settling her on his lap. She blinked her eyes open, startled at the new position. Patrick watched her personal guard whisper something in her ear.

Whatever he said worked. Jo allowed him to place her head on his broad shoulder, her face in the crook of his neck. Thomas looked at Patrick, almost daring him to object to his lack of professionalism. Pat believed that ship had sailed months ago for those two. Patrick shrugged— not concerned.

Another thirty minutes of silence passed while he tried to work out his first move once he reached Dublin. Thomas shifted Jo, pulling a blanket over her body. Patrick wondered if Macgregor knew how far gone he was over Josephine.

Thomas looked at him. "She's barely slept since she saw the pictures," he explained in his heavy Scottish brogue.

"I understand," is all he could say. He hurt so many people.

"I would like to discuss New Year's Eve. At Wolves." As Patrick's body stiffened, Thomas added, "Not to berate you, Patrick. I imagine you are doing that to yourself well enough."

"I do nothing but. What do you want to know?"

"Did you know there was a full spread of photographs from that night in Tulsa World's social section?"

That startled Patrick. Sickened, he asked, "Of the garden?"

"No. There are tons of pictures of various customers enjoying themselves. One picture was of you and that woman at the garden doors."

Patrick could only nod. He might vomit.

Thomas continued. "My people called the paper and asked who submitted the photos. Your father said he wasn't aware of hiring a specific photographer for the event." MacGregor's grim face made Patrick extremely uneasy about where this conversation was heading.

"Did they get a name?"

"No. The paper's editor said the cover letter accompanying the email and pictures led her to believe he was an independent hired by the O'Faolains. She sent the email to the detectives working the Samuel Delton case." He took a deep breath, obviously angry that no one had caught the stalker yet.

"The *SocialOK* blogger is the one who received and posted all the intimate pictures of you in the garden. The lead detective spoke to her personally. She received an email from a person who claimed to work for *Event Photography*, a new company. The email explained that he didn't expect payment, only a shout-out for the new business to help build his clientele. She did as he asked."

"Did the detective find anything from that email?"

"The email was no longer available. The website for *Event Photography* was erased as though it had never been. No searches provided any leads."

Patrick's insides froze. Had that maniac been at Wolves? "What do you think?"

"I think Samuel Delton was there that night. I think he was

in disguise. I think we stood next to him and never knew it. This man is a psychopath, but he's also brilliant."

"If he *was* there... my God, I left River alone to screw around."

"That aside, Patrick, Delton has not given up. He isn't hiding in a dark corner. He is still actively coming for your family, and I assume the O'Connors as well. I spoke with Mr. O'Connor before we boarded. We will keep the same team in Dublin, but he wants protection added to James and Jane."

"Is the FBI still hunting him because of his dark web shit?"

"Yes. All the information from the editor and the blogger have been sent. The security cameras from Wolves are being analyzed now. They hope to peg Sam in the crowd, disguise or no. They have facial recognition software that should flag him no matter the costume," he sighed, "but this guy is a professional. His school records before moving online show he had extremely high marks in business classes, but he also excelled in art."

Ahh, Patrick understood. His disguises might be good enough to fool software. "Why exactly is the FBI interested in him?"

Thomas stared at him for a moment before answering. "I found out," he stated grimly. "Rape. He videos himself drugging and raping women. Sick fucks rent his videos on the dark web."

"Jesus. Have you told Dad and Bran?" They would be frantic.

"I just got the intel before takeoff. I plan on meeting with you three, Mr. O'Connor and James, by video, and my men as soon as it can be arranged tomorrow afternoon. I want to make sure the O'Connors can attend, and they'll be six hours earlier than us."

"I understand." Patrick rubbed his head. It ached worse with each revelation. "You realize, at least for now, River will not let me help keep her safe?" A crushing sense of despair threatened to drown him.

"They will be properly guarded. At all times." Patrick nodded his gratitude. "At our meeting, I plan on discussing with Hugh and Mr. O'Connor the necessity of telling the women of Delton's crimes. They need to know. They'll understand the heightened safety protocols if they understand the gravity of the situation."

"I agree." Patrick looked at MacGregor then. "I don't know if I've thanked you for how well you guard our families. I truly appreciate you and your people."

Thomas nodded. Accepting the thanks. "For what it's worth, in my time around your family, I wouldn't describe O'Faolains as quitters. Is that a correct assumption?"

"Yes."

"Then I hope you stop beating yourself up sooner than later. I learned that lesson the hard way. In the military, I lost friends, good friends, and I almost lost myself to anger and regret."

"How did you get over it?"

"My Granny. I had some leave and went home to visit. During dinner one night, she hit me upside the head with a wooden spoon. Hard. The spoon was covered in stew, by the way. I was pissed and asked her why she did it. Mind me now, Pat, I had been all but impossible to be around.

"She'd had enough of my attitude apparently— asked me if being an arsehole would bring my friends back. I admitted it wouldn't. While wiping bits of tatties and gravy from my scalp, Granny told me that the way to honor my friends was to remember them. Blaming myself put the focus on me. Not them.

"She was right. I wallowed in guilt that I shouldn't have even been carrying. I was getting in my way. Focus on your goal and then do everything you can to achieve it. It's the only thing men like us, who care deeply, can do to carry on."

Patrick had the goal and the beginning of a game plan, but Macgregor was right. Wallowing in pity only put the focus on himself. "Thank you, MacGregor. I'm working on a plan, and I have no intention of losing."

12

Four score and seven years ago...

Try four days and seven hours ago. That's when River's heart burned up, her hopes and dreams nothing but ash.

She'd gone to the blogger's website to see the photos for herself. They'd been removed. River was angry at first and then relieved. Everybody knows self-flagellation is only a good idea if you want to look as miserable on the outside as you feel on the inside. She truly never wanted to see the photos again, but she wouldn't have minded them staying up a bit longer if only to haunt Patrick.

First thing this morning, Raven let her know that Jo and Honey were coming in late tomorrow. Patrick was flying with them.

"What? Why?" River's shoddily constructed emotion box was weakening.

Holding up her 'hold your roll' hand, Raven admitted, "Yeah, I was pissed until Jo explained that James had said he could. She was _not_ happy. He'll be lucky to survive hours in a confined area with Jo."

"I told Jo she didn't have to come back to Ireland so early.

She meant to stay in Oklahoma until late January at the earliest. She wanted to spend time with her family."

"She loves each of us, Riv. You couldn't ask her to not stand beside you. I know you aren't ready to scream and rage and cry and make threats to Patrick's life, but you can't expect those who love you most not to rally. We'll be here when you're ready — and you will be ready," she whispered the last.

River only nodded. Her agreement. Her understanding.

Since returning home, River had been running from dusk 'til dawn. Her sisters created a Herculean To-Do list. One that they knew would leave her too tired each night to do anything but sleep.

There was baby décor, birthday and baby shower planning, and hours upon hours of decisions to be made for the O'Faolain building— the gorgeous four-story hugging Triskelion that the Oklahoma Wolves purchased so that Bran could be close to Raven— next door: paint, décor, furniture... ad infinitum. She was gloriously relieved. Her sisters were taskmasters. They gave her jobs and expected them to be done. No excuses, no time for pity parties, no time for tears in the bathroom.

Raven and Rowan knew her better than anybody else in the world, and they knew she needed the grind as an outlet. Hit the pavement running, no time allowed to... think. Unfortunately, River's daily Shakespearian quote was from *Much Ado About Nothing—*

Balthasar:
Sigh no more, ladies, sigh no more,
Men were deceivers ever,
One foot in sea, and one on shore,
To one thing constant never.
Then sigh not so, but let them go,
And be you blithe and bonny,

Converting all your sounds of woe
Into hey nonny nonny.

River's fist pumped to the 'Surviving a Cheater' passage. It made her feel better for twenty-two seconds— why working overtime and weekends was mandatory so she could eventually shout *hey nonny nonny* at the top of her lungs. And mean it.

Raven happened to be in the office at the same time as River. It was a rarity, as they were all three going in different directions these days. She noticed her sister rubbing her back repeatedly. Raven was due in about five weeks and was still working long hours. River had heard her and Bran argue several times about her needing to step back and let other people take over. That never went well for her brother-in-law. River happened to agree with him, however.

She texted Bran and asked how far away he was from Triskelion. He responded immediately. *Next door*. River replied, come to the shop, please. She then casually asked if Raven had updated lists for the three of them. It was Saturday, so Raven should have updated their lists for Monday, she was sure.

Raven looked up from her computer and smiled— a tired smile. Damn it. "Oh yeah, I finished them this morning. Next week looks like it's going to be a real bitch," she laughed, but her face looked more tearful than cheerful.

Right on time and looking like he ran, Bran burst through Triskelion's heavy wooden door, startling his wife half out of her chair before she recognized that the hatless Norse warrior wearing a black wool Tom Ford Pea Coat was her husband. Bran looked so much like Patrick it struck River hard at times. Swallowing past the lump forming in her throat, she stood.

"Raven, babe, are you okay?"

Looking bewildered, she replied, "I'm fine, Bran. Why?"

Bran moved over to his wife, running his hands up and down her arms and her shoulders. He looked at River in question. Oh boy. "Raven," she waited until her sister looked at her. "I asked Bran to come."

"Well, I don't mind, but why?" she asked while patting Bran's hand in an attempt to calm her overprotective spouse.

"I need him to take you home. As of today, this minute, you are officially on maternity leave."

Her sister was speechless— until she wasn't. "I think that is a *me* decision. Not a *you* decision." Oh, shit, Raven was fighting tears.

River quickly walked to her sister's side, bumping Bran out of the way so she could kneel in front of Raven. Placing her hand on Baby O, she asked, "Is our work more important than your health? Your son's?" River didn't let her answer. "You're tired, Rave. Let Rowan and me pick up the slack."

"There's too much to do," she hiccupped.

"If I were pregnant and you knew I was working too hard, what would you do?"

Silence reigned as Raven digested River's truth bomb. She glanced behind at her husband, who thankfully did not tell her what he wanted her to do. It had to be her choice.

"I would do exactly what you're doing now," she admitted. "But... but I don't want you alone right now," she choked, placing both her hands against River's cheeks.

Damn it, she was not ready to discuss New Year's. "You know I want, no, I *need* to stay busy right now. Think of handing over your tasks to me as a gift," River smiled. When Raven didn't return the smile, she added, "I promise to talk to you and Row. Give me a few more weeks. Okay?"

"Before Baby O gets here. You, me, and Rowan. Promise."

River didn't want to rehash the worst moment of her life, but that wasn't an option in this family. "I promise. Now, for your promise, Raven— and witnessed by your husband— you can make the final decisions for your floor in the building, especially the baby room, but—" River stood up then and leaned menacingly over her pregnant sister, "—you will delegate. You will give us, or anyone else, our marching orders from a chair with your feet up. Do you agree?"

Raven knew she was purposely making her say it in front of Bran. No backing out. "Fine."

"Promise me."

"I promise," she growled. Bran scooped his wife out of her chair and cradling his family in his arms, he swung her around while she shrieked and laughed.

Her family's happiness was healing balm. It *would* be enough. It had to be.

Rowan breezed in all lovely and chic as only her youngest sister could pull off, stopping mid-step when she noticed Bran swinging their very pregnant sister all around the office. Rowan looked at River, like, 'what the hell is going on?'

River heard Bran tell Raven that he had all sorts of amazing things planned to pass the time during her leave of absence.

Jealous? Most definitely.

"This is Raven's first day of maternity leave. Bran's excited," she added with a shrug.

"Thank God." Rowan smiled and laughed when Bran announced he was going home and taking his wife to bed. For rest. Doubtful, that.

When the door closed behind the happy couple, Rowan collapsed in her own chair, resting her head on her desk. "I am more than thankful for whatever voodoo you performed to get our sister to call it quits, but Jaysus, Mary, and Joseph," she said, mimicking their grandma, "how will we ever get all this work done with just the two of us?"

"We'll manage. I hardly sleep these days." River meant it as a lighthearted comment, but Rowan looked troubled.

"I don't want this for you, Riv. Talk to me. Please. Tell me how I might help you, and I'll do it."

"I know you would. I... I need time to learn how to live without him, you know. I need time to find my happy place again. Separate from... him. It's been less than a week." River stared at her sister, begging for understanding.

"I'll give you a few weeks, and then you *will* talk to me."

"Jesus, fine. You sound more like Raven every day, I swear." Rowan's only response was flipping her off. Precious.

Rowan's phone started to ring, and River saw Hugh's name flash on the screen. She also witnessed her sister's blush before she answered.

"Hello." River could hear Hugh's deep, rumbling voice, Rowan's occasional *that won't be necessary, we don't need help,* followed by more growls and a final, *Fine!* Followed by a quieter, *thank you, Hugh,* before hanging up.

Someone else in this office doesn't wish to discuss personal shit— River thought. Talk about the pot calling the kettle black! River hesitated to ask but decided to anyway. "What was that all about?"

"Apparently, in the last five seconds, Bran told his father that Raven was on maternity leave."

"Annnnnd," River prompted.

"He asked Saoirse Kennedy to give him recommendations for personal assistants. For *all three* of us."

"What the fuck? Seriously, that man has no boundaries. Dom officially starts in two weeks!" Dom worked for years as a top-tier butler and concierge for the wealthy who stayed in Dublin's famed hotel, The Fitzwilliam. The older gentleman had more knowledge of the city and its affluent, potential clients living there than anyone River knew. He was going to be key to Triskelion Territory Designs moving into the big leagues.

"That's what I said, but Hugh made the argument that it would take Dom weeks to fully acclimate himself to his job and responsibilities. He's interviewing candidates in the morning. Soooo, yeah, that's that, I guess."

River had to admit, "He's one of the most annoying men I've ever met, but he's also one of the best." River watched her sister smile.

"He is that. Just." Strong emotion brought a hint of Irish to her words.

"Patrick is flying in tomorrow with Jo and Honey." River tried for nonchalance. She achieved stilted. Note to self: casual commentary needed work.

"I know." Rowan's eyes burned into her own. "If you never wish to see him, you won't. *That* is a promise."

River could only nod. She desperately wanted to see his face, which meant she was broken. She had to repair her shattered bits before she was ever near... him.

"He just needs to stay out of my way, but I don't want anything to taint the arrival of Baby O. I will make it work, but he has to give me space."

"Agreed. On a lighter, non-O'Faolain note," Rowan smirked, "Rave and I signed you up for your first blacksmithing class with Josh Ryan. It starts at four-thirty."

Josh was a local blacksmith who specialized in metal sculptures. He was brilliant. Triskelion had earmarked several of his pieces for their clients as well as pieces for the O'Faolain project. He believed in giving back to his community and taught beginner classes for the locals, free of charge.

But that didn't mean she was interested in the equivalent of a paint and sip night— minus the sip.

River's face flamed at her sisters' highhandedness. "Why in

the hell would you do that? Like I have any extra time, and now we need to split Raven's work between us!" River was spitting mad at this point. They were all friendly with Josh. He was a wonderful man. She knew that he set up his classroom workshop specifically to how many people signed up and their experience level, which meant if she canceled now, it would be horribly rude— which her sisters knew— and that's why she was only just hearing about it.

"You need to switch shit up. It's all a part of Rave's and my game plan. I won't apologize for making you realize you have an amazing life. You had one before Patrick, with Patrick, and you'll have one without that prick."

"You are being... extra. I. Am. Busy." River was shaking, she was so furious.

"Hugh's handling the extra help. I trust him. You, on the other hand, don't do *anything* that's good for you."

"You aren't my fucking mother, Rowan. Stop already." River regretted her harsh words as soon as they left her mouth. Rowan's face fell. Her earlier attempt at joviality was gone. "Shit, Row, I didn't... mean—"

Rowan stopped her by standing up and walking over to her desk, standing at River's knees. "I'm not your mother, River, but I sure as hell am your sister. Raven and I wanted you to have something fun. Something fun that was just yours. You've always loved the art of smithing, and we thought... it might make you smile." She frowned at River. "A real smile."

They were right. The longer River hid from her emotions, the more closed off she would become. Of course, they would know this. Of course, they would force her hand.

Breathing out slowly, River stood so that she and Rowan faced one another. She took her hands and brought them to her chest. "Forgive me for being an asshole. If it were you or Raven, I would do the same thing for the same reason. I love you."

"Will you go?"

"Yes, damn it. I'll go. Try not to call Raven before I've left the building."

Rowan grinned. "I'll try really, really, really hard."

RIVER WAS the last of the class's six attendees. Josh was in the middle of helping a middle-aged man organize his workstation but noticed her entrance and smiled. River smiled, waving awkwardly before taking a seat in the rear. River saw printed instructions— with pictures— thank you little tiny baby Jesus.

Her sisters were right in that River was obsessed with hand-forged art. Blacksmithing was cool as hell, but come on, she never thought to try her hand at it. She would never admit to Raven or Rowan, but she was secretly a tiny bit stoked about the class. This was exactly what she needed to move past... him.

As River flipped through the directions for a 'Twist-Forged Bracelet in 5 Steps,' Josh stopped by her desk. "Hey, River."

"Hi, Josh."

"So, were you surprised your sisters signed you up," he grinned and chuckled.

Thank God, at least he knew it wasn't her idea, so when she bombed at being a blacksmith, he wouldn't be too hard on her. "Found out a few hours ago," she answered with a laugh. "They really need hobbies."

"I delivered the Wolf sculpture yesterday for the O'Faolain's main floor. Hugh helped me set it in place. I admit, it's been one of the most creative projects I've worked on for months."

"Oh my God, Josh, you finished it? I can't wait to see how it looks in the space."

"For an artist, it was a treat to make a statement piece for a specific space versus creating art for an unknown customer. Not that I don't love it all, but there was something special about being a part of the entire creative process."

"It's why my sisters and I love interior design so much. We get to see our vision become reality." Looking down at the bracelet instructions, River said, "I'm excited to give this black-smithing thing a go."

"You'll love it, trust me." He smiled at River one more time, making her feel more comfortable before he turned and addressed the class, "Okay, everyone, tonight we will try our hands at twisted-forge bracelets."

Josh went through a practice demonstration first. He explained what each tool was called and how and when they were used: tongs, steel stock, anvil, forge, hammer, punch, vise, twisting wrench, essential to tonight's project, and the finishing metal wire brush. Information overload, but River was wholly committed.

Furiously scribbling notes and videoing Josh with her phone as he demoed the process was such a sweet relief from her recent depressing thoughts River could have cried.

This was healing.

This was moving forward.

This was leaving Patrick O'Faolain behind.

Damn it. River realized she'd allowed a few tears to escape, now trekking down her cheeks. The class stood around Josh as he helped each student create their bracelet. It was hot and hard work. If anyone noticed her ridiculous tears, she hoped they thought it was sweat.

"River?"

Double damn. It was her turn, and she had spaced for a moment. Damn it all to hell. She'd been doing so well too. "Oh, sorry, Josh. I'm ready." Josh gave her a steady look. She hadn't fooled him.

River got through her turn— and— drumroll— she loved it! Damn her sisters. As everyone was packing up their things, she was still turning over her lovely, twisted bracelet, amazed she'd made something so pretty.

River hadn't realized Josh had walked up until he spoke. "You're a natural, River." His smile and kind words made her feel good.

"Your exaggeration skills are top-notch," she laughed. "Regardless of my skill level, I truly enjoyed myself. You are a great teacher."

"You enjoyed yourself so much you cried?"

Startled, River started to flail her hands in the air and stutter out excuses about sweat or a possible eyelash. When her excuse train derailed, she awkwardly, very awkwardly, finished with, "Well, thanks so much, Josh. I'll make sure to go to the O'Faolain's tomorrow to look at your sculpture."

River kept backing toward the exit, inanities still dripping from her stupid mouth. All the while, Josh just listened and watched, arms crossed over his broad chest, probably waiting for her to shut up. She didn't blame him.

While she'd been mumbling incomplete thoughts, the rest of the class had already said their goodbyes. "Why did your sisters sign you up for this class?"

Umm, could they go back to a lighthearted mood? "Oh, they knew I've always been interested in the craft. Okay," River tried once more to bow out, "thanks again."

She'd gotten the door open this time, and then Josh asked, "Hey, you want to go to O'Donoghue's? Some of my friends are meeting there to watch a good friend's band play?" At River's hesitation, he added, "Only friends, River. I mean it. You obviously have stuff going on. I do, as well. I could use a friend."

River thought about running until she was in her bed with the covers thrown over her head, but that wouldn't fix her broken parts. She did need friends and friendly outings. "Oh, actually, that sounds great."

Josh looked surprised his offer worked. "I've been in the smithy since six this morning. I hope you're hungry because I'm about to order the menu." She laughed, and he did too, but admitted, "I actually do plan on ordering... a lot," he smirked.

Raven laughed. Like, not a fake one, but a real laugh. It felt amazing.

～

O'Donoghue's was crazy fun. Josh's friend was the lead singer for a traditional Irish band, sounding just like the music her father had loved so much. She'd thought never to enjoy this type of evening again... without him.

Josh leaned into her side and asked, "Why did you cry tonight?"

It might be the whiskey shots, but River wasn't embarrassed like she probably should be. Everyone had an off day. Being cheated on wasn't a 'Breaking News' story. It happened all the time, and she refused to be ashamed of someone else's awful behavior.

She looked at Josh then, really looked at him. He was a very handsome man with tight brown curls buzzed close to his scalp and caramel skin— the muscles were a given in his profession.

She knew from earlier visits with her sisters that his father was a native Dubliner, and his mother was a Nigerian who had moved to Ireland to be with her love. It was a romantic story. River had seen a picture of Josh and his folks hung in his shop earlier that evening. He shared his father's build, close to six feet, but Josh was way more bulked up. His beautiful chocolate eyes and wide smile came from his mother. In the picture, Mrs. Ryan wore a bright blue kaftan with a navy and gold silk scarf wrapped around her head. It was a great family photo.

But just because Josh was nice and came from a nice family didn't mean she wanted to answer his private questions. "Why do you want to know?" River countered.

Josh took a sip of his drink, staying silent for a moment. "Something, or someone, hurt you, and your sisters added you to my class because of it. You seem sad. I'd like us to be friends, which means I want to know *you*."

Well, put like that... River tapped her fingernail against the top of her glass, contemplating how to answer. "I was in love with a man who cheated on me New Year's Eve. The same night he first told me he loved me." The truth, apparently.

"Did he *tell* you?" Josh asked, eyes wide.

"The pictures were all over social media and the Tulsa newspaper the next morning. I haven't spoken to him since. My sisters and I flew home that day."

"What a dick. Seriously, what a fucking cocksucker." Josh seemed genuinely floored. Join the club, she thought.

"Pretty much," River shrugged. "I'm trying to move on. Your class was an incredible distraction. I did really love it." Josh flushed at the compliment.

"Does this man live here or the States?"

"Both now, I guess." At his questioning look, River decided on full disclosure. "He's Raven's husband's brother."

"Ahh, I see. An O'Faolain then?"

"Yes."

"Awkward."

"Yes," she smiled then and even chuckled. A lovely lightness touched her bones, which had felt unusually heavy. Her sisters would be so happy. Josh drummed his fingers on the bar as his friend started his last set. He was pensive, and it wasn't because of River's woes, she was sure. "Why do you want to be friends with me? Besides the fact that I must appear semi-pathetic and in need of support," she smiled.

Josh took a deep breath, his chest swelling beneath his tight, black t-shirt. "My mother died last month. I'm having a difficult... a very difficult time."

Before he finished his confession, River had slipped off her barstool and was standing in front of Josh, her arms wrapping around his waist. Josh stiffened, surprised, but then his body deflated, wrapping around her much smaller frame. A gush of air huffed out of his mouth, stirring her hair. River rubbed and patted his back for a few minutes before stepping away.

"Oh God, Josh. Thank you for telling me." Once she sat on her stool, their knees touching and a world of vulnerable thoughts between them, River confessed, "I know how you feel."

"You can't possibly know, River. I get your boyfriend hurt you, but it isn't the same," he spoke low, clearly struggling with his emotions.

"Raven, Rowan, and I lost our parents when we were in college. Car accident. We were a very close family. Without my sisters and our grandma, I'm not sure how I would have moved past it. I'm so glad you have your father still with you, Josh. There are moments during the day when I grab my phone to call mom or dad about something. Remembering they are gone is brutal."

It was Josh's turn to crush her into a hug. She hated the public tears, but her parents were worth all her emotions.

"I didn't know, River. I'm sorry. To lose both," he swallowed hard, "I'm barely keeping afloat, and I still have my da, thank the Lord."

Once they eased apart some, River asked, "How did your mother die?"

"Cancer. She fought for three years."

She lost the battle. Damn. River wasn't sure what was more painful. Losing a loved one suddenly or being given an expiration date. Cruel, cruel, cruel either way.

"Oh, Josh. Only a month. Damn. I'm glad she got to see what an amazing artist her son is, though."

Josh finally let River go but stayed tight to her side. He seemed to find comfort in her. It must have been a relief to discover someone who understood his grief.

Josh admitted, "She was very proud of me. My father is as well." He stopped speaking abruptly, scuffing his hand across his scalp, trying to get his emotions under control. "Da's having a tough time."

River wove her fingers through his, squeezing in comfort. "You are *both* having a hard time, Josh, not just your father and it won't end anytime soon. There is no way around it. Grieving is sorrow and anguish and, at times, despair. You have your father. Lean on him. He'll lean on you too, and together, you'll find a way to bear it."

River and Josh just looked at one another while patrons laughed and the band played. In that moment, it felt like they'd been close for years. This friendship could very well help them both through their current trials.

"You can lean on me, River, when you need to. I would appreciate you letting me lean on you once in a while."

"I would really like that. I can text you all the embarrassing things my sisters do, and you can complain about clients and stinky students," she laughed, making him laugh too.

"Oh, so you noticed Mr. Tom's fragrant hair balm? Christ, it smelled like lard. I was afraid to have him stand so close to the flames." They laughed, toasting to Mr. Tom's greasy head, and shot back the rest of their drinks.

River touched Josh's arm briefly to get his attention. "And you can always talk to me about your mother. I would love for you to tell me some of your memories, and I can do the same with my parents."

Josh's eyes were glassy, but he nodded in agreement. "And you can talk to me about your ex-boyfriend. If you need to."

"Maybe."

"You still love him, even after what he did?"

"Unfortunately."

"Do you think you'll get back together?"

"Listen, Josh. Patrick has his own personal demons. They don't excuse his behavior with me. I plan on taking a long time to heal and assess my life, what direction I want it to go in, and who I plan on spending it with. It's only been a few days."

"It's good you are taking time. Did he stay in the States?"

"He's flying in with one of my best friends tomorrow." At Josh's raised brows, she added, "Jo wouldn't have brought him, but her brother happens to be Bran and Patrick's best friend."

"Jesus."

"Right? My sisters won't allow him near me." Changing gears, she told Josh she would run by O'Faolain's place before work in the morning to see his wolf sculpture.

"Text or call me and let me know what you think. I admit to being proud of it. I get why Hugh wanted a wolf since O'Faolain in Irish means wolf."

River laughed. "Yeah, growing up in Oklahoma, every woman with a pulse, and probably just as many men, ate up any bit of gossip about The Irish Wolves. That's what they were known as in the Tulsa oil circle." Geez, she had to stop talking about Patrick's family.

"Sorry, sometimes my mouth isn't synced with my brain. You need to pinch me every time I bring up the world's biggest douche canoe. Pain therapy. It supposedly takes twenty-one days to break a habit. Are you ready to commit to at least that many days being my bestie?"

He laughed, "I'll do your twenty-one days and raise you an extra ninety." They both chuckled, shaking hands to seal their new friendship. River's phone buzzed, the screen reading Rave. Instant panic that her sister was still up.

"I've got to take this. It's Raven." She answered and told her sister to wait until she walked outside so she could hear.

"Go on out. I'll pay our tab and meet you."

"Thank you." As soon as she reached the street, she asked what was wrong.

Raven laughed, "Jesus, nervous Nancy, nothing's wrong. Lynx, your guard for the night, reported that you were at a pub. So, on the off chance you're still with Josh, I was hoping to talk to him about work."

River knew she was guarded, but since she only caught fleeting glimpses of the men, she forgot about them.

Josh walked up and grabbed her free hand to lead them under an awning beside the main entrance. She smiled as he let her hand drop. It was much warmer out of the wind and sprinkles.

"Why is Bran allowing you to work this late?"

"First, Bran doesn't *allow* me anything. Second, my feet are up, and I thought I would tick off some of the list. Third, it's only ten-thirty. I'm pregnant, not a step away from a nursing care facility." In the background, River heard Bran say, "Hurry up and come to bed." That man was obsessed with her sister.

River loved that about him.

"Fine, I'm handing the phone to Josh now." River held her phone out. Josh's eyes got wide, but he took it. After a moment, Josh leaned his back against the brick façade.

River went in for her own lean, tuning out the one-sided conversation between Josh and her sister. Patrick would be in Dublin tomorrow night. Regardless of what he did, his fault in it, his utter disregard for her feelings, she knew, without a shadow of a doubt, that he would seek her out. Leaning her head against the wall, River sighed. A problem that wouldn't be solved standing outside a Dublin pub.

River knew she wouldn't be able to resist Patrick if she saw him. She would have to count on her sisters, and now Josh, to keep her on the straight and narrow.

Speaking of her new friend with Patrick-blocking benefits, Josh was saying goodbye to Raven. He handed her phone back. "You look slightly flustered, big guy. Was my sister weird or what?" Honestly, River and Rowan had learned quite quickly that pregnancy hormones were unpredictable.

Slipping his arm through the crook of hers, Josh said, "If you aren't too tired, let's share a cab, and I'll tell you all about your sister's proposal," he answered, grinning like a maniac.

13

———

Patrick should have been asleep. He'd been staring at the ceiling of his hotel room at The Fitzwilliam for hours, having been forced to come here with Jo and MacGregor. Bran had called Patrick as soon as they'd landed to let his brother know that he couldn't stay at the house they leased and that he'd made him a reservation at a hotel.

It was a blow. Bran said River had planned on moving out of their rental before Pat got to town, but the sisters said if she went, they would follow. "And damn, Patrick, I couldn't let Raven upend her life like that. She just started maternity leave, and she needs to rest." He paused, blowing out a deep breath. "Please understand," he begged. "I've been where you are. I know you're desperate to see her. It just can't... not yet, Brother."

Patrick told Bran he understood, and he did, damn it. He did fucking understand! He didn't deserve to be near her, but God, how he wanted to see her. Bran said he and their dad would talk to him before the meeting MacGregor set up. They were using a small conference room at The Fitzwilliam, again, because he wasn't allowed in the family home.

Patrick groaned, rubbing his temples and swiping his too-long hair out of his eyes. His bangs came to his nose, and one side needed shaving. Why bother fixing it? The only person he gave a shit to impress refused to see him. He'd asked himself repeatedly; how had his life had gotten this fucked up. But he knew *that* answer better than anyone.

The meeting about Samuel Delton didn't start until one to allow James and Dean O'Connor to join. And it was— Pat touched his phone screen until the time lit— only seven. If he took an hour to shower and dress, that'd put him at eight. Break-fast— forty-five minutes maximum. Write a letter to River, part of his grand plan to win her back— one hour. So, that left three hours and fifteen minutes before the meeting.

He wanted to check out how their building was coming along, but he'd have to ask Bran if he could. Fuck, that grated, but again, he was only reaping the rewards of his stupidity. Throwing the covers off, he grabbed his toiletry bag, digging around until he found the electric razor. He shaved one side of his head on the second to the lowest setting before taking a quick shower. Patrick dressed in brown trousers and a fitted off-white, long-sleeved shirt. His white hair fell to one side. River said he looked like a Viking with his hair like that. Since she'd kissed him after saying it, Pat figured she must like the look, so he would be keeping it.

Only twenty minutes had passed. So much for wasting an hour on grooming.

Patrick was just considering the benefits of having a whiskey with breakfast when someone knocked on his door. As he moved to open it, he assumed it was Dad or Bran, or both come early. As the door swung wide, his body clenched so tight he felt close to shattering.

It was Raven and Rowan. For the barest moment, Patrick

thought Rowan was River. That she'd come to him. Christ. What an idiot.

He must have stared overly long because Raven asked, "May we have a moment of your time, Patrick?"

Her voice startled him, jumpstarting his brain. Stepping back, he indicated that they should come in. "Sorry, of course. I didn't... I didn't expect you to come see me." He felt his cheeks heat and sweat start to bead on his forehead. Casually, Patrick turned the air down a few degrees. "Would you like me to order tea?" He offered lamely.

The two women sat at the dining table that was set in front of the glass balcony doors, early morning light sending beams of warmth across the room. Dark shadows and chill would have been more welcome. This was not a casual call. With Rowan's first question, he *definitely* knew casual was not on the menu.

"Why did you do it?" Before he could come up with a reply — not that anything had automatically jumped into his head— Rowan continued. "You kissed another woman, had your hands all over her not thirty minutes before you had your tongue down *my* sister's throat, confessing your undying love." She stood then, shaking in her fury. Patrick was physically ill. He was shaking too. Not with fury but shame.

"I... I don't—" He tried to get out that he *hadn't been* thinking. But Rowan wasn't having it.

"She's loved you since the moment she met you. Did you know that? Do you even care? You played with her, Patrick, like one of your easy club girls," she choked on the last. Whirling to face her sister so Patrick wouldn't see her tears, he guessed.

"I'm sorry. So sorry. There are no words to describe how crushed I am that I did that to River. Fuck," he moaned, holding his head. Agony. "To your sister. Christ. I won't ask for forgiveness because I don't deserve it." Patrick walked to the glass doors, looking out at the cool January Dublin morning.

"I would do anything, sacrifice everything, to rewind those minutes." He turned then to face the sisters. Rowan stood behind Raven, watching him warily. Leaning his back against the cool glass, he crossed his arms over his chest, letting his head fall backward a moment before focusing on the sisters once again.

"The truth is," his voice faltered. "Damn it, why is this so hard to say?"

"Just be honest, Patrick," Raven said, watching him with uncomfortable intensity.

"I've loved River probably as long as she's loved me. It just took me months too long to admit. When we talked on the phone or texted... I don't know how to say... how to... to make you understand that... that it was the best part of my day. River was— is— the best part of every day.

"Friends, I could understand. I told myself that being friends was so much better than dating. Relationships were a joke. You— Raven, and Bran— confirmed being friends was safer. Helen and Dad." Patrick would never call that woman Mother. Never.

"I remember, I couldn't have been but a few years old. I was playing with a new monster truck Dad got me around the living room fireplace. I was jumping the truck off it and tripped, cutting my forearm on the sharp ledge," he absently ran his thumb over the scar. "Dad was at work, and Bran was in school. My Nanny was... I'm not sure, actually. I ran to Helen's room. I was bleeding and crying because it hurt. She screamed at me to get out before I stained her carpet.

"I remember, too, before she yelled at me that I thought she looked so beautiful. Her white hair reminded me of a fairytale princess. After she told me to get out and find Nanny, I heard her say what a waste of time it'd been to have two." Patrick clenched his teeth at the memory but forced himself to finish. "She meant two children. It had been a waste to have two children. To have me."

"Oh, Patrick," Raven started, her eyes glossy.

"No, Raven, don't. Don't feel sorry for me. Helen did mess up some of how I felt about relationships, but it was me and me alone that hurt your sister. I knew I was pushing her away. I'm sure Helen's rejection is the reason I've always run from commitment." Listening to himself, he couldn't believe how screwed up he was. "I guess I'm scared of being left. I'm more scared of not being good enough."

Patrick looked at both women. He was laying it all out. It was a revelation. He felt— relief at admitting his deepest fears. He needed to get through the rest, though. The worst. "That night, at Wolves, I felt cornered, caged. After River and I... after we... we."

Rowan cut in. "Had sex."

"No. It was never just sex with River," he corrected. "After we were together, I had this overwhelming urge to drop to my knees and beg her to marry me. That's when I freaked out. I hid in the bathroom like a cowardly asshole. I let River think she didn't matter when she's the *only* thing that matters.

"You both know that I avoided her until New Year's Eve. I watched her all night, thinking of ways I could apologize. I wondered if she would forgive me and, if she did forgive me, what that would mean. You all were dancing with each other. River was smiling and laughing. She was the most beautiful woman there.

"And then the first bad thing happened. Miranda, a wannabe socialite that I'd had sex with once about a year ago, was standing in front of me. I hadn't noticed her because I was watching River. Miranda put her hands on my chest right as

River looked at me. She looked hurt, and I was about to push the woman off me and go to River when she grabbed a random guy's hand and pulled him onto the dance floor with her.

"I was jealous. Furious. That kind of rejection was exactly what I expected from attempting an exclusive relationship. So, when Miranda asked me to go to the garden, I did. Before I stepped outside, I knew I was screwing up. When I sat on the bench, I was thinking I needed to go back inside and find River. I didn't want to be out there with a woman I didn't care about.

"All these thoughts were rushing in my head. Miranda was sitting on my lap and kissing me— and I *did* kiss her back briefly. Out of habit, not desire. Cheating all the same. I stopped and told her I was in a relationship. That I wouldn't be hooking up in bars anymore. Miranda was annoyed but didn't really care either way. Any man would do, so she left to find someone more willing. I was disgusted thinking that I used to be that way.

"I had planned on telling River what I'd done. I *told* her I needed to tell her something. But then, we were dancing, and she was in my arms, and I confessed I loved her. I decided to tell her about what happened with Miranda once we were back in Dublin. I was afraid and wanted a few days of being a real couple. And then the pictures." Patrick grimaced, recalling the moment River saw them.

"And you know the rest. She's blocked me from everything. I understand, but how will I ever convince her to give me another chance?"

"She isn't ready to see you. I don't know if she ever will be," Raven explained. It was crushing to hear, but he knew Raven wasn't intentionally trying to be cruel. She was only being honest.

"I have decided to write to River. I thought or hoped that it would be a way to express how I feel. My regrets but also what she means to me." Neither sister gave Patrick any indication of what they thought of his plan. "Would either of you agree to give the letters to her?"

"She's going to need a lot longer than a week to stabilize. Her emotions are raw, and though she's trying to hide it from us, River is wrecked. I won't give her any of your letters." Rowan started to object, but Raven shook her head, "Let me explain. I needed the separation after Bran hurt me. I never stopped loving your brother, but I did need to find my own way without Bran's influence. I didn't want to see him or talk to him. I didn't want his apologies or his touch." Raven looked at Bran and then Rowan. "She needs more time."

"I don't disagree with you, Raven," Rowan said. "I was with you in Switzerland. I was with you when you cried. I was with you when you were quiet. I lived for your smiles, then.

"Bran didn't immediately recognize how badly he screwed up. He may have hated he'd hurt you so badly, but he felt justified in breaking up with you. Patrick admitted his mistake the moment it happened." Rowan's stern gaze met Patrick's. "You were a total coward for not telling River that night. I don't forgive you for that or what my sister is going through now."

"You are correct, and your anger at me is justified." Patrick was amazed that Rowan had something positive to say about him.

"My point is, though I think that your healing process was exactly what you needed for you, Rave, it may not be what River needs." Touching Raven's cheek, she admitted, "I'll only do this if Raven agrees, but I will give River your letter on one condition."

"Anything." Patrick didn't care what it was.

"You might not be so quick to agree once you hear my proposal. I know you have a meeting with MacGregor, but after that, you'll pack and go live with Nan, and you won't come back to Dublin until Baby O arrives."

Patrick had not seen that one coming. "But that's weeks!" He was shocked she'd ask that of him.

"Yes. Five weeks. I would think a few weeks is not much to ask after what you did to my sister."

Noted. "Have you even spoken with Bébinn?"

"This morning," Rowan replied smugly.

Raven looked shocked. "You didn't tell me."

"No, I didn't. I wasn't sure how this would go, and you'll recall, I didn't even want you to come. Stress isn't good for you or my nephew."

Patrick winced at the reminder that his actions hadn't just affected River and him. "What did Nan say? Did you tell her... umm, how bad I fucked up?" So far, Patrick had avoided thinking of how disappointed River's grandma would be when she found out. His Gran. Jesus. He prayed she never knew.

"I told her everything. Keeping secrets is pointless with Nan. As Raven knows," she smiled at her sister then.

"She's a bloodhound," Raven smiled back.

"Nan said you could live with her for the five weeks. She needs work done around the house, and her neighbor, Mr. Dunn, would likely hire you to help him with some repairs around his farm." Rowan glanced at Raven, lifting her brows in thought. "Something is going on with Nan. She sounded weird when she mentioned Mr. Dunn."

"That's something else Patrick can do while he's away. Discover if Nan is keeping a secret from us," Raven poked her sister.

Rowan sobered. "Listen, Pat. If we weren't family, I would never speak to you again, and happily after what you did. But we are family, so we all have to try harder. If River loves you still, a few weeks away won't change that. Make an effort. Write to River. By abiding by her wishes to stay away, you're letting her know her feelings matter to you.

"Let our grandma care for you. Talk to her. She's suffered a lot of loss in her life. She didn't only lose the love of her life like your grandma did, but also her only child. She knows suffering, but she also knows how to heal. Let her help you, and maybe you can help her too."

Patrick thought about everything the sisters had said. It was a lot to take in. It was drastic, and admittedly, a little daunting. "I'll leave after the meeting."

"Are you alright with this, Rave?"

Raven sighed. "I let my past pain shadow my reaction. I agree with the proposal." She stood and faced Patrick, smoothing her dress over her swollen belly. "You're willing to work for River, so I'm willing to support you." Raven stared at him a moment longer before adding, "I believe you didn't *want* to hurt River... but Patrick, you can't imagine what it's like to see a part of your very soul, my sister, in so much pain."

Patrick barely swallowed his tears before they fell. He looked at River's sisters, beyond fortunate to have their support, let alone their help. "Thank you, both, for not giving up on me completely. Truly."

"We've taken up enough of your morning, Pat. Come on, Rave, you know Bran is probably pissed you left the house without telling him," she laughed.

"Hey, we took a guard, and Bran surely doesn't expect me to tell him what my plans are every minute of the day." As Rowan snorted her disbelief, Raven added, "Laugh it up. If Bran is annoyed with me, then I bet there is someone else equally annoyed with you."

Patrick watched Rowan's face turn red. Was there something between her and his dad? Pat wouldn't be mad. It was just weird to consider his dad was almost thirty years older than

Rowan. As if it was choreographed, someone pounded on his door.

"Jesus, save me from O'Faolain testosterone," Raven moaned.

Rowan only whispered, "Told you."

The girls followed Pat to the door, standing slightly behind him while he opened things up for, yep, a worried Bran and a scowling Dad. Bran didn't even acknowledge Pat, stepping around his brother to latch on to his wife.

"What the hell, babe. Why didn't you ask me to bring you? You know I don't like you to go out alone."

Raven gave Bran a quick kiss. "Rowan and I wanted to come by ourselves." She didn't say anything else. Just looked at her husband like he should understand and move on.

Before Bran could reply, his dad crowded in, staring past Patrick, presumably at Rowan, before he barked out, "Let's go eat downstairs. I assume neither of you ladies thought to eat breakfast before sneaking out of the house."

He thought he heard a *Jesus Christ* from Rowan. She didn't argue openly. This time, at least. She was learning to pick and choose battles with the old man. Truly, if a person were to fight him every time he annoyed them, it would be a full-time job.

Dad looked at Patrick then. Putting his hand on his son's shoulder. "Did you and the girls work anything out?" It shouldn't, but it always amazed Patrick at what a loving father he had.

"We did," Pat swallowed. Embarrassed and ashamed that it'd come to this, but also slightly hopeful. "I'll be leaving town after the meeting today and won't be back until the baby comes."

"What the fuck, Pat! That's five weeks." No surprise, Bran was not happy.

"Come on, I'll explain at breakfast." Rowan walked up at

that point; his dad immediately watched her. He growled something at her about a second guard, after which she ignored him and walked on out the door. At the elevator, Bran leaned down to Raven and said, "I don't like this." To which Raven replied, "I know, babe. This was Rowan's idea, and I think it might work."

Please let it work.

14

After breakfast, and after he'd told his brother and Dad about staying with Bébhinn, Raven mentioned to Patrick that River was meeting with a client at a textiles shop and wouldn't be back to the office for an hour or two. She said it would be a good time to check out the progress on the O Building, as the sisters referred to it.

"I really need you to do a thorough walk-through of your floor. I'll help you make a final checklist of things left to do. Make sure the colors suit you, etc." As they got up from the breakfast table, Rowan sighed, obviously not wanting to say what she was about to say.

"Everything River picked out last year that you okayed was finished while we were in Oklahoma. All the furnishings have been ordered. Some of the more personal items, like linens, bedding, window treatments, rugs, and things of that nature, are in River's notes that she handed over to me. Would you like to go over the items before you leave town?"

It should have been River and him picking out everything together. In an attempt to stifle the pain, Patrick clenched his jaw before replying to Rowan. "Thank you, Row. I don't need to see the list. I want everything River chose. I know you and Dad are busy doing the top floor. I can surely figure out how to order the stuff if you give me River's notes."

His dad's head slowly turned toward Patrick, eyes wide like he'd said something weird. "What, Dad? River knows exactly what I like." Jesus, the moody fuck.

Stiffly, Dad only said, "Good thinking, Pat. Rowan won't need to do all the ordering herself. The girls' new assistants start today."

Raven guffawed at Rowen's, "What? Today?"

"Yes. Today. I told them to be at Triskelion by ten."

"You are a piece of work, Hugh," she shook her head, glaring at Raven for laughing.

"Raven, your assistant is already waiting at the house rental. One of MacGregor's men let me know ten minutes ago."

Oh, his dad was good. Now Raven was all puffed up, asking Bran, "Did you know about this?" And to Dad, "I'm on maternity leave, Hugh! What in the hell do I need an assistant for?"

"Driver's here," Bran announced, not making eye contact with his wife.

Patrick quickly got into the front passenger seat. He wasn't sitting by Raven or Rowan. It was too painful when River was missing. Raven wasn't letting the assistant thing go. Surely, she knew she'd lose against Hugh the Indomitable.

"I don't need an assistant," Raven repeated.

As usual, his dad was unruffled by dramatics or censure. "You're on maternity leave, but you are still working. Your three assistants need to work together from the beginning. They need to be a team. When Dom comes on board, the four of them need to be a team. Also, your assistant, Bre, used to be a nanny, I believe. She is divorced, and she has never had children of her own. When I asked if she would be willing to help with your son should the need arise, she said, and I quote, "It would be the highlight of my day."

And just like that, Dad went from asshole to angel. In the rearview mirror, Patrick could see Raven blinking rapidly and... sniffling. She cried a lot lately. River said it was pregnancy hormones. Just thinking about River, that she wasn't a part of this conversation, almost had *him* sniffling. Christ. He had to get her back.

"She really said that?" Raven asked quietly.

"Yes."

"Seems like Bre might be a pretty amazing fit for you, Rave. Don't you think?" Bran asked carefully.

Raven sighed, the caving inevitable. "She does. Thank you, Hugh."

From the front seat, Patrick only heard a grunt. It was decided that Raven and Bran would be dropped off at their leased house to meet Bre. Since Patrick said he wouldn't make any changes to what River had decided for his floor in the building, Rowan would head on to Triskelion while he and his dad checked on the building's progress.

Tim Daniels had done a damn fine job on his first monster contract. Patrick already knew that if they bought the distillery outside of Dublin, Daniels would be involved. He and his dad stopped in the foyer to admire the giant metal wolf sculpture. "I had thought I might do some research on the distillery while I'm at Bébhinn's. Perhaps set up a meeting to meet with the seller in a few weeks. Would you be able to meet me?"

"I don't want you to leave town," was his answer.

Patrick blew out a deep breath, shoving his hands in his front pockets. "I don't want to leave, Dad, but Rowan's plan has merit." Dad continued to stare at the sculpture. "She won't talk to me in person or by phone. She refuses to be near me, but I'm hoping she'll read my letters and that they might soften her toward me. Rowan promised to give her the letters."

"Raven and Rowan surprised me today. I had no idea they planned on speaking with you. I didn't expect them to give you a chance to contact River."

"I didn't either. I fucked up. The sisters are my only hope at the moment."

"I still don't want you to leave."

Dog with a bone, as usual. "Maybe in two weeks you'll meet me in Longford, and I can brief you on the distillery?"

"Fine."

"Dad, can I ask you something?"

Hugh stopped staring at the wolf and focused his dark eyes on his son. An eyebrow lift was Pat's consent to ask. "Are you... I mean... Christ. Are you and Rowan together?"

Patrick didn't think he'd ever seen his dad turn such a dark shade of red. Various emotions crossed his features— surprise, embarrassment, and finally, shame. "She is younger than my children. Absolutely not."

So, he was in denial. Interesting. He'd never seen his father back down from anything or anyone. "I can't speak for Bran, but I think she's good for you."

"The subject is closed," Dad growled ominously.

Patrick dared to add, "I was a coward with River, and I've lost her. I've never known you to run away from something you wanted."

No answer. Patrick didn't expect one. He did hope that his dad would rethink his stance. He deserved happiness. It had been a long time coming.

~

AT ONE THAT AFTERNOON, MacGregor used the flat screen on the conference room wall at The Fitzwilliam to connect with Mr. O'Connor and James. None of MacGregor's team was there. They'd already been briefed. Thomas decided he didn't want to pull any of his men from their stations unnecessarily.

O'Connor nodded to Dad, "Hugh."

"Dean."

As Dean O'Connor was the first person to hire MacGregor, he began with, "Where is Josephine?"

Thomas seemed to swell twice his normal size. As if Dean were calling his abilities into question. "Safe."

O'Connor nodded. "Tell me everything you've learned."

"It seems Delton has been creating more rape videos for his dark web account. The FBI has gotten close several times, but the bastard has managed to elude capture. The Tulsa detective I work with hoped that Delton had moved on from stalking you and the O'Faolains. However, after the photos surfaced from New Year's Eve taken at Wolves, we believe that he was there that night."

"You believe he took the photos of Patrick?" His dad was a breath away from exploding.

"Yes. The Tulsa newspaper editor of the social column received an email with the pictures. The photographer led her to believe he'd been hired by Hugh. The pictures were all typical grand opening stuff. There were a few of all of us and only one of Patrick and the woman he took to the garden as they were about to walk out." At Patrick's flinch, Thomas dipped his head in apology.

"The detective sent me pictures of who he believes is Samuel Delton." Here, MacGregor pulled up several security camera stills taken from inside Wolves. It was of an older woman with big hair and loud clothes. There were several pictures of her, or him rather, standing around all of them. Jesus.

They had stood right next to a predator. Rowan was at the bar, standing shoulder-to-shoulder with him at one point.

"Obviously, he hasn't moved on. The blogger that posted the pictures of Patrick got them from a new photography business hoping to grab clients' attention. They only asked to be given credit. The blogger, *SocialOK*, immediately handed over the email address, which was no longer valid, and the name of the business, *Event Photography*, which has also been erased without a trace. They shared the information with the FBI. There's a chance they might be able to trace it back to Delton. Even without the confirmation, everyone believes it's him."

And then another bomb. "The detectives are combing through the video and pictures from the Oklahoma Historical Society's gala last month. There is a possibility he was a photographer."

Patrick went cold. He remembered something then that made him sick. "He took our pictures." Bran and Dad both sat forward, the revelation shocking. "I'm sick. I didn't realize it then, but he knew our names." Looking at Bran, he asked, "Do you remember? I thought it was off the man knew our first names. *All* of our first names."

"Christ almighty," Dad whispered.

"I get the O'Faolains are well-known in Oklahoma, in the papers once in a while. Whatever. But he called the sisters by their first names too."

"I know," MacGregor's jaw clenched in anger. "Your guard that night stayed with the vehicle to ensure it wasn't tampered with. At the time, I didn't believe you would be unsafe as a group and surrounded by other people. Now we know his behavior has escalated. It changes everything and how we react.

"There is a real chance he will follow you to Dublin. It would be an easy thing to track your families for someone like him. Which reminds me, I have one of my top digital forensic specialists flying in. He'll be here in a few hours. I need everyone to give me their laptops. I took Ms. O'Connor's this morning. I need everyone at this meeting to turn theirs in today. Joel will call a colleague in the Tulsa area to look at yours, Mr. O'Connor's, and James and Jane's."

Bran said, "I'll get Raven and her sisters and mine as well, but what are you looking for?"

"He seems to know your schedules. He may have planted software on your computers months ago. If you got new computers but transferred all your data and apps, he'd be able to get in with no problem. My people will clear your laptops. If anything is found, your desktops will then be cleaned. Until they've gone through your electronics, you can still work but do not make any personal communications. Doctors and the like need to take you off all emailing lists.

"There's one more thing that I just was made aware of this morning. I warn you, it isn't good, and it's the reason the FBI is asking permission to bring a few agents to Dublin. Everyone is aware that they've been after Delton because of his dark web crimes long before James got the pictures of Jane. They'd just zeroed in on Delton's real identity when the Tulsa detectives' search popped up and they realized they were looking for the same man. Of course, the son of a bitch had already fled his home."

Here, MacGregor paused, his normally steely facade showing definite cracks. "Though his face is always covered, and his voice is always modulated, Delton, performing as *@SammySoGood*, has been promoting a 'Coming Soon' video featuring a long-legged blonde and a dark-haired Native American with an affinity for long walks in forests."

It just kept getting worse, Patrick thought.

Dad exploded out of his chair, slamming his fist on the table. "Over my dead fucking body."

They were all shaken. They knew Delton was unstable, but this was next-level frightening. And Patrick was to leave his family? Now?

MacGregor didn't even flinch. Patrick had a feeling the man was thinking of ways to kill Delton himself and hide the body.

James asked, "My God, is the blonde woman Jo?"

MacGregor's jaw flexed. "We believe so. There are more than one promotional videos referencing both women. He's trying to stimulate his audience. Ramp their interest to a frenzy. And, fuck, I'm sorry to have to tell you this, but he has a photo album, faces blurred, but definitely Rowan, Jo—Ms. O'Connor, and," MacGregor glanced briefly in Patrick's direction, "River. They were taken around the time Raven's were. Some from Ms. Stade's gym."

Oh God, he meant from the locker room. The violation. Patrick felt his stomach clench with nausea at the thought of the 'album.'

Pandemonium reigned. Disbelief. Anger. Dean and Dad asking for more manpower.

When the men took a breath, Bran, hands visibly shaking, asked, "Should I move Raven out of Dublin? Fuck! We're weeks away from our son's arrival, and there's possibly a psycho stalking us even here in Ireland!"

Dad walked to the room's only window, leaning on the sill that overlooked a small, manicured courtyard. Speaking toward the window, he said, "MacGregor, tell me what you suggest, and I'll do it." He sighed deeply, heavy shoulders rounding in despair. "My actions caused this. Tell me what I can do to fix it."

Patrick and Bran were out of their chairs and by their father's side immediately. "You weren't the one to embezzle. You couldn't have foreseen Delton's son becoming a psychopath. Don't blame this situation on yourself. You gave the man's father leniency when he should have gone to jail."

"Pat's right, Dad. No one can predict a lunatic's actions. I'm worried. I'm scared for my wife and child if I'm honest, but there is no blame to be laid on you. Only at the feet of that animal, Delton."

Dad took a deep, shuddering breath before turning back to the room. "Dean, what are you willing to do to keep the women safe?"

"Anything."

"MacGregor. Do you have people, or know people for hire that we can bring in to find this motherfucker?"

"Yes."

He meant mercenaries. Guns for hire. Patrick was all for it.

"Do you think Jane and I are still targets?" James asked.

"The Tulsa detectives, the FBI, and I all believe that you and Jane, and Bran and Raven are no longer targets. The women are firmly attached, and none of you will be falling for his tricks. Add to that, you are almost always together. Patrick and River are still unknown. He has an interest. We just don't know how much.

"The biggest threat is to Rowan and Jo. They are unattached women but still very much loved by the O'Faolains and the O'Connors. His MO suggests he enjoys chasing women with no permanent male protection." MacGregor dragged his hand down his face, his frustration evident. "And... and he really enjoys hurting your families."

All sound and movement ceased. Patrick voiced what he and MacGregor had previously discussed. "The women need to be called in and briefed. They cannot be left in the dark any longer."

No sooner had the words left his mouth than the conference room door was thrown open. Josephine, Raven, Rowan, and... fuck... River walked in. She looked at Patrick for the briefest of seconds before averting her eyes. She never looked back. He would know. He never stopped watching her.

Bran went straight to Raven. "Baby, why are you here? I would have told you everything."

"Bran," she whispered quietly, tears clumping her lashes, "we should have been invited to this meeting. We should have known all along that Delton is a predator, not just a stalker."

"You're right. I'm sorry." Bran tightened his arms about his wife, his distress over her safety clear.

Josephine advanced toward the screen. Thomas was out of his seat, watching her every step. "Were you ever going to tell me I was a target, Father?"

"I won't apologize for loving you, Josephine. Your life means more to me than your anger." Dean O'Connor was about as blunt as his own father, Patrick thought.

Turning to MacGregor, Jo asked, "Honey?"

Dean and James both leaned closer to their camera. Unsure why Josephine was calling her guard, honey. Obviously frustrated at being so far away.

MacGregor ignored the O'Connors. His sole focus was Jo. "I would have told you. You *are* safe with me."

"The website? The... the... the pictures of Rowan, River, and me?" Tears started to leak out of the corner of Jo's wide eyes.

Thomas, uncaring of their audience, whispered, "Do not cry, Josephine. No one, and I mean fucking no one, will touch you."

Josephine nodded. Satisfied. She sat in his abandoned chair, at ease with MacGregor at her back, and didn't utter another word.

Rowan was clearly distraught. His father stood at the side of the room like an avenging angel. Rowan looked at his father then. "Hugh?"

He walked to Rowan's side, obviously wanting to take the youngest Byrne into his arms; his muscles were bulging, and his jaw clenched. "You are safe, Row." That was the first time Pat had ever heard his father call Rowan by her nickname. "Trust me." They stared into one another's eyes for a moment longer before she nodded and sat at the table.

Thomas stood behind Jo. His father stood behind Rowan. Bran had his wife in his arms. Patrick was left staring across the conference table at River. She was standing alone. She should never stand alone. "River." He couldn't help but utter her name. Her eyes briefly flicked to his before settling on the window behind him.

"Patrick, I understand you are to travel to Boyle this afternoon," MacGregor announced.

"I am." As he never stopped looking at River, he saw her stiffen. She hadn't known. Her sisters instantly moved to comfort their sister. "I will postpone the trip if I'm needed here." Rowan briefly shot Patrick a look but didn't speak her thoughts out loud.

"We are good on men at the moment, and I already sent word to some... freelancers that their presence was needed here in Dublin. However, when your business in Boyle is finished, an extra set of eyes wouldn't go amiss."

Patrick looked at Thomas then. "We don't know if Delton will even come to Ireland, but there is a chance he's already here. The Tulsa airport is being heavily surveilled. Nothing has pinged the system. Yet." God, let that piece of shit not be in Ireland, Pat silently prayed,

Please, River, please look at me. She didn't.

"I won't rehash what type of psycho we're dealing with since you ladies have been eavesdropping since...?"

"The beginning," Jo helpfully supplied. "The girls and I

figured something big was happening when all our men were holed up together."

"Right then, lass," Thomas grumbled. "Is everyone in agreement with the plan? We bring in more muscle— more eyes. No one, including the men, goes anywhere alone." He looked at Rowan and Raven before adding. "No sneaking out. Even with a guard. From here on out, everyone needs to know where each other is. At *all* times. I need everyone's agreement before the meeting breaks."

All nine agreed. "And you, Thomas? Will you promise to never be alone?" Jo turned so she could look directly at her guard.

They stared at one another for several seconds before he caved. "I promise." Other people in the room, especially Jo's father and brother, were probably surprised at the interaction. Having flown to Ireland with them, Patrick was not.

A few more details were made before the O'Connors signed off. As everyone stood to leave. Patrick tried to catch River's eye. She was the first to leave. He would go to Bébhinn's because he had promised. He would stay the five weeks and trust MacGregor and his people to keep River safe... because he'd promised.

Once that five weeks was up, he would never leave her side again.

15

____

Thanks to Ms. O'Connor emailing her flight itinerary to Mrs. Raven O'Faolain née Byrne, Sam knew Josephine, her guard, and— my, my, my— Patrick O'Faolain left Oklahoma yesterday. Which meant that Patrick didn't fly to Ireland with his family.

Red flag, anyone?

Thank God Patrick got in a kiss and fondle before having a crisis of conscience. The entire tryst lasted no more than ninety seconds, including Patrick explaining he was turning over a new leaf and changing his way of life. Pathetic.

After the little lady with the hard tits and loose morals left the garden and the sulking Patrick behind, Sam was thrilled to see that he wasted no time meeting the middle Byrne sister on the dance floor.

River must have seen Sam's pictures and realized her New Year's Eve kiss was just a heaping helping of sloppy seconds.

If only he could have witnessed the embarrassing reveal. Ah, well. Sam couldn't be everywhere. For his last bit (maybe) of small mischief, he was more than pleased.

Sam's current situation had him waltzing through Tulsa's

airport. Today, his disguise was what he dubbed 'Travel Drag.' He wore a long, flowy, floor-length batwing maxi. It was a purple, pink, and yellow plaid number with dark pink velvet half boots— understated gaudy chic.

No wigs or facial hair. He wasn't about to travel all day itching in an uncomfortable plane seat, though he was flying first class.

In case the Tulsa police were monitoring the airports, waiting for his face to pop up on camera, he went with a bright purple head scarf, copious amounts of heavy foundation, outlandishly long eyelashes, rainbow glitter eyeshadow, and bright pink lipstick. He'd drawn the lips on, exaggerating the shape and size. The best part of fully covering all his features was the bejeweled, oversized, bright pink glasses.

Wearing his version of Travel Drag was a perfect mix of 'Look at me, I'm glorious' and 'Don't you dare stare, you Neanderthal.' Sam lengthened his stride, added an extra bit of hip swing, and made the airport terminal his personal runway.

DUBLIN WAS A BEAUTIFUL CITY. He looked forward to exploring, but there were a million things to do— like destroying Hugh O'Faolain's family —before he could fully relax. As soon as the plane landed, Sam went straight to his decently clean hostel where he'd prepaid three months' rent online.

Hostels weren't as easily tracked as traditional hotels, so it was an obvious choice. Once he checked in, he was pleased to find that the proprietress, or hostel 'mom,' was a geriatric, walker-scooting, foot-dragging, vision-impaired woman. He quickly ditched the drag and morphed into his new, long-term disguise. Meet Robert Smith, Robbie to his friends— if he'd had any.

Sam met some interesting clients through his dark web

@SammySoGood business. He made a few inquiries to his video renters about finding a source for false identification, and one gentleman came through big time. The man he recommended asked exorbitant prices— worth every dollar.

Robert Smith had an ID, an education, and several jobs with references. Most of the references were no longer valid, or they went to one of the fraud specialists' teams, who would give Robert a glowing review. That service was only available for three months. Sam wouldn't need the provision longer than that.

He planned on screwing with Patrick's ex-girlfriend, River, while planning the ultimate Twisted Love Story featuring Rowan Byrne, Josephine O'Connor, and Sammy, of course.

He seriously could not think about that for very long, or he'd be rash and try to get to the women before he'd had enough time to learn the lay of the land, so to speak. The lay of the land involved reconnaissance of the family guards and their routines.

Sam tried not to toot his own horn, but come on, who wouldn't feel honored that such privileged families had to hire professional guards because of little ole him. It would be fun to see how close he could get without them being any the wiser. His new persona was going to work perfectly.

Robert Smith was a thirty-five-year-old with a ridiculously nondescript pageboy haircut dyed a mousy brown. He kept his natural blue eyes, so he didn't have to mess with contacts, but he was sporting thick tortoiseshell glasses, no prescription, of course. His attire would consist primarily of skinny jeans, Vans, and oversized sweaters. A wannabe hipster without a clue, bless his heart.

Sam already researched businesses in close proximity to the Byrne sisters' design firm, Triskelion Territory Designs. There were a few coffee shops and bookstore combos in the vicinity that would be perfect for Robert. One of the jobs on his resume included several years as a barista. In reality, he once owned a fancy coffee machine.

So, a coffee shop should be an easy hire, and hopefully, the Byrne sisters and Josephine O'Connor would frequent the establishment. He planned on laying low, scouting the area to get an idea of where the Byrnes hung out— and letting their guards get used to seeing him in the neighborhood.

This was the stake out of a lifetime. Patience. Patience. Patience. Sam needed a bicycle. He needed to establish a routine for Robert. Grocery shopping, haircuts, restaurants. It would take a few months to blend in.

Challenge accepted.

16

Dear River,

I miss you. I don't want to hurt you further by bringing up New Year's Eve at Wolves, but I need you to know.

After we made love the first time, I've never been more afraid in my life. I had always believed relationships couldn't work. We made such a good team as friends, something that I believed could work. When we went past friendship, the very real possibility of me losing you because of that— scared me.

So, New Year's Eve, I was still running scared, but I decided I couldn't live without you either. I never noticed the woman in front of me until she touched my chest. I was only looking at you. You saw her touch me and grabbed a man's hand to dance. You thought I hurt you so you would hurt me back. Proof in my mind that relationships didn't work. They couldn't work. And what we had, our friendship, was ruined now too.

When she asked me to go outside, I did. I knew it was a mistake before I stepped out those doors. She was someone I'd hooked up with the year before at some club. She didn't matter to me, and I didn't matter to her.

And I... damn it... I would rather die than hurt you again, but I read that the wronged person often wants full disclosure — that it's better to know everything than imagine it worse.

I sat on the bench. She straddled my lap. I did place my hands on her, an automatic response. I didn't want to be there. I didn't want to be doing what I was doing. I thought of you. That I'd rather be inside where I could still watch you. Which, I think, makes what I was doing even more disrespectful to you. She kissed me. Her hands were on my chest and in my hair. I kissed her back for the <u>barest</u> moment before stopping the whole charade.

I told her I was committed to someone. That I wouldn't be doing casual hook-ups anymore. Though after my behavior, who would believe that? How will *you* ever believe that?

As I sat there in the garden alone, I realized something very important. I do love you. Deeply. I am completely committed. I will remain committed to you for the rest of my life.

I will never give up.

I don't deserve you. Yet. But someday, River, I hope to.

All my love,

Patrick

17

Patrick was gone.

Rowan and Raven explained their 'Rehabilitate Patrick' plan to River after the meeting with MacGregor.

He would live with Nan. Rowan admitted it was her suggestion. He could work on himself and help their grandma around the house.

River wouldn't have to work at avoiding him.

Raven said he would be welcome to come back to Dublin when she had her baby. Bran would be devastated without him, and Raven would be devastated without River. Could River please be in the same room with him for Baby O?

She'd assured her sister that, of course, she could.

Five weeks. He would be away for five weeks.

She didn't feel relief. Which was the whole flipping reason for the separation and proved she wasn't rational when it came to Patrick O'Faolain. She would have caved and seen him if he'd stayed. That wouldn't have been healthy for her.

But, oh God. He'd looked so lost in the meeting. It hurt her to stand across from him. He'd been so still, so unanimated. Not normal. He had been trying to make himself smaller in her presence.

There was nothing about this situation that pointed toward a happy ending.

And then— Rowan handed her a letter— from Patrick. She told River that it had been a part of their deal. Patrick would not try to see or talk to her if Rowan would give River his letters.

She read it five times. It was painful each time. He was right about one thing. She had imagined worse. It had still been debilitating to know what he'd done. She'd cried for over an hour as her sisters sat silently next to her.

Normally, River would have given them the letter to read. She didn't— couldn't. It was personal and raw, and Patrick's inner thoughts. He still deserved privacy.

Washing her face with a wet washcloth one of her sisters got her, she could tell her eyes were swollen and raw. Someone had also put a closed sign on the door, thank God. Sitting straighter, she tried to get her bearings. Her body felt all wobbly and jittery. Carefully, River folded the letter and placed it in her purse. She knew she would find a safe place to store it at home.

"Okay, then, Row. No more letters at work," she tried to chuckle, but it came out choked, another tear slipping down her cheek. She heard *Oh, Riv* and *River* spoken low while she once again blotted her eyes.

"Sorry, guys. I don't even have pregnancy hormones to blame." This time, she was able to smile.

"Riv, did I screw up? Should I not have committed to delivering the letters?"

Rowan was clearly distraught, her hands clasped tight on her desktop.

"No, you were right to do it. It hurt to read about that night... but now I know. I think imagining and wondering was much worse. It was just hard to read."

"Well, the worst is over. I hope," Raven smiled. "You know, River, I didn't want him to have any chance at contacting you again. He hurt you, and I was angry. It reminded me too much of me and Bran. I was wrong, and I'm glad Rowan did what she did. Whether you ever take him back or not, every person deserves the chance to apologize and change."

"Okay, Raven," Rowan said, "call your husband and go home. River, you and I are meeting Josh at the Murphy's pub to hammer out Raven's proposal of working more closely together with him on future projects."

"What the hell? It was *my* proposal! I'm going too." Raven jumped from her seat, wobbling side to side before she found her center of balance. Baby O was— BIG.

"We've been sitting here for hours because of me. You—" River stopped mid-sentence when she noticed Raven getting more upset.

"I've seen you rubbing your feet and ankles, lower back and neck for hours, Rave." Rowan added with raised brows and a 'Deny it' attitude.

"Oh my God, Raven. Jesus, I'm selfish! Damn it, I didn't think... shit!" River heard the click of the door unlocking, assumed it was a guard checking on the racket, and never turned from her sisters, who were now all three in a face-off.

"Don't you dare apologize to me, River Aster Byrne! How dare you act like you put me out for supporting you while you cried," she sniffled. "Now look what you've done," she wailed. "I'm crying, and you won't even let me go to the bar with you. You two leave me out of EVERYTHING!"

Oh, Jesus, shit was getting deep. "I didn't tell you to go home, you asshole! That was Rowan! Rowan is the bitch, not me!"

"I didn't tattle on Raven to make you feel bad, River, but

now I wish I had! I can't believe you guys, and Rave, you literally almost toppled over just standing up for the love of God!"

Raven's eyes bulged at Rowen's truth bomb. "I wish I would have let you go on that date our freshman year with that absolute douche canoe football meathead— WHO HAD VENERIAL WARTS!"

Silence of the Byrnes. And then she and her sisters burst out laughing, literally bent in half, tears of absolute delight and release. Jesus, they all needed to yell at each other. River grabbed her wet rag to dab at their faces, still laughing when she noticed their guests.

"Oh, sweet baby Jesus," River whispered. Rowan and Raven whipped around, finally seeing them too. Bran and Hugh.

Raven laughed awkwardly before addressing her husband. "Oh, Bran, what a nice surprise," she smiled and batted her still wet lashes. "Are you and Hugh taking us to Murphy's? *We're* meeting Josh Ryan, the blacksmith?" Raven glared at Rowan over her shoulder, daring her to contradict.

Hugh and Bran looked like they'd just witnessed an apocalypse.

Bran recovered first. "I thought we might just go home, babe."

Wrong, wrong, wrong answer, Bran.

"You thought wrong. I'm going out with my sisters. I'll meet you at home if you're too tired." Raven tried to put her hands on her hips, but well, there really wasn't room.

"My mistake, Rave. Dad and I would love to take you ladies out," Bran sent a desperate, 'bail me out' look to Hugh.

"That's why we're here." He could have left it at that, but when he looked at Rowan's red face, he added, "An evening out with absolute assholes and bitches sounds like a perfect night." His eyes twinkled, and an almost nonexistent smile graced his lips. Rowan smiled back.

Damn, River wished Patrick was there. Five weeks.

Cormac and Ciaran Murphy, brothers and the owners of Murphy's Pub, hailed Raven, River, and Rowan when they walked in. Josh waved to them from a table by the windows; appetizers already lined up. The Murphys were friends with Josh, so they knew they were meeting up. As the five of them joined Josh, Raven sat close to the loaded chips, moaning as she shoved one in her mouth.

"Bran, oh my God, your son has wanted loaded chips all day," she laughed as she licked a bit of sour cream from her lips.

Bran laughed, giving her a smacking kiss. "You know I would have brought my baby mamma fries. You only had to call," he laughed, dodging her teasing smack.

"Baby mama, my ass. This baby mama has a ring," she grinned, holding up her middle finger. "Whoops, that wasn't my ring finger."

"You'll pay for that later," Bran teased.

"I like how you make me pay," Raven purred.

"Jesus, you two. Please turn off the soft porn channel," Rowan admonished while River laughed.

Before River and Rowan could take their seats, Cormac and Ciaran Murphy swaggered up to the table. Two handsome, red-headed Irishmen. Cormac grabbed River by the waist, swinging her around before giving her a hug. "You are such a shit, Cormac," River admonished, blushing at the attention.

"Hey, I've missed ye, girl," he teased. Just as his brother brought a tray of drinks over and set them on their table.

"Ciaran," Rowan laughed. "It's good to see you, boyo!"

Ciaran wrapped an arm around Rowan's waist, squeezing her against his side. His smile was broad and perhaps a bit hopeful. "I brought you a Slane and River a Bushmills." Laughing, he winked at Raven, "And a Shirley Temple for Mama. Extra cherries, lass." Looking at Bran, he stuck his hand out, the one not holding tight to Rowan, toward Bran. "You must be Raven's other. Nice to meet you, and thank you for stopping in. I'm Ciaran, and this is me brother, Cormac."

"Bran," he answered as he shook both brother's hands. "You have a great place here."

"We know what the lassies drink, and Josh, of course," he grinned at his friend. "What'll you two have?" he asked, glancing at Bran and then Hugh.

Hugh looked ready to kill. Ciaran still had an arm wrapped around her sister's waist. River had already taken a seat by Josh, Raven next to him, still shoveling chips in her mouth at an impressive rate. The last spot available was in the partial bench next to Hugh. Rowan would have to sit by Hugh eventually, which River knew she really wanted to do, but she also really didn't like being treated like Hugh's young daughter. She and her sisters certainly didn't make it easy for themselves.

Bran, the ass kisser, said he'd take a Shirley Temple, to which Raven rewarded him with a kiss. God, those two.

Hugh didn't answer the Murphy brother. He stared at Rowan, jaw locked until she relented to his silent demand and extricated herself from Ciaran to sit next to Hugh.

"The water is fine," he gestured toward the glasses already on the table, "and a double shot of Teeling Small Batch, neat." He never smiled. He never said thank you. He just stared at the man who dared touch Rowan. Ciaran left without another word. Great.

River saw Rowan frown at Hugh, raising her brows like, *what the hell* was that? Hugh looked away, taking a sip of his water.

Save them from O'Faolains.

Thirty minutes later, Raven rolled out her proposal to Josh in more detail.

"So, basically, Raven, you're saying that you would have me consult directly with your clients? I would see the space, and *I* would decide what piece to create?"

"Exactly." Raven smiled as she leaned heavily against Bran. She was exhausted. Bran knew it, too, and was fighting against the need to force her to leave.

Josh grinned at River, wrapping his arm around her shoulders. She saw Hugh and Bran stiffen, assumably not liking a man who wasn't Patrick touching her. Raven side-eyed Bran. Rowan did something under the table to Hugh that she didn't even *want* to know about, but it did divert his gaze from Josh momentarily.

"What do you think, River?"

River lightly thumped his forehead with her knuckle. "I think you'd be a fool not to accept. It's your chance to create one-of-a-kind pieces for one-of-a-kind spaces. An artist's dream." She smiled softly at Josh before adding, "It's a challenge I think you need Josh." This type of new venture would help him not dwell on his mother's passing as much.

Josh leaned his forehead against the top of River's head. "She would have been so proud."

River touched his cheek until he looked at her. "She *is* proud, Josh and your father will be too when you go home tonight, drunk and bellowing at the top of your lungs about the deal you just struck," she teased, hoping to ease Josh's melancholy.

"You're right. They'll both be proud." Turning to Raven, he said, "I accept Mrs. O'Faolain, and I thank you for the chance."

Raven whooped in excitement, grinning ear to ear before

turning to Bran. She admitted, "I'm tired. Will you take me home?"

"Of course. Dad, will you get Row and River home?" Hugh dipped his head in affirmation. River and Josh stood, allowing Raven to scoot out, followed by Bran, who stuck his hand out to shake Josh's hand. "Welcome to the team, Josh."

Josh grasped his hand, smiling. "Thank you. I'm totally stoked. Seriously."

Once everyone was settled after Bran and Raven took their leave, Rowan lightly elbowed Hugh in the ribs. "We won't get served another drink if you keep scowling at Ciaran."

"Are you two dating?" Hugh gritted out.

"No, we aren't," Rowan snapped, looking at River for help.

"Then why did you allow a man you aren't dating to touch you like that? Do you let every male acquaintance hold you?"

"Hugh, enough," River admonished. Hugh stared at her sister for several more uncomfortable moments before turning his gaze to the bank of windows.

Trying to rally, Rowan told Josh how excited she was for him. "The wolf sculpture is stunning. Isn't it Hugh?" she nudged Mr. Belligerence.

"It was exactly what I wanted," Hugh relented. Having Josh in his sights, the eldest O'Faolain asked, "You do realize, Mr. Ryan, that River loves my youngest son, and he loves her?"

Shock and Awe. Shock and fucking awe. The absolute bull-shit nerve of this man! Before Josh could summon a reply, Rowan said, "I'm ready to go home, Hugh."

River saw Rowan blinking away furious tears and inter-jected. "Row. Do not be upset. I'm fine. Josh is fine."

Hugh's startled expression landed on River and then settled on Rowan. Hugh's hands fisted on the table. "Damn it," he sighed. "I'd like to apologize to you, Josh, and especially Rowan and River for my behavior." He paused, rubbing his temples.

"The meeting today has put me on edge. The threat that shadows our family is because of me." He looked at Rowan then. "Will you let me take you home?"

Rowan sighed, dabbing her eyes. "Yes, but Hugh, this isn't your fault." Her sister took Hugh's hand between her own.

Geez, what a day. She'd told Josh about the stalker, so at least he wasn't completely in the dark. "I'm tired too, Josh. Sorry for the short night, Hugh. Would you take us both home?"

Josh was gracious. He told Hugh he hated what they were going through, and he told River that he would call her tomorrow. "I plan on staying out long enough to have a few shots with Cormac and Ciaran to celebrate my new business venture," he grinned. Obviously excited.

"Okay. Don't drink too much, Josh," she grinned. "Raven's birthday-baby shower is in two weeks, and you promised to have Rave's birthday present finished."

"What did you decide on?" Rowan asked.

"Josh is making a wall hanging of the Muscogee Nation logo. And since it has a bit of green, the green shamrock in the center should look super cool."

"I can't wait to see it. Raven will love that it represents both our parents." Rowan sighed, her eyes a bit glassy. Their eyes always got a bit glassy when their parents were mentioned. "You know it crushed Mom when she found out her mother's family had either passed away or moved with no forwarding address."

"Family was everything to her, and to not have her own to meet her husband and us— it was a blow." She and Rowan were standing by then. They touched each other's hands in remembrance of their parents. An acknowledgment of their loss. Hugh stood behind Rowan, not touching, but there if her sister needed him.

"I was sorry to hear about your mother, Josh. She is watching, you know, and is so proud." River had told her sisters. They were devastated for the blacksmith.

Josh nodded his head, not trusting himself to speak, she imagined. Hugh shook his hand and thanked him again for the wolf sculpture.

Then... her heart aching that Patrick wasn't next to her, River third-wheeled her way home.

18
___

Patrick had been sitting in his rental for hours, or perhaps it was only minutes. Getting out seemed so final. Grabbing his luggage seemed so permanent. He wanted to turn the car around— go back to Dublin... to River.

A soft knock on his window got things moving. Startled, Patrick looked out the driver's side glass. Bébhinn Byrne, with her intricate white braids and soft smile, stood in the drive, waiting for Pat to get out.

Pathetic, Pat. It was only for five weeks. He would work on himself. He would continue to write River. In fact, he'd stopped and posted another letter to Rowan when he passed through Longford.

Attempting to embrace the inevitable, he got out of the car. "Hello, Bébhinn." He was sure his cheeks were red. Rowan wouldn't have held anything back from her beloved grandmother.

"Well, young man. You've made a right mess for yourself, haven't you?"

"I have, yes," he admitted.

"Do you love, River?"

165

"Yes." Patrick barely got the word to pass his constricted throat.

"Well, then... well. I suppose I can work with that."

And then the most unexpected of things happened. River's grandmother opened her arms, inviting Patrick in. He stepped forward tentatively. Nan was having none of that. She wrapped her arms around him, bringing his head to her shoulder. And that was that.

Deep, guttural moans— the pain he'd been holding in from the minute River saw the picture— came pouring out. Patrick didn't know how long he cried. Bébhinn held him through it all. Only when the tsunami of emotion washed out of him and away into the Irish countryside of Roscommon did the older woman pull back.

Patrick was embarrassed at the... whatever that was, but Bébhinn acted like she held wailing grown men every day. "Come, now, Patrick. Grab your bags. I've got beef stew warm on the hob. The rolls are all but done."

He followed the older woman inside. He'd barely paid attention to the outside, but the inside was beautiful. The sisters must get their eye for design from their grandmother. And God, the house smelled of everything delicious, his stomach rumbling in appreciation. The room was comfortable, with the white-washed walls and floors. There were cream-colored thick wool rugs, blankets, pillows, and paintings done in greens and yellows, oranges, blues, and reds. It looked like a garden. River had told him Bébhinn was an avid gardener.

River. Christ, he wanted to talk to her. Wanted to see her smile again. Smile at him. Taking a deep breath— refusing to cry again —he followed Bébhinn to the second floor where the bedrooms were, or the first floor as the Irish called it. Apparently, they entered their homes on the ground floor.

At the top of the stairs, she pointed to a closed door. "That is my room. Across the way is the guest bedroom. The girls' room is the last. It's the largest of the three since they all end up sleeping in the same room anyway," she smiled fondly. "You'll probably have noticed how they gravitate toward each other."

Patrick huffed out a laugh as she opened the door to their room. "Dad, Bran, and I are very close. We noticed right away, after meeting your granddaughters, that they were next level close." The room held one large bed placed in the middle of the longest wall, with a comfy-looking couch at the foot. Three desks held knickknacks, makeup, and perfume. Each desk and the surrounding space were decorated in different color schemes.

"Ha, next level. Well put. Okay, then, I've made some space in the walk-in for you to hang your clothes. This," she indicated a large middle drawer in the only clothes chest, "is Rivers. I moved most of her things to the side."

"Why are you having me stay in here and not the guest room? I don't want to invade their space, Bébhinn."

"Call me Nan, please. We are family. As to the room, it's homier in here." As she explained, Patrick moved toward River's desk. Picking up and setting down some of her things. "You'll be living here for a while, and I want you to feel comfortable. The girls have a nook in my attached garden room you also might enjoy of an evening. It's where their parent's ashes rest." That last part was said more quietly.

"Thank you. This room is great." He meant it. It made him feel not so alone. Closer to River.

"How did you know that desk is River's?"

Startled, Patrick put down the delicate gold bracelet he'd been holding. "Oh well, that was easy. River's favorite color is blue. Slate is her favorite shade, but any blue will do. Blue and white rug, pale blue lampshade, and" he picked up a squeeze tube, "she always carries this lotion in her purse for her hands.

River's favorite time of day is when the sun has set, and the stars make the dark sky appear deep navy."

He pointed toward another desk. "Raven loves everything green. She says it reminds her of your garden. And the last one, of course, is Rowan's. Yellows. She told me yellow is a happy color." Patrick looked at Bébhinn, shrugging.

"You know my granddaughters. I didn't even know why they preferred one color over another. You care about all my grandchildren, don't you?"

He sighed, admitting, "Yes."

"I hope you win River back, Patrick. I hope you *deserve* to win her back."

"It's all I want, Bé— Nan."

She patted his arm. "Why don't you unpack, and I'll get dinner situated."

Patrick made quick work of unpacking. He put his notepad, pens, and envelopes on River's desk, looking at himself in the attached makeup mirror. God, he looked defeated. And that needed to change. If he felt defeated, then he was sure to lose.

He wanted his letters to make him and River closer. He wanted his words to show her how much he loved her, how hard he was willing to work on himself for her. So, he had to change his attitude. It was as simple as that. He had five weeks to convince the Byrnes that he was worthy of being let back in.

Five weeks.

19

Dear River,

I miss you.

This is my first night at your grandma's. I'm sitting at your desk as I write this. Nan— she asked me to call her that— insisted I sleep in your room.

I like being close to your things.

God, how I miss you— and what a boring letter this must be to read.

Since it's still cold as hell outside, I'll be washing the windows inside. I admit the attached greenhouse, with all that glass, gave me pause.

I saw your parents' memorial cabinet. It's beautiful. I think I'll try sitting there some night. I hope you don't object.

I hope you find something every day that makes you smile. Not a smile to appease others, but a genuine smile. A smile that proves you're happy. I hope Raven and Baby O continue to do well. I am excited to be an uncle. Bran is nervous. I would be nervous too.

Have you noticed anything... something between Row and Dad?

I imagine everyone is about to move into the 'O Building,' as you call it. Would you consider asking Raven to send me a picture of the baby's room? And maybe a picture a week of her ginormous belly?

I better sign off. I'll be starting early. I'll write you tomorrow and let you know if my window washing skills are up to Nan's standards.

All my love,

Patrick

Three weeks had passed since he'd left Dublin. Missing River hadn't gotten easier, but living with what he'd done had. He and Nan spent hours together. She told him of summers with the girls, about her husband's goofy sense of humor, and of what a proud father Daniel had been.

Patrick told her about Bran and him sneaking out of the house when their nanny fell asleep so they could slip off to the old gardening shed. They worked hours for over a year using wood scraps to build a pirate ship. Bran said he would be captain, and Patrick, his first mate. They would sail anywhere they pleased. He still laughed at the memory. He told her about how his dad had helped with school craft projects— about his big hugs and stories at bedtime. And he told her about his mother's indifference.

It felt good to talk. He never thought it would. He thought sharing his vulnerabilities would make him weak, but Nan had a way of making him feel proud of opening up.

Living here had been a revelation.

Patrick had just got home from working for Mr. Dunn, Nan's neighbor. He was a gruff, no-nonsense man. His property was even nicer than the Byrne plot and meticulously maintained. Pat's body was on fire after the day's labor. It felt amazing. The gym or his daily runs didn't compare to actual outdoor physical activity. Patrick's time here had been a revelation in more ways than one. He felt more connected to, well, himself. More than he'd ever remembered being. Living with River's grandma was like signing up for a spiritual retreat-boot camp; hugs and tough love.

Before heading to his room to write to River, he and Nan shared a whiskey before the fire.

"Nan, can I ask you something? You don't have to answer."

"Of course, Pat." Sipping her Jameson, Nan waited while he got his thoughts in order.

"How is River?" He quickly added, "If it's against the rules to talk to me about her, I'll understand."

Nan stared at the fire's flames for a few minutes before answering. Taking a sip of her whiskey, she admitted, "She's afraid for her family because of that Delton man," Nan grimaced, shaking her head in disbelief. "She works all day, seven days a week, which I am very upset about. She is beside herself excited about becoming an aunt. Raven is restless. River thinks she'll go early. She tried to tattle on Rowan. She wanted me to ask her sister about the man she was secretly in love with. I refused. I know better. She asks about you every time we speak."

Patrick set his glass of whiskey down with a shaky hand. Christ. She asked after him. Was that good? Bad? Patrick pinched the bridge of his nose, willing his eyes not to leak. There were moments when he thought to himself, *you've got this, Pat,* and then moments like this. Damn.

"Patrick," Nan gently patted his hand. "She still loves you. I don't know if she'll take you back, though."

Patrick breathed through the strong emotion. He was finally able to say, "If she loves me even a tenth of how much I love her, I have hope."

"Hope is good." Nan twisted her glass of whiskey round and round on the side table. Lost in thought.

"Is something on your mind, Nan?"

Her startled look was proof enough that something was weighing heavily on her shoulders beside him and River.

Tapping the rim of her glass with a blunt fingernail, she obviously debated telling Patrick anything. "If I asked you not to tell the girls what I'm about to tell you, would you promise not to?"

Patrick thought about her request. Recent events with Delton made him cautious about keeping secrets. "I would keep whatever you tell me in confidence if your news had nothing to do with your health or safety."

Nan sighed, "Okay then. Okay." She took another sip of whiskey. Twirled her glass several more times and fidgeted with the collar of her robe before she spoke again. "Mr. Dunn, Devlen that is, he... he asked me to marry him, and I said yes," she finished her confession in a rush. Then, promptly burst into tears.

Oh no, Pat thought. Now what? Oh, shit. He needed to channel his dad and Gran's comforting skills. Covering her small hand in his much larger one, he asked, "Nan, isn't this good news? Happy news?" He grabbed the tissue box, plucking several out and handing them to her.

"I'm being ridiculous, Pat. I know I'm being ridiculous," she sniffled. "I'm worried about what the girls will think. I'm worried about leaving the house I raised my son in and then his daughters. I'm worried about what my Sean would think if he knew I... that I fell in love with another man."

Patrick tried to comfort Nan. A pat here, a there there... there. She was beside herself. Why did she have to open up to *him*, of all people? Then he realized what a dick he sounded like. Fine. She told him, which meant she trusted him, which meant he was going to help.

"Bébhinn Byrne! That's enough. Pull yourself together." That got her attention. "Okay, first, and most importantly, did Sean love you?"

She was so shocked at his question that she answered immediately. "Of course, he fecking loved me! Desperately! As I loved him." At least her crying had stopped.

"And do you think he's in heaven, thanking the Lord every day that you're lonely?"

She puffed up then. "Now listen here, young man, I will not have you speaking ill of my Sean."

"You didn't answer the question."

"Of course, he wouldn't want me lonely, you little shite. What exactly is your point?" She huffed.

"You just made it, Nan. Sean, the man you loved all those years and who loved you the same, would probably rather die all over again than see his precious Bébhinn unhappy for even a moment. Is that true or not?"

She deflated with that. "It's true. Oh. God, it's true enough." Dabbing again at her eyes, she admitted, "I am happy, Patrick, don't mistake me. I love my home, and my granddaughters are everything to me."

"But you'd like something or someone that's only yours?"

"Yes. Exactly. Someone I can fuss over and someone who wants to fuss over me."

"So then, let's put your other worries to rest. And you should be ashamed, honestly, for even thinking it. You know very well that the girls will be beside themselves with joy. Don't you tell me for one damn second that they won't be."

"Patrick O'Faolain, you will watch your language, but fine, I'll give you that. The girls are nothing but love."

"I believe your final worry is this house." At her nod, he

continued. "What do you think of me buying the house and putting it in your granddaughters' names?"

"I could never— I *would never* ask you to do such a thing."

Cupping her hands between his, Patrick replied honestly. "Nan, it would be my honor to do this. Our families are bound. Let us keep this home. Let future Byrne generations have the same happy memories as your son and his daughters got to have."

"Oh my. Oh my, oh my, Pat, you've settled me as nothing has for months. Thank you. I feel like a great weight has been lifted from my shoulders, and I can tell you, Devlen will be right pleased to see the last of my tears."

"When will you tell them?"

"Hmm, how about we head to Dublin first of next week. Devlen and I will drive ourselves, obviously. Raven has asked me to come already, but with you staying and my own silliness, I wasn't ready. River wants me to look over my new apartment and make a few final design decisions. I would love for Devlen to be a part of that."

Patrick's heart was beating out of his chest. "I'm not supposed to return until Raven goes into labor, Nan. And though I want to go so bad, I won't risk upsetting River."

"I'll speak with the girls, not about my news, mind, but I do want to be close in case Raven goes early. I had Daniel three weeks early, though the doctor could have gotten the date wrong. Anyway, I'll speak with them. You can stay at the hotel again, at least until the dust settles."

And that was, apparently, that.

Four weeks, not five. Thank God.

20

―――――

Dear River,

I miss you.

I hope I'm not writing too often. I've tried to continue some of the letters, but I can't stop myself from posting them. I worry you might think I'm not thinking of you. I always am. Raven sent me some pictures. Thank you for asking her.

I talked to your mom and dad last night. I sat in the nook you and your sisters created. I looked at all the pictures and mementos in the cabinet. I... well, I decided to talk to your folks. You always say they're watching over you. I wanted them to know that I love you. That I want to marry you. That I hurt you. That I don't deserve you. That I hope one day, you will love me again.

I fixed the toilet today. I had to watch a YouTube video, but I must say, I think I nailed it. I've also been in touch with the distillery that's for sale outside of Dublin. I've been going over the seller's portfolio— financial statements, legal documents, etc. The property is beautiful. The distillery itself was built in the mid-1800s, but some of the outlying buildings are much older.

Once I'm back, I'll be talking to Dad and Bran. With the whole Delton situation, I decided not to add to their plates, but I think this would be an excellent venture. I would love to hear your ideas for naming the distillery. O'Faolain Distillery? Dark Wolf Distillery? Triple R Distillery? I hope someday you will look at the property. With me.

I'm about to fall asleep sitting up. I'll continue tomorrow night.

Think of me.

Nan made me pancakes this morning. They were better than mine, which I'd be totally offended by, except she gave me her recipe. I hope you and I can make them together one day.

I worked for your grandma's neighbor, Mr. Dunn, today. His property wraps this one and is really nice. I chopped wood, sharpened mower blades, and patched a roof on one of his sheds.

Do you think I should give up entrepreneurial endeavors and just become a handyman? Patrick Patches Shit?

Bran called earlier. I was washing dinner dishes— it was my turn. I don't mind. Your Nan always has a whiskey waiting by the fire for me.

I miss you.

I dream of you every night.

Bran was good. He's excited and scared equally. The baby shower is in a few days, right? I hope Raven and Bran aren't too busy to send me a pic. I have a present, but I'll bring it with me when Baby O decides to get here.

I haven't asked yet, but how was your day? I hate to sound like my dad, but are you eating enough? The last time I went to town to post your letters, I bought a bottle of Jameson Black Barrel in your honor. It was delicious.

Tell Raven and Rowan I said hello.

No need to tell Dad. He calls me every day. He mainly just sits on the phone saying nothing, but... it's his way of letting me know he's thinking of me. So, I don't mind if he doesn't talk.

Did you get the daisy dishes from Stella? Will you use them?

I told your grandma some personal stuff. It wasn't as horrible as I thought it'd be. I mean, I didn't die.

Nan is excited to see the progress in her apartment. I wondered how much is done or if you guys have been too swamped to work on the grandma properties. I would help if you needed me to. You know I can fix toilets.

All my love,
Patrick

Dear River,

I miss you.

Nan wants to come early. A week early. Next week. She desperately wants to be in town before Raven goes into labor. Mr. Dunn is going to drive her as the weather is unpredictable.

I will stay back if you would rather me not come early. If you don't care, I promise to stay away. I'll stay at the hotel until the baby comes.

Would you let Nan know, please? I don't want to come if you aren't ready.

I want you to know that I haven't considered my time here as a punishment for hurting you. I think Rowan meant it to help me, to heal me, and it has. I have cherished every moment. It doesn't mean I don't miss you desperately.

Please, please let Nan know. I won't be angry if it's no.

All my love,
Patrick

21

———————

Sam paced his small room at the hostel. Furious! He was fucking furious. Three weeks had passed since Sam landed in Dublin— and nothing. Sam's faultless patience usually worked. He'd been doing everything right. He blended. He shopped locally. He went to the same places to eat. People began to recognize him.

He got a job at one of the coffee shop bookstores less than a block away from Triskelion, Literary Latte. And River and Rowan Byrne had even come in a few times. Never alone, though. They each had their own bodyguard. Just this past week, he noticed that their guards went into the coffee shop. They stood right next to them while extra guards stood on the sidewalk. There was no chance of initiating a conversation.

He hadn't seen anyone else. At all. Not at the restaurants, or pubs, or on the sidewalk. Nowhere. They were definitely on lockdown.

The O'Faolains were not going to beat him at his own game. They were not going to kill his father and not suffer the conse-quences. Oh no, they had to pay. Some way. Only— this was the first time he truly felt like his dwindling options were fast drop-ping to nonexistent.

Adding insult to injury, his computer remote access apps were discovered. No more itineraries or doctor's appointments.

He basically had no access to ANYTHING!

And then there were his @SammySoGood fans. They'd started leaving comments that he wasn't following through with his special video. Where was it? Why was his site still up if he never had new content? No follow-through. Taunts, all of them. He'd even lost a few subscribers. Not good. Not good at all.

His pacing continued. He had to think. THINK! He had to come to terms with the fact that his original plan was no longer viable.

He could figure this out.

He would.

He wouldn't let his father down.

22

Tonight was Raven's baby shower and birthday party. It should have been a joint birthday party for Bran, too, as his birthday was February 8, but he wanted the night to be all about his wife. He said we could have lunch or dinner on his day. River was beyond excited.

Her and Rowan's assistants had just left Triskelion, and she and Rowan were about to walk over to the O'Faolain Building. The cake and catered food would be arriving within the hour. They had enough of the four-floor complex decorated to handle throwing the party on the ground floor. They hadn't let Raven see the party décor. She was so mad because she wanted to help. Too bad.

"Josh should be here before we head over. I can't wait to see how the Muscogee Nation piece turned out. The asshole hid it from me. He said it was a surprise."

"I can't wait to see what he did either. He's a truly talented metal smith. Hey, before I forget. Dom is moving into the loft this weekend. I thought maybe we could put together a house-warming basket of goodies to leave upstairs as a surprise."

"I should have thought of that! Let's make a quick list of

what we want to add, and you and I can get everything picked up first thing in the morning. He isn't moving in until Saturday afternoon, so we'll have a few hours. Glad you're a thinker, Row," she chuckled while she gathered up Patrick's newest batch of letters.

"Patrick writes a lot, huh?"

"He does," River answered as she smoothed the crinkles from some of the envelopes. She looked at Rowan then. "Nan wants to come to Dublin on Monday."

"Oh, really? That's perfect! I can't wait for her to see the progress to her apartment. Too bad she didn't come early enough for the shower."

"She told Raven weeks ago that she, Matilda, and Diana Gaines wanted to have a simpler shower at The Fitzwilliam. In Diana Gaines' speak, simple meant black tie. We'll need to take Nan shopping for a few special event dresses."

"Definitely. Diana is lovely, but even when we decorated her penthouse, I kind of felt like I had spinach in my teeth, and a brown stain on the seat of my pants."

River snorted at the visual. "Pat said Mr. Dunn would be driving Nan to town."

"Really?"

"Something about unpredictable weather conditions. Umm, we're not looking at an Oklahoma winter here." River raised her eyes in obvious disbelief, mirroring Rowan.

"So... driving the same roads for half a century hasn't prepared her?"

"Mmmhmm. I guess."

"What of Patrick? Is he coming home early?"

Having gone back to fidgeting with the letters' edges, she had to glance up. She would prefer not to say, but she would never lie to her sister. Sighing, she admitted, "He asked me to let Nan know if he could come too."

When River didn't continue, Rowan prompted, "And?"

"And— I told Nan this morning that he could come." It was a huge, ginormous, and momentous decision.

River knew it.

Nan would know it.

Patrick would know it.

"He said he would stay at the hotel, at least until Baby O's arrival."

"I've given you space. I see you read Patrick's letters like they're manna from Heaven. I see you reread them, and reread them, and read them again. You smile. Did you know that, Riv? Your smile is the brightest when you have one of his letters in your hands."

"Do you think I'm making a mistake?" River's resolve waffled a hundred times a day at least.

"Nan believes he's been doing the work. He talks to her about personal things. She would never break his confidence, but she believes he's changed."

River stared at Rowan for a moment. "I asked if *you* thought I was making a mistake."

"No. I don't. That said, I hope you don't go too fast. Get to know the man he is now or is trying to be. Make sure he is what you want. But," and here Rowan rubbed her eyes, sadness flashing across her features— there and gone, "if you decide to keep him. It will be forever. No takesies-backsies." she grinned then. The sisters' childhood pact made them both smile. "I think you and Patrick have what Bran and Raven have. I do. It's been rocky, and he hurt you badly, River, but I think he will spend the rest of his life proving his love to you and you to him."

It was like pure peace washed over her, head to toe. She had promised Patrick that night that she would love him forever. She meant it, then. She felt no different now. Though River felt giddy inside, she didn't celebrate. Rowan's attempt to hide her own sadness tempered River's joy.

"And what of you, Row? Who do you think will bring you a lifetime of love and happiness?" River knew who that person was, and damn it, she wanted her sister to live her own love story.

It had to be Hugh, though her sister had never said a flipping word. It was a shock to consider, River admitted, but love was love, and her sister wasn't some flighty woman who would decide on a different man next week. No, River knew that once her sister had chosen the O'Faolain patriarch, it was over for her. It was him or nothing.

She didn't answer.

"You want to know something?"

"What?"

"Hugh is the biggest of fools if he doesn't love you back."

Rowan's eyes widened, her face blazing red. She opened and closed her mouth a few times. Speechless. Yeah, that's right, babe. Your big sisters know your secret.

"That's not... no, you... he won't... I absolutely do *not*..." Finally, her painful denials died on her tongue when Josh walked in. Her relief was embarrassingly apparent.

"This isn't over, Rowan," she whispered, "only postponed."

"Josh, oh my God, tell me you brought Raven's prezzie!" River jumped up, crowding his space. Poking the package wrapped in brown shipping paper.

"Back off, damn it," he laughed, sweeping the gift over his head where River didn't have a chance of reaching.

"Give it over, Josh!" In the middle of jumping up to reach the gift, the door swept open, and Raven and Bran breezed in.

Raven laughed, asking, "What in the hell are you doing, River?"

"None of your business. It's a surprise. For the party," she smirked.

"I think you should let her open it now," Josh interjected.

"No one cares what you think, asshole. Give it to me." River jumped again, missing by about two feet.

"Is that my birthday present? I want," Raven made grabby hands.

"Before the party? And... I haven't even seen it yet!"

"Give me. It'll be more fun to open a present with just us." Raven was grinning, her eyes bright. How could River say no to a happy pregnant woman?

"You have to open mine too, then," Rowan protested. "Otherwise, it's favoritism of presents. Plus, I'd planned on giving it to you in private anyway," she grinned mischievously. Rowan reached into her tote and pulled out a bright red, festively wrapped box.

Hugh walked in just as she laid her present on the desk with a flourish. River and Raven's eyes widened when they saw Rowan snatch the present back, trying to shove it back into her bag. It ended up landing on the floor, where she finally kicked it under her desk.

What in the *hell* was that all about?

Bran, ignoring the sisters' antics as usual, told his dad he was just in time to watch Raven get her birthday presents from the girls early.

River heard Rowan whisper a *fuck me* under her breath.

Better and better. "Mine first," River sniped. Elbowing Rowan in the side. "Okay, Josh, give it over now."

"Gladly," he laughed, enjoying himself. He handed it to River, who immediately handed it to Raven.

"Happy early Birthday! Let's go sit on the sofa." Once they were situated, Raven tore off the wrapping paper, such that it was, and then promptly burst into tears. If Raven weren't so predictable, River might believe she wielded prophetic power.

She and Rowan crowded Raven to get a better look at the piece. Josh had killed it. It was a true representation of their Native American logo. The centralized Irish shamrock in green was stunning. Perfectly integrated.

"Look," Raven touched the three green leaves.

Josh had burned the Native American symbols for a raven, river, and rowan tree in the leaves. It was... beautiful.

"Josh."

"Wow, Josh."

"Oh, Josh. It's better than I ever imagined it."

"That will be perfect to hang in our foyer, Rave, where it's the first thing anyone sees." Bran patted his wife's shoulder, surreptitiously handing her sister a tissue. He probably kept every pocket stuffed with them.

"Oh my, River. Thank you so much. It's perfect. And thank you, Josh. You are beyond talented."

Josh blushed at the praise. While Rowan was taking a closer look at the sculpture, River went back to her desk and tugged out the present her sister had punted beneath it. Walking over, she started to hand the present to Raven. Rowan saw and lunged for it.

What can only be described as a birthday present tug-of-war ensued.

"Give it back. I told Raven I wanted to give it to her another time."

"What's the big deal? It's just us!"

One more pull, tug, and jiggle— and then... buzzing?

"What is...?" Josh's voice trailed off.

"What the fuck?" Bran asked.

"Oh my God. Is that...?" Rowan's scarlet face finally brought a dawning realization to River.

River let go of the box. Rowan fell back on the sofa by Raven. Her arms firmly cupping a very vibratey box. Her face burning, Rowan shoved the box toward Raven. "Christ, please open it so you can shut the damn thing off." Her face was a hundred and eighty degrees of fiery red.

River glanced at the men. Josh's shoulders were shaking in silent laughter. Bran looked— uncomfortably —interested. Hugh was staring at Rowan.

Raven got the lid off, and several highly inventive sex toys joined the party, including lubricants and oils. She stared in the box with a look of horrified wonder. "This is... this is... wow, Row. Thank y—"

Before the thank you left his wife's mouth, Bran was leaning over her shoulder, digging in the box. Truly, a kid in a candy store moment. Rowan looked resigned. "Holy shit Rave, this one has a remote control!"

Raven found the off button on the rogue vibrator, shooing Bran's hands away before quickly placing the lid over the stash.

Rowan was dying, but come on, this was funny shit. "Damn, Row, been shopping the naughty stores without me?"

She gave River a 'go to hell' look. "Remember the sex toy party Saoirse invited us to before we went to Oklahoma— that you canceled on? Well, I went."

"You went to a sex party?" Hugh choked on the words. Like River said earlier, it just kept getting better and better.

"Not a party to have sex. Jesus, Hugh. A party to buy sex *toys*," Rowan explained. Hugh actually blushed. Priceless.

River hated Patrick wasn't there to witness the pandemonium.

Raven stood, which took a minute, and thanked both sisters for the amazing presents. Bran especially thanked Rowan with a great deal of enthusiasm.

"Oh," River began, "did I tell you that Saoirse is bringing

her sister tonight? They swung by my house earlier. Her name is Sadhbh. She's so great. You guys are going to love her."

Bran asked, "What is her name again?"

"Sadhbh— SAH-eev. Speaking of the party, we better head over. I see one of the catering vans pulling up now."

That got everyone moving. Raven took a moment to grab her and Rowan's hands, squeezing them tight. "Thank you. For the presents, for the party, and mostly for loving me."

"Always." River and Rowan answered together. Rowan added, "Just please don't tell me how the toys worked out for you and Bran."

Laughing, the sisters walked out of Triskelion. Hand in hand in hand.

THE PARTY WAS PERFECT. All soft greens and creams. Delicate shortbread cookies, mini cakes, and tarts. Crab and artichoke dip, veg for days, mini beef Wellingtons, whiskey, and sparkling water. The guests praised the renovation and were wowed by the wolf sculpture, earning Josh even more recognition.

Sadhbh Kennedy was everything Raven had promised. Hell on heels like her sister. A history professor instead of a real estate agent, but equally passionate and ferocious. River knew the moment Josh fell in love with the petite redhead. He looked at River once eyes rounded, and mouthed, *holy shit*. Well, he wasn't wrong. When you found your person, it was life-altering.

Rowan walked over to join River. "It turned out perfect. Raven is so happy."

"It did, and she is," River agreed, smiling. She leaned against a door frame at the edge of the room. Rowan sighed, then fidgeted, then sighed again. "What is it? Will you tell me?"

River held her hand. They were always comforted by one another's touch.

Rowan stared at Bran, slow dancing with Raven. "They'll be completely moved in here in a few more days. They should have already been moved in. Hugh is, but Raven doesn't want to leave us, and we've never discussed where we'll live."

"I know. Damn. If that Delton wasn't an issue, we would have more options. But you're right. We're holding everyone back. Patrick will eventually move into his flat. I won't rush into anything with him. I don't know, Row. What do you think?"

"I don't want to live in the guest rooms here." Her face flamed. "I feel like I would be taking advantage of the O'Faolain's generosity. But River, you realize it's only a matter of time before Patrick convinces you to marry him. Then you'll live here too."

River leaned her head on her sister's shoulder. "We stay together. At least for now, Row, we stay together."

"Well, then," Rowan hesitated, "I do have a possibility."

"Really? What?"

"You remember my client last fall, Mrs. Adamson?"

"Oh yes. I loved what you did in her sitting room. That wallpaper was to die for."

"Yes, well, she emailed me Monday and asked if I might know anyone to house-sit for her. She's visiting her daughter and family in Japan for at least four months. Her grandson is expecting his first child, and her daughter asked if she would be up for an extended stay."

"So, it would be rent free?"

"Yes." Rowan grabbed her hands, squeezing in excitement. "We wouldn't be a financial burden, and Mrs. Adamson's home is gorgeous. Plus, while we still need guards, there are plenty of bedrooms to comfortably house them."

"Holy cow! Why didn't you say something before now?"

"I... I... shit, Riv, I didn't want you to move in with me out of sympathy. I want you and Patrick to work things out as much as you do. And believe it not, I *can* live on my own."

"Let Mrs. Adamson know we accept and ask when we can move in," she grinned. This would truly be the best thing for both of them— and Patrick. He could move into his apartment without worrying about keeping his space from her. River saw Rowan scrolling through her contacts. "What? Are you calling her now?"

"Yep."

Mrs. Adamson was ecstatic. She adored Rowan and was so relieved. She was actually flying out next Tuesday. She asked if Rowan and her sister could bring their things over this weekend. She would go over security codes, Wi-Fi, etc.

"And just like that— we are house sitters!" River squealed. Raven walked up, asking what all the excitement was about.

Rowan explained. "Oh, Rave, you'll never guess. You remember Mrs. Adamson?"

"I remember. She was so sweet. Very good taste."

"Well, she offered River and me to live in her home for several months, rent free! We'll be house-sitting. Her home is stunning. River will die over her chef's kitchen that's never been used, I'm sure. There are rooms for the guards too."

"But... but... we've always been together. I thought... I guess I assumed we'd be moving here together."

"Oh, Raven. We'll see you and Baby O every day. Every day, I promise. We both promise. I do have hope for Patrick and I. Someday."

"The rooms on this floor are all ready for you, though," Raven insisted.

"Patrick and I may be together again someday. But not today. I want him to be able to move in with his family. And he won't as long as he thinks it would bother me. I still need space without pressure."

"You guys are *my* family, damn it. Patrick can go hang!"

"Please, try to understand," Rowan pleaded. "I never wanted to hurt you. Ever. But... River's situation is... it's a situation. And I refuse to be a mooch. Just because you married Bran doesn't mean the O'Faolains are responsible for your siblings."

Raven was visibly distressed. And, oh Jesus, Bran and Hugh were coming in hot.

Bran pulled Raven to his side. "What's all this, babe? Why are you upset? You know I hate when you fucking cry," he admitted while rubbing a soothing hand down Raven's silky hair.

"Please, Rave. Don't make it a big deal," River begged.

"Don't make what a big deal?" Bran asked.

"Rowan?" asked Hugh of Few Words.

"My sisters are moving out. Without me. Because they don't want to be a burden. But they aren't burdens. They wouldn't even know how to *be* burdens." Turning to her sisters, she implored, "Would you feel better if they charged you rent?"

Hugh did not speak. His eyes drilled into Rowan's. She met his look. Defiant. Good girl, Rowan. If that stubborn man wouldn't claim one of the most amazing women ever to be born, then he could suffer the consequences.

Separation.

"Raven. Look at me." River waited until they were eye to eye. "A different address doesn't matter. This is you being nervous about having Baby O. You know this. Rowan and I will see you every single day. Let us do this. Please." River touched her fingers to Raven's cheek. Then Raven touched Rowan's cheek, and Rowan touched River's.

"Okay."

"Okay."

"Okay."

23

———

Dear River,

I miss you.

I don't know if you'll get this letter before I'm back in town. Thank you, thank you, thank you for letting me come back to Dublin. We don't leave for three more days, but I already packed. I tried to fix your clothes back the way they were.

I touched your panties. I'd like to say I'm sorry, but I'm working on honesty.

Have you moved into the new building?

I dream of you moved in to~~my~~ our apartment. Your daisy dishes are sitting on the open shelving in the kitchen. Your citrus shampoo in the shower. Your naked body lying against the sheets you picked out. In our bed.

I think a lot of inappropriate things where you're concerned.

I hope the baby shower was a success last night. I'm getting as antsy as Nan for Baby O to get here, I swear. I also want to see Bran cry and video it.

Dad called me this morning. He seemed, I don't know,

upset, which is hard to tell with him. Lost maybe? If something's happened that might explain (him), would you let Nan know so she could tell me?

Nan wanted to go to the fabric store in town and buy material to make washable 'gag' diapers. Tell Raven she owes me a giant thank you for talking your grandma out of that (literal) shit idea.

Do you ever look at the picture I gave you for Christmas? I have the one you gave me next to your bed. You have the best smile.

I dreamed that I asked you to marry me. You said yes.

I dreamed that you were round with my child. It was my best dream ever.

Nan and I spent the day cleaning the deep freeze and fridge. Apparently, that's a necessity before leaving town.

Nan's also been baking. She had to make everyone's favorite. My guess is she'll be baking until we leave Monday morning. She even called Jo to ask what Mr. Bunny's (her words, not mine) favorite treat was.

Nan said that Jo's been feeling under the weather and didn't want to go near Raven until she was sure she wouldn't pass any bug along. Nan said Jo seemed down. She invited her to the second baby shower next week with her, Gran, and Diana (aka The Beast).

Tomorrow, I'm helping Mr. Dunn do a full detail wash and wax on his truck. The bed has a cover, but it still needs a thorough washing.

Nan promised to bring me and Mr. Dunn lunch. I see where you learned how to cook so well. (If you married me, we'd never starve at least). Devlen, that's Mr. Dunn's name, has an amazing patio and outdoor cooking space. Much more modern than I would have expected from the man. He's thawing toward me— finally— but he could give Dad a run for his money on stern looks.

Please keep following MacGregor's rules on safety. Please allow me to help in watching over you when I get back.

Will you talk to me again? Once I'm home, I mean. I won't rush you. I swear it, River. If I could only hear you say... say something like, Hello, Patrick, it would be enough. For now.

All my love,
Patrick

24

Bran called Patrick first thing in the morning while he was helping Mr. Dunn pack all of Nan's things— a lot of things. Dunn remained stoic even though his truck was a potholder away from exploding.

Pat answered, "Hey, Bran."

"You headed this way yet?"

He laughed, "Not quite. Nan just ran back inside. She forgot the hospital nightgown she bought for Raven. And let me be the first person to wish you condolences." He heard Dunn snort in amusement from the other side of the truck.

"Oh God, and you know Raven will wear it," he chuckled. "I'm glad you're coming back early."

"Yeah, me too." When Bran didn't speak again, he thought they'd gotten disconnected. "You still there?"

"Yeah, sorry. Come straight to the O Building. We finished moving all your things in yesterday."

"I hope not everything. I'll be living at the hotel for a while, remember?" Another long silence. "Jesus, Bran. This is like talking to Dad on the phone. What the fu—heck is going on?"

Patrick did a quick glance around for Nan. The f-word got Bran's dessert taken away.

Sighing, Bran admitted that he would have preferred to speak with him once he was back in town, but he also didn't want Patrick to be blindsided. "River and Rowan moved into their own place. I believe, and so does Rave, that the situation is temporary. You will get her back, Pat."

Patrick wasn't sure how to feel. He wouldn't have been living with River either way, but it felt like he was keeping her from living with the family— where it was safer. And he didn't like that at all.

"Why didn't you stop her, Bran? She and Rowan are safer with the rest of you, damn it! I would have kept my distance. I promised I would until she was ready." If she ever was.

"Making a Byrne do a damn thing they don't want to is impossible, and you know it. Since you've been away, the new protocol is always one guard per person. At *all* times. The extra hired men MacGregor brought in continually walk the perimeter of their house, Triskelion, and the O building. They are safe, Pat. I swear it."

"Yeah, okay, I understand. Thanks for letting me know. I'll come straight to our building. Damn, I just wish they could catch that sick bastard so we could all start living normally again." Nan was locking the front door— finally. "Hey, is this why Dad was extra weird when he called me this weekend?"

"Yeah. It's weird, right? Please tell me you think it's... weird. Not like weird, weird, but hard to wrap your brain around, weird."

"I want Dad to be happy. We both do. I guess it's just so— unexpected," he laughed. "Listen, we'll gossip about Dad more when I get in town. Nan is walking up."

"Okay, Pat. See you in a few hours. Drive safe."

As Pat slipped his phone into his pocket, he heard Nan ask

Devlen if he would mind waiting in the truck for a moment. Then she headed back to Pat's ride. He momentarily froze, then burned. Surely, she wasn't going to ask him to stay behind after all. River hadn't changed her mind.

Nan smiled. "Stop looking like a lad about to get a spanking." At her laughter, Pat relaxed. "So, now. Here we are, then. I wanted a moment before it was too late, and we're surrounded by family to tell you how much I'll miss you around here." She started to tear up, instantly pulling a handkerchief from her pocket. Dabbing her eyes, she continued. "Now look, ignore the waterworks, Pat. I'm just that proud of you, boy."

Patrick needed to carry his own handkerchief. Damn. "Nan, from the bottom of my heart, thank you for taking me in. If I could choose a mother who loved me and that I loved, it would be you."

She gave him a fierce hug. "Remember Pat. This homecoming isn't going to be easy for you or River. Have patience. Work on communicating your feelings. All of them. When you're nervous or scared or angry or upset. It's the only way to have something— real. Do you understand?"

"I do."

"Then let's go see our family. Oh, I meant to ask, umm." Clearly flustered, Pat didn't rush her to finish, letting her get it out at her own pace. "Did you mention anything about Devlen's proposal?"

Nan's blushing was priceless. He would tease her someday. "Mr. Dunn proposed, and you said yes. That isn't a proposal. It's an engagement. I told them nothing, however. I would never speak of your personal business without permission, Nan. Can I give you a bit of advice?" At her nod, he finished. "You are happy with Mr. Dunn. Very happy. Which means your girls will be very happy. My advice is this. When you tell the family of your engagement, don't act unsure or embarrassed. I think it would devastate Dunn. He might think you're ashamed of him, and I know you aren't. Tell them the news with all the joy and excitement you feel."

Nan looked truly shocked that her nervousness at telling her family might make her fiancé feel like she was embarrassed by him. "Oh my. My goodness. I never thought... I never considered that. Shite. I've been... not who I *am*." Looking at Pat with a big grin, she told him, "You're dead on, boy. I've been a ninny. I am proud of Dev." With a small laugh, and twinkling eyes, she said "Let's get going."

Patrick smiled as he got behind the wheel. He was headed home.

To River.

~

ROWAN WAS SITTING at the stunning copper kitchen island. The plush cream-colored high-backed barstools even had copper bases. No question, Mrs. Adamson liked nice things. The guest rooms were comfortable and chic. The bathrooms were gorgeous, with giant, open showers. Long benches were installed if they wanted to steam. Walk-in closets, soft beds with feather toppers, fluffy duvets, and silk sheets.

The kitchen was better than advertised. A chef's dream, let alone a home cook like herself. All the appliances were Wolf, the red knobs were a beautiful complement to the copper. So high-end, River wasn't sure how she felt about making scrambled eggs on all this amazingness.

She and her sisters had designed the O building's kitchens using the Viking Tuscany line. River had picked the slate blue for Patrick's. All the countertops were pure white granite, white walls with cream vertical tile from countertop to ceiling. She was very proud of the finished space.

She *may* have pictured Pat and her cooking together. Beginning a life. Creating a home. A family. River shut those thoughts down. She couldn't afford to... remember. She wouldn't wallow in regret. What happened would happen.

The colors he'd used in his Muskogee home, the one time she'd seen it, were similar to the palette she'd used in his new Dublin flat. They happened to be one of her favorite color schemes to work with. After seeing his personal space— New Year's Eve night —she believed she'd nailed his aesthetic. Each room was light but cozy. A home.

River attempted to speak about something— anything —that didn't remind her of Patrick. "Did you notice Josh literally making a fool of himself over Saoirse's sister? Oh my God, I was dying. I texted him first thing this morning and asked him if he ever stopped stammering long enough to ask Sadhbh out."

"Oh God, I noticed. What did he say?"

River pulled up her messages and showed Rowan the screenshot of Josh and Sadhbh's text chat. River laughed as Rowan grinned and then laughed. "Obviously, love at first sight," she giggled.

Rowan asked the most important question. "Does Josh know he has to pass the big sister interrogation? Saoirse can be— intense."

"I wasn't about to ruin the surprise," she grinned. "Before I forget, remember Dom is rolling out some new app to keep us and our assistants connected. It is supposed to 'streamline' our whole business. That man is a wonder."

"Bran's best idea yet," Rowan agreed.

"Oh look, Josh is texting again." She and Rowan leaned over her screen, watching the waving dots until his words popped up. "Oh, fun! What should I say?" Josh asked if she and Rowan would meet him and Sadhbh at Murphy's.

"I'm totally down. Thursday afternoon is Nan and Matilda's baby shower, so we're free Friday night. Oh, did Raven tell you her doctor advised against any more morning workouts with us? She's supposed to be doing light yoga to help with her hip flexibility. Yikes.

"Consider me a birth control believer after seeing the size of Baby O and the size of our sister. No thanks," she smirked. "My next gyno appointment is in March. I'm getting on birth control then." Rowan laughed.

River raised her brows in question. "Thinking of hopping in bed with someone?" That would come as quite a shock to Hugh.

"It's a 'just in case' plan. I do *like* Ciaran."

"Well, you better have stronger feelings than just 'like' if you're thinking of sleeping with the man," River advised. "Row. What of Hugh?" She knew Rowan didn't want to speak about the O'Faolain patriarch until she was ready, but for Heaven's sake, surely their current conversation would allow a bit of prying.

Rowan tapped her teacup, spinning the lovely floral china slowly in its saucer. The flowers reminded her of Patrick's gift of the daisy pottery. She'd mentioned it only once, and he'd remembered.

She loved that gift.

"Hugh and I are... not anything. We are connected because of Raven and Bran. And eventually, you and Pat. There will never be anything between us."

Her sister looked so pained. River was devastated she hadn't pushed her sooner. "But, Row, I don't understand." She really didn't understand. "The way he acts with you. He's overprotective and, just proved the other night, he was jealous."

"He made it very," Rowan looked straight at her sister so there was no misunderstanding, "*very* clear that because of our age difference, he would never consider dating me." Grimacing at the memory, she obviously had to force out the last. "I kept hoping, because of the things you mentioned yourself, that he might change his mind. He won't. I'm trying to move on. I *need* to move on. And I need to see him as little as possible."

River sat beside her, placing the plated eggs on the table. "Have you ever wondered, Row, what it would have been like if the O'Faolains had never hired us?"

Rowan picked at her eggs, moving the soft bits of yellow around her plate. "No. No, I don't wish that. For one, look at Raven. Bran loves her to distraction. And second, or first, I suppose, we have Baby O. Third, and I am a firm believer in this one— *It's better to have loved and lost than never to have loved at all.*"

"You're right. Definitely right."

"For what it's worth, I think you and Pat are going to make it."

"For what it's worth, Hugh better watch himself around you. He doesn't want to have a relationship, that's his loss, but he'd better stop trying to dictate your life."

"Agreed."

"Patrick is coming in today. How are we feeling about that?" Rowan smiled.

"*We* want to see him, but we *aren't* ready to talk to him."

"Agreed."

25
___

P atrick called Nan before they reached Dublin and asked if she would mind stopping at the new O'Faolain building first to see the apartments. Raven was there with Bran. She was dying to show her grandma the baby's room. Then River and Rowan would meet everyone at Nan's new apartment. A great place for Nan's big reveal, Pat encouraged.

She approved the plan. It would all fit, she said, before her three o'clock appointment at The Fitzwilliam to finalize the second baby shower.

Bran and Dad were waiting for him inside the front door of their new Dublin home. The door was an impressive mix of dark, heavy metal, and thick wooden planks— very medieval and a total statement piece. He couldn't remember which sister had found it while antiquing.

He ushered Nan and Devlen in before him, making all the appropriate introductions. Nan gave big hugs to Bran *and* Dad, much to Dad's consternation. Patrick smirked at his discomfort, and when he noticed, he gave Pat a discreet middle finger.

Bran went to his brother and told him he'd missed him. Patrick knew his brother loved him, but man, the confirmation felt amazing. His father pulled him into a hug. Before letting him go, he quietly said, "I missed you too. Are you okay?" He really regretted the lack of a pocket hanky. His time with Nan had really done a number on his feelings. Swallowing hard, he whispered back, "I'm better."

If River took him back, he would be a whole lot *more* than better.

Bran told Nan and Devlen he would give them a tour of the floors, ending with the third floor where Raven was waiting. The second floor was Patrick's. It was everything he didn't know he even wanted. Whites and creams with subtle touches of blue. The kitchen was extraordinary. The dark blue appliances were pieces of art.

The rest of the floor was just as thoughtfully done. The light wood floors, thick rugs, and off-white leather furniture with cream and soft blue striped pillows invited a person to sit and relax.

He didn't want to leave.

He wanted to find River, bring her back, and never leave.

There were other areas and rooms to explore, but he would rather wait until River walked him through her design. He had to believe she eventually would. He passed two guestrooms, giving them only a cursory glance before he reached the master. It hadn't been anywhere near done when he'd left for Nan's. It was done now.

The same crème and white were here, but the blues were darker, more intimate. More night sky. All Raven. Cobalt glass lamps and simple tan suede bedding topped the massive wooden frame, and the most amazing part was a giant painting of The Irish Wolves pub. It was painted to make the tall brick building look old-fashioned, sepia with hints of slate. Three men dressed in traditional cut suits circa 1920s with newsboy caps stood outside on the stone sidewalk. A seriously cool Peaky

Blinders vibe. The men were painted from a side perspective, but clearly of him, Bran, and Dad.

"River commissioned the painting from a local artist in November," Bran stood leaning against the doorframe.

"It's one of the coolest things I've ever fucking seen." Pat would have continued, but from behind Bran, Nan huffed, "Patrick O'Faolain, watch your language, young man." Bran was laughing silently, so Nan didn't discipline him either.

"Sorry, Nan. Let's go to Dad's place on the fourth floor."

"Yeah, Bébhinn. Raven is probably about to come find us if we don't get a move on," Bran laughed.

Nan and Patrick were the last to walk out his door. She lightly touched his arm to stop him before reaching the elevator. "A lot of beautiful blues in your apartment. Interesting, that."

"Very," Patrick grinned. Patrick liked blue just fine, but nothing close to River's fervor.

They toured Dad's penthouse, then went to Bran and Raven's. No matter the floor level, each apartment was expertly done. Timothy Daniels had delivered. With the O'Faolains as investors and this job on his resume, Daniel's construction business was about to reach new heights. Pat couldn't wait to toast his success with him and Saoirse. Also, since Daniels finished on time, he got his father's half-million-dollar 'push gift' bonus. They finally reached Bran and Raven's third-floor apartment, and Patrick could tell they'd be there a while.

Raven and Nan were busy looking at every pair of socks and mittens Baby O would be wearing, trying out the rocking chair, and crying over how tiny the diapers were. A lot of hormones bouncing around. He was happy that Dad and Bran were getting to know Devlen. Mr. Dunn was a quiet man; mid-seventies would be Pat's guess. Bébhinn was closer to seventy.

At one point, Raven held up the *Little House on the Prairie* cotton hospital nightgown, smiling and telling her Nan how much she loved it. Bran's eyes were bugging out at the high-necked embroidered collar. There were days Pat wished he was a videographer.

Nan kept glancing at her secret fiancé, smiling but twisting her simple gold engagement band in nervousness. Raven had yet to notice the ring. Pat truly wasn't nervous. He knew all three sisters would be thrilled.

The Byrne's touch could be seen on each floor of this building. Patrick chuckled to himself when he saw that Bran and Raven's kitchen mirrored his own except in color. Raven chose all Viking appliances in a muted green. Their accent colors were green, of course. His dad's apartment had Rowan written all over it. His appliances were a creamy yellow. The colors for his apartment were all shades of yellow, pale to mustard, and accented by dark cherry wood.

Whether purposeful or not, except for Raven, since it actually *was* her apartment, the girls had placed their stamp on the other two men's spaces. He loved it.

Once they were finally finished looking at every bit of baby paraphernalia, Raven said she had called her sisters, and they were headed to Nan's apartment. Flushing at the coming awkward 'parting of ways,' Patrick quickly announced he'd see everyone tomorrow so no one else had to inform him he was no longer wanted.

Nan looked at him in near panic. "I thought you were coming with us, Pat."

"You'll have to show me another day. I don't mind," Pat assured.

"But... but that doesn't make any sense. Come with us now."

Obviously, her nerves were getting the best of her, and she was forgetting why he wasn't welcome to join the family. "Nan," he tried gently, "River will be there, and she doesn't want to see me."

Nan blanched. "Oh, Patrick. I'm sorry. I'm flustered and wasn't thinking." She grabbed his hand like she might not let go. Devlen looked like he wanted to comfort her himself, but he was allowing her to do the reveal at her own pace, which Pat admired.

Pat leaned close to Nan's ear so no one would hear and whispered, "Remember how much you love Devlen. Be brave for him."

She took a deep breath, blinking her eyes rapidly to stop the tears from falling. Raven had grabbed Bran's hand in distress. She knew something was going on. It wasn't Pat's place to tell her, though, or Bran, for that matter.

Nan said, "I'm ready to go now."

"I'm staying with Pat." Dad could literally make an awkward situation worse with absolutely no effort whatsoever. Pat was about to object when he added, "We're going to grab lunch and a drink so he can tell me about his progress on the distillery."

Patrick only nodded. Bran said to text him where they were, and once they were done at the apartment and he got Raven settled, he'd meet them because he wanted an update on the property as well.

"Did you just say, 'Get me settled,' Bran?"

"I... no, I... I didn't mean it that way," Bran cringed, probably hearing how pathetic he sounded. "Rave," he began, taking his wife's hands, "you know I worry. I can't help it."

Raven's expression softened. "I worry for you too, Bran. Love goes both ways." Once they were done staring into each other's eyes, Raven announced, "So, that's settled. After we see Nan's apartment and she finalizes a few details, we'll all meet you wherever you guys end up."

∼

PATRICK COULD BARELY FOCUS. He was in the middle of discussing the property details with his dad, but his focus was on whether River would be coming with everyone else. Surely not. Her sisters would tell her that he was here.

"What had Bébhinn so anxious?"

He shouldn't be surprised his dad noticed. The man noticed everything. He would know soon anyway. He might as well tell. "She's engaged to Mr. Dunn and worried the girls won't approve."

"They will."

"I told her that. Several times. Devlen is a nice man."

"He is."

"I told Nan I would buy her property and put it in the girls' names. Nan will be moving in with Devlen. His property connects to hers."

"Of course. Should I call our attorney to start the paperwork?"

"Not yet. We need to ask how they feel about it first. They may want to go together and buy it themselves, though I believe Nan's property is worth a considerable amount, and it may strap them for cash."

"Why not just tell them after it's done?"

Sighing, Pat rubbed his head. The beginnings of a headache were forming. "For starters, I like my balls where they are."

His dad sighed then too. "True." Drumming his fingers against the table in agitation, Dad finally told Patrick, "The FBI monitoring Delton's rape page said that he was starting to take some online heat from subscribers pissed that he hadn't produced the video he'd promised... of Rowan and Jo."

"What is the FBI saying? The detectives?"

"That he may feel pressed to act sooner than later—encourage rash behavior. He is probably manic that he hasn't been able to get near us. No computer access. Nothing. We're too heavily guarded. They're definitely worried about him escalating."

"I guess the only comfort is knowing how well guarded we all are. Delton will show himself eventually, and they'll catch him. They have to, Dad. For fuck's sake. This nightmare has gone on long enough. I hate that Bran has to worry about the safety of his wife and child every moment."

"I don't like River and Rowan living on their own. Even with guards."

"Why did they insist on it? Everyone knew I was going to stay at a hotel. They could have stayed with you guys where it was safer. I promised River I'd keep my distance, and I would have kept that promise."

Dad rubbed his hand several times over his face and beard, clearly frustrated. "I believe it was more Rowan than River. They told Raven they didn't want to be burdens. Just because Raven was married to Bran didn't mean we were responsible for her sisters. Total bullshit."

Patrick almost snapped that he had more reason to hate the separation than his father, but he managed to refrain. His dad was obviously going through something too. "Did you tell them they would never be considered burdens?"

"No."

Alrighty then.

"Let's set up a tour with the distillery's seller," Hugh announced. Topic change. Noted.

"I'll send an email this—" They were walking in. Raven, in all her big-bellied glory, Bran, Devlen, Rowan, Nan, and— oh fuck— River. "Christ."

"Steady, Pat," Dad growled.

Pat watched the three sisters laugh and hug their Nan and Devlen— probably for the hundredth time. The announcement went well, apparently. He wasn't sure what he should do.

Leave? Ignore River? Go to the restroom and stay there? *That* would bring back lovely memories for River.

River made eye contact with him then. Her steps slowed. She took a deep breath, and then another, and another. Patrick was standing. He hadn't intended on standing. The family chatter ceased.

River broke eye contact first, so he quickly sat while he decided his best course of action. River announced to the waitress when she approached, "Shots all the way 'round, minus one, pointing at Raven, we're celebrating an engagement."

"That's grand," the waitress grinned. "Any preference?"

"Your choice," River answered, smiling. The smile almost reached her eyes. But not quite. Everyone took their seats. Chatter resumed. Wedding plans for Nan. Raven's Braxton Hicks— and yes, he knew what those were. Bran insisted he and their dad read *What to Expect When You're Expecting.* "In case of emergencies." Patrick didn't state the obvious. Emergencies would begin and end with a 911 call, but whatever.

He didn't want River to have to force good cheer during such an important celebration. So, he stood again, causing everyone to go quiet. Again. The opposite of celebratory. "No, everyone, don't let me interrupt. I have to get back home and send off some emails." Bran looked at Patrick and nodded. He understood.

Dad said, "Be sure to ask for the end of this week or the beginning of next, Pat."

Patrick nodded, stepping away from the table when River froze him like Medusa. "Hello, Patrick. Could you stay long enough to toast Nan?"

Stunned. Elated. Patrick slowly sank back into his chair. "I would really like to. Thank you." She didn't address him again, but her smile seemed less forced. What a first day back. Better than he ever dreamed. He got to see River, and she spoke to him.

Nan was sitting next to Patrick. She patted his leg under the table.

Rowan was sitting next to River. She looked at him and shrugged, but she did give him a small smile.

Raven only looked at Patrick with speculation. He knew she would take a while to forgive him.

Bran was staring at Raven. Dad was staring at Rowan— who was studiously ignoring him. Their blended family was not for the faint of heart.

Devlen placed his hand over Nan's on the tabletop. She blushed. The old man winked at her. The sisters whooped in joy.

Patrick didn't say anything or join in the banter. He smiled and was thankful to be a part of the group again. The truth was, though, Patrick was unsure where he fit. He felt like they were all puzzle pieces, but his piece was bent on one corner. Close, but not quite right.

Shots were passed around, something sweet and gross. Everyone grimaced while congratulating Nan and Devlen.

Patrick excused himself after another thirty minutes, not wanting to overstay, and he truly did need to email the distillery people. He said his goodbyes to the table at large, briefly touching on River but not allowing his eyes to linger.

As he stepped outside, he froze. The first thing River said to him was, *Hello Patrick.*

Oh my God. River was quoting his letter.

26

___

Thanks to information from one of his dark web acquaintances, Sam found himself standing outside a derelict warehouse on some back street in Tallaght, South Dublin County. T, which Sam could only assume wasn't his real name, dealt in arms and drug trafficking. T knew somebody, that knew somebody, that provided weapons to the person who sold guns to Mickey, the man he was supposed to be meeting tonight.

The warehouse looked abandoned. Sam's excitement started to dim. Surely, this wasn't another dead end. He had to take several deep breaths, so he didn't lose his shit. He was tired of nothing going his way. Tired of working at the coffee shop. He'd considered quitting, but it did give him an excuse to be in the area of Triskelion. Working and shopping. He wanted the guards to see him every day.

The cons outweighed the pros in favor of quitting, but God, he was tired of the comments from the people who used to be his fans. He'd lost another ten subscribers. He couldn't chance making any videos while he was here. He wanted to go back to the States. He missed the freedom of life in the motor home.

The O'Faolains, yet again, ruining his life.

215

Fuck them, and fuck Dublin.

Meeting Mickey was supposed to be the first step in taking back control of his revenge narrative. He'd been waiting on this shadowed sidewalk for twenty minutes, a duffle slung over his shoulder, shivering in the cold damp.

The rattle of metal sounded to his left. Sam spun at the sound. A dingy, white metal door creaked on its ancient hinges as it was pulled open. A man with spiked hair was illuminated by the low light behind him.

"Who are you?"

"Someone ordered a pizza." Literally, the most ridiculous thing to have someone say as the code to make contact with an arms dealer. Sam might need a Plan C and D if this was their highest level of professionalism.

The man opened the door wider so Sam could see his acne-scarred face, and unlike when Sam had them, he didn't believe it was makeup. Acne-Face's smirk was annoying. No matter. Sam wanted a gun.

"Follow me. Mickey's in the back. Wish you had really brought pizza. I'm starved," he laughed. "I'm Petey, by the way." Was it a job requirement that names need to end in 'y?'

They walked by four vehicles in various states of dismantling. Grease, rags, and tools littered the floor. If they were attempting to make this appear like a legitimate car repair shop, they were failing miserably.

They passed through something resembling an office/employee kitchen— but dirtier— a long hallway with doors here and there— bedrooms maybe, surely not a janitor's closet, as no one here cleaned— finally coming to a newer looking door, heavy-duty metal with a fancy looking keypad. The first thing in this shithole with promise.

Petey covered the pad while he entered the code, presumably so Sam wouldn't learn the code. Spoiler alert: Sam would never lower himself to come here again.

The door opened with a pressurized *shhzz*. Petey waved Sam forward. This room was— a surprise. A good surprise. Modern, cold, and full of weapons, big, small, and everything in between. A big man sat at a metal table in the center of the room, a laptop and three monitors arranged at precise angles, each casting a flickering light show across his scruffy, square jaw. Sam knew computer equipment. Consider him impressed.

"Mickey, I'm Samuel. T is the man who gave me your contact information. I appreciate you meeting with me." It never hurt to kowtow to people who dealt in death.

"I have something important in fifteen minutes. What do you want from me?"

This man's voice held zero inflection. He was neither aggressive nor bored. Nothingness. Sam believed himself relatively impervious to those who resided in society's underbelly— he was a dark web affiliate, after all—but this Mickey... he sent chills up Sam's spine. "I need a high-powered, long-range rifle with a scope and suppressor."

"Fifty-thousand US."

What the fuck? Sam might not be extremely knowledgeable about the cost of weapons— but come on! His thoughts must have shown on his face.

"Problem?"

What was fifty grand to finish the O'Faolains and return to the life he loved most? @SammySoGood had taken a long enough hiatus.

"No problem. I'll transfer the money now."

Without another word, Mickey went to one of the gun walls and started pulling things off the shelves like it was Black Friday at Wal-Mart. He gestured once at Sam's duffel, which he immediately pulled from his shoulder and handed to Mickey, who,

shocker, held absolutely zero resemblance to the Disney character. Mickey placed the rifle and its accouterments inside.

Before handing Sam the bag, Mickey went to his computer,
flipping through several pages before finding, presumably, his
payment of $50,000.

Nodding his big, shaved head in what Sam presumed
signaled satisfaction, he shoved the now heavy duffel into Sam's
chest, knocking him back a step. "Leave."

Sam might have been incensed at the man's rudeness, considering he'd just paid a premium for the weapon, but he wasn't. He
wasn't even a tiny bit put out because things were starting to
finally go his way.

The O'Faolains were back on Sam's revenge menu.

27

River and Rowan sat at their desks in Triskelion's office, sorting mail and answering emails. They'd given their assistants the day off and purposely didn't schedule any meetings so that she and Rowan would have time to get ready for their night out with Josh and Sadhbh. Before going home, they wanted to get their nails done. Dom was even out. He had a doctor's appointment this morning. River suggested he take the afternoon off as well and get the rest of the décor purchased to finish his flat upstairs.

Dom jumped at the chance, taking several vendor payments with him. Triskelion bought locally for their clients, especially for the O Building, unless they required a specific design found in other areas of the world. Dom liked to personally deliver the checks from Triskelion whenever possible. He said he enjoyed ensuring the vendors, especially the artisans, that their services were appreciated. Yeah, Dom was irreplaceable.

"Nan and Matilda did an amazing job with Raven's second shower."

"It was beautiful. To be fair, Dom did most of the work,"

Rowan laughed. "That man knows The Fitzwilliam Hotel better than the owners, I imagine."

"Did you see when Hugh and Bran left before the shower started, the big hugs and kisses they gave Matilda? I could tell she melted at their show of affection." As soon as the question left River's mouth, she mentally kicked herself.

Rowan's shoulders stiffened briefly, but she still managed a small smile. "It was sweet of them."

"Row." Her sister only shook her head no. She didn't want to discuss Hugh today. So, they wouldn't. This was not a day to push.

"Speaking of sweet gestures, are Devlen and Nan, not the cutest couple? He is very attentive, and Nan blushes literally every time he so much as touches her hand."

"Never in a million years did I think Nan would get remarried, let alone move into his house. It's crazy and wonderful, and I bet, if Dad were still alive he would be happy for his mother too."

"I agree. So does Raven. She mentioned that same thing at the shower. You know, we should really tell Nan that. I imagine she's wondered if her son and husband would be happy for her."

"Definitely."

Before River could ask what Rowan planned on wearing that evening, her sister asked, "Have you spoken to Patrick since we all met for drinks Monday night?"

"No. I've seen him walking into the O Building a few times." She wanted to talk to him. Desperately. Rowan picked up an envelope from her desk, a very familiar style of envelope, and waved it back and forth. River was mesmerized, like a cat watching a feather bouncing on a string. She didn't pounce, but it was a close thing.

"I know we agreed to save the letters for home, but since I've personally witnessed your cheesy smiles and blushes when you read them now, I figured I'd give it over now. Plus, you've been moping."

River didn't bother denying the charge. She *had* been sulking. Enough with patience, River shot out of her chair and snatched the letter from her sister's fingers. Sitting back down, she flipped Rowan off for smirking before running her fingertips across her name on the front. Patrick had distinctive handwriting. After all his letters, she imagined she would be able to pick out his style easily. She carefully broke the seal, pulling two pages free. Her hands shook in anticipation.

River wasn't sure if she'd forgiven Patrick. She wasn't sure when she admitted he was the only man she would ever love. She did know she couldn't trust herself, but God, she wanted to. He had wooed her with letters. Letters! No one could read Patrick's letters without feeling his honesty. His truth. She hoped... commitment. Regret.

Patrick held nothing back. His vulnerability was beautiful. His mundane was mesmerizing. His erotic descriptions... heart palpitating.

Dear River,

You said hello to me, just like I'd hoped to hear from your mouth, your lips— Hello Patrick— you said it, and I'm still hearing it. I hear your voice all the time. I wake up in the middle of the night hearing your voice.

When it's dark, I hear you breathe. When I close my eyes, I hear you moan. I hear you ask me to kiss you. I hear you ask me to go faster. You demand I go harder. I'm hard for hours... after.

How has your week been? Are you getting plenty to eat?

Is it wrong to admit how jealous I am of the ~~fucking Murphy~~ the Murphy brothers feeding you?

I'm meeting Dad downstairs later for a drink. We ordered

a food delivery. The wolf sculpture takes my breath away whenever I'm on the ground floor.

Dad has been extra... well... extra everything lately— quiet, sullen, angry. I think it has to do with Rowan. I plan on trying to get him to open up tonight. I don't believe he will.

Do you wish I would go back to Oklahoma?

Do you dream of ways to avoid me, or do you dream of me sliding into your body? Do you wake up feeling my naked chest pressed against yours?

My floor in the O Building is better than I could have ever imagined. The kitchen is everything. I haven't cooked in it yet. I just can't bring myself to use anything. I want the first time to be with you. I think your daisy dishes will look perfect on the open shelving. What do you think?

The painting in the master is, Jesus, River... I can't describe how I felt when I saw it, but I'll try. It makes me think of the past, the present, and the future. I feel such a connection to my dad and my brother. I see us standing together, just like that, forever. When we're nothing but spirits in the wind, I know the three of us will always stand side by side. Thank you.

I also see you and I standing together. We're strong. We're faithful. We're each other's everything. We're in love. It's forever too.

I had lunch with Jo and MacGregor yesterday. I've never seen Jo go after another person like she goes after her guard. No matter what she says or does, he ignores her— he's pretending. He notices everything— it drives her crazy. It's pretty entertaining.

Example: Our waitress asked for our drink orders. Jo ordered a gin and tonic, and before Thomas could order his drink, Jo started petting his hand on the table and told the waitress (and here, I feel I should relate that the waitress appeared to be drooling over the Scottish giant), "Oh, Honey would *adore* a Cosmopolitan." I give the man credit. His expression never changed. Only a slight side-eye toward his charge. Clearly, Jo was marking her territory. She is *not* subtle. I don't think MacGregor minded.

I ordered a shot of Jameson Black Barrel. With every swallow, I pretend that it's your tongue in my mouth, tasting of whiskey. It makes it hard to concentrate.

Will you meet me for breakfast? Lunch? Afternoon tea? Dinner? Will you ever be mine again? I am forever yours.

All my love,

Patrick

River pressed the letter back into its trifold, slipping it back into the envelope. Her face had to be red. Her entire body felt hot. Patrick's letters... his letters were an addiction. They were love poems written only for her, mixed with the subtlest of erotic meanderings. Patrick dropped the spicy curveballs so randomly. Did he know what he was doing? Did he know she felt every single word?

"Do you need to take a break? In the bathroom? With loud music?" When River jerked her gaze to Rowan's, her sister was watching her with a cheeky grin. Her dimples were deep and judgy.

River laughed. She wouldn't even try to deny how the letters affected her.

"I take it Patrick has literary skills?"

"God, Row. He's... he... Lord, I feel like I know him better through his letters than all the months we've spent in each other's company. I know what makes him happy or sad, or what his favorite foods are, and what makes him laugh out loud. What he thinks of his family and ours. How much Nan helped him. He... damn, I don't want to ever transgress his privacy, but he told me some childhood stories. Some made me laugh, and... several made me cry."

"Will you give him one more chance? You love him. He clearly loves you."

"I want to run to him. I want him to wrap his arms around me and never let go. I want to tell him that I still love him."

"But?" Rowan asked.

River stared at her sister. Describing her inner turmoil was difficult at best. "But? There is really only one but. He destroyed me that night." River blinked rapidly to stem the tears.

"Bullshit, River." Rowan's harsh expletive got her attention. Rowan slammed her palm flat against her desktop, making River jump. "He did *not* destroy you. He *hurt* you. Terribly. He did not, however, *destroy* you. You are stronger than that. Bran didn't destroy our sister, and Patrick sure as hell didn't do that to you.

"I vote, well, if I get a vote," Rowan raised her brows at River in question. When River nodded yes, she continued. "I vote you give him another chance. I also vote you write *him* a letter. Explain your feelings. How he made you feel. How you want to feel. What you need from him and what you're willing to give him in return. Write it all down, River. You just said you know him better now than you ever did before. Give him a chance to *know* you."

River was shocked. Rowan was, well, wow, she was right. She didn't want to give up on a possible future with Patrick. A letter, though? "A letter? Do you really think—"

"I do."

"But... but what would I say in it?" Panic. This definitely felt like panic.

"It sounds like Patrick simply writes what he feels. What he's doing. What he thinks about. And, I assume he thinks of you. A lot. If your blushes and heavy breathing are anything to go by, his thoughts aren't purely platonic."

River's tension eased. "You are a real asshole sometimes, Row." Rowan shrugged.

"I'll write it before we leave the office and before I chicken out."

"I'll drop it off before we meet Josh."

28

───────

Dad and Patrick decided to have dinner in tonight. The sports channel played on the flat screen behind the bar on the ground floor, where they sat on comfortable bar stools. Patrick swiveled his chair to look more closely at his dad who was nursing his drink while staring moodily at the bar's woodgrain.

"Dad." Once Patrick had his father's attention, he wasn't sure he wanted it. His father seemed lost, and that was alarming. He wished Bran were here, but he and Raven were having a quiet dinner with Nan and Mr. Dunn. Taking a deep breath, Patrick went for it. "Are you in love with Rowan?"

If looks could kill... "Never ask me about her again." Dad's voice was so low, so angry, Patrick was momentarily thrown by its intensity. If the tumbler in his grip wasn't made from heavy crystal, it would be in shards with the white-knuckled grip his dad currently strangled it with.

"I thought we could ask each other anything. You know my secrets and all my fuckups. Why can't you tell me something as simple as whether you're interested in a woman?" Good Lord, his dad had an intense stare. Ball shriveling. Pat watched several emotions cross his stoney face— anger, frustration, defeat. With a sigh, he stopped his attempted tumbler murder, letting the glass go entirely so he could rub his palms over his jean-clad thighs.

"I don't like to discuss my... personal... my... Christ! Women. I don't like to discuss them."

"Not a huge newsflash, Dad. Bran and I aren't toddlers, however. We've known some of the women you've slept with over the years. We never asked you about them because they weren't important to you. Or we didn't think they were."

"They were not," he huffed, crossing his arms across his massive chest defensively.

"So?"

"So, fucking what, Son?"

Patrick groaned in frustration. A normal occurrence when talking to his father. "So, *Dad*, Rowan isn't someone you're interested in for casual sex. Do you love her, and if you do, then why in the hell are you doing your damnedest to keep her at arm's length?" Since he was on a roll, he finished with, "You've been different for months. Bran and I have both noticed. I'm asking you now because it looks like you're going to continue ignoring your feelings. Bébhinn taught me a lot of things these last few weeks, but her biggest lesson was not to hide from feelings. Good, bad, scary, or sad."

Dad could barely answer through his locked jaw. He was angry. Really angry. No one liked to be confronted. Patrick didn't say anything else. They stared at each other another minute before Dad broke the silence by slamming his hand down on the bar top, rattling their glasses.

Patrick was beginning to think he'd royally screwed up by asking, but finally... finally, he answered, and it was like watching a dam break under pressure.

"She is a young woman, Patrick. A *very* young woman! I am

twice her age, for fuck's sake. More than twice! Jesus, Patrick, what kind of man would I be if I pursued a woman so young? Younger than my own children." He went silent, shaking his head as if he disgusted himself.

"You only hurt yourself and Row by treating her like you do. You are possessive as fuck over her, and you know it. Look at what I did to River. I warned her not to date anyone even though I had no plans of dating her myself. I was so selfish, and I hurt her! I hurt the woman I love. Do you not see that you're doing the same thing?"

Dad deflated, leaning against the bar. He picked his whiskey up and swallowed the shot. "Christ, I know I'm hurting her, and it's killing me. I *cannot*... I *will* not have a relationship with someone so young. Rowan deserves to find a man that she can grow old with."

Dad ran his hand over his face several times. He was clenching his empty glass once more. The other hand was fisted in his lap. Patrick thought he wouldn't speak again. Which was his normal way of ending conversations.

Pat was wrong. Never taking his eyes from the glass, he admitted, "We've... I've... damn it! Things have been... or rather happened. No," he swiped an angry hand in front of his face, silencing himself. "I've made up my mind, Son. I know you're trying to help, and I appreciate your concern, but nothing will come of me discussing her further."

Patrick had pushed as far as he could. He wanted his dad to open up. He didn't want to cause him pain. "Consider the topic closed. I do hope you realize if you ever did want to discuss this or anything else bothering you, that I would be honored if you trusted me with your thoughts." When Dad looked at him again, he nodded and even went so far as to pat his son's leg.

The next half hour saw both he and his dad relax back into comfortable camaraderie. Patrick refilled their drinks and found an old John Wayne movie to watch with dinner. *The Quiet Man*, funnily enough.

Patrick had just finished shuffling a deck of cards, placing them between him and his dad to try a game of Slap Jack while they waited for their food 'buffet' delivery, when the front door knocker thudded against metal. One of the guards stepped forward, stating, "It's Ms. Byrne, Mr. O'Faolain."

Patrick's body went into instant overdrive. River. Was River on the other side of that massive door?

His dad's jaw clenched, but he kept his stress under control. As he walked over to the entrance to open things up, he was asking, "Do you know which Ms. Byrne, Daniel?"

"No, sir."

With a sigh of irritation, Dad sprung the deadbolts and master locks, opening the behemoth door to reveal... Rowan. Her "Mr. O'Faolain, I've come to see Patrick if it's convenient," had his dad clenching his jaw all over again. The teeth-rattling door slam after she entered was his only show of temper.

Rowan jumped at the slam. However, her stride remained steady and she made her way to the bar as if undisturbed by his dad's rudeness. Patrick watched her face for any clue as to why she wanted to speak to him. Did River want to see him? Did she want him to stop writing to her? Dread, the sick churning in his gut, was definitely dread.

Rowan glanced at the cards and raised her brows in question. "Slap Jack?"

Patrick smiled sheepishly. "Well, you did make it sound fun." When she didn't say anything right away, Pat asked her if she would like a drink. "We ordered an entire menu of food too. It should be here soon if you're hungry."

"No, thank you, though. I'm meeting River."

Gut punch. "Of course," he mumbled like a bumpkin. Dad

was helping his anxiety tremendously by standing at the end of the bar, arms crossed and staring. Jesus.

Rowan unbuttoned her long wool coat, butter yellow, of course. He noticed his father was no longer leaning against the counter but highly attuned to Rowan's small reveal. Patrick was about to offer to take her coat, but before a word passed his lips, she pulled an envelope from her inner pocket.

His name was written across the front. Patrick. Oh God, oh God.

"I only came to drop this off." She offered him a small smile. "I didn't want to wait until tomorrow." He nodded his thanks as words were beyond him. His hand shook as he reached for *his* letter *from* River. With quick efficiency, Rowan buttoned her coat. "Well, I'm off. River is waiting for me to pick her up."

Patrick hoped he said thank you, but he wasn't sure if his lips were working. He barely acknowledged his dad walking Rowan to the door. He placed the envelope on the bar in front of him, smoothing its edges while praying it was... a good letter.

Not a goodbye.

~~Dear~~ Hello Patrick,

I'm at Triskelion. Row and me. I miss Raven, but I'm so glad she isn't here. It means she and Baby O are resting. I'm ready to be an aunt. I'm ready to hold my nephew. I'm ready to try out my Auntie name on him and see what he thinks.

I miss you.

Rowan and I are going out tonight with Josh and Saoirse's younger sister, Sadhbh. I think Josh is already half in love with Sadhbh. We're closing early to get our nails done before we go home to change. The house we are staying in is incredible. Mrs. Adamson, the owner of the house and a former client of Rowan's, is quite a character and very generous. She has a fancy kitchen that I'm sure she's never touched. I've been cooking some for Row and me.

It's weird not always being with both my sisters. I have a lot of quiet time. I lot of time to think and reflect on... me, I guess. Did you feel that way when you stayed with Nan? She always makes me feel better.

I'm glad you like your apartment. I'm really glad you loved the painting. Besides the kitchen and the master bath, it's my favorite piece in the whole place.

I'll tell you a secret. I bought the painting with my own money. I worked with the artist, and I think he captured my vision perfectly. I wanted you to see the painting every day and know it was from me. Only me.

That *sounds* presumptuous, and I'm only writing it. I shudder to imagine how it would have truly sounded if I'd had the chance to tell you personally.

Rowan's getting antsy to leave the office.

I dreamed of you last night. I don't wish you would move back to Oklahoma.

Are you wondering about my dream?

Your father is aggravating. Don't get me wrong, he's one of the best men I've ever known, besides my own father and grandfather, but... still aggravating. I believe he has been attracted to Row since the moment we all met each other. I won't tell you of Rowan's feelings. She barely tells her sisters, so I would never break her trust. I wonder what your dad would think if he knew my little sister will be seeing Ciaran later.

I thought you destroyed me on New Year's Eve. My sisters have helped me realize you didn't destroy me, but you did hurt me. Badly. You've explained your feelings. Some days it helps to know them. On other days, I'm still hurt. Badly. Sometimes I wonder, would you feel the same as I did? Would you be as hurt if another man's hands grasped my body and pulled me tight against him? Would you mind if I rubbed my core up and down his cock? If I let him put his tongue down my throat?

Would it hurt you? Badly?

The daisy dishes are perhaps the most fantastic gift I've ever received. I use them. Every day.

Did you know that I smile and laugh when I really want to cry? I go out with friends when I really want to curl up in bed? That I say, 'No problem' when I really want to say, 'No?'

Has Bran hinted at Baby O's name? Raven won't give me anything. I adore how Rave decorated the baby's room. My sister and your brother are going to be the best parents in the history of great parents.

We were both naked. In your bed. In your master suite. In my dream, that is.

I love Mr. Dunn (Devlen) already. He is everything I would have wished for Nan. I will worry for her less. I don't understand her giving up her house, though. She loves that house. I plan on speaking with my sisters after Baby O gets here about seeing if we can swing buying it from her. Rowan and I can stay where we are quite a bit longer, I imagine.

That house is... where my parents are.

I got a new client that wants one-of-a-kind furniture. I love that. Money is no issue. I love that more. I have planned a quick trip to Scotland with Jo and Thomas. There is a master furniture builder in Nairn that I'm dying to meet. I've heard he's quite the grumpy recluse, but his work is worth any amount of 'tude. I plan on flying to Inverness and renting a car. Lord, I wish that Delton shithead would be caught already. I hate dragging MacGregor out of Dublin, but Jo wanted to go, which means Honey Bunny is definitely going.

Do you think Jo's guard will continue to stand by her side even when the stalker is caught? I do.

In my dream, your body was curled around mine. My back to your chest. My head rested on your right bicep. Your left arm wrapped around my middle. My breasts grazed your skin. My bottom pressed tightly to your sex. I pressed against your hardness. You moaned and pulled me tighter. I wanted you inside me.

I might meet you. Sometime. Before Baby O.

In my dream, I feel safe. I feel loved.

But you hurt me. Badly.

I wonder, every hour of every day if I can forget.

I want to, Patrick. I want to forgive and forget.

I want to hear you say, "I will never hurt you again, River. I vow it."

I want to believe you.

Still yours. Maybe,

River

The highest of highs and the lowest of lows.

The high— River missed him. She didn't want him to leave Dublin. She had the painting done— for him, from *only* her. She would meet him. Sometime. She dreamed of him, of them, together. She wanted to forgive him. She was still his.

The low— River was going out with friends. Patrick isn't one of them. He'd hurt her. Badly. She made him visualize her with another man. It was a cruel punishment. He deserved it. She wanted to forgive him. She might not be able to. She was still his. Maybe.

He didn't look at his dad. If he met with sympathy, he would crumble. He noticed all the food containers on the bar. He hadn't realized it had been delivered. He refolded the letter and gently placed it in the envelope. More deep breaths. There were hard things in the letter, but there were a lot of amazing things too. Really amazing. He had to focus on the amazing. The alternative... No.

How would he ask her to meet him without her phone number? Would it be a date? After she mentioned Ciaran, he figured River and Rowan were going to Murphys tonight. Would it be a mistake to go to the pub if it was only for a moment? Just long enough to ask her for a time to meet.

He looked at his dad, who was now sitting quietly by his side. "Let's eat. I'm starved." She said she would meet him. Nothing else mattered.

29

———

Murphy's was packed. The pub's live music on Friday nights always drew a crowd. Josh and Sadhbh arrived early to get a table between the band and the bar. Prime real estate. Ciaran and Cormac kept their table full of appetizers and drinks. River could eat the mini crab cakes here for breakfast, lunch, and dinner. They were *that* good. Cormac told Josh earlier that once the kitchen slowed down, they would come join their table.

They were all laughing and singing, taking shots, and stomping their feet to the bodhrán's beat. River was doing her best to keep herself present, but wondering what Patrick thought of her letter was distracting as hell. Oh God, she'd told him she'd dreamed of him. She admitted she missed him.

River said she'd meet him— full body shudder. That was either the worst or the best part of the letter, depending on the angle she studied the words. It had been her attempt at reconcil-iation. *And* she said she'd see him *before* Baby O's arrival. Was she weak? It didn't feel weak. It felt... not right exactly, but inevitable. After several weeks of contemplation— contem-plating her life in a gazillion different scenarios —Patrick was in all of them! No matter where her ponderings wandered, River's mind introduced Patrick as a keynote speaker *consistently*. At this point, she expected his presence in her dreams, night or day.

Daydream Example A. She was enjoying a breakfast muffin and hot tea alone at a local cafe. She was reading a romance novel, and the early morning sun warmed her face through the windowpanes. She was content. She looked freaking content, for crying out loud! Happy. Satisfied with life. A second later, she was tilting her head to the side to accept Patrick's kiss against the tender skin of her neck. He sat across from her, his own muffin and coffee before him. It felt right.

There were several X-rated night dreams, of course. River knew better than pulling *those* out *now*— in public.

Daydream Example B. River was visiting Nan for a quiet weekend getaway. While her grandma repotted several plants in her attached greenhouse, River spent hours weeding the flower garden and pinching and pruning all the brilliantly colored shrubs and flowers outside. Kneeling amidst the fragrant plants, she looked around with a sense of peace and accomplishment. She looked to the left and smiled at Pat, who was bringing out a cold glass of water. That felt right too.

River was shaken from her musings when Ciaran and Cormac brought more shots and loud greetings, their energy high and smiles bright. They must have gotten a break from their duties finally. Cormac sat to her left, giving her a good-natured bump to the side. She smiled, taking the offered shot with a happy, "You're the best, Cor!"

It was tons easier to be around the oldest Murphy once he realized River was not interested in dating him. Ciaran was still hopeful where Rowan was concerned. If his constant close proximity and heart emoji eyes fixated on her little sister weren't enough, he touched Rowan's hand, arm, or hair at least once every two minutes. It didn't look like she minded, but she certainly wasn't encouraging— more.

Daydream Example C. She was jogging in the park before work. It was still cool enough that her breath puffed white clouds with each exhalation. Earbuds firmly in place, her feet pounding to *The Kill* by Thirty Seconds to Mars. She loved her morning runs. No meetings, no clients, no expectations other than making her body feel strong. Then, River realized she was jogging in perfect step next to Patrick. She knew he liked to jog, but they had never run together. Sighing, she admitted to herself that it had felt... right.

Before she could trek further down *that* rabbit hole of alternate reality dreams, Rowan elbowed her side, not gently. "What the hell?" River hissed.

"Sadhbh tried to talk to you. Twice. You were totally zoned out. What is going on with you?"

"Crap. How rude of me." River started to holler at Sadhbh and apologize for not paying attention, but Rowan said that the youngest Kennedy could tell River was in deep thought and was in no way offended, especially with the attractive blacksmith's arm casually draped around her shoulders.

Rowan still waited for an answer. River considered lying about what was going on but discarded that route quickly enough. She and her sisters didn't lie to one another. They might choose to stay silent but not outright lying. "The letter. Oh, God, Row. Do you think it was a mistake? I think it was a mistake. I wrote some of my *real* feelings," she whisper-wailed in her sister's ear. Thank God the band distracted everyone from her semi-meltdown.

"It's about time Patrick knew, you idiot. You hide your true self all the time," she held her hand up to stop River's denial. "No, River. You do, and you know it. He needed to *hear* you, even if the words were written. He needed to know you better, like you know him better through his letters. I wish I'd have thought of you writing back sooner."

Daydream Example D: River was enjoying a night out with Rowan and their friends. She was dressed in a dark blue knit jumper Nan had made for her birthday last year. Her Nan's sweaters made her feel loved. She was listening to music and taking shots of God knows what. She loved nights out with friends. She didn't need a significant other to complete her. She could be a one-woman wolf pack. *That* is how flipping solid she was. So why... *why* was she imagining Patrick walking through the pub's front door? With Hugh?

Okay, no need to panic. This clearly wasn't a daydream of 'the wishful thinking' variety. This was real life, and currently playing. "Row?" River nodded toward the front of the pub. "Is that... are they... really here?" Her body was an inferno. Fire and heat licked over her skin. So hot she felt cold shivers prickle her neck.

"I told Patrick I was meeting you. But not where!" Her unblinking eyes were anime-large. Rowan looked sick. Like she'd done something that could potentially hurt her sister.

"No, Row. No," Rowan repeated, shaking her head. "I did it. Jesus, it was me. I told Patrick in the letter that we were going out tonight. He'd mentioned Hugh in *his* letter and... he said... shit." River sighed. Hugh's treatment of her youngest sister had pissed River off. "I'm sorry, Row. I shouldn't have said it or written it, I guess, but I asked Pat if Hugh would care that you would be seeing Ciaran tonight." Rowan visibly flinched. "Oh God. Please forgive me, Row. Please tell me you forgive me," River begged. She'd basically waved a red flag in front of an alpha O'Faolain.

Rowan's cheeks puffed up as she sucked in air and held it before slowly exhaling. "I would forgive you if there was something to forgive. Hugh made it clear that we will never be...

anything. Who I see is none of that man's business," Rowan waved her hand between them. Moving on. "The important bit is Patrick. Hello! Your ex is here, and I don't think he came to Murphy's for any reason except to find you. So, decide now. Hide or Seek?"

River could see the two men edging the room. Looking for them. She had only a minute before he found her. Maybe less. And, oh wow, Pat looked— like he always looked. Handsome, dangerous, and delicious. His messy white, blond hair partially hid his right eye, the amber gold of the left eye reflecting the pub's light. He wore a brown leather jacket, crème sweater, and denim jeans. O'Faolain casual was runway-worthy.

Hide or Seek? It was her favorite childhood game. She wasn't a child anymore. Grabbing her sister's hand and squeezing, she took her eyes off Patrick for a moment to focus on Rowan. "Seek."

"Are you sure?"

"I'm sure." If River's voice trembled, her loyal sister didn't comment.

"I'm coming with you." Rowan looked fierce. She wasn't taking no for an answer. She caught Josh's attention, completely ignoring the Murphys, and told him they'd be back. They stood, and in the dim light, they could have been twins. Rowan placed her fingers against River's cheek, a brief touch, a moment to remember she wasn't alone.

Hand in hand, they walked toward the two men they'd been avoiding— the two men they wanted most in the world.

THERE SHE WAS. The woman Pat loved. The only woman. The woman he would die a thousand times for. The woman that he had hurt. Badly.

She and Rowan were looking right at him and Dad. Patrick nudged his dad's side. There was no mistake. They weren't looking for the restrooms. Those were in the opposite direction. Halfway across the pub, Ciaran Murphy stopped Rowan. He wrapped a hand around her arm, stopping her momentum. He felt his dad's fury swell. He took a step toward the sisters, but Patrick grabbed his arm.

"Reel it in, Dad. They are coming to us. Do *not* make a scene. Please." Patrick's desperation must have gotten through. He reluctantly stepped back against the bar. Patrick wasn't foolish enough to believe a crisis had been averted between his father and River's sister. Rowan was patting Ciaran's arm, smiling and laughing.

Oh, Christ. Ciaran looked up, making eye contact with the berserker standing beside him. Don't do it, Murphy. Don't fucking do it. He did it. He hugged Rowan, pulling her into his body, a possessive hand at her back. The nail in his coffin was the kiss he placed on her cheek. His dad was an ethical man, but in this, Patrick could envision his father ruining Murphy and his bar for the insult.

Patrick barely caught his dad before he lunged toward the enemy. Patrick placed a hand on his chest. "Don't, Dad. He's trying to get under your skin. Rowan considers him a friend. Don't do something you'll regret." His dad didn't move. He didn't acknowledge Patrick's words either, but he was still. For now.

River looked confident, but she was white-knuckling her sister's hand. A sure sign of her nerves. He was beyond nervous himself. If she was angry that he crashed her night out, it would crush him.

And here she was. Standing right in front of him. "Hello, Patrick." Christ, his whole body felt those words. River had added extra black liner around her eyes, accentuating her feisty cat vibe. How could a woman look wicked and innocent at the same time? That was River, though. Unique in every way.

Patrick lifted a hand to touch her but stopped. Instead, he made a gesture toward her sweater. "Fisherman's rib stitch. Your Nan taught me that one." Tragic. Karma for making fun of Bran's sourdough starter. He would pay a hefty price for a *Last of the Mohican's* mercy kill about now.

River ran her hands over the dark blue pattern. "I love it." That was all. She didn't ask him why he was there. She didn't look mad or sad. A good sign or the calm before the storm? Hmm.

Patrik took a deep breath. It was now or never, really. He'd come here for a reason, and there was no way he was leaving without at least asking, "Would you step outside for a moment? With me?"

River's eyes rounded before turning to Rowan, who looked to be having a tense standoff with his dad. Patrick watched River take a deep breath, presumably to calm her nerves. She told her sister that they were going to go outside for a minute.

River had Rowan's full attention. "Are you sure?" she asked. At River's nod, she added, "I'll meet you at our table then." With a strict look at Pat, she added, "If your plans change. Text me so I don't worry."

"Rowan." One word spoken through his father's clenched teeth had Rowan's cheeks flush red. She refused to look at Dad. This was quickly turning into a train wreck.

River moved around Patrick and stood toe to toe with his dad. It happened so fast that Pat felt like they were on the *Matrix* set. River practically hissed. She was so angry. Pointing at his father's chest with one hand while Rowan grabbed her other, she demanded, "No, Hugh. No. You can't have it both ways." River glanced at Patrick for a moment, an apology in her eyes before she swung her attention back to Dad. "Your son tried that with me, and guess what? It hurts. Go home. Rowan can do whatever the hell she wants. With *whoever* she wants."

Forget the train wreck. They were living through atomic bomb fallout. "Dad, would you please go home? I only wanted a word with River, and then I'll follow you. I don't want to ruin their night out." The pleading look on his son's face must have registered.

He nodded before glancing at River and Rowan. "I apologize for coming." He looked directly at Rowan then, who took a hesitant step forward before shaking her head and whirling around to head back to her table. His dad watched her go before walking out of the pub.

Patrick wrapped River's hand in his, entwining their fingers, tired of second-guessing whether he could touch her. "I'm sorry, River. This wasn't what I intended when I came here tonight. Will you still step out for a minute? Only a minute." At her nod, he kept her hand and led them out the front. It was cold but not horrible once they ducked under an awning with wind protection on two sides. There were a few wrought iron benches, but Patrick led River past those to the only quiet corner.

RIVER LOOKED UP AT PATRICK, but his face was in shadows. The outside lampposts only highlighted the breadth of his shoulders. She might not be able to see his expression, but his body language screamed with determination. He probably wasn't aware that he'd blocked her in with his big body like she may change her mind— as if she wanted to be anywhere else.

"I'm sorry about Dad. He's... well, I'd like to say he's not always such a Neanderthal, but you know better."

She could hear the band's music filtering out of Murphy's. It was kind of a romantic moment, all things told— 'all things' referring to Hugh's drama and a potential reconciliation between her and Patrick. Blended families were *hard*, especially if they slept with one another. "You don't need to apologize for your dad." Patrick took both her hands, bringing them to rest on his chest. "Why are you here, Pat?"

His hands shook slightly where they cupped hers. He was nervous. "I read your letter." Now, it was River's turn to tremble. "You said you would let me see you. Before the baby gets here."

That was all true, but "Why are you here *tonight?*" Patrick had started gently rubbing her fingers, pressing her hands more firmly against his chest. Distracting.

"Well, I was going to wait to call Rowan tomorrow, but while Dad and I were eating dinner, I realized I couldn't wait to know."

"Know what?" Patrick moved forward, trapping her hands between their bodies. His new position allowed a stray beam of light to cross his face. River had wanted to see his face... see what he was thinking, and oh, wow. Her breath constricted, short pants of air hitting her lips— the intensity of his stillness— predator and prey. River was definitely the prey.

Having forgotten she'd asked him a question, River was startled when he answered. "I want to know *when* you will see me. The day. The time. The place." As Patrick spoke, his hands moved to her sides, a slight pressure to her ribs, before sliding around her back where he splayed his hands. His head had lowered so that when he spoke, his lips tickled her ear.

Deliberate seduction. River applauded the approach.

The words fizzing in her throat, begging for release, were not going to win her a Pulitzer, but she said them anyway. Turning her lips to the side of Patrick's mouth, River threw caution to the wind. "Take me home, and we can talk about it."

Patrick's hands flexed against her back. She heard him murmur, *Thank God.*

Because he was Patrick, he said, "Text Row so she doesn't worry. Should I have Dad come back to walk her home?"

River already had her phone out, texting her sister. "No. She has a guard that lives with us. She'll be fine." Rowan would not thank anyone for a Hugh escort.

Pat is walking me home. Yeah... Meet me in the kitchen in the morning. 8. Promise deets.

River hit send at the same time Patrick's mouth crashed against her own. Her phone almost dropped to the cobblestones before her nerveless fingers dropped it into her open crossbody. And oh, God, he tasted delectable.

Patrick broke the kiss, presumably to breathe. His teeth nipped her bottom lip before his tongue followed in a soothing caress. They were in public, leaning against a pub's cold stone, and River couldn't have cared less. Thank God Pat still possessed a brain cell. He pulled his phone out to call his guard to ask that he let Peter, the girls' guard for the evening, know that he was to stay at Murphy's with Rowan.

"Let's go, babe." He licked into her mouth in an almost desperate frenzy. River was half a second from wrapping her legs around his waist— public bedamned. "Christ. No. Not here," he moaned into her ear. "We've got to get out of here. Now." Grabbing her with one hand, he raised the other for a taxi.

A compact, four-door silver Ford with a yellow and blue Taxi sign on its roof pulled to the curb in front of them. Patrick's guard, whom River hadn't met yet, climbed in the front, and she and Pat tumbled in the back, neither willing to let go of the other.

~

THIS WAS HAPPENING. This. Was. Happening— now. Holy shit, River was taking him home. *Calm the fuck down, Patrick.* He couldn't stop glancing at her profile. She wasn't looking at him anymore. Maybe she regretted asking.

"River." He waited until she met his eyes. Christ, she was beautiful. The smokey ring around her cat eyes enhanced the green in the hazel. She was biting her lip. Anticipation or regret? Leaning close to her ear, he spoke low, hoping his words wouldn't carry to the two men sitting in front. "We don't have to do anything. I will walk you to your door. We can set up a time to meet, and I will go home." When she only watched him, her eyes slowly blinking, her teeth still worrying her bottom lip, his own doubts began to bubble up his throat.

Finally, she leaned toward him, her mouth at his ear, and said, "What if I want to do *something*?" River followed that bomb with a lick to the shell of his ear. Hot, wet torture.

Patrick barely swallowed his groan. Every place on his body that had held even a particle of softness hardened— especially the mindless beast between his legs. He could not believe she'd done that when they weren't alone. Christ, he wanted her to do it again. He also wanted to give her a taste of her own medicine.

In a normal voice, he asked, "You never said whether Mrs. Adamson is married." When River opened her mouth to reply, Patrick slipped his hand between her legs, putting slight pressure on her jean-clad core, causing her to inhale sharply. His guard instantly twisted in his seat to make sure there wasn't a problem, noticed Pat's smirk, and shook his head slightly before turning forward.

"I'm sorry, babe. What did you say?"

Shooting him a 'you're going to pay for that,' look, River attempting to answer again. Patrick increased the pressure and made sure to move his palm just that smallest bit over her most sensitive spot. She coughed, tried to move his hand, and even elbowed his side. He only smiled. Paybacks.

Squirming in her seat, River tried again. "Divorced. I... Ahh," she gasped, shooting him a death stare, but her hips were beginning to move against his hand. "I don't believe it was ami-ahh-cable."

The guard spoke slightly louder than necessary to the taxi driver. "The house on the corner." Patrick heard River mumble a *thank you, Jesus*. After one last squeeze, Patrick released his grip. Her gasp this time seemed less like relief and more like regret.

Patrick paid the driver before exiting the car. He helped River out his side, keeping hold of her hand. His guard, Sim, told Patrick that he was going to check in with the house guard on duty tonight and let him know Peter was bringing Rowan home later. That settled, River used her phone app to unlock the front door.

The red-brick Georgian townhouse on North Great George's Street was all of two centuries old, solemnity on the outside and all bright and airy on the inside. "Wow."

"I know, right?" River grinned in answer. "The house is a stunner. I'll give you a tour during the day sometime. The original architectural designs throughout the house have been preserved with much love and care. Which they deserved. Homes built like this one are true works of art. It used to be all about the details," she sighed.

Patrick watched River look passionately about the house as she led him across the spacious foyer. She loved everything about design— and he loved everything about her.

She stopped at the entrance to a hallway. Even in the dim light, Patrick could see her cheeks pinken. "Would you like to see my room?" Her question had his body picking up right where it had left off in the taxi ride. Hard.

"I would. Yes." She took his hand this time, leading him through a maze of hardwood floors and priceless art. When her hand finally landed on a copper doorknob, Patrick placed his on top, stopping her from turning it.

At her questioning look, Patrick had to make a decision. He could let this happen, or he could make his feelings known and see if it still happened. He touched her face, turning her eyes to his. "Would you give me a minute to tell you something?" Eyes wide, she nodded. "If... if we do this, River, you need to know that it isn't just sex.

"It never was just sex with you. If we do this," he repeated, "I need a commitment from you because I plan on giving you one. So, if you aren't ready for that yet, which I would understand and respect, I would want to wait until you *are* sure.

"I would wait forever for you, River, but you have to understand, once you take me into your life— your body —it *has* to be a forever thing."

RIVER WAS STUNNED. This was not the same Pat she'd known these many months. This was an older, wiser version. A man, and one who no longer ran from feelings! She was equal parts elated and scared of trusting him again... trusting herself. If her sisters, and especially Nan, had warned her away from him, the decision would have been easy. It would be an unequivocal no.

But they believed in Patrick. River wanted to believe in this new Patrick too. Her heart was beating louder than the bodhrán player at Murphy's. This was it, then. She'd felt all along, even in the midst of her crushing hurt, that she and Patrick O'Faolain weren't simply an exception. They were the rule.

"I never stopped loving you, Patrick. Even when—" River hesitated.

"I hurt you. Badly." Patrick finished.

Air whooshed out of her lungs. He understood. He'd *heard* what she'd written. But... yes, there was still a *but*. River closed her eyes and leaned her head against the door. The day, or night, of reckoning, had come faster than she'd anticipated. She wanted— desperately —to make the right choice.

Was there a choice, though? Or only an answer.

Raising her head up, River looked at Patrick. She reached up, brushing his shaggy bangs from covering one of his eyes. Now, his twin amber gaze watched her. He was so still. River felt he was preparing himself for rejection. She knew Patrick. Perhaps better than anyone else. He wanted to believe in redemption. In changing the story. In happily-ever-afters. He just didn't believe he was worthy. Not deep down where his mother had destroyed a young boy's self-esteem.

He *was* worthy. Patrick was worth every— damn —thing.

"Mr. O'Faolain, I agree to your terms. I accept your commitment and give you my own." River laughed at his shout of triumph, which would probably have the guards running, but she felt only joy as he scooped her up, hugging her close to his heart. He pressed his face against her neck. Stunned, she felt hot tears against her skin.

"Pat? What...?"

"Thank you, River. You've made me so happy. I don't deserve your forgiveness, but... thank you for it."

"Everyone deserves love and forgiveness. That includes you, Pat. I love you."

Hugging her even tighter, he whispered, "I love you too."

"Will you take me to bed, then?" Twisting the knob at her back, they practically fell through the doorway.

Picking her up, he strode to the bed, tossing her in the middle before jumping in after. Straddling her legs, he grabbed her hands and stretched them above her head. "Oh, I'll take you to bed, then, love," Patrick mimicked her slight brogue. "I'll take you in the shower, on the floor, and against the wall." The last was breathed against her mouth before he nipped her lower lip, one of his favorite things, and at her gasp, his tongue found her own.

This kiss felt different. Slow, methodical, thorough. He touched every part of her body with that one kiss. She felt cherished, loved, and full of hope.

Patrick paused from ravishing her mouth to ask, "Will you come to my apartment tomorrow? I have something for you." Before she could reply, his mouth was fused to hers again. When he left her mouth for her neck, he asked again.

"I will," River answered with a moan.

That was the end of all conversation for the evening.

Commitment felt really, *really* good.

30

Sam loved the cool weather. It made it so easy to keep his thin leather gloves on. Fingerprints in his line of work were a no-no. His line of work, he chuckled. If revenge wasn't considered a job, it should be.

Pushing the glass door open to exit the antique shop— thrift store would be more accurate— was gratifying. Sam held an old wooden photo album under his arm. What a perfect 'Remember Me?' gift to River Byrne. He wouldn't be able to watch her open the present, but his imagination was more than enough.

The pictures weren't even the best part of the gift... Surprise!

Sam knew he was poking the bear, but he couldn't help himself. Life in Dublin with no outlets was slowly draining his creativity. This small token would tide him over while he practiced and practiced... and practiced some more. Boom.

31

———————

Waking up next to Patrick felt like a dream. River had been so afraid that being intimate with Patrick again would trigger memories of him and that woman from New Year's. It had... and maybe it would for weeks, months, or years. It might not ever happen again. All she knew for sure was that she would fight for their love. Her parents had still been very much in love when they died. However, River wasn't naïve enough to believe their relationship had been twenty-plus years of never-ending rainbows. Both her mother and Nan had taught her and her sisters that any relationship took a lot of love and double the work.

River propped herself up on her arm to get a better look at a sleeping Pat. His tousled white hair covered half his face, as usual, with the barest hint of stubble texturing his chin. A beard grower, Patrick O'Faolain, was not, she smirked. She needed to remember to tease him.

River let her eyes slide over his high cheekbones and chiseled jawline down his neck toward her real obsession. Damn, but Patrick had an amazing chest and abs. His golden skin, so much darker than her own— of course, cream was darker— had a sprinkling of white hair. The trail on his stomach was thicker, not much, but enough she didn't need a compass to lead her to the... really, *really* good bits.

When the sheet draped across his groin started to shift, River's eyes jumped to Patrick's. He'd obviously been awake while she'd been admiring him. Heat flared in her cheeks, but she ended up laughing. "You're such a shithead, Pat."

"You like what you see, baby?" All cheese this morning, obviously. Yanking the sheet off to reveal the thick erection previously camping under the covers, he invited her to climb aboard the 'Pat Express.' "No worries, Riv. The name has nothing to do with performance."

Grinning, he grabbed River around the waist, lifting her body until she straddled his hips. "Tell me all the things you like most about my body. Spare no adjectives."

River was thrilled with Patrick's playfulness. Previously, they'd loved to tease, but as platonic friends. Naked and in bed teasing was a side of Pat she'd never experienced. Deciding to do a little teasing of her own, River pretended to ponder her options.

"Hmm, perhaps I'll start with your eyes." She leaned down, her mouth almost grazing the lashes of his right eye. "You have lovely eyes, Patrick. Have I ever told you?"

Huffing out a laugh, he told her, "I don't recall. Tell me all about them."

She placed delicate kisses around each eye, the bridge of his nose, his forehead, and cheeks while describing their beauty. "They look brown most of the time. Not an ordinary brown, not dark, more caramel, and when the light hits them just right, they glow like amber." She placed a kiss on the side of his mouth, barely touching his lips with her own. She traced the shape with tiny licks from the tip of her tongue. "Have I told you the thoughts your mouth conjures?"

Oh, ho, Patrick was breathing a bit heavier. "What thoughts?" he growled. It seemed Patrick's humor had left the building.

Still tracing their shape, River admitted, "I've had very dirty dreams about your mouth." She nipped his bottom lip, causing him to swallow a moan, but his mouth parted oh so slightly. "Your mouth on mine. Your mouth on my breasts. Your mouth at my core. Yes, I admitted, your mouth is wicked."

River was thoroughly enjoying her attempt at verse— 'An Ode to Pat.'

Patrick's hands gripped River's hips, pressing her firmly against him. His hips moved just that slightest bit.

Never breaching his lips, River ran her tongue down his neck, collar bones, and the sternum between his developed pecs before flicking his nipples, nibbling, and sucking his chest.

"River," Patrick warned.

All innocence, River teased, "Oh right. I'm supposed to be describing your attributes, not tasting them. Let's see, I've always admired the golden sheen of your skin. Your chest is smooth and firm. I dream about sucking on it until I leave love bites. Purple would mar the gold, but every time you looked in the mirror, you would know that it was my mouth that had marked you."

Patrick's hip thrusts were becoming harder, more deliberate. River tutted in admonishment, "Now, now, Pat. Settle yourself. I'm only partway through my 'Admiration of Pat' tour."

"Finish," he growled.

Hiding a smile, River licked and sucked her way down his abdomen, causing his muscles to spasm and contract. She used both hands to touch and caress his stomach, sides, and thighs in tandem with her mouth. Patrick was writhing, fisting the bedding, and bracing his feet against the footboard.

Creating a vacuum with her mouth, she left a mark on his

lower stomach next to his delicious alabaster trail. "Your abs... I could play in the ridges for hours."

Patrick fisted her hair then, forcing her to look into his face. "I can't take much more. I'm warning you now."

"But, baby, I haven't even gotten to one of my favorite parts," River murmured as she moved lower, letting her hot breath puff against his engorged skin. "I've fantasized about taking you down my throat again. A million times at night while I'm in bed. I've gotten myself off just from the thought," she whispered, her lips barely touching his length. "I've wondered," River paused to lick a drop of precum off his head as her hand fisted his length, "if I'm tall enough to reach between your legs, if you're between mine." River looked directly into his bright, burning eyes before sliding him slowly into her mouth.

River had yet to get into a rhythm before Patrick whipped forward and grabbed her body. He held her over his sex before pressing in. A curse passed his lips on a moan. "No more teasing. No more, baby. I'm about to explode, and it's going to be inside you."

Patrick looked fierce as he used his strength to lift her body up and down, sliding and plunging deep. She cupped her breasts, tweaking her nipples at Patrick's urging. He loved watching her pleasure herself, and like a preening cat, River loved Pat watching.

Only an hour had passed since Patrick had left, and River's body still tingled. They had both experienced near-death orgasms, and after fifteen minutes of breath-catching, they showered together— water conservation always a consideration —before they kissed their way to the front door, where Patrick practically fell onto the sidewalk before catching a taxi to his apartment. Soon to be *their* apartment. Crazy. She'd better call Nan today and fess up. Nan had a vested interest in the status of her new relationship with Patrick. Those two had definitely bonded over chores, crocheting, and whiskey.

Fiddling with a Hexclad frying pan— Jesus, these pans were legit— and hello... Gordon Ramsay approved— River wondered for the hundredth time where in the hell her sister was? They were supposed to meet this morning. River texted her fifteen minutes ago, and still no reply. She'd already knocked on her bedroom door with no results. She found a guard outside, and he told her that Rowan had left the house an hour ago.

River's phone pinged. Finally.

Sorry! I had a ton of errands to run today, and I left early, but I want ALL the details over lunch. We're meeting Jo and Rave at Queen of Tarts—noon.

Np. Patrick asked me to stop by his flat this morning anyway. See you at QoT. (bring mail from Triskelion if you stop by there), leaving for Scotland tomorrow-take it with me).

One hour. One flipping hour and River felt Patrick's absence— deeply. They were back together— it didn't seem real yet. They were back, but they were both different... their relationship was different. Where the banter had always been easy between them, it was effortless now.

Patrick had begun a journey of healing. It was brave and probably scary as hell, but he'd done it. Pat would have had to face a lot of ugly truths and buried fears. They made a pact last night to talk things through. To never let an argument come between them. To never walk away. Ever.

Byrnes kept their promises.

O'Faolains had better.

Through Patrick's security camera, he saw River, her long black hair in an intricate twist that showed off her delicate throat. She wore some sort of long, ropey sweater dress thing and boots. Her cat eyes playfully winked at the camera.

Oh, fuck. This was it. Patrick's hands hadn't stopped shaking since he'd left River's house and climbed the stairs to his apartment. They shook worse after opening his safe. He was wearing a suit. Christ, she'd know something was up right away. Tearing off the wool blazer, he tossed it over the closest chair, straightened the cuffs of his black button-up, rubbed his palms over the front of his wool trousers, and pulled the door open to reveal, hopefully, the woman who would become his fiancé today.

She was about to say something, but Patrick had his mouth slanted over hers before a word crossed her lips. Slowly moving into the apartment, he kicked the door shut behind them. He didn't stop kissing her until they reached the master.

In one quick pull, he took the cozy dress off her body and flung it to the floor. Boots, wool socks, panties, and bra were next. He was breathing heavily. River was breathing heavily.

Yeah, it was *not* the finesse Patrick had envisioned. He had planned on going down on one knee in the middle of their new kitchen and asking for her hand. Romantic. Her smile detoured him, damn it! He sure as hell wasn't stopping now, though.

His attire went the way of River's.

"I take it you missed me," River teased as he tossed her on the bed.

River watched as a very naked Patrick placed first one knee and then the other on the bed. She would almost call his countenance grim, except his lower anatomy screamed elation. Pat never took his eyes off her while he slowly started to stroke his sex. Perhaps grim wasn't the right word. Determined? Hungry? River could feel her core start to pulse in time with his strokes. Her knees, oh so slightly, parted. Waiting.

"I *did* miss you, Riv." Patrick's voice was low, even. River didn't think he was talking about the hours that had passed since he'd left her bed this morning. "You're finally here. In *our* apartment. In *our* bed. I've dreamed of hundreds of things I've wanted to do to you once I got you here." He paused, looking at her body like he truly couldn't decide where to start.

"Get on your knees, River. I'll start there. You can look at the picture you gave me while I take you."

River felt close to climaxing already. Pushing up so she was kneeling in front of Patrick, she pulled his head down to swipe her tongue inside his mouth— once, twice— before she obeyed and turned to look at the painting, positioning her body on hands and knees.

"Jesus, babe. I wish you could see what I see right now. Your thighs are already wet. You want me inside you so bad."

River yelped as Patrick squeezed her bottom, almost painfully rough. Not rough enough. "I need you in me, Pat. Now," she begged.

She felt his shaft sliding between her legs and lowered her arms even more, pushing her ass higher. An offering.

"This is going to be hard and fast. After is for gentle."

"After?" Her answer was Patrick grabbing her hips and fully seating himself. They both groaned at the fullness, the tight, hot friction. Patrick pistoned faster and harder until, "Oh God, Patrick. Right there, baby!"

Patrick groaned. River felt his sex swell further, setting her channel to pulsing, squeezing. "God," she whimpered. It felt so good. Her orgasm forced Patrick's own. He shouted, thrusting deep once more before his body stilled.

River was boneless, her face smooshed into the bedding. Zero fucks were given for her hair and makeup. Patrick laid his back gently over hers, curling his arm around her middle and pulling them both sideways. He wrapped his big body around her own and pulled her tight to his chest.

River sighed. She was so content she could cry from the beauty of it. "I love you, Patrick."

He kissed her neck and bare shoulder before replying. "You are everything to me."

"Is this why you wanted me to drop by this morning? And just so you know, if it was, I'm totally okay with it." River was rubbing his arm when she felt him stiffen at her words. That made her instantly wary. "What's wrong?"

"Nothing's wrong. I swear, but this," he squeezed her breast, "was not why I asked you here, but I'm not mad about bonus sex either."

River could tell he was smiling from the teasing note in his voice, so she dropped from a Code Red to Yellow. "Why then? Did you get me a prezzie? You know I love them," she laughed.

"I'm aware, Miss Byrne. You and your sisters can sniff out anything with the smallest bow." He slid from her body... and the bed. "I do have something for you. Hang on a sec, and I'll grab it."

Interest piqued, River scooted against the headboard, pulling the sheet over her breasts. Patrick was trying to play it casual, but his body language was anything but. He was nervous. This 'something' was important.

River tracked Patrick's naked ass until he stepped into his, no, *their* colossal closet. He reappeared less than a second later, and oh wow, the front view was fun to watch as well.

"If you keep staring at me like that, babe, you'll distract me again."

River smiled and shrugged. Letting the sheet dip enough to

show a hint of nipple, she asked, "What exactly will happen if I distract you?" She laughed when he briefly closed his eyes and moaned.

Undeterred, Patrick asked her if she could stand by the bed. *What in the hell?* She complied... naked. At least Pat was nak— He was kneeling. "Oh my God," she breathed aloud.

River's heart might give out. It was pounding in her chest as she and Patrick looked at one another. "Shit, sorry, Riv. Would you grab the sheet or something to cover up? Your body is distracting, and I need to concentrate." Holy shit, Patrick was nervous and blushing. Why, oh why, could this not have been recorded for posterity? Oh, right— they were naked. River snatched Pat's button-up off the floor since it was closest and practically tore the fine material when she punched her arms through the sleeves.

Decent now, or decent enough, she stood back in front of the still naked and kneeling Patrick. He took her left hand in his slightly shaking one. Truth— hers were shaking too.

Patrick cleared his throat. "River," another throat clearing, "Damn it. This is *not* how I pictured this going."

River used her other hand to sandwich his hand. "Whatever you're wanting to say, and however you say it, will be perfect to my ears, Pat."

Briefly touching his forehead with their joined hands, he visibly got his bearings. "You're right. Love doesn't need perfection, but... you've given me everything by giving me a second chance, and I will always strive for perfection, even if it only appears perfect to *you*.

"There will never be anyone for me but you. It was the biggest, but simplest, truth to understand." River felt faint, and her legs were shaky as Patrick raised his free hand, unfurled his fingers, and presented— a ring. Not *My Precious*, but THE RING.

PATRICK OPENED the palm that had been gripping River's engagement ring so tight its grooves were imprinted in his skin. She wasn't running, and Patrick knew she was an extremely intelligent person, so she had to have guessed where all this was going.

Deep breath, Pat. "I won't go on and on about my love and devotion to you, but I could. I won't tell you that you saved me, but you did. I won't tell you that I will devote my life to your happiness, but I will.

"River Aster Byrne, will you marry me?"

River didn't answer right away. She knelt before him, her eyes glassy with unshed tears, a wobbly smile gracing her lips. She hadn't said yes yet, though. Concerning.

"Patrick Brandon O'Faolain." River's voice wobbled over his middle name, which made Patrick want to tear up— dang it, Nan. "I won't tell you that I can't breathe unless you're by my side, but I don't. I won't tell you that I see your face for every important occasion I will ever have for the rest of my life, but you're there. I won't tell you that you are the only man I will ever love, but you are.

"I will, most happily, marry you."

Patrick almost passed out in relief. With an unsteady hand, he slipped the ring on River's finger and explained why he'd chosen it. "The blue sapphire because it's your favorite color. The black titanium band represents your inner rebel, which I hope is always in you. No diamonds... because nothing could ever outshine your beauty." Gently kissing River's lips, he made her a promise.

"Forever, Riv. You and me."

"Forever, Pat. You and me." And then, because she was... River, "You just proposed to me in the most romantic way imaginable— naked. Not really a story we can tell our children," she snorted gleefully.

Pat looked down. Yep, swinging dick, party of one. There was nothing to do about it now, but... take advantage of his fiancé. Slowly, Patrick started unbuttoning his shirt, currently covering River's body. "That shirt was custom-made for me. Perhaps we should get it off you now so it isn't ruined."

"Oh goodness," River feigned distress. "I would feel terrible if I stained it. After all, it was neatly *wadded* up in a pile on the floor when I found it." Shrugging out of the shirt, River was now as naked as he was. "Whatever will we do now?" She smirked and pretended to think it over.

Patrick grabbed River around her waist and pulled her close until his mouth feathered hers. "I'm going to make love to the woman who just agreed to be my wife."

32

After she and Patrick celebrated their engagement— naked —River walked into Queen of Tarts fifteen minutes late and received a heaping helping of ribbing from her sisters and Jo.

"Back in the saddle, I see," Jo teased as River sat down.

"Sorry, guys," River was flushed with her secret. The sapphire in the room was currently hidden under her jacket, which was strategically draped over her left forearm. She couldn't decide whether she should just come out and tell them or wait to see if they noticed the ring.

It turns out she needn't have stressed. "Oh my God!" Raven literary yelled, drawing all eyes to their table before she jumped out of her chair— there was no *actual* jumping. Her very pregnant sister pushed out of her chair, knocking it over in the process so that she could pounce on River's hand. "When? And why didn't you call us immediately?"

At this point, 'spectacle' would have been a kind description. Thomas and the two other bodyguards on duty surrounded their table, backs to the women as they scanned the surroundings. Rowen was out of her chair hovering over River's head, while Jo was elbowing Thomas out of the way to squeeze up to River's free side.

River laughed. Spectacle or not, she was too elated to care. "I didn't call because it only happened a couple of hours ago, and—" River cut off her sisters' rebukes, "—I didn't call you then because I knew I was meeting you for lunch."

Raven was crying. *Oh, Baby O, let up on the hormone surges, big guy.* "Riv, this is... a sapphire... your favorite color... you took him back... you said yes. You're happy?" By this point, Raven had clasped River's hand against her 'generous' breast, a look of worry and hope.

"Mr. MacGregor," Jo interjected, "everything is fine here if you would like to return to your table." Jo wasn't looking at 'Mr. MacGregor,' but River was. He stared at Jo for what seemed like minutes, jaw clenched. He was *not* happy, but he did finally—stiffly —leave. Something had happened there, and if Jo thought, for one flipping second, that they wouldn't demand answers, she'd lost her mind.

Returning her attention back to Raven, she admitted, "It is my favorite color. I did take him back, and I absolutely, with zero hesitation, said yes." River couldn't help the desperately euphoric smile on her face.

After the three women gave River hugs and kisses and best wishes, they resumed their seats— and the interrogation began.

"How many times did you have sex since last night and this morning?" Jo.

"If we don't call Nan in the next thirty minutes, we'll be in big trouble." Rowan.

"Tell us every detail of the proposal. Was it so romantic?" Raven.

River felt her chest and neck heat to match her cheeks, but with these women, one had to be *all* in. River waited to answer until the waitress set down... the entire menu. "I was hungry," Raven admitted sheepishly.

"You have to feed Baby O, Rave," River reassured. "So, in answer to your questions. Jo, too many times to count. Row, I'd planned on meeting Nan as soon as we're done here— we can all go. Rave, it was incredibly romantic, but we were naked."

Jo choked on her burger, and Rowan laughed out loud— more attention from the other patrons, yay. Raven was wide-eyed and slack-jawed. "You lie," she insisted.

"No lie. Naked. He *was* on one knee. So... nakedly romantic?"

"This is just... oh my God." Raven waved her hands all over like she'd been working with Pat Sajak on *Wheel of Fortune*. "Bran proposed to me when we were... naked too."

"O'Faolains!" Jo rubbed her temples as though the three adult O's were too much for her psyche. River was dying inside, but she totally agreed. However, a family inclination toward nude proposals sounded like glorious blackmail. Hmm, what would Patrick be willing to do to keep this information from his grandma?

"Wow. You two won't be telling your children your proposal stories in the future," Rowan shook her head, grinning.

"Auntie Jo will, though!"

Raven gasped, "Don't you f-ing dare, Josephine O'Connor!"

"We'll see in eighteen years or so, won't we? Now everyone inhale this spread. We have granny minds to blow!" Jo smiled, attempting to keep the side glance she sent Thomas undetected.

AFTER LUNCH, they decided to head straight to Nan's and surprise her with the news. River tried to imagine how she would react. Definitely thrilled. She'd texted Patrick to meet them at Nan's apartment. River wanted to go all out with the news, plus they could Facetime Matilda too.

Minutes into the visit, Nan and Matilda were crying and talking over each other, and even Devlen was thrilled to learn of her and Patrick's engagement. Both grandmas were knee-deep in wedding planning— no input from the engaged couple was necessary. They stayed for a couple hours. They were saying their goodbyes and about to stand when Patrick asked everyone to stay seated for another minute. He and Nan exchanged knowing glances. What was this about? Jo and the sisters looked equally flummoxed.

Nan and Patrick disappeared into her bedroom, coming out a moment later with a wrapped present and an envelope. The same style of envelope as her letters. Patrick handed Raven the package. She took it gently, a bemused look on her face. "I wasn't here for the baby shower to give this to you. Nan's been keeping it for me."

Patrick was blushing. Oh my. River might have fallen even more in love with him at that moment.

Everyone in the room leaned toward Raven as she unwrapped the gift, except for Patrick, who backed up a few paces. River stretched her hand toward him. "Come stand by me, Pat." He relaxed when River wrapped her hand through his.

Raven took the top off the box, peeled back the tissue, and pulled out... every woman there, except Nan, gasped at the crocheted baby blanket. It was soft and green. Lovely and thoughtful. Raven was crying.

Raven tried to scooch off the couch. Whether to get a better look at the blanket or hug Patrick was anyone's guess. Patrick walked to Raven, placing a hand on her shoulder. "Stay sitting, Rave. Here," he took the box off her lap and laid the small blanket over her lap. "It's pretty small, and one of the sides is wobbly," he mumbled something about the stitch count being off. "It's a lemon peel stitch. Umm... good for baby blankets."

"I love this, Pat. What a beautiful blanket. I can't wait to snuggle Baby O in it."

Jo handed Raven the hundredth tissue of the day to blot her ever-present tears.

Patrick looked at Nan desperately. River just realized why Patrick was so out of sorts. Wobbly... stitch count off... lemon peel... River recalled last night, Patrick mentioned her sweater was a fisherman's rib stitch. "Oh my God, Pat! Did you *make* the blanket?"

Nan was the one to answer the question. "Well, of course, he did. He barely needed but a few hours of instruction." Nan was obviously proud of her student. "Patrick is quite a skilled crocheter. He even picked out the yarn by himself from the craft store in Boyle."

"One hundred percent cotton," Pat quietly added.

Raven stuck her hand out to Jo and Rowan. "Get me up." Once she was vertical, she crushed Patrick in a huge hug, her behind stuck out at an exaggerated angle due to her belly, and the blanket squished between them. "I loved it before, but, oh Patrick... this... I will cherish it always. And... oh, Bran... he'll cry over this. It'll mean so much." Raven was patting Pat's back while she wet the front of his shirt.

River doubted Bran would break down quite like his wife currently was, but who knew, because damn it, River was sniffling her own tears. Rowan and Jo's eyes even looked glassy.

"Ok, Raven, my love, let the boy go," Nan chuckled. "Patrick has something else." Nan handed the envelope to Patrick, who only said, "Oh right," like he'd forgotten about it.

He handed the heavy, white envelope to River, her eyes widening in surprise. "It's for you and your sisters, babe." Nan took Jo's hand, tears sparkling in her grandma's lashes. Devlen stood close to her Nan's free side. Rowan and Raven moved next to River.

River carefully slid her finger under the flap, loosening the bit of glue before pulling out a sheaf of tri-folded paper. Unfolding things, the girls put their heads together and read until River's hands shook enough that Rowan had to take over holding them.

They all looked at Patrick, who was grinning. Rowan asked, "Pat, did you buy Nan's house?"

"And put it in our names?" River needed clarification. Raven was so shocked her tears never stopped from the blanket reveal.

"I'll be moving in with Devlen," Nan smiled at the man standing to her left, "but I hated to give up my home where I'd raised my family. Patrick and I discussed it at some length, and he wanted it to stay with the Byrne family as well, and though he insisted on paying a ridiculously overpriced sum, I agreed."

"I had planned on asking you three if you would want the house, but in your letter, Riv," he stopped to smile at her before continuing, "you mentioned wanting to talk with your sisters and see if you all could afford it. So," Patrick shrugged, "I just went ahead and did it."

They rushed Patrick as one, laughing and hugging and loving him for the generous gift. He hugged them all and gave River a soft kiss and an *I love you* before telling them all it was time to head to the O Building. Hugh and Bran were apparently blowing up his phone since someone, Raven most likely, told her husband about the engagement.

Nan hugged everyone once more as they filed out of the apartment, including MacGregor, who wore a look of pain, but everyone knew he secretly loved her hugs.

They were outside Nan's, waiting for their cars to be

brought around. Noting Jo's continued stiffness around her personal guard, River moved closer to her friend.

Making sure no one could overhear, River whispered to Jo, "We leave for Inverness tomorrow, and I *do* expect an explanation for what's going on between you and Honey Bunny." Using MacGregor's former nickname brought a brief, very brief smile to Jo's mouth.

"No need to wait until tomorrow," Jo whispered back. "There is nothing going on with Mr. MacGregor. We had a disagreement. It's now tense. I asked to switch guards with one of yours. He refused."

"I see." River paused and then added, "Actually, Jo, I don't see. That explanation might work on a stranger, but we aren't strangers, are we?"

Jo's shoulders sagged. "I'll talk to you tomorrow." Her words were grim. Her face was grimm*er*. River clasped her hand briefly, giving it a squeeze. Before she could say anything else, the man of the hour, or more accurately, the man of the scowl, crowded Jo from the front.

"What is wrong?" MacGregor grumbled, leaning his hulking mass low enough to put his face on a level with Jo's. Jo wouldn't meet his eyes, which River could tell bothered the guard tremendously.

"We were discussing when we needed to be at the airport in the morning." River could tell Jo was on the verge of tears and would die of embarrassment if she cried in front of everyone. River caught Rowen's eye, who joined them. "We also were finalizing Jo moving in with Row when we get home from Inverness next week. She's taking over my suite since I'm moving into Patrick's flat."

Speaking of her favorite O'Faolain, her future husband slid his arm around her waist, kissing her neck as he did so. "Our flat, Riv. Not mine. Ours."

"Ours." River agreed. "Jo and I were just discussing how she was going to take over my suite at Mrs. Adamson's when we get back from Scotland."

Jo's eyes were huge. She kept nodding even though we had been talking about no such thing. If things were this bad between Jo and her personal guard, then she needed to have another woman around to talk to.

"Good news, Jo. The bed is *super* comfy," Patrick smirked. River smiled at him. He probably didn't know it, but he cut the tension in half.

Rowan, not slow to pick up on the weird tension, glared at Patrick. "Jesus, Patrick," she rolled her eyes, but they were twinkling in amusement. "I'm so happy to not be alone in that big house, Jo. Thanks for not leaving me hanging. Like River," she added with a wink and smile.

Everyone chuckled less awkwardly this time. River gave a soft pinch to Patrick's side so he wouldn't ask any questions, and bless him, he was one step ahead. "Hanging my ass! You, Raven, River, and Jo are interchangeable with each other, four peas in a pod." Jo's cheeks pinkened, Patrick's words pleasing her. "You'll be just as happy living with Jo as you were with the other two. But seriously, I don't care what living arrangements you end up with as long as no one is alone. I'm only pissed Dad, Bran and I have a meeting with the distillery people next week, and I can't go to Inverness with my fiancé."

Raven overheard part of Pat's rant and, laughing, asked, "Holy cow, Patrick, how many times are we going to have to endure hearing fiancé come out of your mouth?"

"Until we're married, and then I'll say, wife. Tell me, Raven, how many times, in the past five minutes we've been waiting for the cars, have you and my brother texted each other."

Raven's face blazed red.

"Exactly."

Everyone laughed at her look of chagrin. "Hey, Riv," Rowan got her attention while they were still laughing at Patrick and Raven's banter, "I'm not going to be able to meet you guys. I know we're celebrating your engagement at the O Building, but I have a huge design consult I'm working on. I meet the clients Monday, and I'm unhappy with some of my choices and want to spend some quiet time looking back over the initial notes."

Rowan's words were everything sensical, but her eyes were begging River to excuse her from the impromptu party— from being near Hugh. It crushed River that her sister and Jo were struggling with love when she and Patrick were in the best of places.

Knowing her youngest sister was hurting, River reassured Rowan with a nonchalance she didn't feel. "Oh my God, Row! I totally forgot you were meeting the Smythes so soon. I thought your design was flawless, but I know what a perfectionist you are. No worries about tonight, for heaven's sake. I feel like we've already celebrated for hours already." Rowan's entire body relaxed. Her relief was evident.

"Thomas, Row has to go back to the Adamson house. Can someone go with her?"

"Yes," Thomas agreed.

Thomas MacGregor and Hugh O'Faolain *had* to be related. Some way. Somehow.

As the cars arrived, Rowan handed a woven tote to River. "I forgot, Riv, I brought your mail from Triskelion."

"Perfect, thanks. I'll bring it with me tomorrow. And fingers crossed, I land some exclusive designs from the hermit furniture designer."

~

"Your brother may not have cried as Raven predicted, but I swear when he held the baby blanket, he was blinking awfully fierce," River noted, a smile infusing her words.

"If my bruised ribs are anything to go by, Bran did like the 'it's the thought that counts' gift." Patrick was relieved the blanket was received well. He'd been ridiculously nervous about giving it to them.

"Enough about crocheting projects, babe. Have I told you today how beautiful you are?" They'd just come up to their apartment. Everyone else had gone home or retired to their own floors. His dad had retired quite some time ago. He didn't offer any excuses, just tossed back the rest of his Macallan 18, shook Pat's hand, gave River a brief hug, told them congratulations, and got in the elevator. He was probably on hour two into one of his brutal workouts, attempting to put a certain woman out of his mind. Good luck with that.

As Patrick paused to turn on the alarm system, River leaned into his side and placed a kiss against his throat. She whispered against his skin, sending heat straight to his groin. "Have I told you today how addicted I am to you?"

"Tell me more, baby." Patrick had already maneuvered River's back against the front door and pulled her legs up to wrap around his waist.

With Patrick's lips gently kissing and sucking River's neck, she breathlessly continued. "When we were sitting by each other at the bar downstairs tonight, you placed your hand on my thigh." Patrick took her mouth then. It was desperate and frenzied and had them groaning at each sweep of the other's tongue.

Breaking the kiss, River continued. "All I could focus on—what I wanted desperately —was for your fingers to move closer, dip deeper between my legs. For your thumb to accidentally brush my center. I was so turned on by the thought that I could feel myself grow wet." She nipped his bottom lip, licking across the seam.

"Christ, River." Patrick was so turned on he would swear his vision was flickering. Grabbing her ass with both hands, Patrick ground his erection against her center, loving the sound of her moans inside his mouth. "Is this what you want, River?"

"God, yes. Now, Pat, I can't wait."

Patrick used one hand to release the metal button on his jeans and unzipped. Pleased River had changed into a dress earlier, he had to do nothing more than bunch her skirt and pull her panties to the side before he was sliding into her body. "Fuck, baby. You *are* wet for me. So hot and tight."

"Oh, that's it," River panted. "Harder... that's... right there!"

Patrick continued to slam into her until he felt her body stiffen; a keening noise escaped her lips as her body spasmed around him, milking his body until he tipped over the edge. Resting their foreheads together, he attempted to calm his racing heart. "Holy fuck, babe. That was intense."

Before his body completely gave out on him, Patrick stepped back from the door, keeping River wrapped around him. He walked them to the bedroom, gently laying them against the mattress.

"I plan on taking your body in so many ways, and so many times you'll feel me inside you for days."

"I won't stop you," she smiled and kissed the side of his mouth. "How about we start by getting these clothes off.

33

River, Jo, and *Mr. MacGregor* were in the air. It was only an hour and a half flight to Inverness, and once there, they would rent a car. Driving to Nairn the next day was just one of the several small excursions she and Jo had planned while they were there.

She tried to relax, recalling memories from her first night staying with Patrick in *their* apartment... River sighed. Patrick really disliked that she was going away, though he'd definitely made good on his word. River felt him in every part of her body, and her lips still tingled from his almost X-rated goodbye kiss.

Unfortunately, this wasn't the fun flight she had anticipated when they'd first planned it. There was certainly *no* laughter *or* mimosas *or* Jameson Black Barrell. Jo pretending the goliath in the room— or cabin rather —was invisible... double inner eye-roll.

Not only did Thomas MacGregor look like a relative to Tom Stoltman, the Scottish strongman competitor and all-around behemoth— and yes, River and her sisters were *huge* strongman competitor fans —MacGregor was also *staring*. As in, the guard had not once taken his eyes from Jo. She knew it too if

279

her stiff shoulders, pinched lips, and the line that rivaled the Suez Canal between her brows— were any indication.

Determined to ignore the two combatants currently sharing the jet, River started to replay her and Patrick's first time using the kitchen together— spoiler, there was no cooking. Unfortunately, Jo's voice cut through her Pat Porn.

"I booked rooms at the Loch Ness Country House Hotel. It's supposed to have gorgeous views. And they have a hothouse on the property with tons of exotic flowers."

"Sounds perfect. How far is it to Nairn?" River asked.

"Oh, only about twenty min—"

Thomas cut Jo off mid-answer. "What do you mean *rooms*, lass?"

His Scottish accent must increase in tandem with his emotions because his words were barely comprehensible. Jo acted as though he hadn't spoken.

"I got the Garden Suite only because there was a last-minute cancellation. Can you believe it?" Jo gushed with excruciatingly false cheer.

Christ have mercy, Lord have mercy, River prayed. Where was her rosary when she needed it? "A garden suite sounds wonderful, Jo."

"I asked for the hotel information before we left Dublin, Josephine," MacGregor stated, speaking more Scots than English.

"Ms. O'Connor," Jo quietly reprimanded. "I sent all the accommodation information to your business email before we took off, per the agreement my father signed with your company. I believe I've done my due diligence. If you have further issues, please take them up with Mr. O'Connor."

Whoa. River was not comfortable witnessing the... hell, she didn't even know what to call the fallout between Jo and MacGregor. Catastrophic failure?

River placed her hand atop Jo's thigh in what she hoped conveyed, *I'm here.* "Jo, I love you. Thomas, I'm undecided at the moment because you've hurt Jo somehow. If something needs saying between the two of you, I suggest using this evening to your advantage. Tomorrow is work. We'll all three be together the *whole* day, and I would prefer... not to witness this... friendship implosion. I hate seeing two people I care about hurting."

Jo took a deep breath. "You're right, Riv, except there isn't anything to discuss tonight that I can't say right now. I've been overreacting *and* acting childishly." Jo looked directly at Thomas then. "I'm sorry I've been so unprofessional. I will communicate with you again and stop making your job harder. Truce?"

MacGregor opened his mouth, shut it before opening it once more, and said, "Fine." His grip on the armrests would be considered leather abuse in most parts of the world, but at least he agreed to a cease-fire.

River gave Jo a look before she changed the subject. She wasn't getting off the hook in telling River what the hell was really going on. Jo's eye-roll was her way of saying she understood.

"Tuesday, Jo, I have an appointment to meet with a local wool weaver. We have several clients who are always interested in one-of-a-kind textiles. I want to cement a working relationship with some of the weavers in the Inverness area. I thought you might also be interested."

"Definitely," Jo said, perking up— finally. "My mother will be traveling to Switzerland soon. She is managing the décor team and opening of a retreat spa in Zürich. Hand-woven textiles would be right up their alley. Mom loves adding new contacts to the O'Connor Hospitality Files."

The rest of the flight passed with making plans and combing

through Jo's own list of vendors and artisans she'd collected from her parents or past interior designers— and River finally got a Jameson Black Barrel... winning. This trip was going to be a lot more abbreviated than she and Jo had originally planned. Bran had shared with River Saturday night that Raven had not been sleeping well. She was restless and moody... moodier.

Bran really didn't want River and Jo to be away from Dublin too long. They agreed to fly home Thursday, but Jo asked her pilot to stay in Scotland, so if they needed to make a quick return, they could.

THE GARDEN SUITE *WAS* GORGEOUS. It was a large cottage completely free-standing from the hotel proper but with the same amenities. The surroundings were stunning, and once they'd unpacked their bags, she and Jo went to have a look around. River had already taken a million pictures to send to Patrick and her sisters.

The two women were walking through the hothouse, situated between the hotel and their cottage. It was warm and fragrant— the profusion of colors and scents was magnificent. It reminded River of Nan's home, *her* home now thanks to Patrick. Relaxing and earthy, a natural beauty that perfumed the air.

"Since MacGregor is patrolling the perimeter and scaring off the other guests from entering, why don't you tell me what in the hell is going on." There was a comfortable bench that River made a beeline for. Jo reluctantly followed.

Her friend took a good two minutes to situate her purse. River waited. Finally— the Josephine O'Connor dam broke. "River," she clasped their hands while her face turned red, and a sheen of tears sparkled in her gray eyes, all of which freaked River out. How bad was this going to be, FFS?

"Jo, you're still breathing, so whatever happened didn't kill you. Just tell me. Whatever's happened, we can figure something out between the two of us, surely. You're freaking me out," River pushed.

"I wish it would have killed me so I didn't have to live every moment of every day in this constant state of mortification." Jo pulled a tissue from her purse and pressed it against her eyes—blotting tears and attempting to force the rest to rethink their appearance. Another deep breath, and then the entire sordid tale spilled out.

"I know you know that MacGregor and I verbally spar. A lot." At River's nod of confirmation, Jo continued. "He's become, I don't know, one of... one of my favorite people. A confidant— a trusted friend...." Her explanation petered off after that.

"More than a friend?" River nudged.

"Yes. Well, on my part, but he would look at me sometimes or touch me in a way that... I thought or hoped, I guess, meant more... *something*. After all these months, I thought *he* felt what *I* felt." Jo dropped her chin to her chest, her cheeks blazing red. "Oh, Riv, I went to his room at The Fitzwilliam. It adjoins mine, and... and... oh God, I only wore a short, silk robe. Thomas was shirtless, fresh from a shower.

"I touched his chest. I pressed my body to his. He put his hands on my hips. I... I... Oh, Lord, how I hate remembering that moment. I raised up on my tiptoes to kiss him. My mouth was about to touch his lips. He moved me away. That's why he'd placed his hands on me. Not to further an intimacy that wasn't there to begin with but to stop me from touching him. I wish it could have stopped the burn of rejection.

"Christ, River! How will I, or rather, how *can* I ever not be embarrassed?" Jo practically wailed. "I haven't been interested in men since college, and when I finally give it another go—THIS HAPPENS!"

River was momentarily speechless because she would have bet money that Thomas MacGregor was as infatuated with Jo, as any man could be, but he'd seriously hurt Jo whether it was intentional or not. River didn't believe he would ever do that unless something else had stopped him.

"Okay, yes Jo, I agree that what happened was embarrassing — crushing even —but I just can't believe there wasn't a reason why he reacted that way. Did he say anything after? Explain?"

Jo's eyes and nose were both leaking at this point. She was a mess. Having just come off her own heartbreak, River couldn't blame her.

"He said this couldn't happen." Jo air quoted the 'this.' "He was working. I was... I was... a job, a client," she whispered the last in a painful exhalation.

No way. No way in hell did he say that! Instead of speaking her thoughts out loud, River asked instead, "Are you sure he meant it the way it sounded? He could be really, really, *really* bad at feelings and explaining them... maybe," River finished with a wince.

"He told me to go to my room and put some clothes on. He let me leave and shut the adjoining door without ever saying another word. He meant it. I'm mortified. I have feelings for a man who only ever considered me as his current *job*. A client that he'll leave the moment that asshole stalking our families is caught."

"I won't blow meaningless fluff up your butt, Jo, but I believe there was a reason for what he did. I've seen him look at you when he thinks no one is paying attention, and it certainly isn't someone calculating your safety. Bullshit! I call bullshit on that stubborn Scottish asshole."

River couldn't take the look of dejection on her friend's face a moment longer. She stood up and pulled Jo with her, wrapping her arms tight about her waist. "I love you, Jo. Raven, Row, and I will always be there for you and on your side. Whatever that jackass guard's existential crisis is, it's his problem. But in the spirit of honesty between us, I think there is more to why he reacted the way he did."

"I'm still embarrassed, but I do feel better telling someone. Thanks, Riv." Jo hugged River tight. "I just need to move on. Surely, it will get easier. Surely," she grimaced. "Just do me a favor. Help run interference. I know it sucks to babysit this debacle, but just don't let us be alone. It's worse when we're alone."

"Consider me your new tick buddy. An annoying blood sucker, but harmless for all that. Rocky Mountain Fever free, I swear," I laughed when Jo gagged.

"What a disgusting analogy, but fine. I'd appreciate you burrowing your head under my skin for the duration of the trip."

Chuckling, the two women started to make their way to the hothouse's exit. "Oh, before we have company," Jo grimaced but didn't turn red or cry— progress. "Did you and Rowan mean it about me taking over your suite at Mrs. Adamson's?"

"We did. Rowan needs another woman there to talk to, and so do you, Jo. We should have moved in together sooner. The day we get back, once I check on Raven and Baby O, I plan on moving my stuff out and to the apartment. I was hoping, if you didn't mind living there, that is, that you would consider moving your stuff in the same day."

"I love the hotel, but I am ready to live in a house again, and... I would like to have an all-access pass to a friend."

As she and Jo left the hothouse, Thomas MacGregor loomed under the arbor-vined path. It looked like he was trying to fit his giant body in a floral bedazzled Barbie House. Jo stiffened, but I'd already taken her hand and gave her a squeeze of encouragement.

"I saw you crying, Jo... Ms. O'Connor," he corrected.

Ahh, River felt slightly vindicated on her friend's behalf. This wasn't a reaction from a disinterested, *You're only a job*, man.

Jo, however, wanted a shield, and River would damn well be that safeguard. Chuckling, River shook her head in a self-deprecating way. "I gave Jo all the details of Patrick's proposal. He was extremely romantic, and Jo got choked up."

Macgregor looked unconvinced and upset when Jo wouldn't look at him. "Hey Jo," River said, "should we order in or eat at the hotel's restaurant. I checked out the dinner menu, and they have a breaded cod with all my favorite veg sides I'm dying to try."

"Let's eat at the restaurant. We can check out the bar for drinks and dessert after we eat. We aren't leaving early in the morning, so we might as well live it up tonight."

River knew why she'd picked the hotel. Less 'alone' time with a certain bodyguard to contend with.

34

Dougal Donaldson was a... character. He was five feet 'nineish' inches of arrogance, rudeness, and crudeness, and... he was also obscenely talented if the stunning pieces of furniture thrown haphazardly about his workshop/giant old barn were anything to go by.

The black-bearded pirate was surly, and that was *before* River introduced herself and said it was nice to meet him. Now, he was toeing the intolerable line. River silently thanked Hugh O'Faolain for inadvertently teaching her to weather several variations and styles of mantrum. *Foreigners didn't appreciate 'the process.' Women were a pain in every Scotsman's 'arse.' The indignity of 'plebeians' asking about his art.*

Shocking! Commence inner eyeroll.

Donaldson huffed and puffed his way the length of his shop and back again.

After Mr. Donaldson cursed River and Jo eight ways to Sunday for asking to see some of his current work, or rather, it sounded like cursing. MacGregor, who had up until this point stayed quiet and still against the heavy barn wall, said, or what

287

River thought he said... "Yer doin' me nut in, ye lavvy heided tadger."

Dougal stopped his posturing, now looking at Thomas with interest. "Oh, aye?"

"Aye."

"Well then, I'll hae ye in for a cuppa and show you me latest."

River and Jo exchanged looks, hoping the men reverted to a form of English more familiar to the women but ecstatic at being allowed in the man's inner sanctum. Whatever MacGregor *had* said to the grump must have been magic. The guard went from Petting Zoo Honey Bunny to *Aladdin's* Genie. MacGregor was her current hero.

RIVER WAS *euphoric* as they drove away from Donaldson's farm. It was the only adjective capable of describing the current high she was riding. Dougal turned out to be not lovely by any stretch of the imagination but... friendly? All thanks to MacGregor's efforts.

Jo was driving because her guard had had a few shots with their host. 'Necessary' to cement the new relationship, according to the men. It was very nice to see Thomas loosen up. He must miss his family and country. River didn't believe it was necessary for Jo to drive as the owner of a security firm would never allow himself to become inebriated on the job, but she'd insisted, and Thomas relented.

Dougal had offered them tea, which turned into lunch. Since River loved cooking, she helped his housekeeper/cook, Rose, prepare the meal, then snacks, then more snacks, and finally the whisky shots. In between kitchen duty, Dougal gave

River and Jo a tour of his completed pieces and allowed them to peruse no less than ten sketchbooks of his newest designs.

Dougal Donaldson was an extraordinary talent. Extra, extra extraordinary. His pieces ranged from heavy and sturdy to light and elegant. All were expertly crafted works of art. He mixed woods like painters mixed color— elm and ash, Scottish sycamore and yew, oak and walnut.

The gems in his work were the carvings. On many pieces, they were hidden. On one oversized chair made from straight grained ash, Dougal had carved a dragon crawling under one armrest, the tips of its claws the only part visible at first glance. However, there were two pieces that had caught her eye and held every ounce of her fascination. The first was a rocking chair made from pale Scottish sycamore and carved from tip to rockers in flowers— roses, daisies, thistles, heather, bluebells, lavender, and everything in between. The second was an armoire. It was made from American Black Walnut with a French Oak Tree of Life inlay.

Neither piece was sold. She wanted that rocker for her Nan and the armoire for Matilda. So, River did what she had to do. She called Hugh O'Faolain. She wanted to buy the chair as a wedding present for Nan from her, Raven, and Rowan. She wanted Hugh to buy the armoire to give to his mother, Matilda. Rowan had taken a keen interest in helping Hugh's mother with a family tree memory cabinet. This one would be perfect for the project.

Of course, he was next to Bran and Patrick, who instantly wanted to know why River was calling their dad. Hugh put her on speaker, she explained what she wanted, sent pictures, Hugh asked to speak to Dougal, and that was that.

"Okay, guys, to celebrate MacGregor winning over that woodworking genius, I'm ordering the menu to be delivered to our Garden Suite and booking massages."

"Have I told you lately that you're my favorite Byrne," Jo laughed. "Nothing sounds better!"

"Thomas, would you like a massage as well? If you don't want a full hour and a half, they can do target areas like neck and shoulders."

River watched Thomas grow tense. She was in the back seat and watched a blanket of stress wash over him. Damn, massages were supposed to cause the opposite reaction.

"I agreed to only one guard on this trip, so that means I need to be alert while strangers are in the cottage with you two. If you could email me the hotel's massage therapists' information, I'll have my people start on background checks immediately."

River hated that all their happy moments carried a black cloud. Delton needed to go away. "Of course."

Jo was white-knuckling the steering wheel, her head turning left several times to look at MacGregor. Finally, she said, "I apologize for insisting on only one guard, Mr. MacGregor. I... should have realized it would cause you extra work."

He only stared at Jo's profile, jaw clenched. No response.

And just that quick, tense silence filled the trip back to the hotel. Sighing, River texted Patrick. *I miss you. Thursday can't get here soon enough (MacGregor and Jo are... having... a moment... not a good one). I love you. Call me tonight.*

Those two, I swear. Text me when you're in bed. I think we should video call...

I am NOT having phone sex with you, Patrick O'Faolain! Jo's room is next to mine!

Bet you will. Love you, Riv.

~

PATRICK WON THE BET, damn him or her, as she was admittedly weak where that man was concerned. It was almost midnight when the video ended. River's body was warm and languid, flushed and sensitive. Even though they'd just signed off, she couldn't help reliving the experience— every second.

River texted Patrick that she was in bed, unwilling to initiate a video chat, half hoping he'd been joking. Half hoping he wasn't. Her embarrassment wasn't because she was a prude but because she was, even now, inexperienced. Her inhibitions were falling away, but exhibitionism was outside her comfort zone, even between them. Seeing herself on video was way different than being with Patrick in person.

She'd set her laptop up at the foot of her bed, put on a white t-shirt of Patrick's, and turned off all the lights except for the connecting bathroom. Soft glow. Check. Wi-Fi. Check. Tousled hair. Check. Clean face with only lip gloss. Check. Nerves and sweating armpits. Double check.

The video app's old-fashioned ringtone filled her room with bells. Once River accepted the call, Patrick was there, leaning against their headboard— shirtless. His body made her mouth dry and other parts of her body... not so dry.

River pulled her knees to her chest, the oversized t-shirt wrapping her legs to her ankles. "Hey, baby," Patrick's voice rumbled over the computer speakers.

"Patrick," River answered, placing her chin atop her raised knees. Her eyes were probably saucers.

"It's late, love, and you have another long day tomorrow." Patrick's eyes were steady and intense. He was tracking her every breath. "Take off your shirt, baby, and get comfortable." Patrick's gaze never left the camera, but his hands pulled the sheet aside that had been covering his lower body.

River's breath hitched at the sight of his erection. She was mesmerized when he took himself in hand, slowly stroking. Her legs started to scissor in an attempt to provide relief but only managed to ignite her core further.

Pat didn't ask again for her to remove her shirt again. He just patiently watched her, continuing the mesmerizing stroke of his flesh. His stomach was tight and rippling with need. Never taking her eyes from the screen, River pinched the bottom of the tee and slowly, perhaps showboating for a moment, revealed her body to her fiancé one inch at a time.

Her face wasn't free of the cotton when she heard Patrick's breathing change. Harsher. Faster. Free of the cloth, she could see Patrick stroking himself faster than before.

"Let your knees fall open, baby. Let me see how wet you are for me." She did what he asked, the thrumming between her legs a living, breathing dragon. "Wet. God, so wet. Listen to me, River. Run your hands up your body... yes, just like that. Take both your tits and squeeze them." River followed his every direction. "Pinch your nipples, baby. Pretend it's my mouth... my teeth."

River opened her eyes to see Patrick, his glazed eyes and panting breath similar to hers. Without him asking, River left off her breasts to run her hands down her body, skating over the planes of her stomach until she reached the apex between her thighs. Widening her legs further, she made one exploratory swipe through the middle of her heat, her ring and middle finger swirling the sensitive nub at the top.

Patrick's pumping trebled, his hips lifting, mimicking thrusting into her body. "How many fingers can you fill yourself with, River?" Without hesitation, she showed him. She pumped first two and then three fingers in and out of herself, pressing her palm against the surrounding heat. Pat left his reclined position and was on his knees, pumping his body faster and faster.

"Going to come, baby. Come for me. Let me watch you come apart." One last press of her palm and River exploded, causing Patrick to paint his screen with ribbons of white. It was one of the most erotic things River had ever witnessed.

They both lay there looking at each other on their computer screens— Pat's was blurry because... well... opaque body fluids. They were still touching their bodies and breathing heavily. "My laptop buttons may never be the same," he smirked.

I pulled my fingers out— slowly, just to mess with him— and said, "My fingers may never be the same." His eyes tracked... Every. Single. Move.

"Come home, River."

THE WEAVERS MIGHT NOT HAVE PRODUCED the level of shenanigans of Dougal Donaldson, but they reaped a heady amount of satisfaction all the same. River and Jo enjoyed learning about the weaving process, and the owner sent a thick binder of fabric swatches with River. Triskelion's clients were going to flip over the choices.

She and Jo spent the rest of the day scouring through several antique and thrift stores. Hidden treasures could be *anywhere*. She wished Ravan and Rowan were here. Antiquing was their favorite thing to do together. Their mother had gotten them addicted to the hunt, taking them as children to markets and fairs to discover 'treasures.'

River considered both days in Scotland to be a massive success. She was excited to meet a local artist tomorrow whose work was gaining quite a following on social media. He lived in Grantown-on-Spey, less than an hour from Inverness.

Jo appeared to enjoy the day, but the tension was still there between her and Thomas, and she went out of her way not to be left alone with him. River gave a mental sigh, wishing for the hundredth time that Patrick was there.

"I feel like we walked twenty miles today," Jo laughed. "I

plan on taking a hot shower and ordering room service. What about you?

"Your plans are my plans. I'm tired." River slung her bag over her shoulder as they walked toward the cottage. "Plus, I've got a mountain of mail to get through that Rowan gave me before we left. Procrastination hasn't shrunk the pile, unfortunately."

"I bet you're even more tired after having sex with Patrick last night," Jo snorted a laugh when River rounded on her.

"Oh. My. God. I told that shit that you would hear." River covered her red face. Dying. Dying. Dead.

"Oh Lord, why didn't I video your reaction for your sisters. Damn it!" She yelped when River swatted her butt. "No worries!" she giggled, obviously enjoying herself immensely at River's expense. "I put earbuds in when I realized you and Pat decided to make a porn."

"I... no... yep, speechless." It was good to see Jo laugh again, even if it was a mortifying subject. "I admit, Jo, I was pretty amazing in my first feature film." River laughed and hip-bumped Jo. She laughed hysterically at that. Arm in arm, the women followed MacGregor into the cottage.

Thomas checked the perimeter of the cottage before he let them get out of the car, and as was the routine, he entered the cottage first and did a room-by-room sweep. She and Jo were looking over the menu when he quietly walked back into the living room next to the kitchen. Jo's back was to him, so she didn't know he'd come back in.

In a low voice, Jo asked River, "Would you get MacGregor's order, Riv? I don't think I can take any more of his disinterest today." My eyes must have gone round because Jo immediately swung around to see the man in question, one who didn't look anywhere close to disinterested.

His fists were clenched, and his jaw was clenched. His

whole damn body appeared locked up. Until he moved—stalked, really.

Each step was silent. Deliberate. MacGregor didn't stop until he was toe-to-toe with Jo, River, a forgotten barnacle at her side, along for the ride. His warrior body appeared to swell twice its size, her friend a golden doll caught in the maelstrom.

"Since you refuse to give me even ten seconds of your time to *privately* discuss what happened in my room, I'm forced to speak *publicly*." He placed his hands on the counter behind Jo, leaning in so that he could look directly into Jo's eyes. "Fair warning, mo ghràdh, the days of swallowing my wants and needs... that's over, lassie."

"I want to be very, very clear here, Josephine O'Connor. I have wanted you naked, and in my bed since the first day I laid eyes on you.

"One of my best men was supposed to be your guard, but his flight from South Africa was delayed. I own the security company. All the men who work there answer to me. I no longer take jobs myself. But here I am, and here we are. Once you were mine, I wouldn't allow another man to take my place.

"I go to bed hard, and I wake up hard. But lass, I am a soldier still, and temptation will not cause me to let my guard down. Delton got close to you at Wolves because I only had eyes for you. That will not happen again. Your life is worth my best. The day my face is buried between your thighs, or my shaft buried deep in your body, I won't be your guard, I'll just be yours."

He straightened to his full height. "A warning, Ms. O'Connor. Once the threat to your life has been eliminated, if you don't want me to catch you, you better fucking run. Fast." Turning all that intensity on River, he asked her to order two cheeseburgers and two orders of chips for his dinner before walking out the front door.

Holy shit! MacGregor knew his way around a mic drop. Clearing her throat, River suggested, "Let's go ahead and order the food and then shower while we wait." Jo was still staring at where her guard had exited. "Okay," River answered herself. "I'll call dining now."

35

———————

River was dying. She knew she wasn't *literally* dying, but her burning, blistered hands sure felt like the Grim Reaper was lounging somewhere close. The pain thankfully distracted her from the photo album of Patrick's greatest hits—his infidelity.

She'd finally gotten around to opening her mail from Triskelion. There was only one package, which she'd saved for last, assuming it was a sample from a vendor looking to impress her and her sisters.

It wasn't a sample.

Inside the plain, brown box, River pulled out a bubble-wrapped parcel. She picked the box up again to look at the return label. There was no address, only a yellow happy face sticker. Weird.

Underneath the bubble wrap was an old-looking, thin wooden album. River ran her hands over the deep grooves and delicate metal inlay. It was getting dusty crap all over her skin. Carefully, she opened the front board cover— and froze. Oh God, no.

It was an eight-and-a-half by eleven-inch photo from New Year's Eve night of Patrick holding that woman on his lap. Even though the dust was starting to really irritate her hands and forearms, River couldn't stop turning the pages. It was like a child's paper flip book. Each page changed the angle just enough to make them look like they were moving on the page.

The kiss. Oh God, it was like watching Patrick kissing another woman right in front of her. She must have cried out because Thomas stood before her where she was sitting on the living room couch. River was crying and rubbing at her hands and arms. Thomas yelled for Jo before getting out his phone.

"River." She must not have responded quick enough. How could she? She felt like she was drowning. "River! Stop scratching, lass. You've something on your skin, and touching it may make it worse."

Jo rushed into the room, sporting a floppy bun and oversized t-shirt. "What is going on?" She started to reach for the photo album, but Thomas grabbed her hands.

"Don't touch it. It looks like Delton sent this to River. He put something on it to hurt her skin. Okay, Riv, you're going to need to do exactly what I say, okay?" River could only nod. Tears from the pain of seeing the pictures and from her hands made speech impossible.

"Hold your hands up in front of you. I'm going to wrap all this up inside the blanket you have over your lap. Jo, as soon as I have it wrapped and gone, help River to the kitchen sink and have River use soap and lukewarm water to gently wash her hands and arms. Do *not* touch anything except her back if she needs support, Jo."

In a daze, River did as Thomas asked. The water felt soothing. The soap, not so much. She heard Thomas barking orders into his phone. After he ended the call, Thomas informed her and Jo that he had a contact here in Scotland who would be coming by to pick up the album and the box it came in for testing.

"The box was mailed in Dublin, which means Delton is most likely in the city. Carefully dry your arms, River. Jo, go get another shirt for River to change into before we go to the hospital."

That got River's attention. "Please, Thomas. I don't want to go to the hospital. My skin already feels better. Just let me take a shower and see how it feels after that. Please." River wanted to cry alone.

MacGregor stared at her for a long minute, probably thinking of the pros and cons of taking her out of the secure room into the chaos of an emergency room at night.

"Fine. But I will cut the back of your shirt so that you can slip it off and not take it over your face." Jo was already rummaging through the kitchen drawers for something Macgregor could cut with. "Room temperature water. We don't want your pores to open."

"Okay. Thank you." River heard the quaver in her voice. Tonight had been a tough blow to her self-esteem *and* her new relationship with Patrick. "Before I forget to tell you, Rowan gave me the box with Triskelion's mail Saturday after we left Nan's. So, it had been mailed to our office."

He nodded, his face grave. Sam Delton made a big mistake going to Dublin with so many of MacGregor's men there. But then, Delton wasn't mentally stable. He probably thought he was untouchable, and up until now, he had been.

Jo found scissors. Thomas took them from her, holding her hand for a moment longer than necessary. "We will find him." He waited for Jo's nod before adding, "Jo, please make sure River gets in the shower without incident." When River started to protest, Thomas cut her off. "You're shaken, lass. And I don't think it's all because of the rash."

Thomas made quick work of cutting the shirt. As Jo led the way to River's bedroom, he dropped what felt like another bomb. "While you shower, I'll call the O'Faolains and Mr. O'Connor. We won't fly back to Dublin until morning. It's late, and we still need to pack. Shower and rest. But River, if that rash worsens, I want to know immediately."

"I understand." The shower was going to be a short reprieve. River knew that Patrick would be wanting to speak to her before she went to bed.

Jo was fiddling in the shower, making sure the temperature wasn't too warm. River leaned against the bathroom counter. "Did you see what the photos were?"

Turning, Jo eyed her with sympathy. She'd seen then. "I'm sorry you had to see those pictures again. I'm sorry they make you feel less somehow— though you are a woman without equal. I'm sorry that sick bastard won't leave our families alone. But you know what I'm not sorry about?"

"What's that?" River was crying but couldn't use her hands or shirt to wipe the tears away.

"Patrick changing his life around. You giving him a second chance. Delton not winning. Now get in the shower, Riv. Nothing's going to fix your wounded heart tonight except for Patrick. So, stop dreading it and recognize how fortunate you are to have a man who loves you so much. So much, in fact, that his brother and father are probably having to physically restrain him from coming to you now."

DAD, Bran, and Patrick were at the bar downstairs when MacGregor called. Dad immediately put the call on speaker.

"Are Bran and Patrick with you?"

The hair on Patrick's body stood on end at the guard's grim tone. "They are, and I have you on speaker," Dad responded.

"Where's River?" Pat asked the most important question first.

"Showering. Jo's with her. River is safe, but something did happen." All three men stood, drinks forgotten, ready to leave immediately. "I would appreciate silence until I give you the rundown of this evening. I'll answer questions and discuss our next play after that. Agreed?"

Dad squeezed Patrick's arm. "Tell us everything."

Once MacGregor finished, Patrick was furious, desperate to get to River, and totally sick that River had to see that. On top of the photos, she'd been hurt. Would she break things off? Would she give him a *third* chance?

"One of my contacts will be here within the hour to take the package for analysis. Delton might think he's untraceable, but I think the motherfucker's luck is about to run out. This reeks of desperation."

"I'm coming. Now."

"I understand, Pat," MacGregor sympathized. "River is shaken up, but she's a fighter. She needs to sleep. Josephine will be with her, and I won't sleep tonight. I'll monitor the property until we leave. The pilot will have us landing in Dublin no later than eight in the morning. Call her in a bit. My man will dispose of her clothes and clean whatever the album was covered in.

"I can't stop you from coming, Patrick, nor would I try. I just think she needs the oblivion of sleep. She will never be alone."

Patrick could barely think. The only thing he did know was that whatever was best for River, he would do it. Dad and Bran were still asking MacGregor questions when Patrick wandered to the opposite side of the room. He had hoped

River would text him when she was out of the shower, but she hadn't.

She didn't want to talk to him. It was as simple and as devastating as that. He called her anyway. He had to hear her voice one way or the other.

"Hello."

"River, baby, please tell me you're okay. Are you in... physical pain?" He *knew* she was in emotional pain.

"My hands and lower arms have red patches, but the burning and itching are almost gone. Jo had some cortisone cream, and it's done wonders."

He heard covers rustling, like River was moving into a more comfortable position, and Jo's voice faint in the background. She didn't offer anything else. Patrick's eyes were hot. He was man enough, at least to admit to himself, that the prickling sensation behind his eyes was tears.

"Riv... can I... do you..."

He heard River take a ragged breath. "I know it's a ridiculous expense, but... I need you, Pat. Can you..."

"Dad," Patrick yelled across the room, "Call Bobby. I'm leaving for the airport as soon as I grab a set of clothes." To River, he asked, "Do you need Row, sweetheart?"

"Yes, please."

Her timid voice ripped his insides to shreds. "Dad, call Rowan and go pick her up. I'll meet you at the airport. Bran, tell Raven what's happened if you don't think it'll upset her too much."

"I'll tell her regardless, or she'd never forgive me," Bran assured.

His dad disappeared upstairs, presumably to grab his own bag. River was still on the phone, her ragged breaths not calming his panic whatsoever. "He made the pictures into a... like a flip book. I watched every second of you kissing that woman." River moaned in pain. "I don't know if I can bear it, Pat. It's all I see—all I *can* see."

Patrick was running up the stairs to their floor, practically bent in two, with the pain of her words ricocheting in his head. He heard Jo whisper words of love and reassurance. "Baby, baby, please don't cry. Don't leave me again, River. I couldn't take you leaving me." He ran into their apartment, grabbed a tote off the kitchen counter, and dumped groceries on the floor as he ran to the master. He wasn't sure what he put in the bag, but he was out the door in less than thirty seconds.

As he hit the main level and the massive front door, Bran yelled, "Your guards have cars out front for you and Dad."

Patrick gave a wave in acknowledgment to his brother, throwing his bag in the backseat of the first car. "Hold on, River. Two hours."

River curled into a tight ball as she hung up. She'd started crying in the shower and couldn't seem to stop. It had nothing to do with the stalker and everything to do with the photos. God help her. She couldn't stop the mental manipulation of the photo story. She still loved Patrick. She'd always love him, but... to have her face rubbed in... to see his mouth against another woman's...

"I'm sorry, Jo. I asked Patrick to come. I... don't know."

"Only you know what's best for you, River. I have... Thomas... you need your own Honey Bunny." She smiled as she hugged River tightly. Apparently, everyone needed a little HB in their lives.

River rubbed her knuckles into her eyes. An attempt to suppress the raging emotions currently burning her body. Her phone started ringing again. She assumed it was Patrick. It was

Raven. River heard her sister take several breaths, probably trying to speak through her tears.

"River," Raven hiccupped, "would you... put me on speaker... just lay me on the pillow next to your head... let me... let me be with you until Patrick and Row get there. Please."

"Okay." And it was okay, or it would be eventually.

36

River's bedroom door swung open, and her youngest sister walked in. Her eyes were red and haunted. Jo hugged Rowan after she slipped off the bed at her approach before quietly leaving the room.

Rowan crawled into bed beside her and placed her fingers gently on River's cheek. "Rowan's here, Rave." River touched Rowan's cheek and took a deep, cleansing breath. Her sisters grounded her.

"I wish I could have come to you," Raven whispered.

"None of that, now. You *have* been here with me. I don't have to see you to feel your love, but Raven, you need to settle now. Let Bran put you to bed. You know it destroys him to see you upset."

"Fine, but promise me you'll come to see me first thing when you get home."

"I promise." After hanging up, Rowan examined River's arms. "They're a lot better. I bet by tomorrow, the red will be all but gone," River tried to reassure her.

Tears started leaking from the corners of her sister's eyes. "I gave you that damn package. God, when I think of how much worse it could have been."

"Don't you dare blame yourself! Of course, you gave it to me. It had my damn name on it!" River tugged Rowan against her side so they could wrap each other up in hugs. They whispered soothing bits of nonsense to one another for another thirty minutes before Rowan pulled back.

"Are you ready to face him?" Him being Patrick.

"I asked him to come, so I imagine I need to." River hated the flutters of conflict. He was the one person she wanted to see the most. He was also the reason those photos even existed. River groaned and rubbed her eyes.

Rowan slid from the bed. "You'll get through this. You *are* a Byrne, after all."

That made River smile. "True. I'll walk out with you." As soon as she stepped outside the protective haven of her bedroom, she searched the room, looking for one man.

"Patrick," she said quietly. He had been staring out the living room window but whirled around when the door opened. He looked destroyed... distraught.

"River." Her name sounded like a prayer, an apology.

While they stared at one another from across the room, MacGregor filled the silence with suggestions, orders, and demands. "Rowan, please take my room. There is a couch you might want to grab, Hugh. Due to the lateness, Hugh and I decided to leave here by nine, which is less than six hours from now.

"We'll have a report on Delton's package in less than forty-eight. Tom, you and Dixon patrol the perimeter until I relieve you. Ms. O'Connor, go to bed now. You're about to fall asleep standing."

River turned to see Jo bristle at Thomas' high-handedness.

She shocked the hell out of her guard, though, when she commented, "You aren't the only guard on duty now."

River had to cover her mouth from letting out an indelicate squawk. HB's whole body turned to stone as if Josephine O'Connor was Medusa. He waited until he heard the click of the front door, meaning his men weren't there to witness their boss toss a squealing Jo over his shoulder, disappearing into her bedroom.

Everyone was shocked but River. After his speech earlier, there were no doubts as to his ultimate end game. Hugh looked at his son, who still hadn't made a move toward River, and asked Rowan if she would mind if he took the couch. He was attempting to give them privacy, which was thoughtful.

"Sure, Mr. O'Faolain. I have no doubt you can resist any wiles I might accidentally throw your way." Rowan's parting shot had Hugh tipping his head back. His eyes closed. Most likely praying for an intervention.

And that left two. The silence was unbearable. All the other bullshit and betrayal, pictures and pain— could not be allowed a second life. She'd already forgiven Patrick. Tonight. The photo album, the tears, the insecurities— all of it —should not, could not, be laid at Patrick's feet.

Patrick and River.

River and Patrick.

"I promised you forever, Patrick."

He rocked back on his feet as if a physical blow had landed a direct hit to his gut. "You did, but... that was before—"

River cut him off. "No buts. I won't lie and say seeing the photographs didn't throw me. They did wound me. They did fucking hurt me again, damn it!" She walked closer to where Patrick stood, looking for all the world like his life was over. Taking his huge hands in her own, she destroyed all doubts about where their relationship stood.

"I promised you forever. I meant it. You promised me forever. Did you mean it?"

"Jesus, River. Forever and a day." He pulled her close to his body. Wrapping his arms tight around her body, he lifted her until she could wrap her legs around his waist.

They stood for several minutes in a silent embrace.

"I've been so worried. It meant everything that you wanted me here."

River pulled back from where she'd tucked her face against Pat's neck. He continued to stroke his hand over her hair and down her back. River thought it soothed him as much as it did her. "From here on out, let us be clear on at least this one thing. You love me, and I love you. That, Mr. O'Faolain, is the present and future for us."

PATRICK and his family were in a meeting with MacGregor in one of The Fitzwilliam's conference rooms again. He, Bran, and Dad hadn't kitted out their conference room at the O Building yet. Dean and James O'Connor were present on Zoom. Holding River in his arms all night in Inverness, then last night in their own apartment, had done wonders for his stress over the Delton situation.

That piece of shit would not destroy his relationship with River. Not. Ever.

"My people confirmed that the package was mailed inside Dublin. Delton could have had someone do it for him, but the detectives and FBI believe he's here. His MO suggests that his ego wouldn't allow others to take part in what he perceives as *his* accomplishments.

"The photo album was old and had several fingerprints, none matching Delton. Unsurprising, as he's always been careful. The powder that coated the album that caused River's skin rash was fiberglass. Its prickly particles are synthetic but contain some glass. The more River rubbed her skin or scratched, the worse it became.

"There are several manufacturing plants in the Dublin area where he could have obtained the substance. The FBI will be here by tonight. Delton made a mistake in giving away his location. Dublin is small when measured against the United States. His stunts, along with his need to brag, will be his downfall."

"Until he's caught, what does that mean for our families?" Dad asked.

"It means we stay in groups. Food needs to be ordered anonymously. Grocery services where Delton can't anticipate how to hurt us in advance. It means, Mr. O'Connor, your daughter needs to stay with me at The Fitzwilliam, where monitoring is easier. It means Rowan Byrne moves into the O Building. There is added security in staying together.

"I believe that with the FBI coming, knowing the perpetrator is here, he'll be run to ground sooner rather than later."

37

———

1. *Stance.*
2. *Sight Alignment.*
3. *Breathing.*
4. *Trigger squeeze.*

Marksmanship. *The fundamental techniques were fascinating.*

Eye dominance— standing, kneeling, or prone. All the online tutorials promised that excellence didn't have to be innate. It could be learned.

And Sam was an excellent student.

38

———

The evening after the meeting, Rowan reluctantly, but without resistance, moved into the O'Faolain building. She understood the gravity of the situation and wouldn't make it harder on MacGregor and his guards to watch the families. No one really thought Delton had followed them to Ireland. It had been a shock to realize their error.

Rowan had settled into a guest room on the first floor. She seemed more comfortable around his dad now, laughing and even teasing occasionally. It was forced. Rowan was definitely trying to lighten the mood between them by pretending that Hugh O'Faolain was just a great friend. Family by marriage. For his father's part, every generic smile she threw his way produced clenched fists.

River told Patrick to let them work it out. Apparently, Dad had told Rowan they would never have a relationship. It had crushed her, so she was trying to get over him. Apparently, the new cringey interactions were supposed to resemble 'getting over it.'

Everyone went to bed early. It'd been a long couple of days — very emotional days for River. She could have left him again over that photo album. Instead, she still wanted forever. Patrick had just wrapped his arm around her waist to draw her closer to his heat when both their phones performed a choreographed light show.

They both lunged for their phones. "Raven's in labor!" River gasped. They both threw off the bed covers and rushed to dress. As they hustled out the front door, Patrick could hear his brother shouting directions, presumably not at his wife.

The first floor— it should be called the Lobby, which made more sense to Patrick— was chaos. Bran was *literally* running around. River immediately went to Raven, who was sitting on a couch, clutching her stomach and grimacing. Then Rowan was there beelining to the sisters. His dad got off the elevator, approaching the scene with caution.

While Bran was haranguing someone about wanting an SUV— apparently more comfortable for his wife, who WAS IN LABOR— Patrick called MacGregor. The plan was to mobilize his guards at the hospital. Plus, the sisters wanted Jo there. He then called Nan and asked if she and Devlen were ready to be great-grandparents. Nan screamed, probably scaring her fiancé to death.

In the meantime, Dad corralled Bran near the bar. "Son. Take a deep breath. I'll make sure we get the right car for Raven. Your agitation is making her more agitated. Now," Dad began with a firm thump to Bran's back that knocked him forward a step, "pretend to have your shit together and go sit with your wife." Bran nodded several times. The jerky nature of his bobbing head was bizarre. He did at least manage to do as Dad suggested. Bran and Raven both visibly relaxed when he sat by her on the couch, rubbing her back.

"Good call, Dad. Bran was going off the rails at an impressive speed," Pat said.

Dad was back to looking at his phone screen, something he'd

been doing since he came down, but at Pat's comment, he finally put it back in his pocket,

"I remember when you boys were born. Scariest days of my life. One day, you'll discover what it's like to become a father," he smirked.

Patrick glanced at River, wondering what it would be like if they had a baby someday. Incredible but terrifying. Shaking his head at the thought, he told his dad, "I called MacGregor and Nan. Will you call Gran or wait until morning?"

His father grunted in amusement. "I called her before I came down. Christ, boy, mom would have my head if I waited. Diana immediately called her pilot."

WAITING WAS TORTURE. The waiting room was currently full of family and guards. River and Rowan paced the white tiled floors, waiting for an update. Months ago, she and her sisters discussed that only Bran would be at the birth. Everyone one hundred percent understood, but it didn't mean it didn't suck knowing *nothing* for so *long*.

Okay, they'd only been waiting thirty minutes, but still! Raven's water had broken on the way to the hospital, and her contractions ramped up hard and fast. The nurse who met them at the sliding doors took one look at Raven and started barking orders, sat Raven in a wheelchair, and rushed off. River didn't even get to say goodbye, damn it.

"What in the hell is taking so long?" Rowan hissed at River.

"No shit," River agreed.

"Girls, for heaven's sake, sit down. You three are so attuned to one another, Raven can probably feel your stress from the birthing room," Nan snapped.

River and Rowan smirked at one another. Nan was obviously just as stressed. River caught Patrick's eye and shrugged. She wouldn't apologize for her Auntie Anxiety. Hugh was gloomy, arms crossed, chair balancing on its back legs. Brooding over the birth of his first grandchild or Rowan? Both? Anyone's guess, really.

"Come lean on me for a minute, Riv," Patrick said, patting his legs. Grinning, River touched Rowan's hand in passing as she went to snuggle on Pat's lap.

"I'm just so worried for Raven and excited to be an aunt. I can hardly stand it." Softly laughing, River lightly kissed Patrick.

"If you think Bran would allow anything bad to happen to his wife or son, you haven't been paying attention," Patrick teased, earning a smile from Nan and a nod from Hugh. Pat nudged River's side. "HB's here, which means Jo is probably bundled up inside his coat." He said this loud enough for everyone to hear, earning a disapproving look from MacGregor and laughter from Jo, who peeked around her guard's massive shoulder.

River jumped off Patrick, and she and Rowan tackled the golden-haired beauty. "We're about to become aunties. Can you believe it?" Rowan laughed, a genuine laugh, not Hugh-approved mirth, thank God.

"Not that this night couldn't get any more exciting, but..." Jo drew out the suspense, "James and Jane eloped! They're on a flight to Paris as we speak. Mom was furious that she didn't get to plan a wedding, but both she and my dad told James not to show his face for at least a month and take his new wife on an extended honeymoon. Mom probably hopes she'll come back pregnant so she can at least plan the baby shower."

"Oh, Jo," River breathed. "I'm so happy for your brother and Jane. They both deserved a happily-ever-after."

Patrick and Hugh both expressed their happiness for the couple. "Bran will be ecstatic to hear the news," Patrick assured.

Jo leaned into Rowan and River and whispered for their ears alone, "Sooo... no sex yet, but Thomas had two of his men stay outside our hotel room for an hour. They were off duty and supposed to be getting some sleep, so that's why it was only for an hour, but I would like to report multiple orgasms were had—on both sides."

River and Rowan both squealed in ecstasy over the news. "Finally, thank you Little Tiny Baby Jesus," River half snorted, half laughed.

"You lucky, lucky bitch," Rowan also laughed and added an ass slap to their friend.

"Josephine," Macgregor growled. His face sported a hint of blush. Adorable.

Jo pooh-poohed his scowl, "It's okay, Honey. Just catching my girls up."

River heard HB mutter, *Christ, have mercy.*

River turned at the sound of footsteps hurrying their way. Oh God. Bran had tears streaking down his face. "He's here."

THEY WERE ALLOWED into Raven and Bran's room forty-five minutes later, a few minutes after midnight. Patrick watched in wonder as his older brother presented his son to the family. Patrick realized at that moment why they called babies miracles. And according to what the women said, Raven's labor had been extremely short.

Bran placed their son carefully back in his mother's arms. River, Rowan, and Nan pressed close, giving kisses to Raven and the baby. They all agreed he was the most beautiful baby ever born. Jo looked like a photographer on Speed, taking photos from every angle.

"Oh, Raven, you won't believe this little shop I found on Etsy."

MacGregor's rumbling voice cut in, "Why wouldn't she believe it? You logged more hours this past month flipping through Etsy vendors than their own content editors."

Jo only rolled her eyes. "Anyway, they will take all Baby O's first photos with family and friends and create a gorgeous album. They can emboss the leather with names or symbols and in different categories, like ultrasounds, pregnancy photos, baby showers, and the one I asked Hugh to take of you before you left for the hospital. That he better have remembered to take." She stopped to look at his dad, who, of course, only nodded.

"What picture did you take, Dad?" Bran asked, smiling at their father doing Jo's bidding.

"One of you marching around in a panic, one of the girls on the couch, and one of Bran and Raven sitting together waiting for the car." Eyes gleaming, he added, "Oh, I also took one of Patrick looking at Bran like his brother had lost his mind. That one was for you, Bran. Something to compare whenever Pat and River are in your position."

Patrick only shook his head, knowing he'd deserved it. "I wondered what the hel—heck you were doing looking at your phone so often."

"So, Raven, in the next few weeks, we'll gather everyone's photos, and you can pick the album color and all the other stuff.

"The best part, which I already had them start, is a family tree for you and Bran. They'll do a coordinating book with all the fancy trees and calligraphy inside. They use more than one genealogy site to gather the most accurate and comprehensive information. Oh, and I told them to make three copies of the Family Tree. One with just your family, Row."

That last part dropped an uncomfortable dollop of awkward in the room. Raven, as sweet as ever, didn't miss a beat.

"Oh wow, Jo! Thank you so much. I never thought of our family trees. Maybe next week you can come over, and we can pick everything out."

Bran finally got his son back and walked over to Nan, who'd gone back to stand next to Devlen. He placed her great-grandson in her arms, making the older woman burst into tears. Gran wasn't expected to land for another few hours, so she would wait to come to the hospital when visiting hours resumed in the morning, but Patrick imagined her reaction to holding the newest Baby O would be just as emotional.

Finally, it was Pat and Dad's turn.

The baby was so... small. Like, move a finger wrong and break it small. Bran looked to their father and proudly held his son out. Without hesitation, Dad took his grandson into his arms and cradled the newest O'Faolain to his chest.

He had the barest bit of white hair glinting over a pink scalp that Dad traced with his blunt fingers. It must be amazing to hold a child from his own child. Patrick wondered in awe if this tiny little boy would grow up to look like his father and uncle.

"Christ, Bran, I wish my father were here to see what you've done. He's perfect."

His dad's rare show of emotion had every woman in the room sniffling— the men, too, if Patrick were honest.

And then— it was his turn to hold his nephew. River and Rowan came over for moral support. He must have been shakier than he thought. As Bran placed the bundle in his arms, the baby's tiny head rested in the crook of his elbow. He opened his tiny, toothless mouth and yawned. "Did your mommy wear you out with all that pushing and nonsense?" he whispered, gently touching a finger to his nephew's cheek.

Tracing the soft brow and scrunched nose, he whispered, "I'm your Uncle Pat."

"Okay, damn it," Jo's exasperated voice cut through the quiet. "You O'Faolains have taken up more than your share of Baby O. Honey Bunny's going to lose his S. H. I. T. if he doesn't get to hold that sweet bundle immediately."

MacGregor looked at Patrick in terror. "No."

Too late, Patrick gently transferred the bundle into the Scotsman's giant arms. Baby O looked the size of a potato. Now Jo was crying. Served her right. Patrick took over photography duties as Thomas, oh so gently; touched the blanket, a look of wonder crossed his tough features. "Congratulations, Bran and Raven. Ye've a name for the bairn, aye?"

It was Raven who answered. Smiling at Bran first, then Hugh, she said," His name is Daniel Hugh O'Faolain."

Bran clasped their dad on the shoulder before adding, "After his grandfathers."

In a raspy voice, full of emotion, Dad responded with, "I'm honored, Son, as I know Raven's father would have been."

Okay... Christ, have mercy already. Are babies supposed to cause this much emotion?

Rowan thankfully suggested they all go home and leave Bran and Raven to settle in. Everyone agreed, though Jo, who was still snuggling little Daniel, looked reluctant to relinquish the bundle.

River and Rowan hugged Bran again before kissing their sister and hugging her tight. "I'm so proud of you, Rave," River murmured against Raven's cheek. Rowan added, "Mom and Dad are so proud of you. I'm so proud of you."

Patrick watched as River pulled away from her sister's bed. She was fighting tears but managed to add, "You'll call Row and me tomorrow when you need us?"

Raven took their hands. "I don't have to need you. I'll always just want you. Okay?"

River and Rowan nodded, clearly biting the inside of their cheeks to keep from bawling. Patrick said his goodbyes and wrapped his arm around River.

His dad followed, but as he closed the distance, Rowan quickly turned her back and preceded her sister out the door. He watched his dad inhale deeply. How could he not see how miserable he was making himself and Rowan by denying his feelings?

He hoped his father didn't learn his lesson in the soul-destroying way Patrick had.

39

As Sam finished making a cortado for the obnoxious, cat hair infested prima donna currently holding out her greased up oil slick of a hand toward him to grab her cup— and really, the brown nails looked like she'd been playing in the litter box with her plethora of cats, and don't get him started on what her wrinkled, scrunched up lips resembled— he smiled, said 'Of course' and 'Have a great day' even after the waste of air gave her parting shot. You better have steamed the milk long enough.

He despised this job, but he had to keep it for his plan to work. The O'Faolain guards were always milling about, especially since they owned the building next to the Byrne sisters' business. He found out that little nugget of information from two gossiping women waiting for their coffees three months ago.

Bran's wife had her baby weeks and weeks ago. The parade of people toting blue balloons, gift boxes with giant bows, couture, of course... nauseating. He'd witnessed it all during his deliveries. May was only a few days away. He could not believe he'd been here for almost four months! However, he wasn't a quitter. Sam had to remind himself of that fact daily.

He was not a quitter.

He made sure, no matter the shitty weather, to jump at every opportunity to make coffee deliveries. His face was becoming more and more familiar. People hailed him on the street. Sam always smiled and waved back. He would make meaningless conversation, or his favorite... reciting a customer's coffee order from memory. It made people feel so special. 'Oh my, he remembered me and my order.'

People were so easily manipulated.

There was another benefit to hoofing around Triskelion's neighborhood— he had a reason to go in and out of the surrounding businesses, a few that had promising rooftops. A simple query here and there got Sam all sorts of intel.

One building in particular had potential. It was a clothing boutique with what looked like apartments or storage above the shop, situated across the street and slightly east of Triskelion and that O'Faolain monstrosity. He'd been watching hundreds of videos on how to use his rifle and scope. The distance wouldn't be a problem. There was enough distance that he knew getting away undetected wouldn't be an issue either.

Hide the rifle, then go right back to making and delivering coffee. Just ole Robbie Smith, everyone's favorite local barista.

Two days ago, Sam scouted behind the boutique and confirmed it had a fire escape reaching the upper levels. Whether it was sturdy enough to use was to be determined. He planned on doing a trial run, rifle included, to see if the rooftop was sniper-worthy. That made Sam chuckle.

He finished adding whipped cream to a customer's Caramel Frappuccino, imagining his revenge would taste as sweet as the decadent caramel swirling in this young woman's drink.

Excitement zinged through his body. A week, maybe two, and he could be back in the States. His enemies— devastated, destroyed, or dead.

Sam would be back on the road in his beloved motor home—

@*SammySoGood would be coming back with a vengeance. Sam was an artist. He needed the creativity his films inspired in him and his followers.*

Unfortunately, that time wasn't now. He knew he'd been more frazzled of late. The ability to sleep had abandoned Sam at least two weeks ago. He could only pace and plan, pace and plan, pace and plan. His body felt connected to a livewire. His father's voice constantly reminded him of his duty. Make them pay.

His father would rest in peace as soon as Samuel, his beloved son, pulled that rifle's trigger— over and over.

40

"Come on, River! Get off your lazy ass," Raven grabbed her hands and attempted to pull her off the couch. "This is my first night out since Daniel was born, and I want a shot of Bushmills stat!"

River hoisted herself up, attempting to shake off the tiredness that had been plaguing her for days. She laughed at Raven, who was practically jumping up and down in her excitement. Everyone was going out for a few hours, men included, since Delton had managed to elude *all* law enforcement. *Nasty bastard.*

Everyone was meeting in the Lobby— the ground floor's newly christened name— River and Raven were the last to go down. River opted to stay with her sister while she pumped more breast milk. She said she'd been pumping extra the last few days so she could actually order a 'big girl' drink. Her assistant, Bre, was staying with Daniel while they went out. Well, Bre and two guards.

It was the new parents' first time leaving their son with someone besides Nan for longer than an hour, but she and Devlen had gone home weeks ago. Matilda was also gone. She and her son had argued because she'd wanted to go back to Tulsa, but Hugh insisted she was safer with Diana, so, in a bit of a huff, she flew to France, where her friend had booked them a suite at the luxury spa, Chateau Des Vigiers. If nothing else, Mrs. Diana Gaines knew how to live a fabulous life.

Raven did one more hot lap to the nursery before gliding halfway to the front door on her return— very Tom Cruise in *Risky Business.* "Damn, Raven, I still can't believe how fast your body bounced back." Raven looked gorgeous in a black and crème wrap dress, which accentuated her hourglass shape. River almost wore a dress tonight but was feeling her black fitted chino capris, tennis shoes, black Deadmau5 t-shirt— the 3D mouse in white— and a light, black leather jacket. She purposely dressed after Patrick left their apartment. This was exactly the type of outfit that would turn her fiancé on.

"Oh, thanks. I hope my boobs remember their former size once I'm done breastfeeding," Raven laughed, "but Bran seems enamored of them."

"He's enamored of all things Raven," River lightly elbowed her sister as they walked downstairs.

"So true, but who could blame him?" Raven's smile was contagious. Marriage and motherhood suited her.

They could hear everyone downstairs, the pre-party in full swing. Raven stopped walking and took River's arm to stop her as well. "Should I ask Bran to ask Hugh to stay home?" At River's wide eyes, she hurriedly added, "I know, I know. Jesus, I would feel horrible, but this will be just another evening of misery for Rowan."

River breathed out a weary sigh and leaned against the balustrade, crossing her arms in thought. "I know. Hugh makes it worse every time too! He runs off men *and* women who get near her. Why does he do that? He doesn't want her, so no one gets her then?"

"I had hoped his... intensity would lessen after he said he wouldn't date her. So far, he seems more solemn, reserved, and miserable." Raven threw her hands up in exasperation.

"The truth is, Rowan wouldn't thank us for discussing this without her or trying to manage the situation."

Raven's shoulders slumped. She knew River was right. "I think we just need to have a few more girls' nights where she has a chance to relax. Really relax. Even if it's here at home. The Delton situation is the real problem. We wouldn't always need the men and guards if that piece of cow shit was no longer a threat."

"Okay, so patience and get Rowan alone time. Good plan. How about tonight? Since you know Bran and I won't be out as late as everyone else, we could maybe get Hugh to leave if you and Patrick leave with us too. Then, even with Thomas and a few guards, Row could enjoy Jo and Saoirse."

The plan was to walk to the Temple Bar pub since they were a big enough group— safety in numbers— and Rowan and Jo would still have plenty of protection once the five of them went home. "I'm totally down for that. Brilliant! I'm tired tonight anyway, so it's a win-win." They restarted their descent, Patrick and Bran meeting them at the bottom of the stairs.

"For fuck's sake, Rave. If you wanted me to go out, then you shouldn't have worn... something I want to rip off," he finished, pulling his wife into his arms for what River assumed was an awkwardly long and inappropriate public kiss.

River *assumed* it because she was in the middle of her own awkwardly long and inappropriate public kiss. When Pat let her up for air, his hands somehow managed to grip her ass and pull her halfway up his body. The hooting and hollering from the Jo Gallery made River snort in amusement.

River traced a finger against Patrick's blonde brow, only slightly darker than his hair. She let her lips linger near his mouth so she could whisper, "Tonight, we'll have to use that third arm between your legs." Laughing, she slid down his body, causing Patrick to moan at the friction.

"Speaking of my 'arm,' give me a minute for it to become unexcited about seeing you in that outfit. Damn it, River, you knew I'd be turned on."

Chuckling, she fed him a truth bomb. "Spoiler alert, babe. Everything turns you on."

Pinching her ass only made her laugh harder, "True, but that knowledge isn't helping me get rid of my... problem."

"Oh, of course. I've got your back, babe. Did I tell you Nan told the girls and me that Devlen is quite the beast in bed and—"

"Don't finish that sentence. Christ, River, that was cruel!"

Laughing, she ducked under his arm to join the family, telling him, "But you're bonerless now. You. Are. Welcome."

"Paybacks," he threatened behind her.

THE NIGHT HAD everything Patrick needed. His father, brother, and... River. They'd walked to the Temple Bar district, stopping at one of Dublin's most popular pubs. Temple Bar Pub's red façade was an inviting sight. Epic live music and whiskey— and River. It always came back to her for him.

She'd explained to Patrick that they needed to leave with Bran, Raven, *and* Dad to give Row a breather. Two hours into the evening, River had nodded off on his shoulder, so leaving early wasn't a problem. She'd barely touched her drink and hadn't eaten a thing. She'd mentioned being tired earlier in the day. Patrick didn't mind. River had roused enough to walk out of the pub, but once they were loaded in the SUV and she was cradled in his lap, it was lights out. He hoped she wasn't coming down with something.

"Bran," Raven started, leaning heavily into her husband's side from her own exhaustion, "Please stop at Spar grocery on the way home."

"What are you needing, sweetheart? I can pick up anything first thing tomorrow."

"I need women's things, Bran. Please don't make it a big deal."

Patrick cringed at 'women's things' and tried to tune out anything else his sister-in-law said. Since his brother wasn't a moron, he answered with a simple, "No problem."

Once they pulled into Spar, Raven insisted on taking only a guard into the store, not wanting to 'inconvenience Bran.' Something was definitely off with that woman tonight. Rounding off the weird, his father crouched in the corner of the vehicle like a *Harry Potter* Dementor— sucking up the evening's happiness. Obviously, he was furious to leave Rowan at the bar. Sucks to suck, as River would say.

Once they were home. Patrick nudged River, but she was stone-cold out. He hoisted her little body against his chest and walked to the elevator with the others. As Patrick stepped out on the second floor, Raven asked him to tell River that she needed her help with something in the morning.

"No problem, I can come too and make us all breakfast."

Raven hesitated, clearly not expecting or wanting his offer. Weird.

"Thanks. Great idea," Raven said, less than enthusiastic.

Patrick wondered if River wasn't the only sister needing extra sleep.

RIVER AND PATRICK walked to Bran and Raven's the following morning. Patrick loaded down with enough breakfast food for twenty. River grabbed the sack of eggs before they were all committed to scrambled.

"Sorry again about sleeping through most of the evening," River laughed. "I must have needed it, though, because I feel amazing this morning."

"Hey, you woke up for the best parts," he nudged her side with the sausage and bacon.

"Ha!" River shook her head at Patrick as she lightly knocked on her sister's door in case Daniel was sleeping. "It was hard to sleep through the extremely thorough disrobing you insisted on giving me."

Repeating River's words back from last night, he said, "You. Are. Welcome." Right as Bran, holding a smiling Daniel, opened the door.

"Who's so handsome this morning? Not you, Bran," River teased. "Come see your auntie, sweet boy." Bran exchanged the baby for the eggs, and he and Patrick put all the groceries on the kitchen counter.

"Thank God, Pat," Bran looked over the bags. "I'm starving."

"Do O'Faolains come any other way?" Raven asked as she walked in from the back, stopping by Bran to give him a kiss. "I see you've already gotten your hands on your nephew, Riv. Did you see his hair? Don't you think it's a tiny bit longer?"

River ran her fingers lightly over the white fluff. "Definitely. Such a pretty color, too, isn't it, Daniel? Just like Daddy and Uncle Pat."

"Come to my bedroom for a sec. I want to show you something." As River followed her sister, Raven told the brothers they should invite Hugh and Rowan. "It looks like you brought your entire fridge, Pat."

Raven walked right into her master bath. She leaned against the counter and held her arms out. "Hand me, Daniel, please." Bemused by her sister's mood, River did. Then Raven dug in a white, plastic Spar shopping bag that was sitting on the counter next to her, pulled out a box, and handed it to River with raised brows.

"Wha—" River couldn't finish as her brain finally caught up to what her eyes were reading. *First Response pregnancy test.* "Tell me you are not pregnant again. So soon!"

"No dummy. I think *you* are."

And just like that, River felt her legs wobble. "Why would you think that?" River whispered.

"You're tired all the time, and that is *so* not you. You pick at, more than actually eat, your food. Again, not you. You've lost weight. You and Patrick have sex like every hour. I mean, you might not be, but... You might."

"I'm on birth control, and unlike you, I haven't swapped my packs with one of my sisters."

"When we got home last night, I did a little research on things that might have nulled your birth control," Raven admitted.

"And? Did you find anything?"

"St. John's Wort. Rowan got you some from the apothecary as soon as we returned to Dublin. It's good for depression and sleeplessness— and apparently, not allowing birth control to... control."

Raven explained all this with a huge grin on her face. Annoying. "I did take it for a couple weeks. I still doubt I'm pregnant."

"Go pee on the damn stick, River! I've barely been able to sleep since I bought it last night." When River still hesitated, Raven brought out her trump card. "If you are pregnant, we can plan a wedding in a couple of weeks, so you aren't the size of the O Building when you say 'I Do.'"

"Oh Christ," River tore the box open, grabbed the directions, and ran to the separate toilet room.

Remove test stick from wrapper and take off the Overcap. Hold stick by Thumb Grip, with the Absorbent Tip pointed down, and the Result Window facing away from body. Place Absorbent Tip into your urine stream for 5 seconds only.

No problem. No big deal. River thought as she finished peeing on the plastic stick. Raven was being dramatic. Gathering her stick, she met Raven by the vanity, who was attempting to pluck a stray eyebrow hair with one hand while rocking her baby with the opposite arm. Lord have mercy. *Am I ready for motherhood?*

"Three minutes. Two and a half now." Raven tossed her tweezers down, and they both stared at the pink and white stick.

Raven turned to River with wide eyes. "Guess it didn't need the full three minutes."

"Two lines. Oh my God, Rave. Two lines!"

Raven grabbed one of River's hands and squeezed. "You are happy, right?"

"I'm a whole bunch of things. Shocked. Scared. Super shocked," she added again and smiled. "But yes, very happy. Patrick is going to flip the F out!"

"Do you want to tell him privately or while he and his brother are cooking our breakfast?" Raven asked, laughing. Obviously giddy with excitement.

"I think now. I don't think I could act normal until we left."

"Okay, text Row and see if she's here or if she's coming."

"She's already here," Rowan said as she slowly walked into

the bathroom. "And very, very hungover. Remind me to kill Jo and Saoirse." Rowan was about to take Daniel from Raven when her gaze landed on all the bright pink trash littering the counter.

River knew when her eyes landed on the stick because her mouth dropped open, then closed, then dropped open again. "Oh my God, Raven. Are you pregnant? Again?"

"Nope," Raven smirked, popping the p.

"Then... who?" Her eyes whipped to River, her alcohol-befuddled mind finally connecting the dots. "River? No way! I can't believe it."

"Shall we go shock another O'Faolain with impending fatherhood?"

PATRICK HEARD the girls coming down the hallway. His dad and Bran were helping with breakfast, but they all three turned at the hushed giggling. They were holding hands and grinning until they realized they were being watched, then quickly pulled their hands away. All three were blushing, their fair skin a map of emotion.

Patrick had just pulled the bacon and sausage and asked Bran to put them in the warmer. Buttermilk biscuits were in the top oven, and the hashbrowns were already crisping away in the bottom. He'd used Bran's new badass Skeppshult cast iron pan. While he'd cooked the bacon, Pat looked up the Swedish company and ordered several sizes for himself. The only thing left were pancakes, eggs, and gravy.

He hadn't planned on making biscuits and gravy this morning, but Bran and Dad pouted until he agreed. Patrick was about to start cracking eggs— Bran had at least made the pancake batter— when he noticed the girls were all standing awkwardly side-by-side, side-eyeing each other, and he even saw Raven elbow River.

"Out with it," Patrick laughed at their identical wide eyes. "You guys are up to something."

"They've been whispering to each other for ten minutes straight." Bran shrugged his shoulders at Raven's, "Hey!"

Dad crossed his arms, a look of boredom on his face that he might have pulled off, except the intensity in his eyes called bullshit. Giving up on his eggs for now, he fully turned, giving River his undivided attention. Rowan and Raven shoved her forward. Patrick was considering that there might be something in the building's water making all the women living here crazy. Raven was off last night too.

River ran her hands along her leggings like she was nervous. Tainted water forgotten; he was getting nervous.

"Guess what, Patrick?

Umm... "What?" Patrick quickly glanced at his father and brother. They looked slightly alarmed.

"I'm pregnant."

It took Patrick less than a second to cross the room and pull River tight against his chest. He couldn't even speak. He was overwhelmed in the best way possible. Their family remained silent, letting them have this moment. "River. Christ," he murmured into the soft hair on her crown. "I can't... believe... How?"

"Do you want the *Birds and the Bees* CliffsNotes, Pat?"

Ignoring his brother, he leaned back to see tears clumped in River's lashes. "You're happy?" he asked.

"Beyond."

Patrick held River in his arms for another ten minutes before he let her feet drop back to the floor. They received hugs and congratulations, followed by Bran and Dad demanding that Patrick finish breakfast. He created a buffet on the center island,

and once everyone had loaded plates and sat down, Raven dropped the second bomb of the morning.

"I texted Dom and asked him who the absolute best wedding planner was that could put together a gorgeous wedding at The Fitzwilliam with only a two-week lead time."

Patrick choked on a sausage link. After pounding his chest and drinking water, he finally asked, "What's the rush, babe. Raven took a lot longer to plan everything, like dress stuff and whatever."

"Because, unlike me, she wants to fit down the aisle, Pat." Raven was giving him a look like he should have known that.

Bran interrupted, leaning toward his wife, grasping her chin gently so she would look at him. "You were the most beautiful bride I've ever seen. Did you not believe me?" he asked quietly.

Raven melted under his tenderness. "I believed you, Bran. I forget sometimes, is all."

"Raven *was* a stunning bride, but I would prefer not to wait... so late."

Patrick took River's hand in both of his. "Whatever day. Whatever time. I'll be there." When she smiled, her stunning cat eyes creased, and the bright hazel mesmerized Patrick.

"I want something simple," River admitted. "Rowan, would you call Jo so we can tell her the news?" Two weeks would fly by, and River would need all the help she could get, and no one was better at event planning than Josephine O'Connor. She flashed a smile at Patrick, who still appeared shell-shocked, but he caught her eye and smiled her favorite mischievous smile.

"Well," Bran began with a chuckle, "I guess we don't have to wonder if Lily Byrne passed along her generous fertility gene to her girls." Everyone laughed — but Hugh, of course.

"Nothing but sparks and drama between O'Faolains and Byrnes, huh, babe?"

"Nothing but," River agreed, grinning at Patrick.

Jo answered the phone on the fourth ring, sounding a bit breathless. "Hey Jo, I've got you on speaker. We've got some exciting news to share." Rowan added, "If this isn't a good time, we can call you later. Sounds like you're in the middle of a workout," she grinned at the table— sans Hugh.

"Oh, no. I was just replying to some emails from Mom. What's the news?"

River couldn't help but ask, "Is Thomas working extra hard on those emails too?"

"MacGregor isn't even here, you bitch," Jo snarked back. Her high horse was hobbled when they heard her bodyguard in the background grumble, "I most definitely am here, lass." This was followed by Jo whispering, *dickhead.*

"Anyway," Jo stressed, "what's the news?"

"I'm pregnant, and I need a wedding to happen at The Fitzwilliam in two weeks." Jo's gasp and then mini scream at River's announcement had her and her sisters bouncing in their chairs with glee.

They spoke to Jo for another twenty minutes while the men cleared the table and started the dishes. They were just about to hang up, having made a solid plan, which included Dom. He had texted Raven back while they were on the phone with Jo and said he would begin making inquiries today, and because it was Dom, River felt all her nerves settle.

During the goodbyes, Jo asked, "Hey Row, did you tell your sisters what you did last night— and where you did it?"

The 'You could hear a pin drop' idiom, yeah, River was experiencing that absolute silence with five other people after Rowan quickly ended the call with Jo. River and Raven looked at Rowan's shocked red face with shocked red faces of their own. And oh God, the three O'Faolains present turned in a synchronized WTF, slow-mo move.

Seeing their sister's horror, River and Raven quickly

jumped up, pulling Rowan with them. Raven let off a pearl-clutching gasp— thank God she didn't try acting as a career path — and pointed to Daniel's behind, "Girls, help me change Daniel."

A herd of Byrnes trampled out of the kitchen like a bucking bull was hot on their asses. Raven practically slammed the nursery door behind them before walking over to the mini fridge, grabbing a bottle, and putting it in an equally mini hot water bath to warm.

"A mini fridge? Seriously, Rave?" The extravagance momentarily changed River's focus.

"Bran." No explanation needed.

Moving on, River looked at Rowan, who was trying to act chill with her face buried in one of Daniel's teddy bears. "What the absolute fffff—heck happened last night after we left, Row?"

"I'm for real going to kill Josephine for blurting that out in front of the guys. Christ, what a mess."

"What is it, Rowan?" Raven asked softly, taking the bottle out of its bath and sitting in the rocker to situate Daniel for his breakfast. She must be concerned her little bit of whiskey from last night could still be lingering in her milk.

"I was going to tell you both earlier," Rowan said defensively. "In the bathroom, but then... the test and baby news... and I... chickened out?" Rowan shook her head, whether it was in disbelief at what she'd done or in waiting to tell her sisters. TBD.

"Row," River began, "you do realize that no matter what happened, we will never judge you. Ever."

"Never," Raven agreed. "Did you have sex?"

"Oh my God! You aren't a virgin anymore. Holy shit!" River whisper-screamed.

"No, for the love of God. I didn't have sex. Geez, I would have called you both last night if *that* had happened!" Rowan's face was turning such a dark crimson that River was concerned her hot skin would split. In a bizarre turn, Rowan began to undress. She unzipped her jacket, and once off, she laid it over the side of Daniel's crib. Next, she pulled her loose t-shirt over her head, leaving a simple white bra with two tiny daisies at the base of each strap.

River couldn't help it. She laughed softly. "Daisies. Love."

That made Rowan smile briefly. She tossed the shirt atop the jacket. Taking a deep breath, River imagined, to fortify what was coming next, Rowan told them, "I got a tattoo. That's what Jo was talking about."

Raven and River gave each other looks. What in the hell was so dramatic about that? "We three already have one. Why are you stressing about getting another? Except, I admit to being jealous Raven and I weren't there to get matching ones!"

Rowan grimaced. "You wouldn't want to get this one. Trust me."

"Oh no. Is it one of those tattoo fails?" Raven asked in sympathy. "I'll schedule laser removal sessions. No worries. Just show us."

Shaking her head, Rowan pulled the right side of her bra to the side, revealing the small Native American tree symbol and triskelion tattoo. She looked at both her sisters. "Good, right?"

The sisters nodded in agreement. Obvi— they both had a similar version on their breasts.

She adjusted her bra back in place, replaced her t-shirt, turned around, and pulled her pants down. She then pulled the right side of her matching daisy panties aside to reveal...

"Oh. My. God!" Raven screeched, momentarily disturbing Daniel's peaceful milk bliss.

"You didn't!" River whispered in horror. On her right butt cheek were three initials done in a fancy, curling black font. HDO. Hugh Darcy O'Faolain. Oh, Christ, have mercy. "Are...

are those your lips tattooed in red underneath... Hugh's... good God, under Hugh's initials?"

"Yes," Rowan admitted as she pulled her pants back up. "Jo didn't know what I got, just that I got one, so she didn't know the possible, *horrifying* consequences of Hugh finding out. That being said," and here, Rowan paused dramatically. "Death to anyone who doesn't keep this secret until I can get rid of it. Death," she stared at her sisters. Rowan could be scary when she wanted to be.

"Promise."

"Cross my heart," River promised. "So can we forget about your ass tat and the fact that you just mooned us and plan my damn wedding?"

41

Where Raven's wedding had been all lovely beige, River's was all white and cream with touches of slate. There were a few white rose bouquets, and that was it. The venue was stunning all by itself. River had asked for minimal, and she did get her wish— for the most part —if minimal also included a small orchestra to play the wedding march and 'ambiance' music during the reception, a caviar bar, three photographers, and a portrait artist.

The wedding team at The Fitzwilliam was exceptional, which, of course, included their office manager, Dom. The penthouse was reserved for the wedding party to dress, drink sparkling grape juice— thank you very much, Baby O-2 —and where River received something old, something new, something borrowed, and something blue.

Something new was sapphire earrings that matched her wedding ring, black titanium posts and all. The something borrowed was from Nan. The same silver comb etched with buttercups that River's grandpa had gifted his wife many years before. The inscription - *Bébhinn, mo grá Always, Sean* - melted her heart just the same as when Nan let Raven wear it at her wedding to Bran.

Then came the gift from her sisters, the same gift she and Rowan had presented to Raven. Something old and something blue. The same antique wooden box with the same Native American symbols representing the three of them was placed in her hands. A raven, river, and rowan tree. Inside held the bracelet with their parents' wedding rings forever soldered to the metal band.

River had to swallow several times before she managed to stop the tears from leaking out. With her earrings from Pat, Nan's beloved comb holding back her slick, black hair, and finished with a part of her mother and father around her wrist— she was ready.

River's dress was 1920s-inspired. It was an ivory beaded silk gown— think Lady Rose's wedding gown in Downton Abbey. It was intricate but had a simplistic beauty. River couldn't imagine wearing any other dress today. It flowed down her body, the majesty of the twenties making her feel like a goddess. Her sisters wore flapper-inspired above-the-knee gowns. Their dresses were the perfect shade of smokey blue to complement the men's navy suits, and they loved the intricately stitched designs and beading.

"Are you ready to marry Patrick?" Rowan asked solemnly.

"I am."

"Are you ready to watch Rowan and I drink copious amounts of whiskey to honor this wedding while you sip lemon water?" Raven asked just as solemnly before breaking into laughter.

"Fine, damn it, I deserved that," River laughed with the three most important women in her life. "Come on, Nan," River took her grandma's hand to head downstairs, "Let's let the drunkards bring up the rear."

Patrick stood next to the priest. His father and brother were keeping him company at the altar. Gran and Diana Gaines were already seated, as were MacGregor and Josephine. James and Jane had flown in yesterday and were seated by Jo. Devlen and Nan were next to Gran. Both Gran and Bébhinn had walked to the front before taking their seats. Giving hugs and kisses to not only him but Bran and Dad as well.

There were a few, very few, friends present because of the continued Delton issue. Saoirse and her fiancé, Tim Daniels. The blacksmith, Josh Ryan, and his date, Saoirse's younger sister, Sadhbh Kennedy. Patrick did not let River invite the Murphy brothers. Cormac and Ciaran had wanted to date River and Rowan. That meant Patrick didn't want them anywhere near his wedding. Childish? Definitely. His father, of course, heartedly approved.

A few artisans who worked with Triskelion were allowed to attend, including Stella, from whom Patrick had purchased the daisy pottery. Bre was there, proudly holding little Daniel until Raven was free from wedding duties. River and Rowan's assistants were invited to the reception. Pat was pleased. It was simple and beautiful, just like River wanted.

He and his two best men wore dark navy wool slacks with matching vests, tweed caps, and off-white button-ups. Their cuffs were sporting new gold cufflinks. The initialed links were gifted to the men at dinner the night before. The only hiccup during rehearsal happened when Rowan laughed at something one of the wedding planners said. Patrick guessed the man was around the girls' age, and with his black hair almost the same shade as Row's, they looked striking standing next to one another. His father, drawn, Patrick was sure, by Rowan's laugh, took his hulking body and dark scowl to stand behind Rowan, glaring over her head until the man finally got the hint and practically ran in the opposite direction.

River and Raven saw what happened, saw Rowan's eyes sparkle with tears, and rounded on Patrick and Bran. Both girls spoke at once. "This can't keep happening, Bran." "Fix your dad, Pat, before I fucking fix him."

Whoa. Hormones were scary. Marching orders in hand, he and his brother cornered their dad. They point-blank told him to cut the shit. Not only was he hurting Rowan, but it was Patrick's wedding.

Dad apologized and said it wouldn't happen again. He appeared defeated. Patrick and Bran looked at each other. Neither liked to see their father upset, even if it was his own fault. They watched him walk over to Rowan and, assumably, apologize to her as well. She nodded once before turning back to her sisters.

Now, here he was, about to marry the woman who possessed every part of him. The orchestra began playing the *Wedding March*, and then she was there... River.

Raven, River, and Rowan walked toward him, arm in arm in arm. Patrick felt tears prick his eyes. Jesus, he was a lucky man. There was no better woman than River Byrne. When she stood before him, and he could take her hands into his own, his body, his entire being, relaxed. He would say yes. River would say yes.

MRS. RIVER ASTER BYRNE O'FAOLAIN. Holy shit. She was married to Patrick Brandon O'Faolain. She had never, not in a million years, believed she would get her own happily-ever-after. River was the one who smiled through drama, joked in the midst of awkward, and laughed instead of cried.

She still felt every emotion; the difference was that now the feelings she showed the world were always real— always real, and it felt amazing. Patrick had his own journey to become the man he was meant to be, the man who'd only moments before slipped that beautiful sapphire ring on her finger, but she'd had her own journey too.

It was her turn to place a simple black band on Pat's finger. River looked deep into his amber eyes and whispered, "I'm glad our journeys ended in the exact same spot."

Patrick leaned closer to whisper back. "The next journey we do will be together. Always together."

42

———

If all went as planned, this could be his last day in Dublin purgatory. Sam had spent weeks tracking the Byrne sisters' comings and goings outside their Triskelion Territory Designs property. It was still tricky, but as his presence in the community had grown, he'd noticed less scrutiny. He hoofed every coffee delivery he could grab, always telling the customers to ask for Robbie if they wanted their coffee hot and on time.

It had been working like a charm. One or more of the sisters— impossible to tell them apart from a distance— went to the bakery only a block from their shop at least twice a week. One of the days might vary, but the second day was always Friday.

Today was Friday.

ROWAN

"I swear if Patrick plans one more party, dinner, luncheon, tea, or picnic, I'm going to scream at the lack of *me* time," Rowan whined to Jo as they meandered down the sidewalk after grabbing some delicious scones and muffins from *Bácús*, a lovely little bakery not far from Triskelion and an easy walk. May in Dublin was lovely. It was sunny and sixty-three degrees that morning.

Rowan hated to complain about the almost *daily* celebrations since the wedding, but seriously. Patrick and River decided to postpone their honeymoon until after the baby was born, which would be near the end of October, so close to Rowan's November 1st birthday— was it bad if she wished for Baby O2 to be late? Pat being Pat, he planned on celebrating their nuptials... for months until they got the 'real thing.'

Multiple get-togethers meant there were so many, many opportunities to practice her 'stealth mode' moves. Avoiding being in Hugh's presence took determination, skill, and frankly, luck. After she humiliated herself back in February... no. No! No! No! Rowan would not think of that night or the flipping tattoo on her ass. Good choices most certainly did not happen after seven whiskey shots. Truer words...

Hugh had cornered her no less than six times over the past few weeks about what Rowan had done that night. What had Jo been referring to? If he only knew... Good God! She'd rather him believe she'd had sex with some random guy versus the truth. All Rowan needed right now was a cinnamon scone— and memory loss.

Jo interrupted her Most Embarrassing Moment reel, thank God, when she grabbed Rowan's arm and yanked her close. "Patrick in love is quite a thing to witness, I must admit, but I don't want to talk about that right now," she emphasized her statement by giving the arm in her grasp a shake. "Thomas told me he loves me. Last night. And I told him I love him too."

That brought Rowan to a standstill in the middle of the sidewalk. Hot scone forgotten, she rounded on Jo, grabbing her shoulders and doing some shaking of her own. The *Bácús* logo on the paper bag bounced off Jo's left collarbone like a door knocker. "We've been talking for twenty minutes. Twenty! And you're just spilling?"

"I know! I was going for drama," Jo giggled, looking over her shoulder to smile at Thomas, who had totally missed it since he and Peter, Rowan's guard, were walking on their left, closest to the street. Neither man stopped scanning the surroundings. It always made her sick to think their Oklahoma stalker had followed them to another country. It had been well over a year!

Sam Delton was the reason Rowan hadn't left Dublin yet. Escaping Dublin meant escaping Hugh. Alas, together, their families were better protected. But God, how she dreamed of working outside of Dublin, at least for a few months. Perhaps absence would make her heart grow... less fond. Whatever the opposite of 'fonder' was, that's what Rowan wanted.

Banishing her depressing thoughts to focus on one of her

best friend's happiest moments, Rowan gave her a giant hug, laughing in delight at Jo's absolute joy. She'd found her happiness just as her sisters had.

It was extraordinarily beautiful and horribly bittersweet.

You have to stop, Rowan. Our age difference is too much. This... will never happen. Ever.

Yeah. Hugh's words from three months ago still took her breath away. How could a man look the way he did at Rowan, like she was *his*, and still believe they weren't meant to be together?

Hugh the Magnificent.

Hugh of the Mixed Signals.

Hugh of the Magic Tongue. *Yeah... Rowan knew.*

Hugh, the Keeper of Rowan's Heart.

Rowan stepped away from Jo, transferring the baked goods to her right hand so she could grasp Jo's hand in her left so she could lead her friend to Triskelion. Jo was having breakfast with Rowan before she left to tackle her workday and before Rowan's first client showed up. River and Raven weren't coming in until ten. Sex must make it challenging to be punctual. Rowan wouldn't know a damn thing about that, she grumped to herself.

"Let's hurry so you have plenty of time to tell me exactly how Honey Bunny professed his—" A shout cut Rowan off. Everything was a blur of speed, but she felt frozen. She knew there was screaming, but her ears were muted.

Peter was on the ground, red blooming on his chest. Thomas tackled Jo, his hand reaching toward Rowan at the exact moment she felt something hit her shoulder, spinning her body around. Thomas was still trying to grab her, but he needn't have worried about making her get down. Rowan felt herself slowly falling toward the cobblestones. All on her own.

ABOUT THE AUTHOR

Anne Gregor is a Contemporary Romance writer and the author of *Raven*, the first book in The Irish Wolves trilogy. Anne loves using her master's degree in history to sprinkle a little of the past into a modern package. When she is not writing, reading, or book reviewing, she is obsessed with true crime documentaries and cooking challenge shows— a combination like fish and cheese— sometimes it works. An empty nester after her three children started adulting, she still loves getting together for family game nights. Quiet evenings are reserved for reading and peanut butter.

She lives in northeast Oklahoma on the Grand Lake O' the Cherokees and is passionate about all things Okie.

ALSO BY ANNE GREGOR

The Irish Wolves Trilogy

Raven

River